Better Dead Than Alive

HENRY FARLEY

ISBN:1542378613
ISBN-13: 978-1542378611

DEDICATION

For Irene

CONTENTS

ACKNOWLEDGMENTS

Several people have given me help and encouragement in cutting my teeth during the writing of this novel:

Belinda gave me encouragement to finish it after stuttering three quarters of the way through the book.

John made sure I steered a clear course with useful advice and a critique on what I'd written.

James who did the new cover design, *GoOnWrite.com*

Above all my wife Irene gave me help, and encouragement especially at times I didn't think I would finish.

Part 1
The Well-Trodden Path

1

Elsa Bartelli could not have foreseen the chain of events that would lead to her premature demise. Her own welfare was the last thing on her mind as she pondered the prospect of making contact with the patsy that would provide her and Jack with enough money to quit their unsavory racket and start afresh. She had played this scene so many times she sometimes felt like an observer rather than a participant. Once this business was over she could return to New York and back to her "normal" life, the sooner the better.

Elsa had been in Miami a little over a week with her lover and "business colleague" Jack Cates. Jack had read about Simon Walsh, a wealthy businessman, who had taken over the reins of the National Mutual Provident on the death of his father, Sean. Although a married man, Simon Walsh had the reputation of a philanderer who always spent a couple of weeks in Florida at this time of year, alone. Now as the chief executive of a multi-million dollar insurance and investment company he would provide rich pickings for Elsa and Jack. Walsh spent his time in Miami sailing and playing golf and often had a drink or quick bite at the Ocean Drop Inn, a bar and restaurant constructed as part of a marina complex, which included various shops, restaurants and a games arcade. The Ocean Drop Inn boasted a 50-foot bar that was only fully utilized after regattas or the annual open yacht race. It was decorated with a nautical theme, with blue and chrome livery, and stainless steel fixtures and fittings. Attempts by the designers to make the décor and artefacts authentic only succeeded in making the place look tacky and artificial.

Sauntering into the Ocean Drop Inn, as she had the previous 5 days, Elsa positioned herself at one end of the bar where she could easily observe the entrance. Automatically she opened her handbag and withdrew a packet of cigarettes. As she was about to put a cigarette to her mouth she asked the barman if he had a light. He lit her cigarette using a book of matches and asked her what she wanted to drink.

"I'll have the usual Jerry, that's a vodka and tonic in case you've forgotten already.

Jerry smiled acknowledging the order. He had seen a number of afternoon drinkers in his time, but none quite like this one. She had a presumptuous manner, like ordering her drink as if she were a regular, after just a few days and only between two and four-thirty at that! But she was a good-looking woman, beautiful even. Her stunning appearance was enhanced by the faintest trace of an Italian accent, complemented by her dark hair and tanned skin to give her the exotic look of a Mediterranean woman. She had large green eyes, high cheekbones and a full sensual mouth.

"Since you're now a regular I should ask you your name," said Jerry handing her a glass of vodka and a small bottle of tonic water. Jerry took the opportunity to take a good look at her close up. She was smartly dressed in a crisp white blouse and a tight fitting skirt, almost like an office secretary, but not many would have looked half as good or sexy as her. She had a full shaped figure but was well toned like a dancer, or even an athlete. Jerry couldn't understand why a woman like her should suddenly become such a regular visitor to his bar.

"Names only get in the way," Elsa replied. "We'll become close friends, visit each other's houses, go to the christening of each other's children and then you'll quit your job."

Jerry laughed thinking beauty and wit, a rare combination. On top of that she could hold her drink. She used one bottle of tonic for 3 shots of vodka, normally having 6 measures without showing any ill effects from the amount of liquor she had drunk.

Before Jerry could reply to Elsa, Simon Walsh walked into the bar. Walsh was a keen sailor and had a boat permanently berthed at the marina, although he usually spent no more than a couple of weeks in the year vacationing in Miami. Elsa eyed Walsh up and down as he approached the bar, then feigned disinterest and turned her attention back to her drink. She didn't want to spend another week as a barfly, or away from work, and was determined to at least set things in motion today, by drawing Walsh's interest. Experience had taught her that the best way of getting a man's interest was to ignore him.

Not that Walsh was an unattractive man. He looked over 6 foot, of stocky build and probably 10 – 15 pounds overweight, but not fat. The white cotton shirt and wool blend pleated trousers set off his ruddy complexion and thick copper colored hair that betrayed his Irish stock. On his wrist he was wearing a Rolex watch that must have set him back $50,000 and his ensemble was finished with black soft leather sailing shoes.

"The usual Mr. Walsh?" said Jerry with a sideways smirk at Elsa.

"Thanks Jerry," said Walsh as he casually glanced around the bar. The place was virtually empty, apart from Elsa and an elderly couple sitting in the corner, who were nursing their drinks as if they had to make them last all day. Walsh caught Elsa in his direct line of vision. He waited until their eyes met and smiled, trying not to register any obvious appreciation of her beauty. Elsa nodded in return then turned back to the bar and lifted her drink to take a sip.

Walsh turned his attention to Elsa again, taking in every detail of her body. He considered himself a connoisseur when it came to the appreciation of women and by any measure this woman was special. "It seems as if we're the only people here, can I buy you a drink?" he asked.

Elsa turned back towards him and cheekily replied, "Do you normally check out the number of people in the bar before offering to buy a round of drinks?"

Sassy too, thought Walsh. "Well I wasn't counting on buying the couple in the corner a drink, but I can if you want me to show my magnanimity."

"Well I wouldn't like you to go out on a limb if the cost of their drinks is going to break the bank."

"Not at all," replied Walsh, "It's costing me $300 to have my boat refueled and checked over, but I think I can still afford a couple of drinks." Walsh found it hard to keep his eyes off Elsa's legs. He liked beautiful women and didn't mind spending money on them to get them to like him too. As the son of a wealthy businessman he had benefited from a privileged upbringing, with a private education and numerous vacations to the most exciting and exotic locations around the globe. Despite this rich background he lacked confidence in his ability to attract women with strong personalities and had given up trying to understand their likes and dislikes. Now he flagrantly used his wealth to woo available females, their affection was optional as long as he was able to get what he needed from these liaisons.

"In that case I'll have another of these," she said pointing to her glass, "a vodka." Thank God things were at last on track she thought, and that she was able to hook him so easily. He was well and truly hooked and now all she had to do was reel him in. Jack should be outside somewhere and would follow them to the hotel of Walsh's choice. She would get Walsh into a compromising situation; Jack would burst into the room as the indignant husband, and bingo - money on tap. It was a well-worn ploy but worked surprisingly well, even these days in which the moral climate is far more forgiving than in bygone times. Not that she looked forward to being pawed by Walsh before Jack's dramatic entrance, but she was a working girl and it was the only way she and Jack could get their hands on a large amount of money, quickly. She crossed and uncrossed her legs to tantalize Walsh a little more.

"I've seen you here before, haven't I?" said Walsh moving down the bar towards her and signaling Jerry to fill up her glass.

"I like coming here for a bit of relaxation away from the hustle and bustle of the city and to fill out my day. I've been visiting my sister on vacation for a change of scene. She was able to take time off last week but has to work this week, so I've been left with having to keep myself amused during the day," Elsa replied blowing out a cloud of smoke. "I guess the vacation's been a bit flat this week, but that's just my bad luck and timing with my sister having to work. I'm actually looking forward to going back home tomorrow."

"It's a pity we didn't meet up earlier. I'm on vacation too and could have shown you around."

"I'm pretty familiar with Miami and know most of what it has to offer. I've been visiting my sister regularly over the past couple of years, since she moved down here with her job."

"Well perhaps I could have shown you areas not on the normal tourist maps. I've got a boat out in the harbor, we could have sailed across to the Bahamas."

Elsa gave him a skeptical look and took another sip of her vodka and tonic. "Do you always make such generous offers to complete strangers? I would have thought there were plenty of people only too willing to go sailing with you."

"Only when they are as beautiful as you," Walsh replied. Elsa was thrown out of her stride by his sudden directness and acknowledged his compliment. For his part Walsh wanted to make her aware of his wealth and the potential benefits a liaison with him could bring. He had taken the initiative to show he was confidant, even arrogant, which he hoped would make him more interesting to her. He was now working outside his normal comfort zone, but he felt that the rewards may be worth the effort.

"Well in that case I'd better introduce myself, so that I'm not a complete stranger to you. I'm Lisa Milllarno," lied Elsa offering Walsh her hand.

Encouraged by her apparent change in attitude Walsh introduced himself in return, adding that he was the head of a large financial corporation just for good measure. He felt any reinforcement of his wealth and position could only help to ingratiate himself with her. He desperately wanted to make the right impression with this woman and get to know her a lot better. His marriage was flat and uninteresting, and didn't provide a fraction of the frisson he was now feeling during this bar room "tete-e-tete". Because of his own innate insecurities and the coldness of his wife, he had grown used to buying the favor of whores who would satisfy his every whim for the right price. Although they were uncomplicated and very accommodating, they couldn't give him the thrill of the chase and ultimate satisfaction of conquest. Lisa was far more sophisticated than the women he usually slept with and it was obvious she would not be easily impressed. Despite that he felt everyone had their price and it would be interesting in finding out "Lisa's".

"Look," continued Walsh, "I'm about to go out in my boat for a brief run out to the reef and back, why don't you come with me? It's a good size at 60 foot, has a range of 260 miles and cruises at 25 knots. C'mon it'll be fun," he said with a grin.

Elsa feigned uncertainty but after a brief pause said, "OK, but I've got to be back at the marina by seven." She was a little uncomfortable about changing the game plan that she had agreed with Jack, but hoped that after the sea jaunt he would be keen to get down to the real action. Naively Elsa never considered the problem her partner would have in keeping tabs on her, or that she would be putting herself in a vulnerable position when alone with Walsh at sea.

"Relax, there's no problem. Just put yourself in my hands for the rest of the afternoon." Turning to the barman he said, "Jerry give me a bottle of vodka and a bottle of Jim Beam, and put this lady's tab on mine." After Jerry had handed him the bottles of spirits in a carrier bag, Walsh took hold of Elsa's arm as they prepared to leave the bar.

Jerry leaned on the bar and rubbed his chin as he watched the pair exit. That was as smooth a pick up as he'd ever seen. He began to wonder if the woman really was a professional, but certainly not the stereotype most people apply to hookers. At least she had provided a little excitement, just by being there. He looked over at the couple in the corner and asked if they wanted another drink. They both shook their heads in unison.

Jack was surprised when he saw Elsa and Walsh walk down towards the quay. They were talking animatedly and Elsa was obviously well in control of the situation. Walsh was being very tactile, guiding Elsa in the direction they needed to go and letting his hand brush against her bottom when occasionally disengaging contact with her upper body. Elsa acted as if she were unaware of his little intimacies and took his guidance compliantly. "What are they doing?" thought Jack, but comforted himself with the fact that Walsh was out of his depth when it came to a woman like Elsa. As he watched them walk away from him he suddenly realized that they were going down to one of the boats berthed at the marina.

2

The day had not started well for Jack as he and Elsa had argued about continuing their search for Walsh. Elsa didn't like hustling for money and now felt she was deeply in love with Jack, which gave her a strong reluctance to using her looks and body to make money. Jack had tried to argue that she wasn't a hooker and that these types of scam only involved light petting before he stepped in to make the sting. Jack had only persuaded her to go for one last payday by promising that this trick would be the last. He was convinced that he could ring a princely sum out of Walsh that would give them sufficient to start new lives somewhere else with a clean sheet.

Jack felt a little out of place on the marina as he wasn't dressed like either a tourist or someone working on the boats or in any of the shops, bars, cafes or restaurants. He didn't look like a tourist, but wasn't conspicuous dressed in blue denim jeans, a white tee shirt and a casual black leather jerkin style jacket.

The prospect of Elsa becoming love struck had never crossed Jack's mind when they first met in the "Blue Cockatoo". Quite the opposite. Her obvious disdain of the club and of the clientele would have been unusual in any service industry, but was particularly contradictory for a stripper. The punters loved her for her stunning beauty and the sexual excitement she generated when strutting her stuff, with a weird combination of arrogance and smut. After several of them had tried and failed to extend their acquaintance with her beyond the confines of the club, they informed their peers that she was a lesbian. Of course in a male dominated audience this only added to her charisma. Jack was as struck by her beauty and body as much as the paying guests.

The first time he saw her on stage she was wearing a beige safari blouse and skimpy shorts, with a pith helmet and towering high heel shoes, which were a little incongruous with the rest of her outfit, but gave her legs a feline grace. Her body was moving sensuously to jungle drums in the "noon day sun", until suddenly two other girls dressed in leotards with a tiger skin pattern and complete with a tiger headdress, jumped onto the stage with her. The three girls circled each other with the "tigers" trying to arrack Elsa randomly. They pulled at Elsa's blouse, which started to tear into strips until it barely covered her torso, with her luscious breasts peeking out from behind the strips. Eventually the tiger girls got her blouse and it ended up with a tug of war between the three of them before disintegrating. The act finished with the 3 girls play fighting, but then fondling and kissing each other in simulated sex. The crowd went wild throwing $10, $20 and even $50 notes onto the stage area to keep the girls on the stage as long as possible.

Jack could see Elsa was a cut above everyone else and no matter how cheesy the act, she somehow managed to give it class. Although he would never admit it to anyone, especially himself, on his part it was probably love at first sight. As he withdrew from his reverie he started to follow the pair at a discrete distance. They walked to the end of the jetty and boarded what looked like a 4 berth sports cruiser. Jack smiled to himself as he took in the size and luxury of Walsh's $800,000 toy, which he probably used just once or twice a year. Yes, this one is going to be the final and biggest payday of them all in their brief, but prosperous, careers.

Walsh took his position at the controls of the boat and Elsa sat down on a chair at the stern, casually looking around in an attempt to catch sight of Jack. Instinctively Jack wanted to give Elsa comfort by letting her see him, but he kept concealed to avoid the chance of her inadvertently acknowledging him. This was too big an opportunity to screw up at this stage. Things weren't going to plan, but this change of events could even prove to be fortuitous should he need to get physical with Walsh. Out at sea he could still play the outraged husband and threaten either exposure to Walsh's wife, or a charge of sexual assault to the police. Either way he was convinced he could pressurize Walsh into parting with a tidy sum of money.

Jack quickly walked back to the central area of the wharf looking for somewhere that he could hire a boat. He couldn't hire a launch or sailboat at short notice and without a skipper, so he hastily looked around the marina searching for a rank of small motorboats usually hired to people on vacation for fun rides around the bay. He spotted a fleet of motorboats on the other side of the wharf and rushed around to the office to hire one. The attendant was still explaining the conditions of hire as he jumped into the boat and turned on the engine. Jack hoped that Walsh wouldn't get too far out to sea as it would be difficult to keep track of him, and a small boat would be difficult to handle if the sea turned rough. Putting the boat into gear Jack turned away from the wharf to head out of the harbor. By this time Walsh had negotiated the reverse out of his berth and was already clear of the harbor. Jack was beginning to think that this was not such a good turn of events after all.

He was confident that Elsa could handle any awkward situation with Walsh, but she was at risk during the time it would take Jack to reach her, and he could not make a sudden burst onto the scene as the sound of his boat would announce his arrival. Jack was a little more concerned than when he first got into the boat, but laughed to himself at the thought of Elsa being seduced by Walsh. She had handled men like him many times before in the "Blue Cockatoo", and had done so effortlessly. She was used to lewd remarks and indelicate touches from her audience during her act, but didn't need to rely on the club's heavies to deter them. She was an expert at the put down remark, which usually entertained all of the customers witnessing the embarrassment of the reprobate. If they didn't take heed of her sarcasm she had the physical strength to defend herself and deliver whatever measure she thought necessary to stop any further unwelcome advances.

Walsh's boat was very small on the horizon now, so having established the direction in which they were headed Jack slowed down to a steadier speed to allow time for Elsa to get him into a compromising situation that would give the cover needed to sneak up on them. As he headed after Walsh's boat, Jack drifted back to his earlier reminisces about his first meeting with Elsa. He had gone to the "Blue Cockatoo" to visit the owner, Roland Bannister, who was a qualified legal attorney but had left the profession for the more lucrative gambling and sex industries in the busy Hell's Kitchen area of New York. He ran a good "no nonsense" club that provided a safe and secure environment for his punters to relax and enjoy themselves and didn't tolerate manhandling of the girls. All of the girls were beautiful and were under strict orders not to mix with the punters on the premises. They did offer private lap dancing sessions but sexual activity was strictly forbidden and the rooms had an alarm button if punters couldn't control themselves. What happened outside the club was their own business. If the girls had no previous experience before starting work at the "Blue Cockatoo" they were given dance lessons to instill basic movements and timing that they could use in their act. The girls were given a portfolio of rudimentary movements to include in their performance and were vetted through auditions before going on stage. Elsa was the best of a very good bunch and had been trained in a dance school before working as an exotic dancer.

Jack had gone to see Bannister about his fee for supplying copies of police records of the Leonard Tuzio disappearance. Tuzio was a "made man" with a strong reputation in criminal circles as someone worthy of respect, and was not a man to be crossed. He worked for Mario Pallacio, the head of the family business on the East side of New York, and who had contacts, which spread from New York to the West Coast and down to Florida. Tuzio looked after finances in the gaming, entertainment and prostitution areas of Pallacio's empire. He had first come to the attention of Pallacio after killing the man that had raped his younger sister, who already had a contract on his head for misappropriating lottery funds. Pallacio had Tuzio brought to his office, but instead of punishing him for interfering in his business, he gave Tuzio half of the contract fee for the kill. Pallacio explained that only half the fee was due as Tuzio had a vested interest in the death of the man who had violated his sister. Pallacio offered Tuzio a position in his organization to control lottery money. After that their relationship grew until Tuzio was Pallacio's second in command.

Bannister had represented Tuzio on a number of police charges for illegal gambling and prostitution, and had managed to keep him out of jail. Mysteriously Tuzio had disappeared following a violent disagreement with Pallacio over the selling of drugs to school kids. Tuzio's body was never found, however the District Attorney ordered a thorough investigation over his disappearance in the hope of bringing down his boss. The DA was unable to gather sufficient evidence to bring charges against Pallacio and reluctantly let the matter drop and Tuzio was eventually filed as a missing person.

Bannister had taken "ownership" of the "Blue Cockatoo" shortly after Tuzio's disappearance. He claimed he had saved enough money in the short period that he had been practicing law to buy a reasonable stake in the club and that he had a silent partner who was a resident of Jamaica. Jack thought that the identity of Bannister's backer must be transparent to everyone, but didn't interfere as he wanted to maintain his friendship with him and retain the use of his club. It was one of the few places in New York that he felt he could relax in safety. If he had too much to drink Bannister would let him sleep it off in the upstairs apartment.

The relationship between Jack and Bannister was mutually beneficial. Bannister could use Jack's police contacts in connection with other business ventures. Although Jack was no longer a part of the NYPD he was still well liked and respected and could get information on the status of police investigations, or access to their records. Many of Bannister's business colleagues were criminals with police records and he perused them to gauge the security of any sensitive business transactions that could be at risk on the basis of the information given in the records. He had asked Jack for a copy of Tuzio's file because of pressure from Pallacio, who suspected that he knew of Tuzio's whereabouts. Bannister eventually gave Pallacio a copy of the file, slightly modified to show that they suspected Pallacio of his murder but couldn't prove it without recovering Tuzio's body. Bannister came to an agreement with Pallacio that he would make sure the police didn't get any leads on Tuzio's whereabouts from anyone at the club, provided he was left in peace. He also agreed to Pallacio becoming the second silent partner. Away from business Jack was one of the few people Bannister could lower his guard with, and the pair spent many drink sodden hours reliving old memories and checking out common friends and acquaintances.

Jack was also popular with the girls in the club. He was a man who enjoyed the company of women and had a voracious sexual appetite. This was largely due to his obvious physical attractions, being over 6 feet tall and ruggedly handsome with thick black hair, sharp angular features and blue eyes. He also had an easygoing charm and innate sense of humor that broke through the sternest defenses. The casual basis of the friendships formed between Jack and the girls was well understood and accepted by all parties, although Bannister was alarmed at the rate he appeared to be going through his staff.

Elsa Bartelli was aware of Jack's reputation as a womanizer and didn't want to become another "notch on his bedpost". She was working at the "Blue Cockatoo" to make money and had no intention of mixing business with pleasure. Although few of the punters looked for the artistic merit in her dance routine, Elsa did the job to the best of her ability and added style, flair and technique to the basic "bump and grind" gyrations. Of course she still had to use the erotic movements required to titillate the punters, but her dance training and natural ability allowed her to convey far more sensuality in emotion and timing than the limited and overtly sexual "exotic dancing" repertoire of the other girls.

Jack saw the seduction of Elsa as a personal mission on behalf of all frustrated men who visited the "Blue Cockatoo". He called her the "Ice Queen" and openly accused her of deceit in purveying sexual innuendo without having a sensual bone in her body. He didn't expect to have the ultimate sexual experience with her but relished the challenge of breaking down her barriers. His early attempts floundered, as he had expected, but it was a chance meeting that allowed him to get a foot in the door.

As a rookie with the NYPD Jack had been called out to a disturbance in a café in Queens. Some local kids were harassing the owners, Gus and his wife Jean, but they decided to move on after Jack threatened to deal with them individually, outside work hours. Gus and Jean were a friendly couple in their mid-fifties who had opened the diner 20 years earlier and had continued to serve good basic "no frills" coffee and food ever since. Their diner became a regular port of call for Jack while he was in uniform. After he became a detective he still visited them often and enjoyed listening to the stories of their lives together as hippies in the sixties. On one of his unannounced visits he ran into Elsa, who had once worked as a waitress for them. They pretended to be friendlier than they actually were for the sake of Gus and Jean, although Elsa was concerned that Jack would try to score points by making oblique references to her dancing at the "Blue

Cockatoo". Jack made the most of the situation that allowed him to pretend to be a close friend of Elsa's. Out of consideration for Gus and Jean she was forced to respond to him in a much friendlier manner than he was used to in their earlier encounters. The shared confidence also created a certain intimacy between them, that was previously absent.

They left Gus and Jean together and Elsa thanked Jack for being discrete about her job. She explained that she had worked at their cafe while training to be a dancer and on leaving she had told them she had joined a touring dance troupe. Jack listened intently and asked her to have dinner with him. Elsa reluctantly agreed because she felt she owed him some kindness for supporting her during their meeting with Gus and Jean. During dinner Elsa discovered that there was more to Jack than the stereotype image she had formed of him from their brief conversations and the lurid gossip she had overheard between the other girls at the club. When she spoke he listened, which encouraged her to tell him more. It had been a long time since she had opened up to another person and she found the experience rejuvenating. She spoke about her aspirations to be a professional dancer and the difficulty in financing herself through dance school. She was easily able to manage the dancing classes but struggled with the theory, as she had little education during her childhood and was too embarrassed to admit she needed extra tuition to improve her reading and writing skills.

Elsa had made a decent fist in her attempt to become a professional dancer but eventually dropped out of school because of the insecurity generated by her poor education. She now felt her childhood dream had passed her by and that she was too old to break into legitimate dancing, hence she was now at the "Blue Cockatoo" getting far more money than she would as an unskilled worker. Initially she had found it difficult to take her clothes off in front of strangers, never mind the overtly sexual movements her routines demanded. If nothing else Elsa was a survivor and she soon came to understand that she could either allow herself to become intimidated by the punters or learn to control them using her obvious sexual charisma. She now wanted to make sufficient money to train as a dance teacher and open a school for children, but knew that the first hurdle would be getting good reading and writing skills.

As she spoke Jack began to see Elsa differently. In a strange way her looks detracted from her as a complete person, as she had many more qualities that weren't on display. She had far more to offer than her face and body and through their conversation she had shown that she was emotionally strong and determined to get what she wanted in the best way she could. Underneath the veneer of strength she was vulnerable and felt alone since the death of her parents in a drugstore robbery. Now Gus and Jean were her only close friends as she didn't mix with the girls at the club and she could only visit their cafe infrequently to live her lie as a dancer with a touring troupe. Suddenly Jack found himself being drawn to her spirit as much as her body. This was a new and strangely liberating feeling for him because he knew he wasn't obliged to play the mating game with her. All he had to do was be himself and hope that Elsa liked what she saw.

Despite her initial resolve, Elsa brought Jack back to her apartment after dinner and allowed him into her bed. Jack had imagined making love to her many times but the reality was different from the fantasy. He felt loving and protective and wanted to be the instrument of her pleasure, rather than concentrate on his own gratification. Elsa found Jack a gentle and considerate lover and tried not to think of him honing his art through his experience with the other girls at the club. His hands and mouth roamed over her body stroking, caressing and teasing, bringing her from one newfound pleasure to another. As he thrust against her she covered his face and chest with kisses, in synchronicity with his movements until they became one as they joined in a final crescendo of pleasure.

Jack was still daydreaming when he thought he heard the faint but unmistakable sound of a gunshot. He switched off the engine and listened and within a couple of minutes heard the shrill sound of gunfire pierce the still air again. Suddenly the loud pulsating throb of Walsh's sports cruiser heading back to the harbor at full throttle broke the silence, creating bow waves that caused Jack's boat to rock violently. Dormant fears re-surfaced as Jack instinctively feared that Elsa must have been hurt, or worse. He reached for the binoculars that were supplied with the boat and turned to look at Walsh's sports cruiser, focusing on the rear of the boat, as it was disappearing into the distance. He could see the back of Walsh's head at the wheel, but there was no sign of Elsa.

Jack had to make a decision to either follow Walsh or head out to sea. It was difficult to determine the exact direction the gunshot sounds had come from, but he turned on the engine of his motorboat and headed to the point on the horizon he had last seen Walsh's boat reappear on the horizon. The thought of finding Elsa's body floating in the water made Jack feel nauseous. His body stiffened and he swallowed to prepare himself for the worst.

3

Elsa was more than a little disorientated by the speed with which Walsh took her from the bar to his boat, and started its engine to set off for the offshore reef. In his eagerness to get Elsa out alone with him at sea, Walsh had swiftly dealt with the mechanic maintaining and refueling his boat and disembarked before she could make Jack aware of the change in plan. She hoped he had seen what was happening. Walking along the quay and down the jetty to Walsh's boat she had tried to catch sight of him, but in between her uncertainty in the direction they were going and trying to avoid Walsh's wandering hands, she was unable to spot him. Jack was a professional she thought, and would only be seen when it suited him, so she wasn't overly concerned about her situation. She didn't envisage any problems as she was sure she could fend of Walsh if he tried to get amorous and was equally convinced that Jack would find a way to follow, although he would have to be a little more resourceful than usual. Despite her slight misgivings, she was confident Jack would rise to the challenge.

As Walsh manned the controls of the boat he began regaling Elsa with its details, hoping to impress her with his knowledge and the obvious size and luxury of the vessel. The boat was elegant with aerodynamic lines to reduce the resistance of the water. There were plenty of timber embellishments and the trims were all stainless steel including hand railing and door fittings. The seated area above the aft cabin comprised highly polished timber framework holding red leather cushions.

"We'll go out to the reef, drop anchor, have a few drinks and enjoy the balmy weather," said Walsh turning back to see Elsa sitting comfortably at the back of the boat. "There's a good selection of wines on board if you fancy a change from your normal tipple," he continued. Elsa had already downed the equivalent of four shots of vodka at the Ocean Drop Inn. Jerry knew the form and was always generous when serving Walsh's female guests. Walsh's game plan was to continue plying Elsa with drinks to get her a little more relaxed and into the right mood after they dropped anchor at the reef. He didn't think it would be long before she was in a condition that would allow him to confidently make a move on her without the risk of rejection. The prospect of having sex with her gave him an erection and he could feel himself flush.

"I don't want to spend too much time on this boat trip, because I promised my sister I'd be back before seven. She's booked a table for dinner tonight. This is my last night in Miami and she wants to treat me to a slap up meal," said Elsa.

"Don't worry we have oodles of time so just relax and enjoy yourself. It's a pity this is your last day otherwise we could have spent all day sailing tomorrow. Let me know the next time you plan to visit your sister and I can arrange a short vacation so we can really put this tub through its paces," replied Walsh, with a grin.

Elsa was beginning to think that the day was going to be a washout and that she and Jack should forget about trying to compromise Walsh. The prospect of Walsh making his play on the boat had finally sunk in. She felt stupid at not being fully aware of the potential danger from the outset, but was determined not to allow that to happen. Men like Walsh were linear in their approach to women and without any subtle nuances that could catch her off guard. The instant he tried to become more intimate, probably in a clumsy attempt to grope her, she would nip his ardor in the bud to prevent it developing into a situation she couldn't handle. There would be some unpleasantness, but she thought she might be able to stall Walsh by arranging some future rendezvous.

As the boat approached the reef Walsh throttled back the engine and coasted into position alongside it. He switched off the engine, pressed a button on the control panel that dropped the anchor and then turned to Elsa. "Let's have a drink," he beamed and produced the bottle of vodka given to him by Jerry. He got two glasses from the galley and poured Elsa a generous measure.

"Not so much," she said, "are you trying to get me drunk?"

"Don't be afraid of having a drink, I can take you back to your sister's place so you don't have to drive yourself. It's your last day on vacation so just relax and enjoy the moment," he replied pouring himself a much smaller measure of vodka. "What do you do for a living?" he asked moving closer to her.

"I work for a financial company as a legal secretary," Elsa lied. "It's not very exciting, but the pay's good and I sometimes get to travel."

Walsh looked her up and down, "It must pay very well judging by the clothes you're wearing. I can see from the quality they're not dissimilar from the clothes my wife buys, so they must be from designer houses." Elsa felt alluring in her white cotton tailored blouse, short, tight black skirt and black high heel shoes. She had examined herself in the mirror before leaving the hotel room and was satisfied that she showed her figure off to classic effect without being "slutty".

"Your wife must be a woman of taste," replied Elsa dispassionately.

"She's able to show off the clothes she has because I buy her everything she desires. Perhaps it's your husband or boyfriend that keeps you so expensively dressed? I'm not complaining because you look great."

"I like to look good, no matter what it costs. If I look good, it makes me feel good," Elsa replied adding, "I also like to be independent."

"Don't be so prickly. You're obviously someone who enjoys and appreciates the good things in life and I could help you get them." Walsh paused to let his words sink in. Elsa made no response to his offer and Walsh took her silence as her approval for him to continue. "I come down here often and try to mix business with pleasure whenever I can. I work hard and like to play hard, especially if I can enjoy myself with someone I like and respect." He immediately devalued the sincerity of his last sentiment by putting his hand on Elsa's knee.

"Do you think your wife would approve of this?" said Elsa with outward calm, but inwardly anxious.

"Do you really care?" countered Walsh moving his hand to the inside of Elsa's leg. "Forget about my wife, your sister or anyone else while we're here together. Relax and let's both have a good time, don't worry I'll make it worth your while."

Walsh's hand was becoming more intrusive as he gained confidence in the prospect of Elsa succumbing to his offer. He began kissing her on the neck and with his free hand cradled her back and pulled her toward him.

Apart from feeling isolated and vulnerable Elsa was starting to get irritated at the liberties Walsh's hand was taking, and his assumption that she was now ready for the taking. She wondered how the hell she let herself get into such a mess and knew she couldn't rely on Jack to come to the rescue because of the speed and aggression of Wash's assault. "Slow down Simon before we get into a situation we may both regret later," she said pushing Walsh away.

"We're not kids Lisa," replied Walsh as he continued stroking the inside of Elsa's thigh, unperturbed at her rebuff. "Whatever happens you won't be sorry. As I said I'll make it worth your while, so no-one loses. I'm a rich man and can get you anything,….anything!"

"That's the same as paying for use of my body," retorted Elsa moving his hand away from her leg for the umpteenth time. "I don't care how rich you are! I'm not a prostitute!"

"We all have to prostitute ourselves in one way or another, so don't be so damn self-righteous. Anyway you didn't display such sensitivity in the Ocean Drop Inn, and the way your clothes cling to your body says you don't mind showing off what you've got," replied Walsh, suddenly becoming more assertive in his tone of voice and body language.

He's not going to be reasonable thought Elsa, bracing herself for a fierce argument and determined she had to stand up to him by matching his aggression. "Don't take me for granted hot shot. It takes more than a few drinks and a boat ride to get inside my pants," she replied standing up to get away from his continual pawing.

"Hey, what's your game then? You come onto me in the bar and then play hard to get. What's so special about you? Surely you can't be saving yourself for Mr. Right."

"No I'm not waiting for Mr. Right, as you put it, but that doesn't mean I'm willing to go with a man with more to offer in his wallet than in his trousers," Elsa retaliated.

Walsh stood up suddenly in a reflex action to her stinging remark and slapped her across the face. The power of the blow knocked Elsa to the deck, momentarily stunning her. Walsh immediately dropped down on top of her and began pulling at her blouse, ripping some of the buttons off in his frenzied rage. As he tried to rip off her bra Elsa recovered her senses and on realizing her situation attempted pushing Walsh away, but couldn't stop the onslaught. Roughly Walsh grabbed her wrists and pinned them above her head. He straddled her body with his legs to hold her more securely and tried to kiss her fully on the mouth. Shaking her head furiously Elsa managed to avoid his lip contact. In an attempt to trap her face with his, Walsh raised himself on his knees and bent forward. As he lifted his body off hers, Elsa brought up her knee sharply into his groin.

Walsh cried out in pain and rolled off Elsa. "You fucking bitch," he screamed trying to control the numbing pain slowly but inevitably building in his groin. Elsa jumped to her feet and tried to circumnavigate Walsh to get to the controls of the boat and fire the engine. As she turned the ignition key Walsh grabbed her by the hair, pulled her away from the controls and slapped her again. This time she saw the blow coming and with her dancers timing was able to ride the force and simply staggered backwards.

Walsh reached downward to a compartment next to the main console and pulled out a handgun. "You fucking bitch," he repeated sucking in his breath to control the pain. He cocked the hammer of the gun and fired it recklessly in Elsa's direction.

"Don't be so stupid," she screamed holding her hands out as if to try and stop the bullet and moving away from him until she was backed up against the rails of the boat. "Nothing's worth murder," she tried to reason with him.

"You're not so superior now," said Walsh regaining his composure and walking toward her as the pain in his groin subsided. "This gun says that you are going to do whatever I want, however I want, and thank me after I'm done." Walsh was standing right in front of Elsa, staring straight into her eyes and sticking the nozzle of the gun into her stomach.

"Well, I don't want to die out here so just put the gun down and we can go back to where we started. I'll be really good to you," she said timidly.

"I know you'll be good to me, you slut, because if you're not I'll blow a hole in your head and fuck you when you're dead." With that he grabbed a handful of hair at the back of her head with his left hand and pulled her face towards his. He forced his tongue into Elsa's mouth and moved the nozzle of the gun down her body and between her legs. Elsa's skirt had ridden up her legs during her fight with Walsh and she could feel the nozzle of the gun rubbing against her through her thin panties as the gun was dragged upward.

Choking under the force with which Walsh's tongue pushed into her mouth, Elsa bit hard on it and pushed him away with all the force she could muster. As he was propelled backwards and fell, Walsh tensed and involuntarily fired the gun in a reflex action and the impact of the bullet knocked Elsa overboard.

Startled by the unexpected sound of the gunshot Walsh stared at the gun in his hand, unable to believe what had just happened. His mind could not handle the shock of Elsa being hit by the bullet, and he feebly staggered to his feet, stumbled across the deck to the rails of the boat and began to look for her in the sea. Frantically he scanned the waves for any sound or sight of movement in the water. The light was fading and it was becoming more difficult to focus on specific areas of the sea in the twilight. As he searched a panic set in when the consequences of what had just taken place started to dawn on him. Turning away from the water Walsh paused to consider his options. If he found the girl and brought her back she might end up charging him with attempted rape. There would be evidence of their fight from bruising on her face and body.

He was beginning to feel more depressed about the furor that would result from police charges, than concern about Elsa's welfare. She could swim back to the marina he thought, but she would have to be one hell of a swimmer. If she did make it back under her own steam she would definitely go to the police just to get back at him, and then he would be accused of attempted murder. The odds on her drowning had to be much greater than on surviving, he thought, especially as she was probably wounded.

As the heat of his fight with Elsa subsided, Walsh concluded that fishing her out of the water and bringing her back would only cause him trouble….big trouble. He picked up her handbag from the deck and tossed it into the water after her. He then walked over to the control panel and calmly switched on the engine. Opening up the throttle, he turned the boat to head back to the harbor without as much as a backward glance. "Let the sharks have the bitch," he mused and calmly put all thoughts of her out of his mind.

4

Jack was getting progressively more anxious about Elsa's wellbeing as he headed in the general direction on the horizon that Walsh's boat had come from. He knew that trying to find her in the water would be virtually impossible, and would rather have had the task of trying to find her in the seedy underbelly of New York. The sun was beginning to set and he could see that the daylight would soon fade. If Elsa were out there in the water he would have to find her quickly. A sudden panic gripped him on the prospect that he might not be able to see her in the dim light and he began shouting her name frantically as he weaved through the water.

As he was shouting Jack began to worry about the possibility of the noise of the engine drowning any shouts for help from Elsa, or of accidentally hitting her with the hull of the boat. Distraught, he switched off the engine and let it glide through the water. A growing silence succeeded the noise of the engine until all he could hear was the lapping of the water against the hull of the boat. His agitation was replaced by a deep, hollow despair that was generated from the core of his soul and manifested itself in an ache in his chest and abdomen. Taking control of his emotions he pulled himself up from his downward spiraling fears and began calling Elsa's name again, praying to catch some sign of her as he scanned the water. As the sound of his voice died it was replaced once more by the lapping of the water.

Jack restarted the engine and began weaving the boat through the water again, albeit at a much slower speed than during his earlier attempts to find her. He spotted a reef 40 yards in the distance and again cut the engine of the boat and glided towards the reef. As the noise of the engine faded he was again greeted with the sound of the seawater lapping on the side of the boat. He resumed calling Elsa's name without any response. A chill overcame Jack as the possibility of Elsa's death became more and more of a reality, and he began to feel the bile building in his stomach. If Elsa was dead, he would have to blame himself. She never liked the business they were in and felt her being fondled by a variety of impatient adulterers cheapened their own relationship. Jack buried his face in his hands and began to sob, regretting every action that had led to this moment.

Suddenly the silence was shattered. "Don't just sit there, help me out of the water!" shouted Elsa grabbing the side of the boat. She looked bedraggled, and weary from floundering around in the sea for the last three quarters of an hour, but at that moment Jack thought she had never looked more beautiful. He put his hands under Elsa's armpits to pull her into the boat. As he took the weight of her body to lift her out of the water, she gasped in pain. "Be gentle, the bastard shot me," said Elsa half smiling at Jack who, on seeing a watery red patch on her shoulder of her white blouse, readjusted the position of his hands to reduce the pressure on her injury. Elsa could not help him much in her weakened state and although Jack tried to be as careful as possible she cried out again from the pain of being manhandled.

Once she was safely in the boat, Jack dropped to his knees, cradled Elsa's head and kissed her firmly on the mouth. The overwhelming sense of relief he felt in finding her alive was unlike any emotion he had ever experienced before. The nausea and tautness that had spread over his entire body earlier, evaporated and suddenly with his sense of relief he felt very tired. As he moved his hand to Elsa's right shoulder she winced in pain from its weight. In the half-light Jack saw the bullet hole through the top of Elsa's blouse and pulled it down off her shoulder to see where she had been hurt. The bullet had gauged a crease in the top of her shoulder, just above the collarbone. The red crease looked deep, but the salt in the water had cleaned the wound. Jack pulled Elsa close to him trying to comfort her and ease the distress she must have felt while she was in the sea.

"The bastard tried to kill me," Elsa whispered. Relief at being rescued was followed by a loss of energy, and she lay in the boat exhausted after believing that she was going to drown. Suddenly she grasped hold of Jack tightly and started to cry, allowing her emotions to pour out of her, now that she was safe. "The bastard shot me," she sobbed repeatedly, before adding "I was thrown overboard into the water. When I realized what had happened I was afraid he would take another shot at me if he saw me bobbing in the water, so I swam underneath the boat. Then he started the boat's engine and almost dragged me into the propeller. I've never been so scared. I was certain I was going to die!"

"Don't worry baby, he's going to pay for hurting you. He's going to pay dearly," replied Jack. If Walsh had been in his grasp now Jack would have snapped his neck like a twig. The anger he felt would soon subside once Elsa was safely on shore and on the road to recovery, but Jack wanted to keep hold of the memory of this feeling so he could use it for future motivation in planning the downfall of Walsh. He looked down at Elsa, who was now comfortably resting her head on his chest. Her wound was still weeping a little but the seawater had done a good job in cleaning it and starting the healing process.

Jack took off his jacket, folded it and placed it under Elsa's head to make her feel more comfortable lying along the clear length at the front of the boat behind the driver's seat. He then went to the rear end and started up the outboard motor before going back to check once more on Elsa, who was now asleep. Satisfied that she was comfortable he put the engine in gear to head back to the harbor. He looked at Elsa again and wondered what kind of man would resort to killing someone merely because of their rejection of him. Nothing could have justified such a black hearted act. He wanted to make Walsh suffer physically as well as financially, but the best and most lasting way to hurt him was through his pocket. The stakes had risen sharply because Walsh, not knowing if Elsa was dead or alive, could now be blackmailed for attempted murder......or even murder itself. Jack shivered again as he realized how close he had come to losing Elsa and he opened the throttle of the engine.

By the time they got back to the harbor the daylight had all but disappeared, and Jack had put together the framework of a plan to get even with Walsh. He looked down at Elsa sleeping. Her hair was stuck to the side of her face and her eyes were stained from the running of her makeup and puffy from crying. He gently woke her as the boat pulled up to the jetty. "Do you think that you'll be able to get to the car park, while I return the boat keys and binoculars?" he asked.

"Of course I will," she replied, feeling uneasy but not wishing to make too much of a drama out of the day's events. She shivered and held her hand out for the car keys, clutching the edges of Jacks jacket, which was draped around her shoulders, with the other hand to keep herself warm. Jack felt bad at letting her walk back to the car on her own, but he didn't want to risk her being seen by the motorboat attendant, or anyone else who may still be hanging around the marina.

As he walked into the office of the boat hire company he saw the attendant slumped in his chair, reading a magazine. The man folded the magazine and stood up as Jack walked to the counter. "That was some joy ride you've had," he said, "I was getting ready to call out the coast guard. Didn't I tell you that you were not to go outside the perimeter marked by the blue colored buoys? These boats should not be taken into deep water as they can't handle big waves."

"I'm sorry," replied Jack, "I lost my bearings and the time just seemed to fly by. I didn't think I'd gone out too far until I lost sight of the marina."

"You've had far more than your allotted time and I should think you've also drained the tank. It's a wonder you didn't end up stranded out there," retorted the attendant who wasn't going to be placated by Jack's lame apology.

Jack took two hundred dollar bills from his wallet and put them on the counter, together with the boat keys and binoculars. "I hope this compensates you for your inconvenience", said Jack trying to appease him. The attendant shrugged his shoulders, picked up the boat keys and dropped them into a drawer behind the counter. Jack smiled and left the office.

Watching Jack walk away from the office, the attendant picked up the two hundred dollar bills and put them in his pocket. His eyes remained fixed on Jack as he made for the exit to the car park. He couldn't remember a woman getting into the boat when he hired it to Jack, so he wondered how and where she had gotten onto the boat, and why she looked so unkempt. She had obviously been in the sea and by the looks of her was much the worse for wear from the experience.

As Jack walked back to his car he felt confident that the attendant wouldn't make a fuss about the late return of the boat, especially as he was $200 better off for a little overtime. When he got to the car he found Elsa fast asleep in the passenger seat, the keys were in the ignition. He opened the driver's door and got into the car and started the engine. Elsa stirred a little but wasn't going to be roused until she had to get out of the car. The vehicle pulled out of the car park and disappeared into the night.

As Jack drove back to the hotel he worried about the mental trauma Elsa might suffer over the next few days when remembering or dreaming about being shot, and how close she came to drowning. He had no doubts about her physical recovery. Elsa was strong and would quickly bounce back from her ordeal, especially as he would get Doc Brandt to patch her up. Yes, Elsa was resilient, he mused, but he still couldn't help but wonder how easily she would cope with the news of her own premature death.

Jack arrived at the hotel where they were staying and asked the reception clerk for a wheel chair, before collecting Elsa. As he passed through reception to the elevator he said, "She's had a minor accident. Fell into the sea but I was able to fish her out without too much damage." Elsa was half asleep but smiled at Jack's simple and under-stated explanation.

5

Simon Walsh got back to his hotel at 7:30 PM. He had a penthouse suite at the Sheraton on Marine Drive that overlooked the beach. Still feeling edgy and irritated after the incident with Elsa, he poured himself a large glass of Jim Beam and found that as he lifted the glass to his mouth his hand was visibly shaking. He put the glass to his mouth took a large gulp of the whiskey and swallowed hard. The whiskey steadied his nerves and he sat down on the sofa cursing "Lisa", rather than himself, for his current predicament. The stupid bitch brought it on herself by stringing him along and then playing hard to get. He shrugged, took another swig of whiskey and decided that prick teasers like that deserve all they get!

But! She had a sister who would now be wondering why she hadn't returned home, particularly as a table had been booked for dinner. His common sense told him that "Lisa's" sister would eventually realize that she was not coming home and would go to the police to report her disappearance. Walsh tried to remember "Lisa's" surname and picked up the local telephone directory and began rapidly thumbing through the pages. His mind was racing as he scanned the pages trying to find "Millarno". Unable to concentrate and focus his thoughts on the task he threw down the phone book, picked up his glass of whiskey and took another large gulp. The sharp bite of the liquor snapped him out of his agitated state and he became calmer as the numbing effect of the alcohol soothed his brain.

He stared vacantly at the wall directly in front of him and smiled to himself at having another panic attack and his fit of anger. If by a miracle he did contact "Lisa's" sister, what on earth could he possibly say to her and how would it help to disguise his part in her sister's disappearance? It would only serve to draw attention to him, rather than deflect it away. "Lisa's" sister was probably unaware of her sibling's movements during the day and certainly wouldn't know of her meeting him and their boat trip together. Mentally Walsh began to reconstruct the events of the day, trying to identify any one factor that could incriminate him. The only people who could connect him with "Lisa" where at the marina and no-one had a complete picture of the time he spent with "Lisa".

Walsh guessed that hundreds of "missing persons" reports would be lodged with the police each year. They couldn't possibly investigate every case and would have no particular reason to go out to the marina. Jerry had seen him leave his bar with "Lisa" and Joe, who maintained his boat for him, saw them sail out of the harbor together, but neither man knew her name, or would have reason to connect "Lisa's" disappearance with him. He had spoken to Joe about cleaning the boat, but it was a brief instruction made in passing as he left the marina and the mechanic hadn't reacted to "Lisa" not returning with him. It was likely that the woman would just become another police statistic. Walsh concluded that the best way of protecting himself from prosecution would be to simply ignore the whole incident and not do anything that could link him to her.

Despite logically trying to think his way out of his predicament, Walsh couldn't forget the shooting or stop worrying about the prospect of his being charged with her murder. Reliving his fight with "Lisa", he couldn't understand how the gun had gone off or the freakish way in which the bullet had hit her. God knows he had no intention of killing her; he only wanted to frighten her enough so that she would agree to do what he wanted. He decided that in future he would avoid unnecessary complications and stick to dealing with prostitutes. They didn't behave like prima donnas and were professional in satisfying their customers, and like any other commodity could be had for the right price. They didn't act as if they had something special between their legs, and if he stuck with the high class girls they could be every bit as attractive and alluring as women like "Lisa". He poured himself another large glass of whiskey and sat back down on the sofa, now more relaxed than when he had first returned to the hotel.

In his relaxed, and now drowsy, state his memory took him back to a similar incident with a teenage whore in New Orleans. Unlike most of the sluts he dealt with, she had balked at the idea of being fucked in the ass and had called him a pervert. Incensed by her refusal he had beaten her unconscious and then taken advantage of her when she was unable to fight back. He thought no more of the episode believing that she'd deserved the beating. When she was discovered unconscious the next morning she was rushed to hospital and had to undergo emergency surgery to relieve the pressure from a blood clot on her brain. The hospital reported the incident to the police, and the madam of the establishment where the girl worked gave them Walsh's name, and he was arrested for assault and battery. Desperate, Walsh called his father to sort out the mess. His father reluctantly called in favors with the police department, who exerted sufficient pressure on the madam of the brothel to persuade her to withdraw her statement about the girl spending the previous night with Walsh. The injured girl was also made a generous payment by Walsh's father.

The girl herself never fully recovered from the beating. After regaining consciousness 3 days later she was unable to remember anything of the events of that fateful night, or even the name of the person she was with. She continued to have blackouts for months after the incident and was eventually found dead in a back street alley, murdered in a petty mugging incident. Apparently two men had taken her to the alley before the murder. Witnesses thought that she was drunk and was being helped by these men. In actual fact she had blacked out while being hustled by them and they had taken full advantage of the situation. There was no real reason to murder her other than the fact that they must have enjoyed doing it.

This jam was no worse than the one in New Orleans thought Walsh, but he overlooked the fact that his father was no longer around to help him. In fact he considered the situation to be much better than the one in New Orleans because there weren't any witnesses and there would probably be no body, and therefore no forensic evidence. The effect of the whiskey was beginning to cloud his thought processes, as he had about a third of the bottle in the two glasses he'd drunk already. He poured himself another large glass and in his light headedness decided he would call his wife. He did not enjoy the best of relations with his wife and hadn't spoken to her during his vacation, which was normal. They led parallel lives, despite living and working together. In his inebriated state he believed that the sound of her voice would give him succor. He picked up the telephone, got an outside line and dialed his home number in New York. Francesca the maid answered the phone and after exchanging the usual pleasantries fetched his wife, Bridget.

"Hello Simon," said the voice at the other end of the line flatly. "I didn't expect to hear from you before the end of your vacation. Is everything alright with you?"

I was a fool to think I'd get a warm welcome he thought. "Yes, everything's fine, I just wanted to call to see how you were."

"That's unexpected, but there's really no need," replied Bridget dispassionately "you should be out enjoying, yourself, sailing or whatever, while you can. I've got plenty to keep me occupied while you're away."

Walsh ignored the brush off and said, "I was out sailing today but wasn't feeling too well, so I only stayed out for a short time. I came back to the hotel and I've had a few stiff drinks to help me get to sleep." Walsh laughed at the thought of the disapproving face Bridget would now be making.

"Well as long as you're alright. Thanks for the call Simon, but I must go now. Enjoy the last day of your vacation and I'll see you when you get back." Bridget put down the phone abruptly not waiting for Walsh's reply. Walsh slammed the phone down onto the receiver, picturing Bridget's face in the black plastic and staring at it contemptuously. Was it any wonder he behaved the way he did when she made him feel small and treated him like shit.

Staring into a mirror on one of the hotel room walls, he noticed a red stain on his shirt. It wasn't a large stain but was unmistakably blood. He put his glass down on a coffee table and started to rip off his shirt, not wanting the blood to come in contact with his skin. Half the buttons were torn off the front of the shirt when he rolled it into a ball and hurled it to one of the corners of the room.

Walsh went back to the sofa and sat in the darkness of his hotel room, decided that he was going to finish off the rest of the bottle of Jim Beam and then go out on the town and sleep with as many whores as he could. He was in no condition to do anything, particularly as far as having sex was concerned. By the time he'd had another large glass of whiskey he would be close to passing out. Before he drifted off into the kind of deep sleep that only large quantities of alcohol can induce, he satisfied himself in his own mind that he had nothing to worry about and by the time morning came round he wouldn't remember a thing.

Walsh didn't appreciate that it's virtually impossible to do anything without people noticing, especially as someone known to vacation frequently in Miami, and with a reputation of spending a lot of money. Most significantly Walsh did not know that Jack Cates was planning to redress the balance by making him suffer for his treatment of Elsa. Jack had far more street savvy than Walsh and was also a strong and determined man who usually got his way.

6

"She'll be alright after a while, once the soreness in her shoulder has eased off," said Doc Brandt. "Make sure she sticks to her medication and don't let her mollycoddle herself otherwise it will stiffen up. She'll be sore for a while but no irreparable damage has been done. There'll be a faint scar where the bullet creased her, but a bit of make-up should cover it up, and it will fade with time." Jack had got in touch with Brandt immediately after returning to his hotel and was relieved that within an hour the doctor arrived to treat Elsa. Brandt had aged since their last meeting and Jack guessed he was in his late sixties. He remembered him as a tall man with a wiry build and angular features. He had the habit of perching his glasses on his hooked nose and looking over the top rim when talking to patients or their friends and relatives. He was now a little stooped and moved with a little stiffness that was probably due to arthritis, but like all medical professionals he didn't address the complaints of his own body.

Doc Brandt was the man who did whatever was necessary to patch up knife or gunshot wounds, or any other suspicious injury that would lead to awkward questions from hospital staff or the police. He was a qualified doctor who had been accused of carrying out back street abortions, before they became legal, and was in serious danger of being dragged in front of the medical ethics committee. Contacts he had already nurtured with senior figures in organized crime syndicates in Florida used their influence to ensure that these allegations were not carried any further. As a consequence he now belonged to them and became a well-known figure in the underworld. Jack knew him from his time with the NYPD when he was assigned to help the FBI with a case involving drug trafficking. The Miami Police Department were also providing a support to the FBI through Gene Tanner.

Cocaine shipped from Colombia to Florida was being transferred to New York by road and the outfit handling the transfer in Miami were given a cut for managing the merchandise, based on the value of the shipment. It was a smooth operation and the ultimate client Mario Pallacio was pleased at the way his Floridian colleagues were meeting their commitments. It was a tried and tested method of importing the drugs and all of the necessary palms had been greased to make sure nothing untoward would happen to the shipments.

Unfortunately one of their gang dealing with the shipments in Miami wanted more than the fee Mario was paying them and decided to cream off some of the cocaine to sell locally. Of course the shortfalls in the shipments became apparent, particularly as the quantities removed grew, as confidence in the lack of detection increased. Mario sent Leonard Tuzio down to Florida to sort out the situation, identify the miscreant and take the necessary action.

Around the same time one of the trucks carrying a cocaine shipment to New York had been picked up on the outskirts of the city during a routine search following a traffic violation. The FBI were called in to handle the investigation but came to rely heavily on information provided by Gene and Jack on the people most likely to be involved in the operation. The two local policemen became friends working in similar capacities in their home towns and being fanatical about the NFL. Gene took Jack to a game between Miami Dolphins and New York Jets and was confident of a win with his team playing on home territory, but he ended up paying Jack $100 on a side bet.

Inevitably Tuzio pruned out the guilty party stealing from the cocaine shipments, but was wounded in the resulting skirmish from a slice across his midriff made by a switchblade. The FBI cleaned up the battle site and weren't too concerned about gangsters killing each other, particularly now that the traffic route was known and couldn't be used in the future. They were unaware of Tuzio's involvement and happy about stopping the Miami end of the operation. Jack had recognized Tuzio from CCTV footage of arrivals at Miami airport and Gene had kept tabs on him and knew the hotel where he was staying. He raided his hotel hoping to get something that would tie his unwanted visitor to the cocaine shipments. Jack accompanied Gene as an observer, but all they found was Doc Brandt stitching up Tuzio's wound. Without any solid evidence to implicate Tuzio with the drug bust they reluctantly allowed him to return to New York.

Later Brandt's name was given to Gene by one of his snitches after a wounding in a homicide case. He had tried to use Brandt as a lead to the contract killer, who was wounded by the police as he escaped the scene of the crime. Nothing had come of the investigation and the killer was never found, despite Gene's harassment of Brandt.

In more recent times Jack had once again come into contact with the rogue doctor through his association with Roland Bannister. A wounding of one of his staff at the Blue Cockatoo led to Bannister asking for medical services from Mario Pallacio, who relished the situation of being able to shower his benevolence on Roland. In Pallacio's world one good turn always deserved another, and therefore his favor put Bannister further into his debt. He decided it would be better to use an outsider to avoid leaving a trail that could be traced. Once contact had been made with Brandt, Bannister was then able to access his services directly, with Pallacio's approval. Jack made all the necessary arrangements to get Brandt to New York.

Jack was relieved at Brandt's confirmation that Elsa had only sustained a minor injury but was worried about how quick the wound would heal. "Could the wound be infected?" he asked Brandt.

"Well, it's generally not a good idea to go swimming in the sea with a cut because the salt water is not sterile and can carry bacteria. This isn't such a problem down here, especially as she was bobbing on the top of the water, not going down to look at the reef. There is a nasty flesh eating bacteria, but provided you keep the wound open and clean it out with the medication I'm going to give you, she should be OK. If the wound starts to look sore and she feels sick, give me a call."

Brandt turned to Elsa and said, "Don't forget to leave it open for a couple of days and let it heal naturally."

The Doctor never let Jack forget their earlier relationship when they were on opposite sides of the fence, particularly when asking for payment, which caused Jack the greatest discomfort. As Brandt walked towards him, Jack picked up the telephone and made a long distance call to New York. Smiling Brandt held out his hand to receive his payment. Cradling the phone under his chin, Jack took out an envelope from the inside pocket of his jacket and handed it to the Doctor, who in turn handed him the prescription for the medication for Elsa. "It's always good to do business with you Jack," smirked Brandt, waving goodbye to Elsa before he left the room.

"Roland," replied Jack as a familiar voice came down the telephone line. "Listen Elsa and I need a big favor."

"Favors cost money Jack, you know that," said Bannister who was used to fencing with his friend and enjoyed the repartee. Although Jack worked for him from time to time he was not entirely dependent on him for his income, as he also had his own interests such as his Detective Agency and the scams he ran with Elsa. They had been involved in a couple of deals together in the past when Jack had made the necessary introductions to useful contacts, but he was strictly the junior partner in these ventures as Bannister had always put up the cash.

"Don't fuck with me Roland, Elsa's been hurt on the Walsh job."

"If Elsa's been hurt on one of your penny ante tricks there'll be hell to pay," interjected Bannister.

"Calm down Roland, she's taken a small gunshot wound in the shoulder. Fortunately Doc Brandt was able to see her at short notice. He says Elsa will be OK as the wound is minor and she'll recover quickly." Jack knew that Bannister would be angry when he heard the news of Elsa's injury, not because she was his main attraction at the Blue Cockatoo, but because he carried a torch for her. He tried to conceal his feelings but the usual tell-tale signs were all evident whenever the two were together.

Jack explained how he and Elsa had become separated after the pick up and ran through the chain of events that led to the shooting, toning down some of the more grisly elements of Walsh's assault. When Bannister heard that Walsh had tried to rape Elsa he started shouting at Jack again, threatening to hold him personally accountable for any post psychological trauma that could affect her performances at the Blue Cockatoo. "Can't you understand she has to be the ultimate sex object to every punter in the club? She can't do that if she's too frightened to get close to them," said Bannister.

"Listen Roland," said Jack apologetically trying to break the barrage of abuse being hurled at him, "how many millionaires or heads of wealthy business corporations do you know that are psychopathic? I had no idea the guy was going to freak out the way he did."

"OK, I know it's not really your fault but you go too close to the line on these scams. It's not always possible to control a guy when he's got his pants around his ankles because all he wants to do is cover up and break free. The real wonder is that no one's been injured before this. Elsa's special, you should know that, but you don't seem to appreciate her," said Bannister with rare sincerity.

The depth of emotion in Bannister's voice surprised Jack who hadn't appreciated the full depth of the affection that he had for Elsa. "It won't happen again Roland. You know I always plan these scams meticulously but in this case things just spiraled out of my control and ended up putting her at risk. But there can still be a payoff from this, one that could be big enough for all three of us." Jack paused waiting for Bannister to either explode again, or consider the potential of making some ready money.

"If that's the case, the payoff has got to be very big," replied Bannister. "That bastard should be eager to pay us handsomely if it's going to save his skin. The inmates are generally not very kind to men sent down for sex crimes or killing women. Someone of his delicate disposition would not like prison life at all, particularly if he were forced to experience rape as a victim, rather than as the perpetrator. Life is full of small ironies isn't it?"

"Don't get too carried away Roland. Your days as an attorney are long gone, but I'm glad you caught onto my train of thought so quickly. Walsh could find himself in a very vulnerable position if we can fabricate a robust case of murder against him, which will have to be based on circumstantial evidence, but may be sufficient for the police to take him to an arraignment hearing, even without a body."

"We need witnesses who saw Elsa and Walsh go out together and who can confirm he came back alone," replied Bannister.

"Yes, but we've got to move quickly before the trail goes cold! If I were in Walsh's position I would want to get away from Miami as soon as possible, especially considering that Elsa's body could be washed onto the beach within a couple of days. Don't forget he probably believes that he's murdered her."

"We need to make a missing person's report to the police to make them aware of Elsa's disappearance. I'll send Julie down to look for Elsa and report her disappearance to the police," said Bannister, taking decisive action to move things forward.

"The police won't act on the strength of a missing person report from a friend unless it can be corroborated by someone at the marina, and I think I know just the man for the job, but it will cost money."

"What's new? I'll wire you twenty grand, although you don't have to use it all if you can avoid it," suggested Bannister, adding, "Let's start the ball rolling as quickly as we can, I can already smell the money."

"You said yourself that we need witnesses who can confirm the movements of Walsh and Elsa at the marina. I'll give you a ring when the pieces are in place and the police have sufficient concern about the reason behind Elsa's disappearance to chase Walsh." Jack replaced the phone on the cradle and went in the bedroom to check on Elsa.

In the half-light of the early morning he could see her lying on the bed with the sheets pulled up to her chin and her knees circling up to her body. She still looked beautiful. She turned her head slowly and beckoned Jack to the bed. Jack sat down on the edge of the bed and Elsa shifted her position to face him, closing her eyes as he bent down to kiss her softly on the lips. "I can't do this anymore," Elsa whispered. "I really thought I was going to die out there." She paused for a second and shuddered at the thought of what might have happened. Jack squeezed her hand reassuringly.

Jack wanted to placate her and tell her not to worry that he wouldn't expect her to prostitute herself like this in the future. He wanted Elsa to know that he was planning one last big job that would set them both up for life and make Walsh suffer for what he had done to her. A sudden feeling of guilt washed over him for the times he had made her play the whore to compromise all of those rich unfeeling bastards that they had ripped off in the past. Roland's words about him not appreciating her echoed in his ears.

"I have to flaunt my body in front of those sad bastards in the Blue Cockatoo," Elsa continued," but I don't have to let anybody touch me anymore." Her voice faded as if she were making a pact with herself. She was still shaken eight hours after falling into the water and was now reappraising her life. With Jack there would always be one more score no matter how big the pay off. They had made a lot of money together from this racket and up to now it had been fairly easy with most of the punters being too embarrassed to make a fuss, or afraid of their wives finding out about their philandering. She had been carefully saving her half of the money while Jack had spent it on lavish gifts to her or his family, or lost it with gambling and reckless spending, or had simply given it away. He was a man that would always need more money.

"Listen Elsa," Jack pleaded, "you won't have to put up with this kind of life any more. Walsh thinks you are dead and that he murdered you. We have got to get some other people to think the same thing, to convince the world you're dead .... you've got to disappear." Jack paused to let Elsa fully take in what he was saying.

"But I thought that you were going to make him suffer for what he did to me. I thought you were going to hurt the bastard," shouted Elsa. "He tried to rape me for God's sake, don't you care about that?"

"Of course I care Elsa, but we've got to be calm, think logically and be smart! There's only a short-term benefit in the satisfaction of me beating him up, which I could easily do. But we would be no better off after it, and you would have nothing to show for the hell you've been through. If my plan succeeds we'll be able to get a small fortune out of him that will get us out of this fucking rat race and let us start over somewhere else on our own terms." Jack stared intensely at Elsa willing her to understand the wisdom in what he was suggesting.

Elsa looked back at Jack searching for a sign that she meant more to him than the money he was expecting to squeeze out of Walsh. The emotion drained from her face when she saw that the excitement of working another angle, another scam, was greater than the anger he felt over what Walsh had done to her. "OK Jack," she said resignedly, "but afterwards things will have to change." Elsa may have reconsidered her decision if she knew what lay ahead of her.

7

Julie's plane landed in Miami at six o'clock in the evening. And she booked into the same hotel as Elsa. Elsa had made the original booking for the hotel, but now Jack had booked into a separate hotel to ensure that he and Julie could not be linked in case Walsh or the police made any enquiries about Elsa. After settling in to her room, Julie made discreet enquiries about her friend's whereabouts and was informed that she had not been seen since the morning of the previous day. The clerk advised her that Elsa should have checked out earlier, before 12:00AM, and that they were storing her belongings so that they could prepare the room for the next guest. He added that they would keep Elsa's belongings until her bill was settled.

Julie then went to Jack's hotel and found his room number from one of the receptionists. She knocked on the door, to be greeted by Jack's smiling face. Instead of returning his smile Julie pushed passed him and went straight into the apartment to find Elsa sitting on the sofa in her pajamas. Julie rushed over to hug her. "Gently," Elsa chided, "I'm still sore."

"I guess this is all thanks to lover boy over there," replied Julie, "who doesn't seem to mind putting your ass on the line." Of course Jack had once been Julie's "lover boy".

"Take it easy Julie; Jack couldn't have known the way Walsh would behave when I was alone with him on his boat. We got separated and so he couldn't step in at the right moment, as he normally does. I feel equally responsible because I shouldn't have got onto Walsh's boat with him. The risks were obvious."

"It could have turned out worse," interjected Jack, "but it didn't and now we've got to make this trip to Miami worthwhile. Roland, Elsa and me have a plan to put Walsh on the spot, and we want you to help us. We'll make it worth your while."

Julie turned from Jack to Elsa who nodded to confirm what he was saying and that Roland supported them. "This means that I've got to disappear to make it look as if Walsh really did kill me and make others suspicious about my not returning with him to the marina," Elsa added.

"I think I understand," replied Julie at a loss to know why Elsa was continuing to do just as Jack wanted. After a short pause she added, "Roland told me to talk to you and Jack and follow your instructions."

"I want you to go to the police tomorrow and report Elsa missing. Tell them you've not heard from her in two days and that she was supposed to ring you before leaving Miami to arrange a pick up at the airport," said Jack.

"But, tomorrow's Sunday, why would I wait to call the police?"

"When Elsa didn't ring on Friday night you became concerned, particularly when you had no word by Saturday morning. You didn't want to ring alarm bells if it wasn't necessary, knowing that sometimes she'd lose track of time if she was enjoying herself, so you arranged a flight to Miami to check things out."

"Doesn't that seem a bit extreme?" asked Julie.

"Normally I would say yes, but in this instance it was important for Elsa to confirm her flight with you because she had made an appointment with her stock broker, before leaving for Miami, to discuss her stock market investments. That bit is actually true and provides a good reason for you to be concerned as she was adamant about keeping the appointment before her body clock changed to suit her working hours at the Blue Cockatoo. What time did you arrive in Miami?"

"About six o'clock," replied Julie.

"Good that fits in with the general framework of the story. In the meantime I'll grease some wheels down at the marina," said Jack.

"What do I do after going to the cops? It would be a shame not to take advantage of the Florida sunshine while I'm here."

Jack gave Julie a thousand dollars to cover the flight ticket and other expenses while she was in Miami. What he didn't know was that Bannister had bought her flight ticket and also given her a thousand dollars for expenses. Julie smiled thinking that she would have plenty of time for shopping before returning to New York.

After talking to Julie, Jack drove over to the marina and waited for the motorboat attendant to collect his car from the car park after work. He spotted the man entering the car park and got out of his car to intercept him before reaching his own car. He put his hand on the man's shoulder as he went to open his car door. The man turned anxiously on feeling the hand on his shoulder, but relaxed when he recognized Jack.

"Hi," said Jack, "how's the motorboat business?"

"It don't matter to me, I don't own the fucking business," replied the man in a matter of fact way, shrugging his shoulders to emphasize the point.

"You know everyone who works at the marina though, don't you?"

"Well I've been working there for the last ten years, so I oughta," the man replied with growing interest.

"Simon Walsh took his boat out yesterday afternoon with a very pretty young woman aboard. Trouble was I heard that he came back alone," said Jack as the man looked back at him impassively. "It must be a long swim back to the marina from wherever they went in his boat and my guess is that she didn't make it."

"What's that got to do with me?"

Jack paused to study the attendant for a moment. He was a typical middle aged under achiever with few interests outside his job other than perhaps sport or DIY. After work he would usually have a quick drink at his local bar where he would tell anyone who cared to listen what was wrong with the world, and what needed to be done to put it right. He probably felt he was underprivileged, but through no fault of his own as he never had the breaks other people had to make a success of his life. Despite his aggressive demeanor Jack sensed that he would be amenable and useful if given the right incentive.

"As responsible citizens you and the other workers at the marina should advise the authorities if you have any doubts about the welfare of the young woman who went out with Walsh yesterday."

"If you're so worried why don't you go to the cops?"

"I could, but then you wouldn't benefit if I went instead of you. Besides, there must be a number of you who would have noticed Walsh with a beautiful young woman down at the marina yesterday and cursed him for having the money to take her out on his sports cruiser. Why don't you talk to the barman at the Ocean Drop Inn or Walsh's mechanic? See what they think"

"Look, I'm sorry if the broad's been hurt," replied the attendant, "but Mr. Walsh is an influential man and I value my crummy job, because it's all that I got."

"What's your name?" asked Jack trying to put the conversation on a more personal footing.

"Al, if it's anything to do with you."

"Well listen to me Al, you don't have to go to the authorities yourself if you can raise doubts in those other guy's minds. Between them they probably have sufficient information to provide the cops with the complete picture. I just want you to make them understand what has happened and the importance of their coming forward."

"That's easier said than done," replied Al.

"Like I said there's something in it for you. Here's five thousand dollars," said Jack handing him an envelope. "If you and your work colleagues find it necessary to report their concerns to the police you'll receive another envelope with the same amount of money in it.

If not I'll be back to collect this," he said pointing at the envelope he had just handed over.

"That's a big incentive," said Al looking into the envelope before putting it into his jacket pocket. "Have the money ready, the job's as good as done." With that he climbed into his car and drove off.

Sunday morning was a nice warm, clear day with a light breeze. At eight o'clock Al was talking to the mechanic, Joe Weaver, who had serviced and refueled Walsh's boat. "Say, Joe that was a fine piece of ass that Walsh went out on his boat with on Friday, the lucky bastard. It just shows what money can get you, doesn't it?"

"Yeah, while I'm up to my neck in grease he's out at sea relaxing with a beautiful broad, where's the justice? Everything he's got was built by his old man, he hasn't earned a penny of it."

"Have you seen that broad before? She's sure hard to forget," pressed Al.

"No, I haven't," replied the mechanic. "And I've not seen her since. Walsh hasn't been out on his boat since Friday and he's leaving today."

"That's a pity I was hoping to get another look at her before Walsh finished his vacation. I bet she looked a little more ruffled getting off the boat than she did getting on it. As I said what a lucky bastard that man is."

"Come to think of it, I didn't see her getting off the boat," said Joe scratching his head. Walsh got back at about six thirty and insisted I clean the boat before finishing as he wasn't going out again and wanted it moth balling for next year. I couldn't see the urgency, so I'll do it when I get round to it."

"But you said the broad wasn't on the boat, that seems strange, doesn't it?" said Al trying to keep the mechanics thoughts focused in the right direction.

"Walsh called me over to the boat as soon as he berthed, I would have definitely seen her getting off the boat if she'd been aboard. I don't know why she wasn't with him," he said as much to himself as to Al. "She couldn't have been on board. It never struck me as strange at the time."

"There must be a logical reason for it, he must have dropped her off elsewhere," replied Al. He knew the mechanic would realize that her disembarking elsewhere was not a likely proposition as they had only been out for about three hours and there were no free berths within one and a half hours travelling distance. The seed of doubt had been planted in Joe Weaver's mind and that was enough.

Mid-morning Al went into the Ocean Drop Inn and repeated his patter about the stunning woman with Walsh on Friday afternoon. "I don't know if she was a hooker or not," said Jerry. "She certainly didn't look like the kind of hooker you'd see downtown, but she latched onto Walsh as soon as he came into the bar. He's always had a roving eye so there was a very strong chance that he'd have made a bee line for her, even if the bar had been packed."

"She didn't look like no hooker to me either," said Al.

"I know what you mean, with looks like hers she wouldn't need to ply her trade on the streets; she'd be into a much higher class of clientele. Sure she was a looker, but she was sophisticated too, you know in the way she dressed. There was nothing cheap about her, but I guess she could have been searching for a high roller like Simon Walsh. Whatever the reason, they left here with his hand on her ass."

"They may have left together, but it doesn't seem as if they came back together," replied Al who went on to recount his conversation with the mechanic. Al was satisfied after talking to Jerry that he had introduced sufficient doubt in his mind to prick his conscience about the young woman's safety and that his concern would grow the more he thought about it. Al was confident that both Jerry and the mechanic would go to the police to report their suspicion of foul play on Walsh's boat. Police enquiries would subsequently lead to corroboration of their stories, and kick off an investigation into

Elsa's whereabouts following her meeting Walsh in the Ocean Drop Inn.

Julie walked into the 10th Precinct Station to report Elsa missing at the same time as Al was talking to Jerry. She strode to the front desk and asked for the Duty Sergeant and made a statement on Elsa's disappearance as Jack had instructed her. Although the sergeant took her statement with a resigned air that said he had heard her story many times before, his attitude would change later when three witnesses from the marina were brought into the station to make formal statements about a missing person.

A police officer had been sent to the marina on Monday afternoon following a telephone call from Joe the mechanic to the police station. Interviews included sessions with Joe, Jerry and Al, although Al kept a low profile by ensuring that his testimony was based on the conversations he had with the other two and would not be admissible as evidence. He did confirm, however that he had seen Walsh and Elsa together at the marina as they walked across the wharf to Walsh's boat.

After taking formal statements the police felt that they had sufficient justification to question Walsh. Walsh had left Miami on the previous Sunday and was now at his home in New York. Detective Tanner rang Walsh on Monday evening to request an interview with him on the following Wednesday. They agreed a time of two thirty in the afternoon, when Walsh knew his wife would be out.

8

Walsh replaced the receiver of the phone quickly when he heard his wife coming into the hallway. "Francesca says that dinner will be ready in thirty minutes Simon, which should give you plenty of time to freshen up and dress ahead of the concert this evening. The concert is scheduled to start at eight o'clock and I don't want to arrive late." Bridget Walsh gave her husband a disdainful look as he smiled and bowed subserviently in acceptance of her instructions. "You can put your business matters on hold for one evening in the year, and at least give me a little support, as I am the President of the charity that will receive the proceeds from the concert. Oh, just please hurry up."

Smiling thinly at Bridget, Walsh watched her as she ascended the stairs without a backward glance towards him. She had spoken and clearly expected him to obey. He followed her up the stairs and went into his bedroom. He poured himself a glass of whiskey and loosened his tie. Tanner had not been specific about the purpose of his visit which caused Walsh to wonder if it was connected with "Lisa Millarno". Tanner had told Walsh that he was following a routine line of enquiry concerning an incident at the marina where his boat was berthed and that he might be able to assist him. Although he felt a little agitated after the call, Walsh decided that he would wait until he heard what Tanner had to say before starting to worry about being implicated in any crime.

Bridget sat at her dressing table and picked up the VIP guest list for their evening's event. She looked into the mirror and brushed a wisp of blonde hair away from her forehead. She was an elegant woman who moved in a natural and unaffected way. Her blonde hair and pale complexion betrayed her North European ancestry. Her figure was slight, even willowy, giving the impression of a delicate frame; however the inner strength she needed to remain in control of her loveless marriage with Simon Walsh was a measure of her strong determination and fighting spirit.

Being the great granddaughter of a Polish immigrant, who had built up a steel fabrication and erection company following his arrival in the United States after the 1st World War, resilience was part of her genetic make-up. Her grandfather began working as a site laborer and rapidly progressed to foreman and then construction manager. It was only a matter of time until he went out on his own, initially with small contracts, but he inevitably built his company into a well-respected and trusted concern with a reputation for delivering good quality work on time. Her father Pavel Koslowski who, like his grandfather had started work after getting an engineering degree at the basement level and had worked very hard to become Chief Executive. He took great pride in the reputation of the company for competitiveness with quality and in his own good name.

The collapse of a partially built steel frame during the construction of an office block, which had resulted in the death of one of the steelwork erectors, threatened legal action for negligence arising from use of sub-standard materials. The public inquiry of the incident had uncovered false certificates issued with the imported steel and that the original overseas steelwork supplier had disappeared following a number of similar complaints over the quality of their steel products. After the findings of the inquiry were released, confidence in Pavel and his company had evaporated and their order book was empty. Pavel's only real mistake had been in not verifying the credentials of the overseas steel supplier before signing contracts. They had been the only firm able to deliver the steel in the very short timescales required by the construction contract. In the few months following the accident all of Pavel's work force had been laid off and many had found new employment elsewhere. His business was now reduced to a hollow shell. Despite this setback Pavel was convinced he would eventually be exonerated and that business would get back to normal.

Bridget's father already suffered from poor health and this incident had visibly aged him to highlight his frailties, and he had lost confidence in his own judgement and his ability to manage the business. Bridget was concerned that further pressure would result in irrevocable deterioration of his health and could even be life threatening, given his heart condition. She found it hard to reconcile the frail body and spirit of her father to the strong, giant of a man that she worshipped in her childhood. She was a qualified accountant and was part of the family business working as the Company Secretary. In dealing with the loss adjuster of the National

Mutual Provident over the company's insurance claim, she met Simon Walsh, their Financial Director, and son of the Chief Executive, Sean.

When Bridget greeted Simon on his first visit to their offices she was pleased to find that he was considerate and sensitive to her company's present circumstance and the poor health of her father. He explained at great length that his involvement in the case was driven by the need to quickly expedite the claim and because her father was a loyal and valued customer. The first day went well and Walsh asked her to have dinner with him that evening. Although her initial reaction was not to accept the invitation, she agreed to dine with Walsh hoping that a friendly working relationship between them might help promote a benevolent approach in his administration of the claim.

Walsh took her to the most expensive restaurant in town and spent the whole evening talking about himself, his father and his important role in the running of the National Mutual Provident. He clearly enjoyed Bridget's company and his single purpose during the whole of the evening appeared to be the need to impress her.

The couple dined together on several occasions during the course of Walsh's investigation into the insurance claim, and she quickly became bored with his preoccupation with himself. By this time she had learned that he planned to take over the reins of the National Mutual Provident when his father retired and had lofty ambitions to enter politics and eventually run for Congress. The more time she spent with him, the more she began to see through the shallow veneer of his public face and recognized a ruthlessly ambitious and egocentric individual. The full depth of his ruthlessness only surfaced during their last dinner date.

"Your father's in a tight spot," said Walsh while he was ordering the after dinner liquors. "He should have arranged for independent testing of the steel by an accredited test house. It's good practice when importing steel and it's also a condition of the insurance agreement. Your father can't hack it anymore and now he's going to lose the company and could even end up going to prison."

Walsh's sudden change of attitude unsettled Bridget and she fought her natural instinct to retaliate. "We don't normally carry out independent tests, unless specifically requested by the client," she replied. "The company who supplied the steel sent us evidence of testing on previous contracts and we checked the company was an accredited supplier in their own country and internationally. We also checked that there were suitable test houses locally available to the production plant to test the steel."

Unfazed by Brigit's interjection, Walsh continued, "You may not be aware of this requirement because you're only a small company and don't normally import your steel. The steel for the other contracts you've undertaken in the past was sourced within the United States. The tight lead in to delivery forced your father to go elsewhere. Your father was negligent in the execution of his responsibilities and did not comply with the requirements of the insurance policy. If I report these facts the insurance claim will not be paid and your father could be prosecuted for criminal negligence."

Bridget began to feel nauseous at the prospect of her father going to prison and feared for the detrimental effect his prosecution would have on his health and on his reputation, which he prized above money. Unable to find an argument that would mitigate her father's failure to carry out independent tests, she pleaded to Walsh's better nature, "My father's been with your company for twenty years without a single claim, surely that must count for something."

"Not as far as my Company's shareholders are concerned," replied Walsh pompously. "But I'm sure that if I'm frugal with the actual details in my report that something can be done about your claim," he continued as he covered Bridget's hand with his. Walsh felt her hand stiffen on his touch and he began to squeeze it more tightly until she winced in pain. "I've enjoyed our time together Bridget and I've come to know you quite well. My initial objective was simply to fuck you, but now I think you can be of much greater use to me."

Although she was feeling very uncomfortable, Bridget's only concern was for her father so she accepted the overfamiliarity and rough handling without complaint. She relaxed and his grip on her hand eased. "My father is due to retire, in fact it would be unwise for him to continue running the firm in his current state of health. He would be satisfied if his current financial commitments were honored by the claim and the matter of the independent test certificates was not taken any further," said Bridget.

"That's asking a lot," replied Walsh. "My father is also due to retire soon and he keeps telling me that it's good business practice to have a wife around when running a company. You're both attractive and intelligent, and also have sound commercial experience from working with your father. I wouldn't expect you to work directly for my company as you do for your father, but you know how business is conducted and that would be useful when entertaining associates and clients."

"Yes, but how does that help my father?" asked Bridget coldly.

"I will suddenly find correspondence from your father to an independent test house requesting sample testing of the steel. I will also find test certificates from the independent test house that verify the quality of the steel. These documents will demonstrate your father complied with the requirements of the insurance policy. Test certificates from verification tests undertaken by my company, will corroborate the findings of the independent test house. The accident will therefore be put down poor workmanship and your father's reputation will remain unblemished," said Walsh confidently. "It's a tall order but there are several people who owe me favors, which I can "cash in" to settle this business."

"That will undermine the insurance claim of Frederick's family, the man killed by the collapse," replied Bridget. She felt compromised at protecting her father at the expense of others, but knew deep down she had no real alternatives.

"Someone has got to lose out, I'm sure you wouldn't like it to be your father. This way he can retire with a bit of money in his pocket," replied Walsh with a smug grin. Bridget nodded in agreement with her eyes fixed on the table, not wishing to give Walsh the pleasure of seeing her inner torment.

"Good! Now let's get things off to a good start," continued Walsh. He called the waiter, paid the bill and took Bridget to his hotel and they consummated their agreement. Walsh used Bridget's body as an object for his own gratification without any consideration of her needs or sensitivities. His discovery that she was a virgin heightened the level of his excitement. In the morning they agreed a schedule for the coming months that would ultimately lead to their marriage.

On her return home Bridget explained to her father that the insurance claim had been settled and convinced him that he should now retire, rather than risking further deterioration to his health. She also told him that she would be marrying Simon Walsh and moving to New York in the near future. Her father lived long enough to see her marry Walsh but died shortly afterward blaming himself for the loss of his own father's company and not providing for his work force.

Walsh and Bridget went on honeymoon to Niagara Falls. After dining together they went to their hotel room. She had endured months of sleeping with an inconsiderate lover and decided to draw a halt to her abuse on their wedding night. They got into bed and Walsh began groping her in the manner that had become normal over the proceeding months. As he buried his head in her breasts she grabbed the hair on the back of his head and pulled it backwards. "Now that we're married don't think that I'm going to submit to your crude pawing and groping, and pathetic excuse for love making."

"But we're married now, you've got to!" replied Walsh pulling his head free. "I'll make you if I have to!" he shouted threateningly.

"You rape me once more and I'll kill you in your sleep," said Bridget with a coldness that made Walsh shiver.

"If that's how you feel, why did you marry after the insurance claim was settled?"

"You took a lot from me," answered Bridget. "Now it's my turn to get something in return. I'll be a good little wife in front of family, friends and business colleagues, but don't expect any more than that. And I also want to be involved in the running of the NMP rather than being a token figure. I'm a chartered accountant and intend to keep on working."

They returned to New York the next day and Walsh moved into a separate bedroom explaining to Francesca their maid that he could only sleep properly when alone in his bed. Bridget took over as Financial Director at the NMP and when at home or at work her personal dealings with Walsh were restricted to business or domestic issues.

9

Detective Tanner was prompt. Francesca greeted him at the front door of the luxury apartment and took him into the study for his meeting with Walsh. Tanner introduced himself, produced his police badge to confirm his identity and the two men shook hands. Walsh invited Tanner to take a seat and asked him if he would like a drink. In response Tanner shook his head refusing the drink and made himself comfortable in the chair facing Walsh, who then told the maid to leave the room. He was impressed by the size and luxuriant décor and fittings of the apartment. The carpets were all pure wool and the walls in the reception and corridor to Walsh's study were clad with wood paneling. In Walsh's study the décor changed with the majority of the wall areas being covered by bookshelves and the remainder being clad either in patterned leather or light wood panels, giving a very masculine feel to the room. The furniture in the room was heavy oak, with the backrests and seats of the chairs clad with dark leather studded cushions.

Tanner being used to the warmth of Florida was wearing a coat to keep out the New York chill. He didn't look like a local cop to Walsh as he was dressed much smarter and wore a dark blue suit, white shirt and blue tie under his gabardine coat, which was belted at the waist. He was a big man and looked to have an athletic build. "This is a very nice apartment you have here. I don't think I've seen anything quite like it in Miami," said Tanner, opening his coat to make himself more comfortable.

"You've come a long way to talk to me Detective, there must be a better reason than seeing my apartment?" As he spoke Walsh poured himself a shot of Jim Beam saying, "I know it's a little early in the day for this but I'm not going back to work this afternoon so what the hell! Are you sure you don't want to join me?"

"No thank you Sir. There's nothing wrong with having a drink in the afternoon, but I'm on duty."

"But you can relax can't you? You're more than a little out of your jurisdiction so who's gonna tell?" Tanner put his hands up declining the offer. "Well, what about a soda?" continued Walsh

"No thank you. This isn't a social call, I'm collecting evidence for a case I'm working on. I have no authority here, but I must warn you that anything you say may be used as evidence, if it's relevant to my case. That also goes for evidence obtained through information you give me in our discussions. You can refuse to answer my questions if you wish."

Clever bastard thought Walsh. He knows with that statement he's made it difficult for me to kick him out, especially as I don't know exactly what he's come to see me about. "I've got nothing to hide. I assume you want to talk to me about my recent vacation in Miami?"

"Yes I do. I'm investigating the disappearance of a young woman called Elsa Bartelli, do you know her?"

Walsh had been expecting to hear Lisa Millarno's name and was relieved and pleasantly surprised at the name given to him. "The name doesn't sound familiar. I really can't remember," he stammered. "I'm sure I would remember her name if we'd met."

"She's not the kind of woman that you would easily forget. Take a look at this picture I have of her," said Tanner handing Walsh a photograph. It was a publicity picture from the "Blue Cockatoo", which showed Elsa in an exotic outfit, posing on stage.

Looking at the photograph Walsh immediately recognized the woman in the picture as Lisa Millarno, which made his stomach turn over. His earlier relief was replaced by anxiety, as he tried not to display any sign of fear that would be picked up by Tanner. An inner anger raged within him at his own stupidity in not anticipating that Lisa Millarno was a false name. Finally he said, "I see what you mean Detective, she's certainly a stunner, but unfortunately I can't place her."

"That's strange," replied the policeman, "you were seen in conversation with her at the Ocean Drop Inn in Miami last Friday afternoon, and later you both went out for a cruise on the sports boat you have berthed at the marina where the bar's located." Tanner delivered his statement in a matter of fact way that was not intended to antagonize Walsh, but nevertheless irritated him because it exposed his lie.

Another stupid mistake thought Walsh as his liaison with Lisa could be easily checked and verified. "Why have you been investigating my movements last Friday, am I suspected of anything?"

"We don't know that any crime has been committed Mr. Walsh. Miss Bartelli was seen drinking with you and later going out with you on your boat, but she has not been seen since and was reported missing the following Sunday. Two independent witnesses confirm your being with her on Friday, both in the Ocean Drop Inn and on your boat."

"You have it all wrapped up don't you Detective, your superiors will be impressed," replied Walsh stalling for time trying to collect his thoughts. His mind was racing beyond control and he was finding it difficult to string the simplest of sentences together. Clutching at straws he asked, "How is Commissioner Connor by the way I haven't seen him for some time?"

"He retired last month sir, and I believe he's enjoying his retirement in Palm Springs. Thanks for your interest, but can we return to my investigation as I have to catch a plane back to Miami at five thirty."

Walsh was getting more and more annoyed with the situation, particularly as he couldn't even use Connor as a threat to rattle Tanner. The face of the Detective was a mask, devoid of expression and emotion and did not betray any doubts or misgivings he may have harbored about the man he was interviewing. Walsh decided to try and treat him as a friend by taking him into his confidence, hoping Tanner could empathize with his situation. He took a gulp of his drink and said, "OK I do know the woman. She called herself Lisa Millarno and said she was in Miami visiting her sister. I went into the Ocean Drop Inn for a quick drink, she was sat at the bar and came onto me. We went out for a short boat ride, but I found out she was just a tease, so I came straight back and that's the last I saw of her."

"Why did you lie when I first asked you if you knew her? How can I believe you're telling the truth now? I want you to answer my questions honestly because if she's not found we will have to delve deeper into her movements last Friday."

"Look I'm a married man and I love my wife. I may party with other women while I'm away by myself but then I'm only human. My picking her up last Friday was like a hundred others I've had. They mean nothing and are quickly forgotten when I get home. I was afraid of my wife finding out, that's why I lied!"

"That's all very well Mr. Walsh, but it doesn't get me any nearer to finding out what has happened to Miss Bartelli and your lying could indicate that you're implicated in her disappearance somehow."

Walsh couldn't contain himself any longer and shouted at Tanner, "What the hell are you trying to say? I've just fucking told you my reason for lying, which is the beginning and end of it! Do you understand?"

Tanner remained calm in the face of Walsh's aggression saying, "I'm not trying to say anything – that's not my job. I only deal in facts and hard evidence. Miss Bartelli has been missing since last Friday and you Mr. Walsh were the last person seen with her before her disappearance. The longer it takes us to establish her whereabouts, or for her to contact her friends or relatives, the more suspicious the circumstances of her disappearance become as there is no obvious reason why she would wish to disappear. I'm sure you can understand that."

Tanner paused to take a breath and let the logic of his reasoning sink in with Walsh, whose anger had subsided, and he was now staring into his drink either looking for inspiration or a place to hide. He couldn't bluster his way through this situation and he didn't have the guile to outwit Tanner.

The policeman continued, "Her flat mate in New York had been expecting a call on Friday evening for a pick up at JFK the following day. She never got the call from Elsa and was unable to contact her at her hotel. Worried, she flew down to Miami on Saturday afternoon to find out if she was OK. There was no trace of Elsa at the hotel, and the hotel staff had not seen her friend since Friday morning."

"A couple of days isn't a long time to be incommunicado. She's a grown woman for God's sake she might have decided to extend her vacation, or gone off with some other sucker," reasoned Walsh.

"If she had done either of those things, her first thought would have been to cancel the return flight she'd booked at the very least. Neither did she check out of her hotel or pick up her luggage," replied Tanner. "You said she came onto you in the Ocean Drop Inn. How did she do that?" he asked trying to understand the circumstances of their meeting and the reason behind her being invited onto Walsh's boat.

"Well it's not too easy to explain. She didn't say or do anything but had an air about her that said she was game for anything. After all she came out with me on my boat minutes after first meeting me."

"Are you saying she was a prostitute?"

"No, of course not. It's just that she was friendlier than you would normally expect after just meeting a stranger. I'm used to girls coming onto me because I'm rich and well connected, so I recognized the signs. They want to be given a good time and have money splashed out on them."

"You have had experience with hookers before though, haven't you Mr. Walsh?" interjected Tanner.

Walsh was startled by the switch in the line of questioning from Elsa to him, and by the faint hint of aggression in the tone of the policeman's voice. "Yes I've been with prostitutes if that's what you mean. I do a lot of travelling and sometimes need a little more than just company from the women I meet."

"Did you want more than "just company" from Elsa, Mr. Walsh?" cut in Tanner.

"I told you she came onto me in the Ocean Drop Inn so I naturally assumed she wanted us to spend some time together, before her dinner date with her sister. It turned out that she was just being a tease so we came straight back."

"Do you mean she wasn't prepared to have sex with you?"

"Yes that's exactly what I mean," said Walsh, once again beginning to show the strain of the questioning on his face. "It soon became clear to me that she wanted money for sex so it was pointless carrying on."

"But you've been with prostitutes before so why was this any different? Why didn't you offer her money?"

"She didn't look like any hooker I've been with, and I thought she was being friendly because she liked me. I was looking for a little more than sex. I also wanted some friendly and witty company after what had been a pretty boring day."

"But sometimes your sexual advances get out of hand, don't they? Rita Alonzo is evidence of that," said Tanner increasing the pressure on Walsh.

"Who the hell is Rita Alonzo?" asked Walsh.

"She's the prostitute in New Orleans you very nearly beat to death."

"Oh yes I remember her now, I caught her trying to steal my wallet after I'd already paid her very well. The incident blew up out of proportion for a short time, but in the end she dropped the charges."

"Yes it's thanks to your father she dropped the charges. You may have made her pay for her mistake, but to my mind the severity of the punishment you meted out doesn't appear to have matched the "crime". Is that what happened to Elsa?"

"No it is not! If you are going to charge me with anything I want to call my lawyer," said Walsh. "I've tried to give you honest answers but you're just twisting everything I say."

"I'm just trying to get to the truth Mr. Walsh and, as I've said, I don't have the authority to charge you with anything. I have to ask these questions to ensure all avenues are covered in my investigation," replied Tanner in an attempt to calm Walsh so that he could carry on with his interview.

"I took Lisa or Elsa onto the boat, but when it became clear she was just after money we had a couple of drinks and went back to the marina," said Walsh having regained his composure.

"What time did you get back to the marina Mr. Walsh?"

"I can't remember," blustered Walsh.

"Nobody can support your statement or remember you returning to the marina with Miss Bartelli. In fact your mechanic Joseph Weaver says that you came back alone."

"He's mistaken, he can't be relied on to put enough fuel in the boat when I go out to sea, so he certainly can't be relied on to observe all of my comings and goings."

"That may be the case, but he seems pretty definite about the fact you returned alone and the time you arrived back at the marina," replied Tanner without giving Walsh the time given in the mechanic's statement.

"In that case it's a question of who you want to believe," retorted Walsh.

"Well I can see you're upset and probably not in a frame of mind to answer my questions objectively, so let's finish and thanks for your time," said Tanner rising from his chair. "Oh, I forgot to mention your telephone call to your wife last Friday. The telephone records show that you called your wife early in the evening so I'll need to talk to her to confirm the time of your conversation and what you said."

"Does that mean you're going to tell her about Lisa, I mean Elsa," said Walsh through gritted teeth. He was seething underneath his relatively calm exterior at the way Tanner had manipulated the interview and at how easily the Detective was able to undermine the information Walsh had given him. Certain that Tanner would now take the matter further, Walsh added, "I'm sure the records show that we only talked for a couple of minutes, hardly enough time for me to tell her that I had met a beautiful woman and subsequently murdered her on my boat!"

"I need to confirm the timing of your movements on that day so that we can build an overall picture of the events as they occurred. If you've nothing to hide, my investigation should help show you are innocent, which is to your benefit."

"Very delicately put, but if you suspect me of murder, why didn't you come straight out with it rather than pussyfooting around?"

"I haven't got all of the relevant information to come to any conclusion and I certainly haven't put you down as a murder suspect yet, Mr. Walsh. I need a lot more information to complete my preliminary investigation. Its outcome will decide whether or not we believe something untoward may have happened to Miss Bartelli, and if the investigation has thrown up any suspects that should be pursued."

"Is that reason enough to break up my marriage?" pleaded Walsh.

I can't promise you anything of course, but I have no desire to create a rift between you and your wife. I'm only interested in finding out what has happened to Miss Bartelli."

"I guess I'll have to rely on your discretion," said Walsh with mock sarcasm.

"Goodbye Mr. Walsh," replied Tanner extending his hand. Walsh refused his offer and remained silent and seated. "We'll be in touch," smiled Tanner ominously as he left the study.

Francesca was waiting in the hall to show Tanner to the front door. As he made his way to the underground car park below the apartment block he picked over the points raised in his interview with Walsh. He was amazed that Walsh had agreed to talk to him so freely and had expected that he would need to go to the NYPD for the authority to question him. Walsh had only raised his concern at the end of the interview when it dawned on him that he was under suspicion. His apparent apathy was probably down to his arrogance.

The earlier picture the Detective had built up of Walsh from delving into police records and his discussions with the witnesses was of a selfish, arrogant man with a complete disregard of other people, particularly women who were simply objects to him. Now after meeting him he had developed a vehement dislike for the man. He knew that it would be unprofessional to let his personal feelings for Walsh influence his recommendation on whether there was sufficient evidence to set up an arraignment hearing and begin the process of prosecuting him for murder, but he felt he would have to be convinced Walsh had nothing to answer for before clearing him as a suspect. He was sure that the department already had the makings of a good case against him for the murder of Elsa. The blood and hair samples taken from his boat were pretty damning evidence of foul play, but without a body it would be more difficult to convince a jury of her murder. Forensic investigation of the boat was bound to come up with more evidence, if a murder had been committed, which Walsh will have overlooked and could build up the case against him.

In weighing up the prospects of a successful prosecution Tanner thought that because Walsh was unaware of the developing case profile and the supporting evidence being collected, and based on his attitude during the interview, he would be in denial about the possibility of having a murder charge to answer. On the evidence of the interview, Walsh's arrogance will make him vulnerable as he is unlikely to offer a robust counter argument to explain events on the boat, and could even incriminate himself when charged. It was an unusual case without overwhelming evidence to prove his guilt or innocence, but in his gut Tanner felt he was guilty.

10

Jack hired a car at Miami Airport, and he and Elsa drove back to New York. Julie flew back to ensure that her return alone became a matter of record. Jack knew he would have to go and see Roland and thought he would go straight away after settling Elsa into his apartment. They hadn't driven at a fast pace just in case they were stopped by a bored traffic cop and broke the journey down into 3 legs, each being less than 500 miles, with two overnight stops at motels. He had paid in cash for the hotels he and Elsa stayed in to avoid his being placed in Miami at the same time as Walsh, which was standard procedure when they were hustling and had also used a false identity. The hire car, gas and motel stops were also paid for in cash, again to avoid using his credit card. Luckily Roland had sent him enough money to pay Al Ferrino and deal with incidentals for Elsa, Julie and himself.

"I'm going over to the Blue Cockatoo," Jack told Elsa as she made herself comfortable on his sofa, sipping a fresh mango and orange drink.

"And what am I supposed to do while you're away? Sit and watch TV?" said Elsa with mock annoyance. They had spent several days together since the Walsh incident and she was actually looking for a bit of free time and a long soak in the bath.

Jack had also felt tied down by the need to stay with Elsa virtually every hour of the day, but picked up on her fake anger, smiled and blew her a kiss as he disappeared out of the apartment.

"Ha! The wanderer returns," exclaimed Bannister as Jack entered his office in the Blue Cockatoo. "What would you like to drink?"

"I'll have a cold beer, in the bottle," Jack replied as he made himself comfortable on the couch. The two way mirror gave a perfect view of the club's catwalk and bars. It was interesting to note the different expressions on the faces of the punters as they watched the girls' parade in front of them. Some were like little kids who had just found some money in their pocket that they didn't know was there, others were overtly lustful towards the girls but knew that they would be in big trouble if they as much as touched them. The majority were there to get drunk, gawk at the bodies on display and tell each other what they wouldn't do to them if they were given the chance.

The catwalk zig - zagged through the main room of the club forming large table areas at every change in direction. Each table area was large enough for two girls to dance and included a pole. In all there were five areas for dancing and the punters gathered around the area where their favorite girl was performing. Elsa always had one of the end areas where more people could congregate around the dance floor, and always performed alone. The other girls didn't mind as they knew she always drew the largest crowds.

There was a bar at the far end of the room and one in the center of the longest stretch of the catwalk. The spirits were the cheapest available and the beer was weak. Nobody complained about the quality of the alcohol being served or the exorbitant prices charged. At the side of the main room were small rooms that could be used by punters who wanted a private performance from one of the girls. Jack mused to himself that the club represented to the entertainment world what McDonalds did for haute cuisine.

Roland Bannister had certainly built on the success of the place since taking it over and certainly appeared to know what his customers wanted. He was constantly changing the dance themes and even had the girls play out little tableaux's from time to time that simulated most of the major male sexual fantasies. Elsa didn't usually participate in this part of the entertainment or give private performances, but that seemed to make the punters want her even more.

Jack turned to Roland Bannister to take the bottle of beer he handed to him. He perceived Bannister to be the antithesis of himself both in appearance and manner, and wondered if his roots went back to one of the rich aristocratic families of England, or on the other hand maybe his ancestors were rich plantation owners involved in the slave trade. Certainly Roland was still pedaling flesh, albeit in a voyeuristic way.

It was a far cry from Bannister's beginning as an attorney in a smart Manhattan law firm, where he had never quite fitted in. He was too slick and smart for the senior partners because of his success rate and the volume of work he was able to get through. He was eventually compromised in a fraud case that involved insider trading and offshore bank accounts, when the prosecution discovered that he had also been investing in the same companies as his client. There was insufficient evidence to bring a criminal prosecution against him, but he was taken off the case and dismissed by the senior partners of the law firm.

After that he set up his own law practice above a betting shop in the Bronx. He had few of the trappings of most law practices, other than a brass name plate on his office door and his framed diploma on the wall. Early clients were not business men or corporate firms, but petty criminals and people with broken marriages. Nevertheless he proved his earlier promise with an exceptional success rate and soon came to the attention of organized crime through Leonard Tuzio, who became one of his best clients. Ultimately Bannister had arranged for the disappearance of Tuzio after his falling out with Pallacio, when he was in imminent danger of becoming another statistic at the City Morgue. He kept Tuzio in a safe place and provided him with a new identity and passport.

Shortly after Tuzio's disappearance Bannister took charge of the Blue Cockatoo. It was already a thriving concern that had begun life as a seedy strip club. Tuzio had changed its image but Bannister was determined to improve on the entertainment, ambience and reputation of the club, and more importantly make it even more profitable. After extensive refurbishment he re-opened the club in a blaze of free publicity, after he had the girls do an exotic routine on a mock up stage in front of the premises. He was arrested but the media coverage was invaluable. Roland gave up his law practice two weeks after the club re-opening.

"Beer is not what successful men drink. Why don't you try and get used to some of the finer things in life, after all we're both on the verge of making some serious money," said Bannister.

"What do you need more money for? You already wear tailored shirts and Armani suits, and walk about in hand made shoes. Besides, I'm only drinking the beverage that befits my station in life."

"This is a celebration, Jack. Soon you'll know what it's like to have to count the number of digits on your bank statement and be able to dress like a gentleman. There was a time I thought my influence would have a positive effect on you. But somehow I don't think it'll matter how much money you have, you'll always be a slob."

"Thank you for that Roland, it's nice to know you hold me in such high regard. Didn't your mother tell you that clothes do not make the man, contrary to popular opinion?"

"Let's not fall out about it Jack, neither of us will care one way or the other when we get our hands on Walsh's money."

"Don't count your chickens Roland, we can't be certain of the money until Walsh is sent down. You know better than me that he has to go to an arraignment hearing before a trial can take place, and even then things can go wrong in a court room."

"I know that! You don't have to teach your granny to suck eggs," replied Roland, annoyed that Jack was trying to dampen his enthusiasm. "If the DA thinks there's sufficient evidence for Walsh to be charged he will take it to arraignment and the judge presiding over the hearing will decide whether there's a case to answer. If he goes to arraignment that will be the first indication of how serious they are."

"OK I'm sorry about explaining the obvious, given the depth of your expertise, but calm down there was no put down intended. I know we've got a very good chance of success, but we'll need to make sure the things outside our control are kept to a minimum. Without a body the forensic evidence and integrity of the witnesses will be crucial to convince the judge that Walsh should go to trial."

"I've been trying to find out who the DA's assigned as lead lawyer for the prosecution from Gene Tanner," continued Jack. "A few attorneys think it will be a high profile case so there'll be a race to get it, but it will probably be James Bantry, who has a good hit rate."

"Bantry spent his early career in New York and I helped him out of a jam when we both worked for the same law firm. He could be an ally," replied Roland.

"Gene has told me that the DNA of the blood found on Walsh's boat matches Elsa's of course, as do the hair samples. It was lucky the mechanic ignored Walsh's instruction to wash the deck. But we're both overlooking one major thing that will work against Walsh, which is he really thinks he's guilty of a crime. That will affect the way he handles himself in court, even if it is just his body language. He believes he murdered Elsa."

"Don't forget the gun Jack. If the DA finds out that Walsh used a gun to intimidate Elsa and it was actually fired, the stakes go up considerably. It doesn't matter if he's charged with 2nd degree murder or manslaughter, the use of a gun will put at least 10 years on his sentence if he's found guilty. That could be a double edged sword. If Walsh decides the stakes are too high not to cop a plea to the murder, he'd still have to do time for Elsa's attempted murder after she shows up, which will reduce his incentive to pay us."

"Don't worry, he won't be harassed into making a confession. After all there were no witnesses to the actual shooting, except Elsa, and she's supposed to be dead! He'll keep quiet expecting to be able to ride it out," replied Jack.

"Well then, why aren't you a little more optimistic about the result? I've seen successful cases prosecuted with far less going for them than this one. Lighten up, you've got me worried that I'm not going to recoup my little investment, which is growing daily by the way."

"C'mon Roland, twenty grand is nothing to you. It's just spare folding money."

"I'm not worried about the money Jack, it's the winning that's important. I've always been a winner no matter how heavily the odds were stacked against me. Even when I was kicked out of Farnshaw and Blythe I came up smelling of roses. So I'm not changing to the losing side now."

"For heaven's sake Roland nothing's guaranteed in this life. All we can do is lay the groundwork as professionally as possible and then hope the plan pans out to meet our expectations."

"Well why don't we go for the short odds and make a deal for Elsa to show before they bring the case to court," suggested Bannister.

"No," rasped Jack, "we won't be able to ask for anything like the amount of money that I want. Money may not be important to you Roland, but it is to me. I want this deal to be my last and make me enough money to kiss goodbye to creeping around the sewers of New York."

"C'mon Jack you know that you can't make that kind of decision on your own. It's my money at stake not yours."

"Look Roland I know that we're a team and any decisions have to be made together," Jack replied heatedly, "but we're in too good a position to throw it all away now. Walsh is in a tight spot and I'm sure that he's beginning to understand that by now. All we've got to do is sit tight and let things develop."

"That's exactly what I've been saying! Cool down Jack I was only trying to make a point. I know you've got this thing planned out in your head, but you've got to let Elsa and me know what's going on. We're all partners and have an equal say in how to manage this deal. Don't worry, I agree with you that it's far better to wait."

Jack was too intent in his desire to convince Bannister of the benefits of his scheme, to be aware that his partner had been playing with his head. Bannister enjoyed taking the contrary position in any argument, which was probably down to his training as a barrister. The two men continued to analyze the case until the early hours of the morning. They concluded that Bantry should be tactfully pointed towards carrying out forensic tests on Walsh's gun. Knowledge that the gun had been fired recently would add great strength to the case against Walsh.

Although Jack normally enjoyed the cut and thrust he shared with Bannister, this time he was annoyed that he had continued the role-playing for the fun of it. More importantly he became aware for the first time that the suave image of Bannister camouflaged the true character of a very ruthless man. So far Bannister had given Jack a lot of slack to let him operate in the way he saw fit, partly because he respected Jack's judgement but also because of his own infatuation with Elsa. But if things went wrong Bannister would be a very difficult man to placate.

Jack regretted having shown Bannister a part of himself he liked to keep private, when he expressed his desire to escape the rat race and the racket he was in. He didn't want Bannister to know how much the success of this job meant to him because he thought it would weaken his position in the partnership. Bannister could afford the diversion of playing his little mind games, but Jack wanted to remain focused until the job was over. He was not the man who had joined NYPD 15 years earlier as a naïve idealist.

Jack had gone to University on a sport's scholarship by playing football. At one time he had considered turning professional but a torn cartilage in his left knee had put paid to that idea. His father was a policeman with NYPD and suggested he join the force when he left university. Unlike his father, Jack's potential was quickly recognized by his superiors and after a brief period in uniform he was given training as a detective and assigned to Homicide. He quickly progressed to the rank of Detective Sergeant and gained a reputation both on the street and in his precinct as a fair and honest cop.

Proud of his reputation, Jack continued to operate efficiently without internal conflict with his peers in the force or interference from his superiors. His one dimensional view of the crime world and the role he played in containing it remained with him until he got involved in the investigation into the murder of a young prostitute, with his partner Charlie Inglewood. Her death was neither shocking nor unexpected as the word on the street was that she had crossed her pimp Enrico Gonzales and taken up with a rival. Neither pimp had any saving graces that would commend them to her, so the reason behind her taking the risk of moving from one to the other was far from obvious, and one which she took to her grave. Her mutilated body could only be identified from dental records. She was tied in a loving embrace to the body of her new pimp, who had also been tortured. The tableau that Gonzales had left in a seedy hotel room was a warning to his other whores not to cross him.

A tip off led Jack and Charlie to another hotel in Harlem only two blocks from the murder scene. Gonzales was arrogant and never considered the consequences of his actions or his need to keep a low profile, following the discovery of the bodies. Screams were heard from one of the upstairs rooms where one of his whores was entertaining a client. Jack knew from her identification by the desk clerk that the woman was one of Gonzales' whores and that Gonzales, who felt the need to keep his girls in a constant state of fear, often visited her. Her john had been seen running from the hotel room, half dressed and with a bleeding lip. Shouting and then screams followed his exit and the desk clerk reluctantly called the police.

On entering the hotel and confirming the hotel room number, Jack took the elevator to the 2nd floor, while Charlie took the stairs. As Jack emerged from the elevator he heard gunshots coming from the staircase. He raced towards the staircase and on opening the door to the landing found Charlie being held as a shield in front of Gonzales who was pointing a gun at his head. The pimp smiled when he saw Jack and squeezed off a shot in his general direction. Jack fell backwards into the corridor and quickly scrambled a retreat, out of view. He heard the squeaking hinges of the door onto the 1st floor corridor and followed cautiously. Gonzales was a giant of a man and the strength in his arm was throttling Charlie, his face was red and the veins in his temples were standing out. Again he smiled at Jack when he appeared, but this time he kept his gun pointed at Charlie's head.

"Stop where you are, unless you want your partner to get his head blown off!" shouted Gonzales. Jack was about 25 feet away from

Gonzales and held his gun in both hands, pointed directly at the pimp's head. "You might get lucky and kill me, but will it be before I kill him," smiled the pimp nodding toward Charlie.

"Kill him and you'll be dead before he hits the floor."

"Well in that case we have a stalemate," smiled Gonzales, "cos if you take me in I'll get life anyway, so I ain't got much to lose, do I?"

Jack was lost for a response. "Put your gun down…" he stuttered.

"No you put your gun down mother-fucker or he dies now!"

For a brief second Jack thought he might get a shot off, but the moment passed and he decided to drop his gun rather than risk Charlie's life.

"Now kick it over here," demanded the pimp. Grudgingly Jack did as he was told. As the gun came to rest at the pimp's feet Jack watched incredulously as Gonzales squeezed the trigger of the gun he was holding. The trigger clicked harmlessly and Charlie nearly fainted. Gonzales smiled again at Jack, pulled a knife from the sleeve of the arm he had around Charlie's neck, grabbed his captive's hair with his other hand and calmly slit his throat.

Jack watched helplessly as blood spurted out of Charlie's neck, unable to stop the pimp from murdering his partner. His muscles suddenly jerked back into life and he rushed towards Gonzales, but before he had made two steps towards his target, the pimp picked up Jack's gun and fired it at him. Jack was hit in the stomach and collapsed before his momentum could carry him to a position where he could grab hold of Gonzales, and he feebly flailed at air, falling face down.

Gonzales turned Jack over onto his back. Jack winced with the pain caused by his movement and grabbed his wound with both hands. "That looks painful" said Gonzales with mock sympathy. He put his foot on top of Jack's hands and pressed down. Jack screamed in pain and doubled up around the pimp's foot. Gonzales lifted his foot and

Jack fell back onto the floor.

Jack looked up into the face of Gonzales who was now pointing the gun at his head. "Go on then you bastard shoot," he shouted deliriously.

At that moment the noise of sirens filled the air as several police cars pulled up outside the hotel. "You're already a dead man," said Gonzales before he disappeared through the staircase exit as Jack saw a red mist descend over his eyes.

Three minutes later armed policemen burst onto the first floor corridor and found Jack unconscious. He was taken to the Mount Sinai Hospital and given emergency surgery to have the bullet removed and stop the internal bleeding. He was moved into intensive care after the operation and at one stage during the first night came very close to death, due to the amount of blood he had lost.

The pain Jack endured from the gunshot wound was insignificant compared to the guilt he felt over Charlie's murder. He had helped Gonzales kill Charlie and escape by handing over his gun so easily. In the police academy and during his early days on the force he had been repeatedly told never to hand over his firearm, no matter what the situation. Nobody had told him how to handle the dilemma of either letting Charlie die or stopping Gonzales, because he didn't believe he could do both. Looking into Charlie's eyes Jack had to shoulder the burden of trust placed on him by his partner. The only time Charlie had shown fear was when Jack laid down his gun. At the academy everything was clear-cut, and in the staged scenarios they used to teach the students there was no undue concern about the obligation to protect others in the handling of such situations. In reality the edges get blurred, especially when a friend's life is at stake.

Jack handed in his badge to NYPD while he was still in hospital and used his outstanding vacation leave to cover the balance of the notice required to quit the job. There was no fuss or leaving party on his departure he simply never went back to the precinct station. He kept his contacts with the NYPD and they helped him operate as a private investigator, giving him an edge the competition didn't have. It was through one of these contacts he got a lead on the whereabouts of Gonzales one wet and cold November night.

Despite an intense manhunt Gonzales remained elusive. The police had put tails on some of his girls but he still managed a covert control over them and get his end of the action. He had been seen with one of his girls in the same hotel where he had murdered Charlie. One of Pat O'Connor's snitches had passed on the information after bumping into him in the lobby. Pat was Charlie's brother in law, and a close friend of Jack. Rather than report the sighting to Homicide, Pat immediately told Jack and they both went over to the hotel to verify the sighting. After confirmation of his room number, Pat kept watch outside the hotel while Jack climbed up to Gonzales' room on the fire escape. Jack prized open the window as quietly as he could and found Gonzales sleeping in bed with his girl. She was awake, her eyes puffy from crying and her lips bruised, probably from beatings by her pimp. As Jack climbed through the window she remained silent, holding his gaze as he came to the bed. He pulled out a switchblade from his pocket and released the catch. The girl remained impassive as the knife sprang out of its holder, and never flinched as Jack placed the blade on Gonzales throat and stabbed downward across one half of his neck, cutting his aorta. Gonzales immediately started retching and grabbed hold of his throat, as if he was trying to stop the torrent of blood from gushing outward. Jacks smiling face was the last image Gonzales saw before he died.

After she was sure he was dead, the girl next to Gonzales sprang from the bed, went round to the opposite side where Jack was standing and spat on the pimp's face. Jack pulled her away from the bed and told her to get dressed and leave. Even though he had gotten revenge for Charlie's death, Jack never lost the feeling of guilt from capitulating to Gonzales.

11

As Jack entered his apartment he was still mulling over the wisdom of including Roland Bannister in the deal, but couldn't see any other way as he didn't have the cash to finance the plan. Bannister had been easily drawn in because of his infatuation with Elsa, but Jack didn't want to capitalize on it. She had been through enough already without adding to her problems by kindling fires within Bannister that could lead to an awkward situation in the future. Jack now knew that despite his education and apparent refinement, Bannister had a dark side to his personality that was not too far beneath the smooth sophisticated surface he showed to the world.

One thing that Jack had learned from his years in the police force was that unscrupulous men do unscrupulous things. He remembered his early days with Homicide and being physically sick at the scene of his first murder enquiry after seeing the state of the murder victim. It was a young boy who had been kidnapped and raped. In an attempt to disguise the identity of the boy the murderer had cut off his hands and his head. In a perverse act the murderer had also removed his genitals, only to satisfy himself. The skull of the boy was found in the furnace used for heating the building where the body was found.

Jack was sure that Bannister could be capable of murder. He had seen him pistol-whip a drunken punter who had tried to grab one of the girls in the club, caving in the cheekbone of the unfortunate man. When Jack had suggested he had been a little severe, Bannister conceded that he might have acted brutally and without any sign of emotion, but only because it was prejudicing business. His business, which he was protecting. The obvious lack of consideration for the physical damage he caused his victim was a familiar trait that Jack had witnessed in a number of evildoers who were at a loss to understand the concern shown by others over the consequences of their vicious acts.

The apartment was dimly lit up from the signs in the street, and in the half-light Jack made his way to the bedroom. He took off his jacket and threw it on a chair next to the dressing table. Looking over towards the bed he could see Elsa sprawled diagonally across it, face down, hugging the pillow. The bed sheet was draped across the bed in the opposite direction, revealing tantalizing glimpses of her body. The part of the bed sheet that covered her clung to her body showing every curve and crevice. He stared at her silently, amazed that the sight of Elsa's half naked body still gave him as big a thrill, as on the first night he had seen her performing at the Blue Cockatoo.

He took off his shoes and gently got onto the bed and lay behind Elsa. He put his hand on her bare shoulder and ran it down her back, pulling down the bed sheet at the same time. Elsa made no move toward Jack leaving him puzzled as he didn't know whether she was asleep or awake. He stood up and pulled the bed sheet down the full length of the bed, still without a sound from Elsa. She turned on her side, clutching the pillow, and the sight of her naked body aroused him even more. He climbed back into the bed and lay behind her, and he put his arm around her waist to draw her closer to him.

Feeling the lower half of Elsa's breast he followed its curve down to her torso and over her flat belly. Elsa kept herself in shape and beneath her silky smooth skin he could feel the ripple of her abdominal muscles. His hand wandered to the fleshy, velvety mound between her legs and he caressed her gently. Elsa sighed quietly half turning away from him, to return to her original position and lie on her front. Jack still couldn't decide if she was awake or just instinctively responding to his touch in her sleep. He kissed the back of her neck and began caressing her body again moving closer to her. He now felt he wanted her so badly that it almost hurt.

He began to be more adventurous with his kisses and caresses, fondling Elsa's right breast and kissing her neck and shoulders, still reluctant to turn her towards him. If she was asleep he didn't want to suddenly waken her by pulling her onto her back. He wanted her to awaken by herself, aroused by his fondling and turn towards him as anxious to make love as he was. He was now up against her body and could feel her bottom pressing into his groin. He was beginning to get a little exasperated at Elsa's lack of response when she softly said, "When are you going to stop playing about and give me what I need?"

Jack turned her sharply toward him and kissed her passionately on the mouth. Elsa started unbuttoning his shirt and loosening the belt on his trousers. Within a few seconds Jack was naked next to Elsa. Every time they made love it felt exciting, almost as if it were the first time and they were still finding out about each other. Jack had been with several women but none had come close to making him feel the way Elsa did. He couldn't remember what sex had been like before he had first slept with her, and now had no wish to remember.

After they had made love Elsa went over to the fridge pulled out a bottle of Chardonnay and opened it. She returned to the bed with the bottle and two wine glasses. Jack sat up took the glasses from Elsa and let her fill each of them.

"You should have just got me a cold bottle of Bud," said Jack.

"The sight of you with a beer bottle stuck out of your mouth is not very romantic. Besides I wouldn't do this with a bottle of Bud," Elsa replied pouring some wine onto her breasts.

Jack leaned over to catch the rivulets of wine running down Elsa's body, lingering on her breasts after the wine had gone. "Stop it Jack, that's enough, or you're going to make me spill the rest of my wine."

"I'll never complain about drinking wine again. Why can't we put the wine on one side and make love again?"

"Because I want to talk about Walsh."

"What! We've only just made love and you want to talk about another man."

"Don't be so crass Jack. Believe me I don't find that the least bit funny," replied Elsa sternly.

Jack sat up at being made aware he had been insensitive. "I'm sorry Elsa, I didn't mean…"

"I know you're just a man and able to pass over what happened in

Miami very quickly! It will take more than a few days for me to get over the incident. When I think of what could have happened, it frightens me. I've never really thought of myself as being a victim before, but now I know I'm no different to anyone else."

"I didn't want the conversation to become serious, so I was just trying to keep things light and not spoil the mood by talking about Walsh."

"Yes but we do have to talk about him. I'm a prisoner in your apartment because I can't be seen and we don't even know if the police have a solid case to bring against him."

"The Miami police have sent someone to interview Walsh in New York. They must think there's more to your disappearance than meets the eye, otherwise they wouldn't bother going to such trouble simply to get a statement. They'd get someone from New York to conduct the interview and send the statement down to them."

"Look Jack I can't stay here indefinitely, and after only a couple of days being stuck in this apartment is driving me crazy."

"If the police drop the case we'll make up some story for your reappearance, but if they decide Walsh has a case to answer at the arraignment, we'll move you out of New York so you can have a bit more freedom to move around."

"And that's supposed to make me feel better? I had a life Jack no matter what you may think of it. I might as well be dead the way I'm living now."

Jack reached out to comfort Elsa, but she just shrugged off his hand and lifted the wine glass to her mouth. The earlier sexual excitement they had generated together had been dissipated and was replaced with tension. They drew a mutual halt to the conversation, not wishing to exacerbate the bad feeling that had come between them after they had started to talk about Walsh.

12

"I'm glad you were able to meet me at such short notice," said Detective Tanner as he greeted Bridget Walsh. Tanner had suggested they meet in a coffee shop because it would be more discrete than him going to the NMP offices. The place he had selected for their meet was only a short distance from her workplace.

"When you said you wished to privately discuss a matter my husband was involved in during his vacation in Miami, I was too intrigued and worried not to meet with you," Bridget replied taking a seat across the table from Tanner.

"Would you like a coffee?" asked Tanner.

"Thank you I'll have an espresso."

Tanner called over the waitress and ordered an espresso for Bridget. "I told Simon that I would be speaking to you without being too specific, have you told him you were coming to meet me today?"

"You asked me not to when we arranged the meeting," replied Bridget, not answering Tanner's question directly and leaving him no wiser. "I don't know what the secrecy is about but I did what you wanted."

"I didn't want him to influence what you might say to me," said Tanner now knowing that the interview was not going to be easy. He decided that he might just as well be direct, rather than trying to fence with Bridget. It was obvious she was too intelligent to be manipulated in the same way as her husband. "Does your husband often take vacations by himself?" he asked.

"He goes down to Florida, about the same time every year for the sailing and golf, neither of which I particularly enjoy. We've been married long enough not to live in each other's pockets."

"But you and your husband have never been on vacation together. In fact your honeymoon only lasted one day."

"Don't judge me and my husband by the standards you set yourself. We like different types of vacation and can afford to vacation separately. Besides we are together at work and at home and probably need a break from each other for at least two weeks in the year. I don't understand what significance our vacation arrangements have on your enquiry. Can we get to the point?"

"Separate vacations could indicate a platonic relationship between you and your husband, which would be very relevant to my inquiry. Did you know that your husband was with a young woman called Elsa Bartelli last Friday, and she has not been seen since going out with him on his boat?"

"First of all, don't be surprised when I tell you that my husband often meets young women when he is far away and on his own. I don't mind provided he behaves discreetly and doesn't bring his habits back to New York," said Bridget coldly.

"That's very understanding of you. Do you have what they call an open marriage?"

"I'm sure we each have secrets we hide from one another, but none that would affect our marriage."

"Does that mean you meet young men when you go on vacation?"

"I can see you are only able to think in straight lines Detective Tanner, which must be very limiting in your job," Bridget replied sarcastically.

"Are you trying to avoid answering my question?"

"No. What I do on vacation is not pertinent to your inquiry and is none of your business."

Tanner couldn't mentally put Mr. and Mrs. Walsh together. She was strong, bright and tenacious, qualities alien to her husband. "Yes you're right it's none of my business. The hotel records show that your husband rang you on Friday evening, what did the two of you talk about?"

"Well we didn't talk about his latest conquest, if that's what you mean? He made a quick call to see how I was and tell me he'd been out sailing. Nothing more, nothing less."

"What time did he call you?" asked Tanner.

"It was about 7:30 PM, he said he had returned to the hotel feeling sick and had gone to bed for a rest before calling me. The hotel records should support me."

"We've checked your husband's movements at both the marina and the hotel. He spoke to the mechanic at the marina at 6:45PM and checked in at the hotel at 7:10PM. It doesn't appear as if he was able to get much sleep, does it?"

For the first time Tanner noticed a trace of doubt cross Bridget's face. She looked away from him, trying to find a good reason that would justify Simon lying to her, and weighing up the possibility that her husband could really be involved in something even darker. Bridget couldn't understand why Simon would need to resort to anything unlawful, other than a traffic offence. She thought he had money to pay for the kind of woman he usually associated with on these trips, and past experience seemed to indicate that he's not too fussy in his choices.

"If you knew his movements, why did you need to see me?"

"I'm just tying up loose ends to confirm that he did in fact speak to you when he made the telephone call. It closes the loop and gives credence to the timings given in the statements of the other witnesses."

"I think you're hoping for more than that. You would like me to go back to my husband with all guns blazing to put him under more pressure, or even get him to do something rash."

"You're making the assumption that we suspect him of injuring or killing Miss Bartelli. Do you think he would be capable of such an act?"

"You have a nice way of turning things around to your own advantage," smiled Bridget, "but no, I don't think he would be capable of murder."

"And I don't think you know your husband as well as you think. Ask him about Rita Alonzo, she's the prostitute he very nearly killed in New Orleans. She refused to submit to him and he hit her so hard that she was in a coma for two days. But if you want to blind yourself to what he could be capable of, so be it. Thank you for your time," said Tanner as he rose to leave. "Oh one more thing, Mrs. Walsh, does your husband own a gun, and does he normally take it on vacation with him?"

Bridget was still reeling from Tanners reference to Rita Alonzo, but his question about Simon owning a gun brought her thoughts sharply back into focus. "Yes, he takes it down to Florida with him. He started taking it with him after he found a tramp sleeping on his boat a couple of years ago. Do you think he shot this woman?"

"I don't think anything yet, because there's no physical evidence to go on. Consequently I have to consider every possibility from A to Z. Thanks again for your time." With that Tanner walked off leaving Bridget in a very confused state.

Bridget's own experience of Simon was enough to tell her that he was a man with little moral fiber, but she hadn't thought of him as being capable of seriously injuring or killing someone. Initially the thought of him as a murderer made her feel very vulnerable, but then she remembered their wedding night and how meekly he had accepted her terms for their marriage. If anything had happened to Elsa Bartelli, she was convinced that it must have been an accident.

Bridget was waiting for her husband that evening as he entered the study. "It's a surprise to find you in here, I'm having a drink, do you want one?" he said walking over to the drinks cabinet.

"No thanks Simon. I've been talking to Detective Tanner of the Miami PD, as he felt we needed to discuss your vacation."

"Yes he said he was going to talk to you, but I expected him to come back to our apartment."

"I didn't speak to him here, we met downtown and he had quite a story to tell. Who is this Elsa Bartelli and did you have any involvement in her disappearance?"

"Don't be ridiculous. I barely knew the woman, she came onto me in a bar and I eventually found out she was just another hooker on the game. I took her out on my boat for the afternoon, but when I found out what she was after I didn't want any part of her."

"I hope you're telling the truth. I know that you're a low, conniving, immoral excuse for a man, but if you harmed her or played any part in her disappearance don't expect to count on my support."

"Look, I'm the victim here. I was reeled in by a woman who was out to get whatever she could from me. She was in the Ocean Drop Inn last Friday afternoon, waiting to latch onto some high roller. I didn't catch on at first because she seemed to be a classy woman and certainly didn't look like a whore. In fact she could have been a business woman who had just taken the afternoon off work."

"Well I think you're saying that she wasn't a stereotype, but nevertheless she was a whore. So go on, what happened next?"

"I've already told you, we went out for a short trip on my boat and that was it!"

"So the Miami police have sent one of their detectives to New York simply to talk to you about an innocent little boat trip? Don't lie Simon, I know it's got to be more than that and I also know about New Orleans and Rita!"

Walsh froze when Bridget mentioned Rita Alonzo's name, "who told you….."

"It doesn't matter who told me about her, but I've done a little investigating of my own this afternoon. In case you can't remember she's the prostitute you nearly beat to death in a seedy New Orleans brothel!"

"You don't understand the bitch was trying to steal my money, I caught her red handed and hit her in anger. She ended up in a coma, but I didn't mean to hurt her, it was an accident."

"And what about Elsa Bartelli? Don't tell me, that was an accident and you didn't mean to hurt her either!"

Walsh looked at Bridget and knowing he was in desperate need of her support, would have to come as close to the truth as he dared without completely losing her good will. "OK something did happen when we were out at sea, but it wasn't something that I did. What happened was completely out of my control!"

"Don't try to elicit my sympathy before you tell the story, just give me the facts and let me decide on your innocence."

Walsh sat down opposite her and took a long drink of whiskey, emptying his glass. He put the glass on the floor in front of him and clasped his hands, looking downward and trying to decide where to start. "As I said we met in the Ocean Drop Inn. She said she was on vacation in Miami, visiting her sister, but was on her own while her sister was at work. I offered to take her out on the boat, which was being prepared for an afternoon fishing trip."

"That was very generous of you. I guess you did it out of concern for her and because of the innate goodness within you to show her a good time," Bridget chided.

"Alright, she was a stunner and yes I was immediately attracted to her. Given our relationship, I don't think it's anything for me to feel guilty about."

"OK carry on," urged Bridget impatiently.

"Everything was straight forward. We got on board and headed out to the reef armed with booze instead of fishing tackle. After I dropped anchor she changed completely. There had been a little flirting up to this point but nothing that prepared me for what followed. She stripped off to her bra and panties, saying she wanted to top up her tan, and then started caressing herself suggestively. By this time I was straining at the leash and I moved next to her and began to fondle her. She didn't object and even encouraged me to go further."

"This just sounds like one of your normal vacations, when did it turn nasty?"

"We were both getting excited and I started getting undressed. Eventually I said I would get a condom from below deck. It took me a little time to find one and when I returned I found her with my wallet in her hand, stuffing money and credit cards into her handbag. I took the wallet from her and slapped her across her face. She went berserk scratching and spitting, and unexplainably ended up jumping overboard."

"Why would she do that?"

"It must have been because I threatened to call the police when we got back to the marina."

"Didn't you try to get her back into the boat?"

"I wasn't able to because when I went to the side of the boat she jumped from I couldn't see her in the water, and searched along both sides of the boat before giving up. Then I started to panic. I saw myself in the very predicament that seems to be developing now. I know that I'm innocent, but I can't convince anyone else that I am. You do believe me, don't you?"

Bridget simply nodded her head in support. She wanted to believe Simon, but knew what an accomplished liar he could be. "Don't let me find out that you're lying," she warned again, "because I can do a lot of damage if this thing goes to court." Bridget suddenly felt that she couldn't bear to be in the same room as Simon and got out of her chair and left without another word.

As she went up the stairs to her bedroom, Bridget tried to be positive about the story she had just been given by Simon. She knew that she could never be certain about his involvement in Elsa Bartelli's disappearance, but cold heartedly consoled herself in the thought that he could never attract a woman of real substance.

13

Elsa opened the apartment door to see the smiling face of Roland Bannister staring back at her as he handed her a bottle of champagne. "Why thank you Roland, what's the occasion?"

"Just seeing you is cause enough to celebrate, especially as I hardly get to see you now that you're in hiding and not dancing at the club anymore. I'm missing you and so are the punters at the club."

"I'm sure there are plenty of other girls for them to drool over, they'll soon forget me," replied Elsa taking the bottle of champagne and walking into the apartment. She put the bottle on the coffee table in the center of the lounge and went into the kitchen to fetch a couple of glasses.

"No you were their favorite, so they won't easily forget you. Your story was given a brief airing in the New York Herald and I've already had several people tell me what they're going to do to Simon Walsh if you don't turn up soon."

"Wait a minute Roland, I can't hear you," shouted Elsa from the kitchen.

Bannister sat down in one of the two easy chairs. "You don't give yourself enough credit Elsa. You're the unattainable woman that they all want but will never get because you have too much class to mix with the riff raff. They'll never feel the same towards any of the other girls because they don't have that extra indefinable something that naturally seeps from every pore in your skin."

"Steady Roland, slow down or else I'll think that you're trying to make a pass at me," said Elsa, putting two fluted wine glasses on the coffee table in front of Bannister, alongside the champagne.

"What if I am?" said Roland picking up the champagne bottle and starting to loosen the cork. "You could do a lot worse than me. I'd treat you far better than Jack, and I wouldn't expect you to keep putting your neck on the line for those chicken shit scams of his."

"Well after this little episode, believe me I won't be doing it again," replied Elsa.

The cork popped out of the bottle and the champagne gushed a little before Bannister started pouring it into the glasses. He handed Elsa one of the glasses.

"I know it's a little early but I really need this drink," said Elsa taking a sip from the glass and feeling the effervescence explode on her tongue. "It's been so boring holed up in Jack's apartment, I'm slowly going crazy."

"Where's Jack?" asked Bannister.

"He's always got something to do, which leaves me stuck here on my own all day and most of the night."

"Why do you put up with it? You know I could give you so much more."

"Well, now you're just as deeply involved in this scam as Jack and me. If I show up and get recognized it will be blown and you'd lose the money you've already put into it."

"I don't care about that, I'd rather see you back to your old self, away from Jack and with me. You know that you could really have been killed down in Miami?"

"I know Roland, but I'm probably as much to blame as Jack for putting myself in harm's way and not thinking of how he was going to follow me."

"There's no need to protect him. It's his cock eyed schemes that put you in danger in the first place."

"I'm not. Jack has always been very professional in the way he's planned these jobs and this is the first time anything's gone wrong. He wasn't to know that Walsh is completely unhinged."

"OK forget about that, and about Jack, and come live with me. You don't need to rely on a pay out from Walsh, I'll take care of you, the way a woman like you should be treated."

"That's a lovely sentiment Roland and I know that at this moment you really mean it, thank you. But I would eventually become just another of your trophies. You're a man of refinement and taste who likes to collect things, simply because you have the desire and money to do so. You like to be surrounded by art or anything else that you put a high value on. When my looks fade, as they will, you will want someone young and fresh to replace me. And so by refusing you now I'm saving you the embarrassment of discarding me later. And besides I really do love Jack in spite of his faults."

"I think that was a brush off most kindly and delicately handled," said Bannister taking her hand and kissing it, "but don't think I've given up."

"What a cozy scene," said Jack entering the lounge. Elsa smiled warmly at him feeling a little relieved that Bannister's love platitudes could now go no further, however her suitor looked far from happy to see Jack. "You must have heard the good news Roland, as you've brought over a bottle of champagne."

"What news?" asked Bannister.

"My contact down in Miami tells me that Walsh is to be arrested tonight and that he will be flown down to Florida immediately with a police guard. Have you another glass for me Elsa?"

"He won't appreciate champagne Elsa, just get him a Bud out of the cold box," interjected Bannister.

"C'mon Roland be nice, we've all got a good reason to celebrate. The DA in Miami has constructed a credible case against Walsh, backed up by eyewitness accounts and forensic evidence. And Walsh won't be the first guy convicted for homicide without the benefit of a dead body."

"I don't know Jack, it's still a tough call," interjected Bannister. "There will always be that element of doubt without the body. The prosecution attorney will have to convince the judge at the arraignment hearing that there is sufficient evidence to take Walsh to trial. It relies on the testimonies of the witnesses confirming she went out with him, but never came back. That's a tall order for anyone."

"But once he gets to trial we'll be in a strong position because Walsh actually thinks that he did kill Elsa and therefore he'll have something to hide. Let's hope he decides to testify and ends up tripping himself up during the cross examination. They haven't named the prosecutor yet, but rumor is that it will be your friend James Bantry, Roland. He's got a fine reputation and won't pull any punches."

"I spoke to Bantry recently and he told me he was lined up for a Puerto Rican drug smuggling case," replied Bannister.

"Yes he was, but that collapsed because the two main defendants were murdered when they were being transferred from their arraignment hearing back to prison," replied Jack settling into the other easy chair and taking a bottle of Bud from Elsa.

"This could be a fortunate turn of events. As you say, Bantry is a good prosecutor and will go for the jugular every time. If anyone can trap Walsh he can."

"If we get through the arraignment, I think we're home and dry," replied Jack.

"Don't be too optimistic. Walsh's attorney will have him well-rehearsed. By the time they get to court he will have gone over his story dozens of times and he will have been coached on how to address any eventuality in a cross examination."

"We can always hope that Bantry gets him in a tight spot and he starts to improvise. If he contradicts himself on the stand, the jury will convict him body or no body," replied Jack.

Elsa sat down on the sofa opposite the two men. "I don't know how he's going to explain leaving the marina with me on board and returning alone. Surely that fact in itself is going to raise a significant doubt in the jury's mind? I agree with Jack. Walsh is going to have a difficult time with Bantry and he just might end up convicting himself."

"I'm not going to argue with a lady. Let's drink to that prospect," said Bannister raising his glass.

14

Walsh and Tanner walked off the Miami bound plane handcuffed together. Walsh had asked Tanner if he would forgo putting on the handcuffs if he promised to obey the Detective's instructions and accede to his wishes during the trip. Tanner refused his request stating that it was strict police procedure to use handcuffs in such circumstances for all criminal suspects, regardless of the embarrassment caused to the individual. Despite the sympathy in his tone of voice, Walsh could not help but notice the relish with which the policeman shackled him. The two men made their way to the terminal building of Miami airport and once inside headed directly to the police car that Tanner knew would be waiting at the arrivals exit.

During their walk through the terminal to the police car they had to run a gauntlet of TV and newspaper reporters, and freelance photographers. The photographers were eager to get pictures of Walsh that would be marketable and pushed to the front of the crowd. At one stage all Walsh could see was a bank of flashlights going off in quick succession and he put his free hand up to his face to protect his eyes, complaining to Tanner about the intrusion on his privacy. The reporters were equally determined to get some sort of statement from him, which made his progress through the terminal very slow. Initially they asked Walsh about his knowledge of the whereabouts of Elsa, and subsequently turned to Tanner to ask if the police where going to charge him.

Walsh was now a minor celebrity as the local papers had been running Elsa's story since she was first reported missing to the police. Jack had instructed Julie to go to the most prominent of the local rags with a broad outline of Elsa's trip with Walsh and her subsequent disappearance. He felt that Elsa's colorful background was juicy enough to generate press interest, which it did. The paper wasted no time in asking Roland Bannister for publicity stills of Elsa, which he gladly provided. After the initial report of her disappearance, the natural momentum of the police investigation resulted in further reports to update readers, which in turn started to refresh public interest. By the time Walsh arrived at Miami airport his arrest was front page headlines in all of the local papers.

Policeman and prisoner were protected from reporters by uniformed Miami police officers in the airport, however Walsh was still horrified at the raw intensity of the media interest in his arrest. He remembered being arrested for his assault on Rita Alonzo, which hadn't generated a fraction of the attention he was now experiencing. Naively Walsh was unaware that his father had stopped the press from printing the story by trading a bigger story on insider dealing on the New York stock market. Sean Walsh was well respected by the press and he fully understood the nature and extent of the serious flaws in the moral character of his son. Sean resorted to relying on the confidence of old and trusted friends in the media to provide a protective blanket around his child, which continued until the old man's death.

On his arrival at police headquarters Walsh was taken through the preliminary arraignment procedures, surrendering his personal belongings and having his photograph and fingerprints taken. He was kept in the "pound" for a couple of hours before his documents were processed and he was marched down to the cells in the basement. His cell was small and dingy, with a cot bed along the wall, a basin in the corner and a slop bucket below it. The police guard escorting Walsh to his cell advised him that dinner would be at 5 o'clock, in two hours' time. The guard then left Walsh in the cell and closed the door. Seconds later he opened the hatch in the door to take a final look at Walsh, and then closed it sharply before going about his normal routine. Walsh shivered involuntarily, suddenly feeling vulnerable, isolated and alone. Still in denial about his own actions leading to his arrest, he dearly wished his father were still alive to protect him.

Simon sat on the bed, resigned to his discomfort and growing hunger. The last 20 hours had gone by so quickly, with one shock quickly succeeded by another. He couldn't fully grasp how he had managed to end up in a Miami police station on a murder charge and was starting to fully appreciate the penalty of not insisting in having his lawyer, Brad Tavistock, present during his interview with Tanner. In his arrogance and misplaced confidence, he had exposed his weaknesses and the police would now try to probe more deeply into Elsa Bartelli's disappearance with the objective of linking him to her murder. For the 10th time that day he went over the interview with Tanner and explanation of his actions to Bridget to see if there were any obvious contradictions that could be exploited by the police, as he planned to use his explanation to Bridget as a brief for Tavistock. And for the 10th time that day he also regretted not consulting Tavistock beforehand who would have offered advice on what questions to answer and more importantly the ones to avoid. Before being whisked away by NYPD and Tanner, Walsh asked Bridget to get in touch with Tavistock and advise him of his arrest and imminent departure for Miami.

Bridget was a little bemused by this sudden turn of events, apparently showing no emotion as her husband was being taken away. She had wrestled privately with the prospect of having to come to terms with the fact that Simon was a murderer, but she was still trying to convince herself that his arrest was speculative so that Miami PD could engage in more detailed questioning before discounting him as a suspect. The thought of his arrest had never crossed her mind during her interview with Tanner. Walsh reflected that Francesca the maid had seemed to show more distress at his arrest than Bridget. He wasn't sure whether Bridget thought him capable of murder or not and didn't really know whether he could rely on her support. If there were a trial and she decided not to appear, he knew that her lack of support would send out the wrong signal to the jury, who could take it as a sign that she believed him to be guilty.

Alone in his cell, Walsh had to face the reality of his circumstances and the possibility of going to trial for Elsa Bartelli's murder. He comforted himself by comparing his current situation with the night he had spent in a New Orleans jail, but his relief was short lived when he remembered that his father was no longer around to clean up after him. Sean Walsh had taken good care of the whore his son had beaten by arranging hospital treatment in one of the best clinics in the city. His father also handsomely paid off the madam of the brothel to make sure assault charges were not made against Simon at a later date. The New Orleans Police Commissioner deferred bringing an aggravated assault charge against Simon as a favor to his father.

Walsh had a lukewarm meal of beans, burned hamburger and runny eggs, before settling down for the night. He repeated re-running the events of that fateful boat trip in his head over and over again trying to find any angle that the police could use to try and pin a homicide charge on him. The more he thought about it, the more comfort he gave himself as he felt it unlikely that the police had any hard evidence against him. Finally having convinced himself that his arrest was just a pathetic attempt by the police to get him to confess to the murder, Walsh closed his eyes and went to sleep.

The next morning he had a visit from Brad Tavistock. The lawyer gave Walsh a nod as he was shown into the interview room. Tavistock was not confident in his Client's innocence, as he knew his history and the lengths Sean Walsh had gone to in protecting him. The lawyer sat down opposite Walsh and was eager to forego the pleasantries and immediately started to question him. Tavistock desperately needed to get a better understanding of the facts behind the police files, and stories he'd read, to get a measure of the challenge ahead of him.

"Hello Simon. I must say you have a rare talent for getting into difficult situations. It always seems to involve ladies of ill repute."

"I know it looks bad Brad, but the police have nothing to go on. They're just flying a kite."

"I'm not so sure Simon. In your interview with Detective Tanner you said that you and Miss Bartelli had returned to the marina together. Evidence from a number of witnesses indicates that you lied to him. The prosecution will make capital out of that lie and your defense will start with you having to establish your credibility to the jury. In addition to that they have forensic evidence and detailed accounts of your movements that afternoon, with and without Miss Bartelli. You were seen leaving the Ocean Drop Inn with the lady……"

"She was no lady, Brad, she knew exactly what she was doing and sucked me into her little scheme before I understood what was happening."

"You were later seen boarding your sports cruiser with the lady," continued Tavistock ignoring Walsh's interruption, "but she was not with you when you returned. They have analyzed hair and blood samples taken from your boat and DNA analyses have proven them to be from Miss Bartelli. The police have checked all of the possible places you could have put Miss Bartelli off your boat and there is no record of you docking anywhere to do that! Finally the police searched your house immediately after your arrest and found your 45 automatic, which has been fired within the last two weeks."

Walsh' jaw dropped and he gazed blankly at the wall behind Tavistock, sifting through the information that his lawyer had just given to him and trying to evaluate the damage. "You've got to get me out of this Brad," he blurted as if the gravity of his situation had suddenly hit him. "I don't care what it costs......whatever it takes."

"Money's not going to help you. The police believe they have sufficient evidence to charge you with homicide. Your best defense is to convince them of your innocence by starting to tell the truth. That is, assuming that you are innocent of course."

"Don't tell me you think I killed her as well."

"Well you're not giving me very much to work on Simon. Why don't you tell me what happened and I can judge the best way to present your case to establish your credibility as an innocent man with the jury and give them an alternative interpretation of the picture painted by the forensic evidence to the one the prosecution are putting forward."

"Everything's more or less the way I said, except that we did have an argument. She panicked and ended up jumping off the boat. I searched for her but she didn't re-surface. I guess she must have knocked herself unconscious when she hit the water."

"Blood stains were found on the deck, how did that happen?"

"OK, the argument turned physical when I found her with my

wallet…..she must have hurt herself in the scuffle."

"Did you rape or attempt to rape her?"

"No I didn't harm her in that way Brad, you've got to believe me," pleaded Walsh sincerely.

"Good that means that the police will not come up with any physical evidence from the boat indicating that you and she had intercourse, which would give you a motive to kill her, if you had taken her by force. At the moment the only person who can tell the true story of what happened on your boat is you. You've got to take the stand and convince the jury that your version of events is the truth."

"It is Brad. I wouldn't risk lying to you. I want you to believe in my innocence because it will make you more committed to getting me acquitted."

"It's not me you've got to convince Simon. In the future don't say anything to the police, or anybody else for that matter, without me beside you. They will want to interview you sometime today, but I want to prepare a statement for them to delay their talking to you before we've had time to get your story straight."

Tavistock still couldn't decide on his Client's guilt or innocence. He didn't really care one way or the other, as he would do his best to protect Simon Walsh no matter what. He owed Sean that much. The media frenzy and consequent muck raking that would follow a conviction, and the subsequent slur that would be put on Sean Walsh's good name, had forced him to accept Bridget Walsh's request to represent her husband. Normally he wouldn't give Simon Walsh the time of day, but he felt he had a duty to defend him for the sake of his dead father. Walsh's story was far from convincing and Tavistock knew that he would need to go over it several times to make it sound plausible and he would also need to prepare Walsh for cross examination.

When he got back to his office he briefed his assistant, John Delaney, on the interview he had with Walsh, his uncertainty about their

Client's guilt, and whether a murder had actually been committed. Despite their reservations they were determined to do the best they could for their Client, however both lawyers were convinced that after a review of the evidence during the arraignment hearing, the case would go to trial.

15

With Walsh under arrest the prosecution team were busy tying up all of the loose ends to make sure there would be no hiccups in court if the case went to trial. Both Jack and Roland had been interviewed to get background on why Elsa was in Miami and to determine whether she drew a line on the things she would do in her act and if she had her own side-line going with the customers of the Blue Cockatoo outside working hours. Jack confirmed that Elsa was in Miami alone because she had decided she needed a break and he was unable to drop everything at short notice due to work commitments. He said he wasn't worried because he knew of the arrangement with Julie to pick her up at the airport and felt "chill out time" would help her as working at the Blue Cockatoo could get claustrophobic.

Initially Bantry had called up Bannister to resume their acquaintance and asked if Elsa was a hooker in her own time and if there was any likelihood that Walsh was telling the truth. Roland assured him that her relationship with the punters of the night club was strictly limited to dancing and that she didn't even do private lap dancing sessions, which were very lucrative for the girls and sometimes led to "private work". He provided Bantry's team with the file he had on Elsa and some publicity photos. Some of the girls were also interviewed who all confirmed Elsa only danced at the club and did not mix with the dancers or the punters outside working hours.

More recently their discussions eventually got round to the probability of Walsh being prosecuted. Bantry told Bannister that the likelihood was that he would be prosecuted for 2nd degree murder including the use of a firearm and that he would go through arraignment in the next couple of weeks.

Jack was getting worried about Elsa being seen in New York and decided to rent a house in the Boston suburbs where she could stay until Walsh had met their demands. She wasn't happy about moving out of Jack's apartment but understood his logic and thought it made sense. They had discussed a number of alternative locations but Boston came out top as it has a good sized population of over 650,000 and is less than 200 miles from New York City. They hired a car for the journey.

There was little conversation between them until they had left the outskirts of the city. "Remind me why I have to go to Boston?" pouted Elsa.

"Now that Walsh has been arrested we can't take the chance of you being seen in New York," replied Jack patiently. "The trial will probably result in your picture being plastered all over the tabloids because of your link to New York, increasing the chance of you being seen." They had discussed the need for her to leave New York several times and he was finding it difficult to control his impatience with her.

"How can I be seen out and about in New York when I've been a prisoner in your apartment for the last two weeks?"

"I know honey, but we've got to be careful. We've come too far with this thing to blow it away through carelessness."

"You only ever "honey" me when you want me to do something that you know I won't like. I know you're being a shit when you call me "honey". Don't try to sugar coat it."

"Listen Elsa, if Walsh goes to prison we are both going to make a lot of money, enough to set us up for life. We can do what we like and go wherever we want afterwards."

"I know you've told me often enough over the past couple of weeks, but he's not in prison yet! Is he? And there are no guarantees."

"I know that, but the prosecution have built up a pretty good case against him. I spent enough time in Homicide to know that!" replied Jack tetchily.

"How can you be sure of that? Besides Miami PD are handling the case and they might do things differently there."

"I've got some contacts in Miami PD. They tell me they have sufficient evidence to take the case to trial from the forensic evidence retrieved from Walsh's boat alone, which is strengthened by witness testimonies. The only weakness in their case is in not having your body as evidence, but I felt providing them with that would be going a little far. Besides let them find their own body, I want yours."

Elsa smiled for the first time on their journey, turning her head away to hide her amusement from Jack. Events in Miami and her subsequent confinement in Jack's apartment had been depressing, apart from odd moments with Jack when he wasn't working or absorbed with Walsh. Surprisingly she had found that she was missing her nightly stints at the Blue Cockatoo. She had come to realize that her work there had provided her with the rhythm and pace of her life, which she had lost over the last few weeks. Even missing the banter with the punters and the other girls and most of all the feeling of power she experienced while she was performing. There was no way of releasing the stored energy built up from her inactivity. Now all she had to look forward to was the distant prospect of Walsh going to jail and being holed up in Boston for God knows how long.

"The best thing we have going for us, is that Walsh thinks that he really did kill you," said Jack snapping Elsa out of her thoughts.

"I know Jack, you're starting to get repetitive."

"I can't overstress the importance of it, because it means he will feel that he has something to hide from his lawyer, the judge and jury, everybody......even his wife. The jury will see him every day of the trial and will pick up on his body language long before he goes on the stand. His attitude during cross-examination will betray him as much as his words. Let's hope Walsh does decide to take the stand, and then hopefully the DA will get him tongue tied and show him up for the liar that he really is."

"OK Jack, let's assume Walsh goes to prison, what then?"

"After he goes to prison we'll need to make an approach to him from the inside. That won't be too difficult as Roland and I have a number of potential contacts in Florida, both inmates and officers. It will need to be delicately handled, but our man will let Walsh know that you survived your ordeal in the water and that for the right price you'll come forward to clear him."

"But won't the police be suspicious about my not coming forward earlier, particularly during the trial?"

"There could be any number of reasons ranging from amnesia to finding a place of sanctuary to recuperate from the experience. The reason could be fear of retribution from Walsh. You thought him to be a vindictive man with the money to pay for people that could have intimidated you, or sought some kind of revenge, making you too frightened to come forward. It won't be difficult to fabricate a story, but we can work out the details later. How does Canada sound?"

"Cold!" replied Elsa curtly.

"On second thoughts it may be difficult to get you out of the country, because you would have to go on a false passport and that might be difficult to explain."

"I don't care what you do as long as I don't end up facing police charges when I return," said Elsa beginning to feel exasperated again.

"We can plan out the timeline beginning with you going into hiding to escape the possibility of retribution, your return to New York and Walsh's going to prison. We have to convince the authorities you didn't have enough time to find out what was happening to him and intervene in his trial. After all the trial is big news in Miami but will barely get a by-line in New York. Alternatively, you could convince the police that you initially had a natural instinct for revenge on hearing of Walsh's plight. That would be understandable, and may even add credibility to your story," said Jack in that matter of fact, analytical way that always annoyed Elsa. In his machinations he didn't stop to think about the strain that a long term stay in Boston would put on her, or the effect on her whole way of life, which she was already missing. While he was going through the options of explaining her return to the police, Elsa became aware that she would end up doing time, just like Walsh.

"Do you think Walsh will readily accept your offer? He may decide to initiate his own investigation if he finds out I'm still alive," asked Elsa.

"He'll have a strong incentive to accept. Let's just say that his incarceration may be fraught with disagreements with other inmates or officers, which will give him the motivation to get out of prison as quickly as possible."

"I don't want him to be hurt, no matter what he did to me," said Elsa, alarmed at Jack's threat.

"Don't worry he won't be seriously hurt, just made to feel a little uncomfortable. He'll be unaccustomed to the stark reality of living in a prison where the rules are so completely different from the outside world. He's been used to being the top dog in his world, but now he'll just be another inmate trying to survive, so he'll find it difficult no matter what I do."

"Yes but he's rich, surely……"

"Money doesn't really count for anything inside," interjected Jack. "Respect from the other "cons" is what really counts and it's the strong and powerful in the criminal world that command the greatest respect. Some crime lords are just as influential when they're in prison as when they're on the outside and they don't hesitate to use brute force to bend people to their will. Walsh won't have any credibility in prison because he's lived his life outside the criminal world, but they may humor, or even, protect him if he promises them money. I don't really know. All I do know is that it will be a massive culture shock for him and that he'll have to tread very carefully until he finds out the lie of the land."

"I'm still worried that he'll be seriously hurt. Do you really think we're doing the right thing?" said Elsa finding another reason to regret the venture they had begun.

"Nobody's going to hurt Walsh unless he gives them a good reason for it. He's just got to keep a low profile and make sure he doesn't annoy anybody," said Jack, amazed that Elsa's attitude had mellowed so much since he shot her. A sign for a diner appeared on the side of the highway and driving towards it Jack said, "Let's pull into that diner, all this talking is making me thirsty."

Elsa and Jack walked into the diner and sat at the table furthest from the door. "I can see why Roland is wary of you Jack. You've got this whole thing planned out to the last detail. Roland and I are just spectators."

"Don't think that, we're a team and we all need each other. We will only be strong, and stay strong, if we have a mutual bond of trust between us. Roland is a control freak, and added to that he's just nervous about losing the money he's already invested in the scam, although that's not his major consideration."

"I know. The money isn't what's really important to him. Roland doesn't like to be a bit player he likes to control things. Power gives him a buzz, so he's uncomfortable with you calling all the shots. Get him more involved or just talk to him more, anything to reduce the tension that's beginning to build up between the two of you."

A waitress came over to their table to take an order. Jack broke their conversation and took two menus from the waitress and handed one to Elsa. Skimming through their menus they decided to order coffee and plain pancakes. The waitress took their order to the kitchen and quickly returned with cups and saucers, milk and a jug of coffee. She topped up the cups with coffee and promised the pancakes wouldn't be long in coming.

Jack took a sip of his drink and said, "Roland seems pleased enough with the way things are going, and with me communicating with Walsh through his wife Bridget. I think Roland's happy for me to take the reins because he doesn't want to get too involved at the business end, and besides he's covering his ass, just in case things don't go to plan."

"Why is his ass any more sensitive than ours? God knows he'll be making as much money as we do."

"Actually he'll be taking slightly more than us, because he's funding the gig. I've agreed a 40:30:30 split, with him taking the lion's share. Together we'll still be taking most of the pot, so I didn't see any reason to argue about his extra 10 percent.

"Well so much for our being a team. Why wasn't I involved in the decision as it's my money as well as yours? You may have invested your time, Roland his money, but I've given up my life!"

At this point the waitress returned to the table with their pancakes. She had heard Elsa shouting at Jack and could see her face was flushed with emotion. "Are you alright," she asked with obvious concern. Elsa nodded pulling a handkerchief from her handbag and wiping her nose. The waitress put Elsa's plate of pancakes down in front of her saying, "I don't know what the problem is honey, but believe me they're not worth the heartache." With that she dropped Jack's plate of pancakes in front of him and turned on her heel. She came back quickly with the syrup and Jack was relieved he didn't end up with having it poured into his lap.

"Obviously you're not such a hit with all women. It's refreshing to see you looking so uncomfortable. There are some situations that you just can't manage, because like it or not, someone will always get the wrong end of the stick," smiled Elsa enjoying her small triumph. "Tell me more about you acting as a go between Walsh and his wife."

"By all accounts she's a very cool customer and her relationship with her husband is not what you'd expect from a recently married or loving couple. In many ways that will be an advantage because she won't be over emotional and won't let extraneous influences cloud her judgement. Besides she needs the support of her husband to operate in her current role as Company Secretary at the NMP. She's an outsider who was brought into the company when she married Walsh. By all accounts she's ambitious and has worked her way up in people's estimation in a very short space of time, so she's bound to appreciate the quick return of her husband as it will take pressure off her from other quarters. I'm assuming some Director's will be calling for her head when he's convicted. If she can fend them off until Walsh is cleared it will motivate her to ensure our transaction moves quickly."

"But why should she talk to you, and why won't she go straight to the police when she finds out the truth?"

"Whoever we get to put the squeeze on Walsh in prison will suggest to him that he gets his wife to contact me to make arrangements for the handover of the money. To Bridget my role will be that of the arbitrator between her and the people keeping you in hiding, rather than as one of the people trying to extort money from her. To do that I'll need to convince her that I've been hired for the job and have no involvement in the scheme, or have any knowledge of your whereabouts. I'll tell her that I only agreed to take the job to help protect her as an innocent party. That way she won't want to take the risk of going to the police and losing the chance to free her husband."

"I don't know Jack, I think it's a long shot. It will take a lot to convince her especially that you're an honest Joe working for her best interests. It seems a risky proposition to me, because if she does go to the police they'll quickly link you to me."

"If Roland talks to her they'll also connect Roland to you. The only alternative would be to bring someone else in and you know that the more people who know what's going on, the greater the risk of Walsh or the police finding out. And it would reduce our pay out."

"All you think about is the money. I hope it gets you everything you want at the end of the day, because it will be a massive disappointment to you if it doesn't."

"It's not just for me, it's for both of us. Don't you really understand that having Walsh's money will mean that we'll never have to work again if we don't want to? You don't want to be dancing every night at the Blue Cockatoo for the next 10 years, do you?"

"I suppose not," replied Elsa. They got up from the table and Jack gave Elsa a quick peck on the cheek before they moved towards the exit. This little show of affection relieved some of the tension Elsa had been feeling since the start of the trip and she began to relax a little.

As she was leaving the diner Elsa turned towards the waitress who had served them, smiled and thanked her for her service. The waitress smiled back saying, "He's only a man honey, don't trust him."

16

The judge appointed to preside over Walsh's arraignment was Wesley Hyam, a man known to support women's rights and to have traditional moral values, abhorring the slide to the current free and easy sex culture in the big cities. He had worked the Florida circuit for twenty years and was now close to retirement. On the basis of the evidence provided at the arraignment hearing he recommended that Walsh be prosecuted for 2nd degree murder, but accepted Tavistock's proposal that a lesser charge of manslaughter could be considered if the jury could not agree to the murder charge. It was anticipated that the trial would not be longer than three weeks and a trial date was scheduled in the court calendar.

The next 6 months to the trial passed quickly for Jack but very slowly for Elsa up in Boston. Jack could feel the tension building between them and he persuaded Bannister to let Julie go to live with her to reduce her feeling of isolation. Reluctantly Bannister agreed, but accepted that if Julie stayed with her, it would relieve some of the tedium of her friend's confinement and help the time pass more quickly. Walsh was released on bail, but he took an extended leave of absence from his company to pacify shareholders and the Board of Directors. He was in no mental state to resume any duties, never mind act as the executive officer of the company. The time passed slowly for both Walsh and Elsa who were bored out of their minds, having to "tread water" until the end of the trial. Although they were both impatient for the trial to begin so that they could get on with their lives, Walsh remained apprehensive of the outcome.

The trial process began with the qualification and swearing in of jurors. Hyam was determined to ensure that the jury would include a reasonable number of women to get an even balance and ensure the female perspective of the case was considered in arriving at a verdict. The prosecution and defense teams had prepared profiles of the likely jurors following the initial coarse qualification process. Tavistock had objected to one well known feminine activist, but generally the process had gone reasonably smoothly with little sign of friction between the two lead lawyers, and Hyam hoped both men would continue to be objective during the actual trial.

The teams from both the Prosecution and Defense had worked frenetically up to the start of the trial examining and re-examining every bit of detail to ensure that their arguments were robust and that they had adequate counter arguments for every unexpected eventuality. Bantry saw himself as an athlete training for the big event, whereas Tavistock had a less romantic view of himself imagining that he was the guardian of Sean Walsh's name and reputation. Both of the lead lawyers wanted to the win the case on their terms. Bantry was relatively young and dynamic hoping to astound the jury with his reasoning and rhetoric, whereas Tavistock expected to adopt a thorough, but measured approach, appealing to the common sense of the jury.

The court usher announced the entrance of Judge Hyam to the courtroom and everyone in the court stood up. The trial had drawn a large crowd because of the revived media publicity preceding it. Most people had come to see the characters they had been reading and hearing about in the flesh. They would undoubtedly be disappointed when they realized there was nothing particularly different or spectacular about them, and attendances would progressively diminish as the trial progressed. Hyam entered the courtroom and took his seat. He was a big man who was not very mobile, even allowing for his advanced years, and he sat down heavily with more than a hint of relief. The court clerk then declared that everyone else should be seated. Hyam announced that the proceedings were for the trial of Simon Walsh accused of the murder of Elsa Bartelli and confirmed the attendance of the defense and prosecution attorneys. He requested a plea from Simon Walsh, which was given as "not guilty". Brushing his forehead Hyam instructed the prosecution and defense attorneys to put forward their opening statements, beginning with the Prosecution.

Hyam was known to give lawyers a free rein when addressing the jury, and Bantry stood up and walked over to the jurors trying to make eye contact with each and every one of them. "Simon Walsh is a man used to getting what he wants," he began, "and when he has difficulty in achieving this he pulls out his checkbook. Consequently he now believes everything and everyone has a price. This reasoning is applied to whatever he wants. It may be cars, yachts, diamonds or women. It makes no difference because to him these things are all "commodities" to be purchased for his use. Bantry noted indignant glances from some of the female jurors, which pleased him as it confirmed that they were already building a personal dislike for Walsh because of his reported attitude to women. "But women, of course, are not commodities, not that recent history can show Walsh making such a subtle distinction. On 16th June last year he took a young and beautiful woman, Elsa Bartelli, on board his sports cruiser for what should have been a pleasant boat trip on a lovely sunny afternoon."

Bantry knew that the jurors would probably have read about Elsa's disappearance and no doubt formed their own opinions on the circumstances leading to her afternoon with Walsh and the underlying reason for her going out with him on his boat. If they had taken any interest in the case they would also know of her colorful background and that she was an exotic dancer. Bantry wanted to portray Elsa in the best possible light, while at the same time destroying any last vestiges of sympathy the jury may still have for Walsh.

"Elsa was on vacation and probably excited at going out with Walsh on his private boat, which was a far cry from the social circles she usually mixed in, at home in New York. But Walsh had an ulterior motive for asking Elsa to spend the afternoon with him," said Bantry, glancing contemptuously sideways at Walsh Pointing directly at the accused man he continued, "this man took the unfortunate young woman on his boat with the intention of compromising her to gratify his own base lust. But she was not a person to be intimidated by Walsh or anyone else for that matter. She stood up to him and a scuffle ensued with him finally shooting her. After dumping her body at sea he returned to the harbor without a trace of remorse or guilt for the crime that he had just committed. His lack of remorse is clearly illustrated by the casual telephone call he made to his wife only hours after killing Elsa and leaving her to rot in the sea!"

Walsh shifted uncomfortably in his seat and chatted to his attorney as if picking errors in Bantry's opening statement or explaining the actual events on the day. Bantry noted that most of the jurors had now focused their attention on Walsh and were trying to determine whether he would be capable of cold-blooded murder. There were four women in the jury who would instinctively sympathize with Elsa's plight, particularly if they themselves had experienced the unwelcome advances of strangers, or been placed in compromising situations. Bantry had to remain diligent throughout the trial to ensure that the women jurors did not lose their sympathy for Elsa by the protracted dissection and analysis of her lifestyle.

"You will hear that Elsa was an exotic dancer in a New York night club and was used to the base attention of men. This aspect of her life has been given a lot of coverage by the media, but don't let their tawdry speculation about Elsa influence your judgement of her, without first hearing the facts. Yes, she was a lap dancer and she was very popular with the customers of the Blue Cockatoo. By all reliable reports she was capable of taking care of herself with anyone who became too friendly, but that was because she was working in a controlled environment and not isolated, on her own, somewhere out at sea. The fact that she was an exotic dancer does not mean that she was a person of low morals or that she deserved to be treated any differently from any other woman. Every woman has the right to say no to an unwanted sexual advance, and no woman should be subjected to the crudity Walsh tried to impose on Elsa. Remember that she was not in her normal environment where she would be prepared for lewd advances, so the attack from Walsh was unexpected. Yes, she showed lack of caution and judgement by going out with him after knowing him for such a short time, but he is an overtly rich and influential person and therefore she could be excused for not anticipating that she would be compromised in such a way."

"When questioned by police Walsh lied to them saying that he had brought Elsa back to the marina. It was only after his arrest that he admitted they had fought, with Elsa jumping overboard. Ladies and gentlemen they were a mile out at sea, does that really seem credible?" Bantry once again turned to Walsh, "I will show you that this man cold bloodedly murdered Elsa Bartelli and believed that his wealth and social position would place him above the law. But he now finds himself in court charged with her murder and I want justice for Elsa."

"Thank you Mr. Bantry, your turn Mr. Tavistock," said Judge Hyam with a resigned almost bored tone of voice. He was used to the theatrics of counsels at this stage in the proceedings, which were generally unimaginative and strangely predictable.

Tavistock stood up and smiled at the jury, "Mr. Bantry would have you believe that Miss Bartelli was an innocent abroad caught up in the clutches of an evil man and unable to defend herself against his lascivious advances. Take off your rose colored spectacles; she was a woman who gyrated semi naked in front of men. She has been described as an exotic dancer, which is a little misleading as that implies that there is some artistic merit in her dancing. The real term is lap dancer, whose job it is to thrust every private part of their body into the faces of men who treat them as fantasy figures. These men reciprocate by attaching money to any brief item of clothing the lap dancer may be wearing. Believe me Elsa Bartelli was hardly an innocent."

"Although I speak of Miss Bartelli in the past tense, a body has not been produced to confirm her death. It is possible that she could have swum back to land although it is probable that she is dead, as she has not been found after extensive police searches and investigations into her whereabouts. If she is dead she brought it upon herself by trying to steal my Client's wallet and then making an irrational attempt to escape when she was caught. She was the perpetrator of a crime and my Client was the victim. He did try to get her back on the boat but there was no sign of her after she entered the water."

From the expressions on some of the juror's faces Tavistock could see that they were questioning the credibility of his last two statements. Tavistock himself had wrestled with the logic of Walsh's story and whether or not anyone would risk their life to avoid a minor theft charge. Tavistock concluded that the only chance Walsh had of beating the murder charge would be to convince the jury that he had no hidden agenda to have sex with Elsa, and that would be the biggest challenge.

"The prosecution have put together a flimsy circumstantial case filled with emotive arguments. I will steer you through the fog created by these emotive arguments and show that there are no hard facts to support the prosecution's case. Members of the jury I will ask you to find Simon Walsh innocent of these preposterous charges."

Walsh turned around to smile at Bridget, who was sitting in the first row of the spectator's area. She had reluctantly decided to attend the trial because she understood that she had to be supportive of her husband to create the right impression for the judge, jury and the media.

Six rows behind her sat Jack Cates, on the opposite side of the courtroom. He had been observing Bridget during the opening remarks of the prosecution and defense attorneys, looking for any reaction to their statements that would give him an insight into her feelings towards her husband and her mental state during this ordeal. Despite the confidence he had in the ultimate success of his plan, Jack recognized that his dealings with Bridget after her husband's conviction would be difficult and the success of the plan hinged on getting her to believe he was working in the best interests of Simon.

With her blonde hair and Scandinavian features the woman was undoubtedly attractive, but in a less earthy way than Elsa's Latin ancestry. She appeared aloof and disinterested in the proceedings. The uninformed observer would never have guessed that she had a personal interest in the trial, never mind that her husband was fighting a murder charge. Jack remembered his father's expression to describe people with her demeanor. He would say that such people went about with their nose in the air trying to avoid eye contact with the people round them. Although he abhorred Walsh's attitude to women he thought he now had an insight into a possible reason for his treatment of them as cold and unfeeling objects.

After a recess for lunch the first prosecution witness was put on the stand. It was Jerry the barman from the Ocean Drop Inn. In fact he was a joint owner of the bar and had worked there since its opening. He confirmed that Elsa and Walsh had left the bar together, and that

Walsh was clearly taken with her. Jerry also confirmed that when vacationing in Miami, Walsh often used to meet women in his bar and take them out on his boat. The implication that Walsh would use his boat to seduce women was clear. When questioned by Tavistock Jerry stated that Elsa had been in the bar every day of that week, drinking several vodka and tonics on each occasion. To Tavistock's delight Jerry ventured his opinion that Elsa was a hooker waiting for a high roller. Despite Bantry's objection and the striking of the remark from the record, the jury would remember what Jerry had said and place another black mark against Elsa.

Other witnesses followed Jerry to confirm the movements of Elsa and Walsh that fateful afternoon, but the next influential witness to take the stand was the forensic examiner of the Miami Police Department. He stated that the DNA testing of blood samples taken from the deck of Walsh's boat matched the DNA of hair samples taken from Elsa's hair brush. He also found hair samples on the boat that had Elsa's DNA structure. His final damning bit of evidence was that forensic tests on Walsh's gun, which confirmed that it had been fired on the day of Elsa's disappearance.

The prosecution presented their case during the first week of the trial and Bantry felt he had done a reasonable job. He had painted a clear picture of the events that had taken place on Walsh's boat and was ably supported by forensic evidence. The only person able to challenge the story he had presented to the court was Walsh himself. If Walsh took the stand he would give Bantry the opportunity to expose the deep flaws in his version of events. Jerry's comments about Elsa being a hooker had tainted the jury's image of her, but on balance he thought he was ahead of the game.

On the other hand the defense attorney was anxious. Tavistock knew he had a mountain to climb to prove Walsh's innocence. Although the prosecution had proven that Elsa had been on Walsh's boat and that a fight had taken place, the circumstances of her disappearance were still open to interpretation and therefore Walsh would have to take the stand to convince the jury that he had not done anything to make her want to jump off his boat. It was risky because his Client would have to weather the cross examination from

Bantry, and if he was guilty, he could incriminate himself.

17

Jack was having a quiet drink before going to his hotel when he heard someone behind him say, "It's a small world isn't it Mr. Cates?" Jack spun on his bar stool to face the man speaking to him. "It's me Al Ferrino, the guy in charge of the motor boats at the marina. Don't you remember me?"

"Oh yes, hi Al. I'm sorry for not recognizing you straight away but you caught me unaware," replied Jack.

"That's OK Jack. I recognized you right off in court. You know I wasn't called as a witness, but my statement was read out. How do you think its going?"

"Who knows? It seems pretty clear to me that he killed the girl, but there's still a long way to go before the jury decide on his guilt. I'll have a better idea after I've heard the defense."

"The girl was on the boat, but isn't it funny they never found a body? Still the tide may have dragged her out to sea..........and then there are sharks. By the way, I got your second payment of five thousand dollars, thanks."

"That's OK Al. You earned it by making sure that the people who were able to bring Walsh to justice went to the police. It was very public spirited of you to do that." The man was angling at something and also starting to get on Jack's nerves. The last thing that he wanted to do was discuss the trial with Al, in a bar within spitting distance of the court house. The attendant had been paid handsomely for his efforts, but it was obvious that he was going to try and squeeze Jack for more money.

"I still say it's strange that a body wasn't found, isn't it?" Al repeated and took another swig from his bottle of beer. "Was that girl, Elsa Bartelli, connected to you in any way?"

"Well you're sure are full of questions today Al. Last time we met I could barely get a word out of you."

"Well that's because I'm involved in the trial in a small way and I've really taken an interest in the case. Most people seem to think that Walsh will be convicted, what about you?"

"My opinion won't change anything that happens in the court, so it's irrelevant."

"Not at all Jack. The defense don't know where the girl's body is, but you do, don't you?"

Jack's body stiffened and he leaned forward until his face was a couple of inches away from Al. "I hope you and me are not going to fall out over a technicality like the resting place of this girl's body. Don't get clever with me and, above all, don't try to threaten me."

Al was visibly shaken by Jack's threatening posture and tone, but he hadn't come this far to stop now. "I know that Elsa is alive and living in Boston. How can a public spirited guy like me keep that information quiet?" he countered.

"Listen carefully. You've been paid well for your help, now don't rock the boat and quit while you're ahead," said Jack coldly.

Al's earlier bravado was quickly dissipating, but he decided to carry on in spite of his natural instinct to turn tail and run. "Look Jack, you paid me and that's fine, but it got me wondering. You gave me ten grand for doing next to nothing, so what's in it for you? I don't know what you're planning, but it must be plenty."

"You're batting out of your league Al. If you stick your head above the parapet then it's likely to get shot off. I'm saying this for your own good, you're moving into dangerous territory."

"Don't fuck with me Jack because I know I've got the trump card. I want more money, not a lot, just enough to buy myself a nice place and retire. You know I've got to push this thing for all its worth," said Al regaining his bravado.

"How much more do you want?"

"One hundred and fifty grand, or the police get a message about Elsa's whereabouts. I know you could move her, but she's bound to leave a trail no matter how careful you are, and my message will give the police sufficient incentive to try and follow the trail. It would certainly blow a hole in the prosecution's case and could stall the trial."

"That's more money than I can get together before the end of the trial," replied Jack calmly. "I'll be in the court until it's finished, so you'll have to wait until then."

Al thought the trial would only go on for another 3 or 4 days and although waiting for the money could reduce his leverage, he was confident he had sufficient information to give him the whip hand in any future negotiations. On hearing Walsh had been arrested he took a few days' vacation, flew to New York and followed Jack around on the hunch he could find out a bit more on what was being planned. Luckily within the first 3 days he had followed Jack and Elsa to Boston to the address where she was to be hidden away, which now was more than enough to make Jack pay up. "That's fine, but please don't get smart Jack. I'll give you two days after the trial to get the money together, otherwise I go to the cops."

"You don't give a guy a lot of choices do you Al?"

"What I'm asking for is probably a pimple on the stash that you'll be making. Walsh must be worth millions. Don't forget Jack it's the money or the cops." With that Al finished his beer and left without saying another word.

Jack pondered the ultimatum given him by Al. He was surprised the little man had worked up sufficient courage to confront him, and he smiled to himself at the thought of being intimidated by a short, overweight, middle aged boat attendant. He was still lost in his thoughts when a lithe blonde headed woman took the stool vacated by Al. Jack turned to look at her, but he was still preoccupied with Al's threat.

"Is your friend coming back?" she asked after giving her order to the barman.

"No it's OK, he's gone and won't be back." Jack smiled again knowing Al would be back with his hand out. Although he was amused by the situation Jack knew that it would have to be handled carefully. If Roland found out about Al's threat to go to the police all hell would break loose, and Jack was sure that Roland wouldn't handle the matter delicately or see the funny side of the situation.

"Well you're a happy man, or are you just drunk?" asked the blonde next to Jack.

"I'm not drunk now, but hopefully that situation will change before the end of the night," replied Jack.

"Well if you're on your own ....so am I....maybe we could spend some time together."

Jack looked quizzically at the woman looking for an angle.

"There's no need to look at me like that man, I'm not a hooker. It's just that Miami can be pretty flat when you're on your own."

"I'm sorry sugar it's just I have a suspicious mind, I'm an ex-cop. Let me make up for that by getting you a drink."

"I only ordered this one a minute ago."

"Hell once we get started it could be a very long night," said Jack lifting his glass to hers.

Lying in bed in his hotel room in the early hours of the morning Jack lit a cigarette, drew in deeply and exhaled slowly. He turned to look at the blonde lying next to him. She was asleep, apparently spent after a frenetic bout of drinking and love making. Jack had been celibate since Elsa went to Boston and he had forgotten just how badly he needed sex. He felt a little guilty about being unfaithful to Elsa, but that was not what was hiding in the back of his mind, he was still thinking about how he would dissuade Al from carrying out his threat. He didn't like using violence to get what he wanted, but resigned himself to the fact that he would have to give the little man a severe beating to make him understand the error of his ways.

18

Tavistock spent hours talking to Walsh to convince him of the need to take the stand and tell the jury his side of the story. The attorney believed it was the only way his Client could credibly present himself as the victim of a crime rather than as the perpetrator. He was worried about how well Walsh would handle himself under cross-examination, but Tavistock had also spent many more hours schooling him rigorously, and they had played out every possible line of questioning that could be thrown at him.

The lead defense attorney was nervous but confident that he had given his Client the armory to defend himself adequately under cross examination, and when Walsh was called to the stand, he strode across the courtroom to take the oath. "What is your name?" opened Tavistock after Walsh had been sworn in.

"Simon Walsh."

And what is your normal place of residence?"

"Suite 5, Manhattan Towers."

"That's a very select address Mr. Walsh, you must be a very rich man."

"I run a major international insurance and banking company, and both my wife and I are on the main board of Directors. I am also the Chief Executive of the company and the combined income of myself and my wife puts us in the top 5 percent of US family income earners."

Tavistock whistled. "You are a very privileged man Mr. Walsh. It's a bit strange that you should put your position and reputation at risk by getting into a fight with a woman of the streets."

"Objection your honor, the defense counsel is implying that Elsa Bartelli was a prostitute and with such innuendo he is prejudicing the juror's opinion of her reasons for meeting with Walsh on the fateful afternoon of her disappearance," interjected Bantry.

"Objection sustained. Mr. Tavistock will you please stick to the facts and not allow yours or anybody else's personal opinions to creep into the evidence," scolded Judge Hyam.

Tavistock nodded apologetically. "Are you in the habit of seeking out the company of prostitutes? This is not a reference to Miss Bartelli your honor."

Walsh had been warned by his attorney that this line of questioning would be introduced early in his testimony, explaining that it would be better to bring it out in the open rather than let the prosecution score points by revealing it later. "I won't deny that I have been with prostitutes and that I enjoy their company when I'm either on business or vacationing alone."

"Does your wife know of your relationship with these women?" asked Tavistock.

"Well if she didn't she does now," said Walsh looking towards his wife in the courtroom. "These relationships mean nothing and are just one night stands. I've always figured that it was better to satisfy my sexual needs that way, than to emotionally betray my wife by getting involved in a complex relationship that could end up hurting her."

"Have you spoken to your wife recently about these liaisons?"

"Yes we had a long talk before my arrest. In the past she never questioned my behavior, provided I acted with discretion. This case has blown open my private life for everyone to pick over and make judgements on the kind of person I am. It has certainly shown me that I've been playing with fire all of these years and that I've been fortunate not to have found myself in a similar situation before this. I love my wife and don't want to risk hurting her anymore."

Bantry bristled at the sentiment gushing from Walsh knowing of Rita Alonzo's fate and also knowing that he would not be able to present the facts of her case to the jury.

"I have noticed that your wife has attended the trial every day and obviously supports you fully," commented Tavistock.

"Yes, she has been very supportive and for my part I've promised to remain faithful to her from now on."

I know you will, thought Jack, because you'll be in prison. He was thankful that Elsa was in Boston and couldn't hear what was being said about her, because so far the impression given to the jury was far from flattering.

"Let me take you back to 16th June last year when you met Elsa Bartelli and took her out on your boat. Had you and she previously met?"

"No we hadn't. I went to the Ocean Drop Inn for a drink while my boat was being serviced and I saw her sitting at the bar. There were no other people in the bar, except for a couple sitting in the corner, and we started talking. There was no intent on my part other than being friendly."

"Why did you end up taking her out on your boat?"

"She told me she was on vacation visiting her sister. Her sister was working that day so she was killing time in the bar. It was the last day of her vacation so I thought a private boat trip would help end her vacation on a high note."

"How did she introduce herself?"

She said her name was Lisa Millarno, so when the police started to question me about Elsa Bartelli I didn't have a clue who they were talking about. When I was shown her picture I recognized her, but started to worry about what I was getting into. Of course I know now that she was hustling me but I had no idea at the time."

"Why do you say that?"

"If she was a hooker she wasn't like any hooker that I've ever met before, not that I go with street walkers you understand. She was refined, smartly dressed in designer clothes, and spoke in an educated way. I mean she had a breadth to her conversation that you wouldn't normally expect to find with a hooker. I don't mean that in a disrespectful way, but normally it's straight down to business with these girls after they've been paid."

"Objection, your Honor," cut in Bantry.

"I know Mr. Bantry. Tell me Mr. Tavistock where are you going with this line of questioning?" responded Hyam.

"Elsa Bartelli didn't look or behave like a prostitute when my Client first met her therefore he innocently took her out in his boat not expecting the turn of events that followed. My cross examination of Mr. Walsh will show that Miss Bartelli's actions on his boat confirm our assumption that she was indeed a prostitute and had sought out my Client to compromise him and also extort or steal money from him."

"Very well Mr. Tavistock, but remember what I said before about sticking to the facts."

"What happened when you got out of the harbor," Tavistock continued.

"We went out to the reef and dropped anchor. We had taken some spirits out with us and we both sat down for a drink and started to talk about this and that, just getting to know one another. She eventually commented on how hot the sun was and would I mind if she took off her blouse. She ended up taking off her skirt and her blouse leaving her just in her underwear, and lay on the deck sunbathing."

"Did she encourage you in any way to lie down with her?"

"Not initially, but the sight of her was very tempting and I suppose I was drawn like a moth to the flame."

"Who made the first sexual advance?" asked Tavistock

"To be honest it's a little difficult to say. All I know is that we ended up kissing and I did start to fondle her. I had been exercising a lot of restraint, after all she had a beautiful body and most of it was on display."

"Did she try and resist you at any time?"

"No. As my kissing and fondling became more intimate she asked if I had protection. I went below deck to the bathroom to try and find a condom."

"Did you offer her money for sex?"

"No, that was the last thing on my mind. By this time I couldn't think straight and I just wanted to get my hands on a rubber as quickly as possible. I found what I wanted easily, but when I came back on deck she was stuffing money and credit cards from my wallet into her handbag. I pulled my wallet and her handbag from her to check what she was trying to steal. After putting my things back into my wallet I threw her handbag at her and told her to get dressed."

"How did she act after you discovered what she was trying to do?"

"She did nothing at first, if anything she acted a little coquettish, as if it were all a game. I told her I was going to report her to the police when we returned to the marina and then she started to cry. She got very apologetic begging me not to go to the police and that she would do anything if I didn't report her. By this time I was completely sick of her antics and told her there was nothing she could do that would change my mind. Then she went berserk. She ran at me trying to scratch my face. I grabbed her wrists holding her at arm's length. She was trying to kick and bite me and eventually broke free of my grasp, then she ran to the side of the boat and jumped overboard."

"Did you try and get her back onto the boat?"

"Of course I did. I immediately went to the side of the boat to see what had happened to her. I couldn't see her in the water and didn't know if she had come back up. I shouted repeatedly but got no answer. I was worried about going in after her in case she got back on the boat while I was still in the water. Instead I circled the area to try and find her, but without any luck."

"Did you kill Elsa Bartelli?" asked Tavistock directly, suddenly raising his voice a few decibels to emphasize his words.

"No Sir," responded Walsh steadfastly, slightly taken aback by his attorney's sudden change of tone, even though the pair had rehearsed this part of his testimony many times.

"Why didn't you report her disappearance to the coastguard?"

"I was shaken by the experience and initially couldn't think straight. I was scared that if anything had happened to her I would be accused of manslaughter or murder. I figured that if she was a good swimmer she could have made it back to shore, and if she wasn't she would be dead before the coastguard arrived, anyway. I know that sounds cold blooded but I was panicking and as I said it was difficult to think straight at the time."

Tavistock continued to elicit from Walsh his well-rehearsed testimony ending with his Client's expression of deep regret at what had happened. The jury seemed sympathetic at times, especially when he referred to the personal suffering he continued to endure in trying to live with the guilt of Elsa's possible death. Tavistock knew the battle wasn't over and would only be happy if the jury remained sympathetic after Bantry's cross-examination.

Roland Bannister had flown down to Miami to hear Walsh's testimony because he too understood that the outcome of the case rested on the man's credibility with the jury and how well he fared under cross examination. He wondered what Elsa would make of Walsh's version of what happened between them on his boat, and the implication from both him and his attorney that she was a cheap whore willing to peddle her body for money. It had been a long time since a case as juicy as this had been heard in Miami and the television and press were making the most of their coverage of the trial. They weren't really concerned with the rights and wrongs of the case, just with sensationalizing Walsh's testimony to satisfy the public's appetite for sleazy drama. Bannister had played his part of course by furnishing them with a range of still photographs of Elsa in action, which he justified to Jack as being publicity for the Blue Cockatoo as at the end of the trial the story would probably be taken up by the national press.

Bannister and Jack were sitting together in one of the bars local to the courtroom at the end of the first day of Walsh's testimony. They were both loath to agree that Walsh had done well on the stand and had probably raised his standing with the jury. It had been a credible performance with just the right amount of naive innocence, remorse and demonstration of affection for his wife. Both men were unconcerned about how the trial was going to finish, and they had every confidence that Bantry would redress the balance. Walsh had to have at least one good day in court.

"Do you think Bantry will be able to tarnish the saintly image that Walsh created for himself today?" asked Jack.

"He'll certainly be able to do that, but I don't know how deeply he can wound Walsh as far as Elsa is concerned. He certainly gave a good performance today, and almost had me wanting to acquit him. And I know the truth! Don't worry he won't have read the script before his session with Bantry. There'll be too many twists and turns in Bantry's line of questioning for him to cope with, and no pat answers that he can churn out. I suppose it all depends on how well he can think on his feet," replied Bannister.

Jack caught the eye of the barman and ordered a Napoleon Brandy for Bannister and got himself a Bud. "It may be a little premature for a celebration, but let's drink to a good outcome," said Jack.

The two men settled down with their drinks, silent for the moment and enjoying one of the simple pleasures of life. The silence was broken by the sound of Jack's cell phone. He pulled the phone from his inside pocket to answer the call. Bannister listened casually to the call from a man called Al.

"I thought we had agreed on the way ahead Al, and that you should be patient…

…Yes the trial is going well but it's still too soon to predict the outcome………

……….If Walsh is convicted he'll get what he deserves…………

………….Don't bring Elsa into this again

……………Look we can't talk about this over the phone we'll have to meet……….

………………After the trial

Jack switched off his cell phone and put it into his pocket, returning to his drink, visibly irritated.

Hearing Jack's side of the conversation Bannister suspected he was trying to hide something as it was obviously about the trial and Elsa. He caught Jack's attention, staring at him intensely saying, "Is this something I should know about? Your phone call seemed to concern Elsa and Walsh, and your deal with some anonymous caller."

"Nobody important Roland, just someone I'm having a little difficulty with at the moment. Don't worry I've got it under control," answered Jack trying to play down the importance of the call.

"Don't give me that Jack, I heard you mention Elsa's name, so what was it all about?"

Jack reluctantly admitted to himself that he would have to tell Roland about Al's attempt to blackmail him for more money. "It was Al Ferrino from the marina, the guy who runs the motor boat concession. He knows Elsa's alive because he saw her with me when I returned the hire boat I used to follow Walsh, back to the marina. He says he wants 150 grand or he goes to the police. I've put him off until the end of the trial, which will give me time to scare him enough to forget about demanding any more money."

"The man is being a little too greedy Jack. He got an easy 10 grand for doing very little and now he has the affront to ask for more. If we don't nip this in the bud the jerk will always put his hand out whenever he needs something, and we'll never get rid of him. He's a loose cannon and we don't know who he could be talking to."

"Don't blow it up out of proportion Roland, the guy's a mouse. I'm surprised he even had the bottle to try and blackmail me. I'll make it clear that if he tries to cross us he'll get his legs broken."

"Now who's being dramatic? Look, I think you're taking this thing too lightly. The man sounds unreliable and unpredictable so putting the fear of God into him may not halt his ambition. When he's safe and thinks about it a bit more he'll either take measures to protect himself or go to the police straight away. Besides he can sink us either by design or just by blabbing one night when he's had a little too much to drink. He's looking at the biggest pay day of his life, so you can't expect him to roll over on your say so. Listen to me, we've got to handle this situation and do it quickly."

"OK Roland, but he won't do anything until after the trial. He said he'd give me a couple of days after the verdict comes in to find his money."

"Well he's certainly got brass, I'll give him that," said Bannister. "Let's hope he doesn't live to regret it."

Roland Bannister flew back to New York late evening, planning to get back to the "Blue Cockatoo" around midnight, just when the night kicks into top gear. Business was as good as ever there, but Roland knew that the punters would quickly go elsewhere if he didn't maintain his high standards. After Elsa's disappearance there was a slight fall in receipts, but takings returned to normal within a month.

Fortunately moral degenerates can be a fickle bunch.

Bannister was less happy about the way Jack was handling Al Ferrino. He was amazed that Jack didn't seem concerned over the risk of the guy wrecking their plans. In contrast Roland couldn't relax knowing the damage this man could do on a whim. By the time his plane had arrived in New York Bannister had decided to deal with the Al Ferrino situation himself, and that he would get Lou and Frank to handle the details.

19

Jack stayed in the bar after Roland had left for the airport, and sat drinking another Bud while he was trying to decide on the best way of dealing with Al Ferrino. The poor guy didn't have a clue about the people he was trying to blackmail. If he understood the under currents of the cesspool he was dipping his toe into, he would never have approached Jack in the first place. Jack wondered how the little man had found out that Elsa was living in Boston. Had he been followed on one of his trips to see her? Al was an amateur and didn't understand how to play the game, thought Jack. A "Pro" would have mentioned the fact that he had registered a letter or other document with his solicitor detailing his side of the story and naming the people involved, as insurance for his own protection. Yes, an amateur, it'll be easy to show him the folly of trying to extort money from me without having to lean on him too hard.

While Jack was lost in his thoughts a woman came to sit at the opposite side of the table he was sat at. The woman had a shock of platinum hair, partially covered by a chiffon headscarf that was tied under her chin. Although it was early evening the she was wearing sunglasses and was incongruously wrapped up in a white raincoat. It was hard to see her face, but her overall appearance was conspicuous in its absurdity and reminded Jack of every femme fatale of every B movie he had ever seen as a kid.

"Do you mind if I sit here?" the woman asked in a light, breathy voice reminiscent of Marilyn Monroe.

Jack nodded avoiding eye contact for fear of laughing out loud.

"I'm from out of town and I just want to know where a girl can get some action," she added lowering her voice as if she were talking about a confidence between the two of them.

Jack's head whipped up to see the woman laughing at him. She lowered her sunglasses enough for him to see that it was Elsa. Without saying a word he stood up, went round to the other side of the table, helped Elsa out of her seat, and the two walked out of the bar.

"You're coming down here was not one of your better ideas," said Jack as he drove to his hotel. "And besides, why wear something like that platinum wig, which will only attract attention to you," he added taking another look at her disguise. "Your whole appearance is ridiculous. You look like the caricature of a sixties blonde bombshell."

"I was missing you and I only dressed up like this to give you a bit of a laugh. I guess I shouldn't have bothered, should I?" replied Elsa dejectedly. "Look it's OK for you and Roland up to your necks in Walsh's trial, but I'm holed up in a house on the outskirts of Boston and it's very boring. It's very difficult putting your life on hold while watching the rest of the world go by."

Jack was more than a little sympathetic to Elsa's situation and had seen a steady downturn in her morale over the time she had been living in Boston. He had tried to visit her as often as possible, but he still had to give the outward appearance of going about his day to day business so as not to attract attention to himself. There had been other things like the memorial service he had arranged in her local church, and commiserating with her friends. The false sentiment was particularly difficult with people like Gus and Jean who took Elsa's disappearance very hard.

When they arrived at his hotel, Jack arranged for dinner and two bottles of wine to be sent to his room. Elsa wasn't pleased, "Do you think I've come all the way down to Miami to spend another night in a fucking hotel room?"

"I'd like to take you somewhere nice Elsa, but if you're spotted everything goes down the pan."

"There must be somewhere we can go with a little atmosphere?"

"It's too risky, there's already someone here who knows that you're not dead."

"Who?" asked Elsa, suddenly feeling the wind knocked out of her sail.

"The motorboat attendant, Al Ferrino. He must have seen you getting out of the boat when we returned to the marina. He doesn't know what's behind our deception, but he's smart enough to figure out it's connected with Walsh's trial, and is asking for 150 grand."

"Does Roland know?"

"Yeah he was with me at the bar when Al rang earlier, so I had to tell him what was going on. He thinks we should sort Al out straight away and I've got a good idea what he means, but I've convinced him it can wait until after the trial."

"I saw you with Roland earlier," said Elsa changing the subject, "but I didn't want him to know that I was down here. I wanted us to spend this evening together, it seems such a long time since we've spent quality time together."

Suddenly Jack and Elsa felt as close as they had before the incident on Walsh's boat when they were constantly together. They hugged and Jack kissed Elsa tenderly.

"I'll just take a quick shower before dinner," said Jack as they broke from their embrace and he went in the bathroom to turn on the water. He undressed in the bedroom, put on a bathrobe and went back into the bathroom.

While Jack was in the shower Elsa switched on the TV and tuned into the local news. A report on the Walsh trial followed the headline news item. The anchorman in the studio handed over to Dee Hamilton outside the courthouse. She had been reporting the trial since its start and gave regular evening updates of the day's events. She began her report by describing Simon Walsh's first day on the stand.

"Today Simon Walsh took the stand to give his version of the events that took place on his boat, which led to the disappearance of Elsa Bartelli. Mr. Walsh testified that Miss Bartelli had tried to seduce him on his boat, but that things turned sour when he caught her trying to steal his wallet. He threatened her with the police and a scuffle ensued, which ended in her jumping overboard. Mr. Walsh confirmed he didn't know Miss Bartelli was a lap dancer or that she also worked as a prostitute. The defense still have to demonstrate that.........."

Jack heard a loud crash in the living room, grabbed a towel and rushed out of the bathroom to find out the cause of the commotion. He was dripping from head to toe and looked a sorry sight as he came into the living area of the hotel room and found himself staring at a hole in the television screen.

"Did you hear what that sanctimonious bitch on the TV said about me?" Elsa didn't pause to wait for a response from Jack, but carried on at full throttle, "OK so I'm a lap dancer, but that doesn't mean I have a different man in my pants every night, and it certainly doesn't mean that I'm a hooker. What sort of person do they think I am?"

"Slow down Elsa. If you had waited until the end of the report before "turning" the TV off, you'd have heard her say that the defense still have to prove that you were a prostitute."

"But what if my Gus and Jean hear of these accusations, it's bad enough that they think I'm dead. The only thing that's holding me together right now is my own self-respect and single-minded determination not to let all of this get the better of me. Nobody has ever, or will ever, own me. But you've managed to take that away from me now, everyone thinks I'm some kind of tramp that can be bought for pin money."

"Don't get upset Elsa...."

Jack didn't finish his sentence because Elsa slapped him sharply across the face and ran into the bedroom. At that moment the doorbell rang. Jack grabbed his bathrobe from the bathroom before answering the door, but was still dripping wet when he opened the door. The bellboy gave Jack a funny look across the door threshold, and looked even more startled when he pushed the dinner trolley into the room and saw the damaged TV.

"I had an accident," said Jack quickly, "I'll pay for the TV in the morning." With that Jack tipped the bellboy handsomely and ushered him out of the room.

Jack walked into the bedroom to see Elsa lying face down on the bed, sobbing quietly. Jack sat on the side of the bed and gently put his hand on her shoulder. "I'm truly sorry Elsa, I didn't realize you'd get such a mauling in court."

Elsa lifted herself onto her elbows and brushed her hair from her face. "Well they're right aren't they? I did try to lure Walsh with the promise of sex, just like all of the other punters we ripped off with this scam. We didn't actually have sex, but that's not really the point, is it? Maybe I'm no better than a hooker and I've just been kidding myself that there's more to me than a good body."

"C'mon Elsa, that's not true and you know it. Don't let a few lurid headlines from a media clown do this to you. The TV people are just trying to cash in on your background because it's an astonishing story and will draw viewers. You know your true worth as a person as I do, otherwise I wouldn't feel the way I do about you."

"Nothing really changes between us, does it? Even now, knowing how depressed I am and how I feel about you, you can't tell me that you love me. Now would be a really good time to tell me, if you mean it."

"What's so important about saying the obvious, you know how I feel," replied Jack insensitively. "OK I love you!"

"That's not how I wanted you to say it, so let's just forget it Jack. You were right my coming down here was a bad idea because you clearly don't give a shit about what I'm going through, or how this business is affecting us. I don't think any amount of money is worth all of this."

"You'll think differently when we get our hands on it, trust me. Now let's eat before the dinner gets cold and the wine gets warm."

Elsa was now even more depressed than she was before flying to Miami. Her joy in the prospect of seeing Jack again was quickly dissipated by his continual hunger for money and unfeeling platitude of love. She was now beginning to question his true feelings for her, and whether she was just a means for him to get what he really wanted. Words of love aren't always easy and she had been waiting so long for him to tell her that he loved her. Now he'd callously taken that dream away from her, because anything he said in the future would be marred by his words and actions this night.

For his part Jack had felt under pressure from Elsa and realized that by not comforting her in the way she wanted, that he was putting a big strain on their relationship. But he couldn't help himself. He knew that Elsa wanted them to settle down and live together, but Jack couldn't picture himself in a conventional relationship, and with just one woman. She was his greatest passion but he still felt he had to cling on to his freedom.

The next morning Jack drove Elsa to the airport to catch a plane back to Boston. They didn't talk much on their trip to the airport and Jack felt distant, and that something between them had died in the hotel room. Give it time, he thought, things will get back to normal when we get the money. His mantra was wearing a bit thin, even to himself.

20

It was now Bantry's turn to cross-examine Walsh. He was keen to put him under pressure, but kept reminding himself that he would have to build his argument slowly and meticulously to avoid being obvious in his lead up to the kill. This case had blown up to be something bigger than he had ever anticipated and was now firmly in the public spotlight, which meant that a successful prosecution could do a lot to further his career. Despite a slight nervousness, which was unusual, he felt destiny was taking a hand.

"Please remember Mr. Walsh that you are still under oath," he began as he walked up to the witness box. Bantry's style was far more animated than that of his defense colleague and he would often walk over to a witness for a face to face interrogation, and then pull away in mock amazement when trying to cast doubt on critical parts of the testimony given. He would also walk over to the jury from time to time and make eye contact with individuals when trying to emphasize a point. Using these techniques he hoped he would establish a personal rapport with the jurors, which would help in reinforcing his closing argument at the end of the trial.

"We've heard a great deal about the moral character, or should I say the lack of moral character, of Miss Bartelli. What was your opinion of her Mr. Walsh?"

"Initially I didn't have any opinion on her as a person. As I said earlier she appeared to be a normal tourist relaxing on vacation, and certainly didn't look like a hooker and I didn't have any reason to think she was."

"Well I accept that statement wholeheartedly because I know you are somewhat of an authority on hookers."

"Objection!" shouted Tavistock, "the Prosecution is trying to make capital from cheap innuendo at my Client's expense."

"I agree Mr. Tavistock," replied Judge Hyam. "Mr. Bantry let me remind you that this is a court of law and therefore your questions must be concise and to the point, and most of all pertinent to the case. Do you understand Mr. Bantry?"

"Yes your Honor," said Bantry respectfully. "What was your intention when you offered to take Miss Bartelli out in your boat?" continued Bantry, turning back to Walsh.

Walsh sat quietly for a moment trying to formulate an answer that would be acceptable to the jury, and also to his wife. "As I said earlier it was the last day of her vacation and I wanted to give her something to remember," said Walsh, which was followed by some quiet laughing around the courtroom. Hyam brought down his gavel sharply and called for quiet. Walsh continued, "When I met Miss Bartelli we seemed to strike up an instant rapport. I was immediately attracted to her and I also wanted to prolong our meeting. I thought it was a nice idea to take her out to the reef and for a run around the coast."

"Yes, but what was your intention in doing that?" persisted Bantry.

"I didn't have any specific intention or objective behind the invitation, if that's what you mean? As I said, I was taken with her and wanted to spend a little more time with her. Taking her out with me seemed a more enjoyable way of spending the afternoon on my boat, than going out alone."

"So your intentions were not completely benevolent, to end her vacation on a high note, as you said yesterday?"

"Yes I did sympathize with her situation, but that was not the only reason I asked her out."

"Let me be clearer then, did you have any intentions of a sexual nature towards Miss Bartelli? Did you want to express yourself more openly when you got her alone on your boat, and far enough out to sea to act on them without attracting unwanted attention?"

"To be honest I didn't know what would happen when we got out to sea. I thought that if we continued to get on well together, that I'd take her out to dinner that evening. She had made arrangements with her sister, but I thought I could gate crash and take them both out." Walsh had gone over that line a hundred times and still couldn't make it sound convincing.

"But you're a married man Mr. Walsh."

"For God's sake I was only contemplating dinner; don't tell me that having dinner with someone of the opposite sex can automatically put your marriage at risk!"

A slight ripple of laughter went around the court again, to Bantry's annoyance. "No Mr. Walsh I can confirm that I often have dinner with female colleagues without any risk to my marriage. The difference being, of course that they are friends I have known for some time, and not people I have just picked up in a bar. I fail to see the difference between your relationship with Miss Bartelli and with the prostitutes you admit to have been with, apart from the fact that there was no financial transaction at the start. Can you explain the difference?"

"Objection, your Honor! Mr. Bantry is trying to harass the witness," interjected Tavistock.

"Objection over ruled Mr. Tavistock," replied Judge Hyam. "I can understand the importance of ascertaining what Mr. Walsh's first impressions of Miss Bartelli were, his attitude towards her and if he expected their relationship to become intimate."

"Well, Mr. Walsh?" asked Bantry.

"As I said earlier, she didn't look or act like a hooker. Yes, she gave off a sexy persona because of her striking appearance, but didn't flaunt it in a cheap way. She was well dressed and could even have been there to have an after work drink. I guess, in the back of my mind, I may have hoped we could become intimate, but not in the way she flaunted herself on the boat."

"But I would have thought that you would be quite used to the brazen behavior of women, in view of your history."

"Not taking her for a hooker at the start, I guess she threw me off balance," replied Walsh, annoyed at Bantry's constant references to his past relationships with prostitutes.

"You agree that she was a sophisticated woman and must have known you were a wealthy man?"

"Yes."

"Then why would she be satisfied with the small change in your wallet, when she could have had far more by trying to develop a deeper, more meaningful relationship with you? You said yourself that she was obviously intelligent, and so surely she wouldn't have sold herself so cheaply?"

"I can't answer for her motives or actions," replied Walsh.

"Quite so, but it's a mystery, especially when you consider the size of her bank balance at that time." Bantry walked over to his table and picked up a piece of paper and then walked over to show it to the jury. "This is the bank statement of Miss Bartelli's finances at the end of the month in which she disappeared. It shows that she had $135,000 in her account at that time. So I ask you again, why should she travel all the way down to Florida for the few hundred bucks you carry in your wallet?"

"I don't know, maybe she was just an opportunist."

"OK Mr. Walsh we had better move on. I would like this bank statement and other documents to be included as evidence as they show Miss Bartelli's assets at the time of her disappearance were worth over $200,000." Bantry then turned to Judge Hyam and explained that blood and hair samples had been taken from the deck of Walsh's boat and a DNA match found with hair samples from Elsa Bartelli's hairbrush.

Bantry went back to his table and exchanged the bank statement for another piece of paper, which he held up in front of Walsh. "This is the summary of a forensic report of tests on blood and hair samples taken from your boat. Firstly, the blood samples taken from the deck of your boat proved to be from Miss Bartelli. Can you explain how the blood got there?"

Walsh's face colored and he became a little restless as he shifted uneasily on his seat. "She must have hurt herself in the scuffle we had, when I found her with my wallet."

"A scuffle sounds like a slight fracas without any real violence. But the samples taken from the deck of your boat indicate that she must have landed on it very hard. She may have fallen to the deck, possibly after being knocked down by you. Is that what happened Mr. Walsh?"

"I don't know…..it all happened so quickly. She may have fallen onto the deck, but I certainly didn't knock her down."

"Well if she was bleeding as a result of your fight, I would have assumed that you would have had blood on your clothes. That is, unless you held her at arm's length during the "scuffle". Did you have blood on your clothes Mr. Walsh?"

"I didn't have any bloodstains on my clothes, in fact I wasn't aware that she was bleeding."

"The blood stains were found on the starboard side of the boat next to the hand railing. Did she fall by the hand railing?"

"I've already told you that I don't know," stammered Walsh.

"Some strands of hair were also found, but nearer to the middle of the deck. These hair samples were also from Miss Bartelli, can you explain that, Mr. Walsh?"

"No I can't, because I can't remember the way things happened in any real detail," replied Walsh. Play dumb, he thought, and limit the damage of Bantry's cross-examination by saying as little as possible. He looked anxiously towards Tavistock, trying to get some comfort from his approval of his performance. Tavistock for his part was beginning to see the threads of Walsh's defense argument beginning to unravel.

Walsh and Tavistock had discussed at length the details of the evidence listed by the prosecution. They knew that the blood and hair samples would be identified as being from Elsa, but they hadn't anticipated Bantry's spin on the locations at which the samples were found, or his interpretation of Walsh's fight with Elsa pinpointing where she had left hair and blood traces on Walsh's boat. They had naively assumed that these samples merely indicated the ferocity of the fight, which they could attribute to Elsa's irrational behavior.

"When Miss Bartelli fell overboard you were reluctant to try and rescue her, in case she eluded you and got back into the boat while you were still in the water. Is that correct Mr. Walsh?"

"Yes."

"But there must have been other measures you could have taken to try and rescue her, without having to go into the water? Why didn't you throw her a safety line or a life saver?"

"I couldn't see her to throw her a lifeline, besides, everything happened so fast I couldn't think straight."

"Let's be clear about this Mr. Walsh, you saw Miss Bartelli go overboard and when you looked over the side you didn't see any sign of her surfacing."

"No."

"How long did you look for her?"

"It seemed a long time. I went to both sides of the boat to try and catch sight of her."

"Was the sea rough or were conditions such that it would have been difficult to see her when she did resurface?"

"No."

"Well there can only be one of two explanations Mr. Walsh. Either she was dead when she hit the water, or you didn't spend any time looking for her and simply left her where she fell overboard. Which was it Mr. Walsh?"

"I've already told you what happened. I don't know why I couldn't see her in the water! The shock of the impact with the water may have knocked her unconscious, how should I know?"

"You have already testified that you did not call the coastguard to report the incident?"

"Yes."

"Why couldn't you have reported your position, so that they could have sent out assistance to help try and find Miss Bartelli? Tell the court why you didn't call the coastguard?"

"How many times do I have to repeat myself? I wasn't thinking straight," stammered Walsh desperate to find something to say that would mitigate the heartless action of leaving his victim in the sea.

"Miss Bartelli's disappearance would have been very convenient for you; after all she may have reported your attack to the police when you returned to the marina?" Walsh shook his head disagreeing with the implication behind Bantry's question. "I know you can't answer that Mr. Walsh, but tell me this, did you think to report the incident to anyone at the marina when you returned?"

"No."

"You didn't tell anyone about Miss Bartellis's accident, what were you trying to cover up?"

"I've already said that by this time I was frightened that I would be accused of harming her."

"Well you're right in that respect, do you own a gun Mr. Walsh?"

"Yes I do."

"Is this the gun?" asked Bantry handing a gun in a polythene bag to Walsh.

"I think it is. It's certainly the same model," replied Walsh.

"I can tell you that it is your gun and that we have checked records to confirm that it is registered to you." Bantry turned to the jury. "This gun was found at Mr. Walsh's home shortly after his arrest and forensic tests confirmed that it had been fired recently. Did you have this gun on your boat the day you met Miss Bartelli?" asked Bantry turning back to Walsh.

"I don't know, I can't remember."

"You don't seem to be able to remember much, do you Mr. Walsh?" said Bantry sarcastically. Walsh hated being humiliated in this way and mentally braced himself as Bantry continued, "Do you normally take the gun with you on vacation?"

"I don't consciously carry it with me everywhere. I originally bought it after hearing about burglaries in my apartment building."

"That's strange, as your wife told the police that you always took the gun to Florida with you, after your encounter with a vagrant sleeping on your boat. I'll ask you again Mr. Walsh did you have your gun with you, the afternoon you took Miss Bartelli out on your boat?"

"Yes I did, but I didn't shoot her!"

"You're jumping ahead of me, Mr. Walsh," said Bantry turning to the jury and smiling at them knowingly. "Let's examine the facts that have been established so far. You claim Miss Bartelli tried to seduce you, but on finding her with your wallet a scuffle ensued in which she may, or may not, have fallen on the deck. Samples of hair and blood found on your boat were from Miss Bartelli. Hair samples in the middle of the deck indicate that she fell during your fight. Blood stains on the starboard side of the deck show that she was injured in that area. Finally, you confirm that there were no blood stains on your clothing indicating she was some distance away from you when the injury occurred."

Bantry paused to let the jury digest the thread running through his brief summary of Walsh's fight with Elsa. "I think you're right Mr. Walsh, the only conclusion that I can draw from these facts is that you tried to force yourself on the unfortunate, innocent Miss Bartelli, and when she tried to escape your crude advances, you shot her."

"That's not true," shouted Walsh, "you've got everything twisted. Elsa Bartelli was not an "unfortunate, innocent" woman, she was a cock teaser on the make who deserved what she got."

There was an audible gasp around the court in response to Walsh's outburst, which made him pause and reconsider what he had just said. "I wasn't talking about the shooting, I was talking about her drowning." This time the response from the spectators was even more pointed as an even louder buzz went around the court. Tavistock sat with his head in his hands feeling utterly crushed by his Client's utterances.

Judge Hyam brought down his gavel sharply and once again asked for quiet in the courtroom. It took a few seconds for the low drone to subside. He turned to Bantry signaling him to continue.

"That's all your Honor," said Bantry, "thank you Mr. Walsh, no more questions."

Bridget Walsh had been stunned, like the rest of the court, at her husband's outburst. A hollow feeling had developed in the pit of her stomach and she felt it radiating outwards, numbing the rest of her body. Her worst fears were suddenly realized. The initial shock she felt was gradually replaced by nausea, when she had to admit to herself that she had been living with a man without a shred of common human decency. Her immediate instinct was to leave the courtroom as quickly as she could, so that she could distance herself from the events she had just witnessed. Without a glance to her husband she rose from her seat next to the aisle and turned toward the rear of the courtroom. Rushing up the aisle she pushed one of the courtroom doors open and took a deep lung full of cool air and started to compose herself.

As she turned to the lobby to leave the court building a news reporter, who must have seen her hurried exit from the courtroom, intercepted her. "Mrs. Walsh, can I have your reaction to your husband's testimony," asked the eager journalist.

"What do you think? Go away and stop asking me stupid questions!" she shouted at him. She picked up her speed but the reporter was not going to be put off, as he followed and cut off her exit.

"But Mrs. Walsh you must have felt something after hearing what your husband said about Elsa deserving what she got?"

"Have you got no sense of decency or is everyone fair game for your cheap rag?" hissed Bridget and with that she briskly brushed the reporter aside before he could deliver any more follow up questions, and strode towards the building exit without hesitation.

Jack had seen the reporter follow Bridget out of the courtroom, and had followed them both to see how she would handle the situation. She had recovered quickly from what must have been a massive blow to her own ego, if not to her emotions, and dealt with the reporter efficiently. A very determined woman thought Jack making a mental note not to underestimate her in their future negotiations.

When he returned to the courtroom Jack found Tavistock questioning Walsh, reworking some of his earlier testimony in an attempt to repair some of the damage he had inflicted on himself by his earlier outburst. Jack smiled to himself as he saw the attorney floundering as he tried to undo the harm. Tavistock knew that his Client's final comments to Bantry would be one of the key influences on each of the jurors when deciding his innocence or guilt. In his own mind he was already thinking about grounds for appeal.

21

Al Ferrino had heard about Walsh's faux pas of the previous day and was expecting a call from Jack Cates, the voice he heard on the other end of the line was unfamiliar.

"Hello Mr. Ferrino, my name is Roland Bannister, how are you?"

"How do you know me and who the hell are you?" replied Al, ignoring pleasantries.

"I'm sorry Mr. Ferrino, let me explain. I'm a business associate of Jack Cates who has asked me to contact you, now that a Walsh conviction seems certain. Jack has asked me to make arrangements for the delivery of your money before the end of the trial."

"You've got my hundred and fifty grand then?"

Bannister paused for a second thinking that Ferrino had as much chance of winning the lottery as getting his hands on that amount of money. "Do you think I'm going to walk through the streets of the city carrying that kind of money?" he replied a little aggressively. "Besides it's quite a large package that I've put in a safe place, so we need to make arrangements for you to collect it."

"OK," said Al who was suddenly at a loss for words. He hadn't really thought through the details for completion of the transaction. He hadn't been sure if Jack would really take heed of his threat and he was also more than a little relieved that he wouldn't have to face Jack again.

"I can come over to your house, or……."

"No there's no need for that," interjected Al, "the neighborhood is not so good and I don't want anyone seeing you make the delivery. I want to pay it straight into a new bank account."

Al didn't want his long suffering wife to know about the source of the money as, despite their desperate financial circumstance, she would have nothing to do with dirty cash. Al and his wife had been married for 25 years and had very little to show for their time together. They didn't own their home, or have any children, or a pension fund for their retirement. Al had worked spasmodically, flitting from one dead end job to another, before finally settling down to his job at the marina. His gambling habit made it impossible for them to save anything from their meagre resources. Al decided that once he got the money they would buy a home in a decent area so that they could have an investment to fall back on if necessary and enjoy their retirement.

"Can we meet at mid-day, during your lunch break? You can take the money straight to whatever bank you like."

"I can meet you between one and two," replied Al.

"Come over to my hotel and we can finish the deal," suggested Bannister

"No I don't want to meet in your hotel room; I want us to meet in a public place."

"That's a little disappointing Al, I've been very open and friendly with you and I thought we were getting on very well."

"We can socialize as much as you like after the money's in the bank, but 'til then it's strictly business."

"Well, where shall we meet?"

"There's an Irish bar in Brickell, which isn't too far from the marina. Meet me there at ten past one."

"OK," agreed Bannister, "but how will I recognize you?"

"I'll be sitting in the right hand corner booth at the rear of the bar," replied Al curtly and then put the phone back on its receiver. Al was amazed at how easy it all was, and was beginning to regret he hadn't asked for more money. Don't be greedy he thought, surely no-one would take any unnecessary chances for a measly 150 grand.

When Roland Bannister entered the Irish bar he briefly perused the décor and tried to absorb the ambience of the place. He walked over to the barman and ordered a brandy, pointing to the right hand corner booth described by Al. The barman was about to explain that there was no waiter service in the bar as Roland strode away, and was left with his mouth hanging open. Roland's training and experience as a lawyer had taught him to prepare a case meticulously and try to catch the opposition off guard. He thought his early arrival would unsettle Al, particularly if this was his own watering hole, which he had probably selected to be in familiar surroundings when closing the deal.

The disgruntled barman delivered the brandy to the booth and set it down loudly in front of Roland, who looked up at him, smiled politely and nodded in gratitude. The barman scowled and returned to the bar. Roland picked up the glass and took a sip of the brandy, but his face creased immediately as the coarseness of the liquor hit the back of his throat. He pushed the glass away realizing that he should have known better than to expect a quality brandy in this type of establishment. He briefly looked around the bar, which was a typical watering hole for tourists, but obviously also a draw for locals working in the area. He wondered how many of regulars in this bar would frequent the "Blue Cockatoo".

As he was still absorbing the atmosphere of the place, Roland noticed a short stocky man enter the bar and collect a beer from the counter. The man looked inquisitively at the booth and took a few tentative steps in its direction not knowing what to expect. Roland stood up and signaled to the man to join him and as the man approached he held out his hand, saying "Hello Al".

Al took his hand, making a weak handshake and moved into the seat opposite. "Have you got the money?" he asked immediately.

"Slow down Al. Have you got any idea how big a one hundred and fifty thousand dollar package broken down into denominations of 100's, 50's and 20's is? I would look conspicuous bringing such a package in here and you would spend the next month explaining to people what it was that you collected and whom it was you met."

"Don't try and be clever Mr. Bannister," shrugged Al bemused by the slick appearance of Bannister and the way words seemed to just roll off his tongue. "We agreed that you would hand over the money here. I can handle any awkward questions, so what's the problem? "

"Listen, I'm trying to do what's safest and best for both of us. I couldn't hand you a large package in this joint without drawing attention to ourselves. I've got the money stashed in a safe place just waiting for you to go and pick it up."

"So where is it?" asked Al briskly.

"I've put the money in a travel bag in one of the baggage lockers at the train station and here's the key," said Roland producing a shiny metal object from the inside pocket of his jacket and handing it to Al. "The locker number is 177, which is on the tab attached to the key. The station lobby is wide open and you can collect the bag in your own time, without drawing attention to yourself."

"The train station's at least 10 blocks away," moaned Al taking the key off Bannister.

"I can drive you there if you want."

"No it's OK, I'll make my own way there," replied Al and with that he stood up and left the bar with his beer virtually untouched.

Al pondered on when to collect the money as he walked out of the bar, but by the time he hit the street he had decided to collect it straight away. He hailed a taxi and gave instructions to the driver to take him to Miami Central Station as he got into the cab. He still had the locker key in his hand and looked down at it smiling to himself and thinking about the change this money would bring to his and Nora's lives. Before buying a house, he would put the money in a high interest account for a couple of years, let it accrue interest and then tell Nora that he had made some stock market investments that had grown beyond all expectations.

The cab stopped suddenly and Al found himself staring at the entrance of Miami Central Station. He got out of the taxi and paid the driver. Entering the station he found it hard to control himself. He felt like a kid at Christmas and his natural instinct was to run as fast as he could to find his present. Restraining his pace he walked to the center of the large lobby and scanned the overhead signs to get the direction to the baggage lockers. The way to the baggage lockers was clearly signed and he made for the ante lobby on the left hand side of the main area, to the side of the departure gates to the train platforms. As he walked into the ante lobby the baggage lockers were arrayed on the two opposing walls leading off the main lobby. His eyes scanned the locker numbers on the nearest wall, looking for a reference from which to find the number 177.

Al found locker number 21 and hurried forward counting locker numbers....33, 51, 73, 91, 103, 121, 143..........177. Al stopped at locker 177 and stared intently at it for a while, catching his breath and trying to imagine what was on the other side of the door. He still clutched the key that Bannister had given him and he inserted it into the door lock, turned the lock anti-clockwise and slowly opened the door. Inside the locker was a cheap brown and cream plastic holdall, zipped tight. Al unzipped the holdall and put his hand inside it and felt a paper parcel wrapped with string. He reached for a penknife in his pocket, pulled out the blade and thrust it into the package. Ripping the wrapping in an upward direction he made an opening of about six inches. Eagerly he stuck his hand through the opening and felt bundles of money inside the parcel. He searched for the edge of a bill, grabbed it and pulled his hand free. Al looked at his hand to see a blank sheet of paper cut into the shape of a dollar bill. He thrust his hand into the package again to pull out a handful of bills, to find they were all blank sheets of paper.

Suddenly Al realized that he had been set up by Bannister and he could only conclude that he had put him in the train station for a reason. He didn't want to hang around to find out what his purpose was, as it would probably involve him being hurt or even killed. On becoming aware of his predicament Al's heart started to pound frantically and beads of perspiration appeared on his face. His early euphoria had completely dissipated and he felt uncomfortable, hot and sluggish. Anxiously he looked towards the main lobby to see if he was being watched. All he could see were busy commuters going about their daily business. He let the pieces of bill shaped paper drop from his hand, sheathed the penknife and put it in his pocket and headed for the main lobby.

Instinctively he knew he had to get out of there as quickly as possible. If someone were waiting to kill him they would have identified him as he went to collect the money from the locker. Reaching the main lobby he headed for the nearest exit, continually looking round about him to see if he was being followed. He would have liked to run out of the station, but in doing that he would only have attracted more attention to himself, and besides he was in no physical condition to run for more than a minute or two. As he approached the exit doors Al's anxiety began to be gradually replaced by a deep sense of relief. The automatic doors opened and he skipped over the threshold, again turning to see if he was being followed. No one appeared to be taking any interest in him and he began to wonder if Bannister's intent was simply to scare him. He had been scared, but instead of running away he would make Bannister pay by asking for more money.

Al started walking up the service road to the taxi rank and was stopped in his tracks by someone calling his name from the direction of the exit he had just passed through. He turned to see a man standing by the automatic doors and holding the brown and crème holdall aloft, and waving him back. The anxiety flooded back, he became flushed and started to run towards the taxi rank, turning intermittently to see the man slowly following him. The combination of his panic and the sudden exertion made him breathe heavily, and he felt as if his heart was going to burst out of his chest. He turned back and ran straight into a man walking in the opposite direction towards the station, knocking him to the ground. The shock of the collision made Al step backwards, rubbing his head, which was ringing from the force of the impact. Looking more closely at the man he had just knocked over, he could see he was a blind, wearing dark glasses and with a white telescopic walking stick, which had retracted. He apologized to the blind man who held out his hand in a gesture for Al to lift him up. Nervously Al looked towards the station to see the man with the holdall still walking slowly up the service road. He won't do anything with witnesses around thought Al and he reached out to grab the outstretched hand of the blind man.

He was heavy and Al strained himself even further pulling him up to his feet. Rising to his feet the blind man groped for an arm to try and stabilize himself, but as the heads of the two men became level, Al felt a sharp pain on the left side of his chest. His legs went weak and suddenly could no longer support him, but the blind man who towered above him when standing up straight, strongly held Al upright to prevent him collapsing onto the pavement. Al stared up at the face of the blind man through a blurred haze and the last image he saw before dying was the parting of the man's lips into a broad smile. With perfect timing the man launched Al into the road, just in front of an oncoming car that was driving toward the train station. The sickening thud of Al's body striking the front nearside corner of the car made the driver stand hard on his brakes. Even though the car was travelling slowly it managed to drag Al's body about 15 feet before coming to a halt. The driver scrambled from his car and rushed to the front of it, to see the mess he had made of the man he had hit, screaming to the passenger that he hadn't seen him.

"That blind man trick never fails Frank," said Lou congratulating his partner as they drove downtown. "You always find the heart with that steel pin inside your walking stick, it's amazing. Man, you're an artist."

"Never mind that Lou, did you clean up?"

"Yeah of course I did. Got the holdall, cleaned the locker, closed it and returned the key. You know I'm reliable, there's no loose ends."

"OK step on the gas I feel hungry."

22

Bantry began his summing up by painting Elsa Bartelli as an innocent woman trapped on a boat with a man prepared to do anything to have sex with her. What if she was a lap dancer, that didn't mean she shouldn't be treated with the same dignity and respect as any other woman, or that she didn't deserve the same protection from the law? He concluded by saying, "the precise details of Elsa's death will never be known to anyone but Simon Walsh. But he fabricated a story of her trying to seduce him for the paltry amount of money in his wallet, and only showed us the true nature of his feelings towards women at the end of his testimony stating that 'she had got what she deserved'.

Bantry paused, letting the jurors remember Walsh's performance on the stand. "There is sufficient evidence of Elsa putting up a strenuous fight, but to no avail. Walsh ruthlessly murdered her to cover up his assault on her body, and concocted a ridiculous story when he was arrested. Don't forget he failed to report her disappearance when he returned to the marina and he failed to call the coastguard for help when he was out at sea. Why? What was he trying to hide? He was hoping his crime would go undetected and that Elsa would just become another missing persons statistic. Members of the jury, I ask you to give Elsa justice and find this man guilty of murder."

Tavistock had a far more difficult task in trying to convince the jury of Walsh's innocence. He tried to portray Walsh as a victim caught up in circumstances beyond his control. "Don't judge the moral character of the defendant. He is being tried for murder, not for his sexual habits or preferences. The only crime he is guilty of is not reporting the incident to the authorities when it happened, or after he had returned to the marina. But surely you can understand his frame of mind at the time and the pressure he must have been under to keep his wife, family and friends from finding out about the incident. He is guilty of gross misjudgment and putting his own interests ahead of his unfortunate passenger, but he is not guilty of murder."

Jack scrutinized the jury as Tavistock was trying to mitigate the callousness of his client's actions. As he studied the faces of the jury members, he was pleased to see that they all had impassive expressions and were clearly not empathizing with what was being said. He also noticed that Bridget Walsh was not in the courtroom, which he thought might also be picked up by the keener members of the jury.

Following Tavistock's closing argument Judge Hyam turned to the jury to instruct them on the points of law that they should consider in coming to their verdict. "Members of the jury," he began, "you will have to decide on whether Simon Walsh took Elsa Bartelli aboard his boat to sexually compromise her and ended up killing her after he assaulted her, or if he was an innocent victim of a petty crime that resulted in tragic consequences. The District Attorney's Office have brought a Homicide charge against him, however the testimony of Mr. Walsh and others has shown that the cause of her death could have been due to any one of a number of alternative scenarios leading to her jumping or being thrown off his boat, if in fact she is dead."

"The true circumstances of her disappearance may never be fully understood as there were no independent witnesses to the events that took place and clearly Mr. Walsh's testimony to the police was aimed at protecting himself from prosecution, which has now taken place. You will have to judge the reliability of his testimony in the same way that you must come to a decision on the real motive of Miss Bartelli in going out to sea with Mr. Walsh in the first place. If Walsh did murder Elsa Bartelli, then clearly it was not a premeditated act as they had only met that afternoon. But if you believe that he could have helped her but left her in the sea to die, to cover up his attempted or actual rape, then you must find him guilty of 2nd degree murder. On the other hand if you feel he was provoked by her actions on the boat, and the ensuing fight with Miss Bartelli resulted in her accidental death, then you must find him not guilty of murder, but guilty of manslaughter. Finally, if you believe his account of Miss Bartelli jumping over board of her own volition and that he was unable to help her get back onto the boat, then you must find him innocent, although charges may be brought against him later for failing to call for help or report the incident."

"Remember that collectively you can only come to a guilty verdict if you all firmly believe that the defendant committed murder or manslaughter. If you cannot all agree on a verdict, then a majority verdict must be presented." Hyam paused to let the jury process the information they had just been given. "Is that clear?" he finally asked and glanced from one jury member to the other for confirmation. They all nodded in agreement. "When you go into the jury room, the first thing you must do is to choose a foreman who will deliver your verdict to the court."

The jury stood up and then filed out of the courtroom. Judge Hyam adjourned the court proceedings until the jury were ready to deliver their verdict. It was just past 3 o'clock in the afternoon and Jack thought he'd grab a quick drink at the bar at the end of the block, before going back to the hotel to call Bannister with the news that the jury were out.

While Jack was sat at the bar with a bottle of Bud to his mouth, James Bantry sidled up beside him and drew his attention with a hearty slap on the back. "I think I'll join you Jack, it's been a difficult trial and I need resuscitation." Jack nodded and signaled the barman for service. Bantry ordered a whiskey sour and Jack asked that the drink be put on his tab. Over the duration of the trial the two men had gotten to know each other quite well as they both were in the habit of going into the bar at the end of the day's events in court. Bantry had seen Jack's daily attendance in court, knew he was Elsa's partner and was able to paint a clearer picture of her through talking to him.

"How long do you think they'll be out?" asked Jack.

"It's difficult to say. We both know that Walsh is a lying, two faced bastard but it all depends on what the jury made of him. Initially the women will have been prejudiced against Elsa, having read all of the sordid details printed in the press before the trial. Luckily Walsh didn't do himself any favors with his testimony. I feel quietly confident."

"The judge gave the jury too many options, do you think that will confuse them?"

"No, the choices are fairly straight forward, and surely no-one can really believe Walsh's ridiculous story of Elsa jumping overboard to escape. I don't know how Tavistock let him come into court with that yarn."

"Maybe they couldn't construe any other plausible reason for her going overboard without pointing the finger at Walsh," answered Jack. "Do you think the jury will be influenced by the fact that the police never found Elsa's body?"

"No, not really Jack as there are a number of precedents of murderers going down without the evidence of a corpse. Anyway, DNA put Elsa on the boat and eye witness testimonies confirmed she wasn't on board when Walsh returned."

"I was looking at the jury while you and Tavistock made your closing remarks. They seemed far more receptive to your argument than they did to his. Luckily Walsh is so obnoxious that even Tavistock couldn't hide that fact."

"I know Jack, but murderers aren't convicted because they aren't nice people, but because they're guilty. Let's hope the jury are convinced of his guilt." With that Bantry finished his drink and bade Jack farewell.

On the way back to his hotel Jack picked up the evening edition of the Miami Herald. He felt a bit tired and the day had proven to be a little anti-climactic after the fireworks of Walsh's testimony the previous day. He had thought about the trial, almost to the exclusion of everything and everyone else. Bantry could have injected a bit more "fire and brimstone" into his closing remarks, heralding old world values for the respect of women. Jack thought that he had been far too restrained in his condemnation of Walsh, and had missed the opportunity to reinforce the negative statements made about him during his trial. Bantry should have tried to eradicate any last vestiges of doubt about Walsh's guilt that there may still be lingering in some of the juror's minds. He put Bantry's lack luster performance down to over confidence.

At the hotel Jack ordered some coffee and sandwich's to be sent up to his room and decided he would stay in rather than go out on the town. There would be plenty of time to celebrate after the guilty verdict was returned. Once inside his room Jack dropped the paper on the bed and turned into the bathroom to take a shower. The bellboy came with his order after he had showered, while he was still in his dressing gown. Jack poured himself a cup of coffee and settled down on the bed with the paper. Half way through the paper he noticed a small article on the death of a local man at the railway station. He sat bolt upright when he read that the name of the man was Al Ferrino.

The newspaper report stated that that Al had been killed in a road accident outside the station. Unaccountably he had fallen in front of an oncoming car and had incurred severe head injuries from which he had died. There were no witnesses to the accident, other than the car driver and his girlfriend. Both were traumatized by the incident and were unable to comment to the paper. The police did not suspect foul play, although they would be making a full investigation into the incident.

Jack dropped the paper and picked up his cell phone to call Gene Tanner. "Hello this is Detective Tanner," came the voice down the other end of the phone line.

"It's Jack Cates, Gene, how are things with you?"

"I'm fine Jack, busy as always….well you know what it's like you've done the job yourself."

"I know and in a strange way I sometimes still miss it, but then I think of the freedom I have now. Tell me Gene, have you closed the file on Walsh?"

"I still have a little involvement, but as you know the jury went out to consider the verdict today, so the case will be closed shortly, one way or the other. Let's hope the bastard goes down for a long time."

"You and me both," replied Jack. "Talking of the Walsh trial, I just read an article in the Herald about the death of Al Ferrino. Wasn't he one of the witnesses?"

"Yes, Ferrino was a witness, but he didn't actually appear in court. His evidence was read out to corroborate the testimonies of the barman and the mechanic. He was a strange little man, very aggressive but genuinely concerned about Elsa."

"What happened to him?"

"He was hit by a guy bringing his girlfriend to the train station. Apparently they were having an argument and didn't see Ferrino until it was too late. No-one knows what he was doing at the station. All we do know is that he was on his lunch break from the marina."

"It's ironic that the poor guy was killed by a car at a train station, but I guess stranger things can happen."

"I'm glad you can see the funny side Jack. It first appeared to be a freakish incident because Ferrino fell awkwardly, hit his head on the grill of the car and perforated his skull behind his left ear. He would have died instantly had he still been alive. What really killed him was a puncture wound below his chest that can't be related to any physical object on the car. The coroner thinks it could have been a stiletto, but the entry of the wound gives a rising trajectory up to the heart. If that's the case Ferrino didn't step in front of the car, he was thrown into its path."

"But the paper said the police didn't think he died in suspicious circumstances."

"I know but that's because we haven't got a clue as to what happened. If the stiletto theory is true it has all the hallmarks of a professional hit.....but for what reason? Al Ferrino had no underworld connections, so we're just keeping a low profile on the case until we can make a few enquiries. What's your interest?"

"I met him at Walsh's trial. We got talking over a drink and he did seem very concerned over Elsa, especially when I told him that she had been my girl. I can't believe he had any criminal connections, he just didn't seem the type."

"It's a mystery Jack. But how are you bearing up now that the trial's nearly over?"

"To be truthful my emotions have dulled. I've been living without Elsa for such a long time that that my passion for revenge has now gone. I'll just be glad when it's all over and Walsh is behind bars."

"I couldn't have sat through the trial like you Jack, listening to the way he treated Elsa on his boat. The man's a low life who will hopefully get what he deserves."

"Yeah the case seems pretty straightforward to me, but you never can tell with these things," replied Jack.

"I'm just glad I was able to get onto the case so quickly and run the rat down. He won't be using his money to compromise any other unsuspecting woman in the future."

"He should be behind bars to protect the public, never mind what he did to Elsa. When I think of the way he manhandled her, I could kill him," said Jack with genuine passion, remembering how he found her in the sea.

"I'm sorry Jack, I didn't mean to stir up things for you again. Look I've got to go now. Let's get together after the trial, bye."

"Yeah, see you Gene," said Jack cancelling the call. Frank and Lou he thought, Bannister had got his two tame gorillas to see off Al. Jack was pissed about Al's murder as it was an unnecessary risk to take at this stage of the trial and because he knew he could have dissuaded him from carrying out his threat to go to the police. Oddly he had grown fond of the grumpy motor boat attendant, who had really provided the initial impetus to get the investigation into Elsa's disappearance off the ground. Jack was also pissed because Roland had taken unilateral action, which was a good indication of his commitment to the partnership, and demonstrated that he would undertake any action he considered necessary without consultation. Bannister would have covered his own tracks to ensure nothing could be used to connect him to the murder, but Jack knew he wouldn't go to the same lengths to protect his partners. If Jack hadn't felt uneasy about their partnership before, he did now.

Suddenly he felt very tired. He threw the paper off the bed, took off his dressing gown and climbed under the covers. He fell asleep without turning off the light, and slept deeply, without dreaming, until the shrill sound of the bedside phone woke him. After several rings he lifted the receiver and held it to his ear. "Yeah, who is it?"

"Wakey-Wakey Jack its Showtime," answered James Bantry. "The jury reached a decision late last night and they'll be delivering their verdict at nine –thirty this morning."

"OK I'll be there," replied Jack and he put the phone down. It was 8:00AM and he had slept through from the previous evening. Clearly some of his recent late night carousing around Miami had taken its toll.

Jack had a front seat in the courtroom to hear the jury's verdict. There was a good attendance in the court, including local and national reporters for both newspapers and television, Jerry the barman and Bridget Walsh. There was the buzz of conversation in the visitor's galleries, but Tavistock and Walsh were not talking to each other, which could have been an indication that they were expecting the worst. Bantry and John Delaney were talking in a relaxed manner, confident of the outcome.

The court usher called the court to order for the entrance of Judge Hyam. Silence followed and the judge took his position on the bench. He turned to the foreman of the jury and asked if they had reached a verdict. "Yes your Honor," replied the foreman in a clear, strong voice.

The courtroom was still as Judge Hyam then asked, "Do you find the defendant guilty or not guilty of 2nd degree murder?"

"Not guilty Your Honor," replied the foreman. Walsh gave a smile of relief and looked across at Bridget who remained impassive, without any sign of empathizing with her husband's situation.

The foreman's answer resulted in a subdued hum circulating around the courtroom and Hyam banged his gavel loudly and repeatedly to bring the court to order. He waited for complete silence before turning to the foreman again. "Do you find the defendant guilty or not guilty of manslaughter?"

"Guilty, your Honor came the reply. Again a quiet hum rose from the courtroom as the spectators passed comment on their opinion of the verdict. And again Hyam demanded silence before continuing.

"Are you all agreed on the verdict?"

"Yes, Your Honor," replied the foreman.

"The jury have come to the only verdict they could have in the light of the evidence placed before them. I take comfort in the legal system and generally the unerring fairness of the juries I have had the pleasure of presiding over. Simon Walsh, you have been found guilty of manslaughter, do you have anything to say before sentence is passed?"

Walsh's earlier relief at the not guilty verdict for murder was replaced with some anxiety, but he was relieved to be facing a sentence for manslaughter and not murder. He thought hard about what he could say to put the judge in a lenient frame of mind. "I can only say how sorry I am that any of this ever happened, your Honor."

Hyam paused after Walsh had finished. Jack wasn't sure whether it was to see if Walsh had anything further to say, or if it was to summon his own thoughts. For his part Jack was feeling dejected about the not guilty verdict for murder and was apprehensive about the sentence that would be given to Walsh for manslaughter.

"It's nice to hear that you are sorry for the events that took place on your boat last summer," began Hyam looking straight at Walsh, "but I am not convinced that the sentiment is genuine. Throughout this episode you have shown that your instincts for your own survival have by far outweighed any concern you have for the welfare of others. There is sufficient evidence on record, preceding the events of this trial, which confirm your intolerable and inexcusable attitude towards women and the appalling manner in which you have behaved towards them. I believe that women should be protected until you have had time to come to understand the error of your ways and can be trusted not to re-offend."

"The exact circumstances of Miss Bartelli's disappearance will never be known, but I am convinced that she would be here today if not for your conduct on your boat. For this reason I sentence you to not less than 10 and no more than 20 years in prison," pronounced the judge.

The look of disbelief on Walsh's face was the first genuine emotion he had displayed throughout the whole of the trial. Tavistock began explaining the appeal procedure to him, but he was too shocked to take in what his attorney was saying. He stared at Bridget who stood up and left the courtroom with just a brief glance in his direction. Even Tavistock was surprised that she didn't come over to console her husband.

Jack found it hard to contain the undiluted joy he felt on hearing the sentence, and imagined he would experience the same euphoria on hearing that he'd won the lottery. It may not have been quite the result he had been expecting, but 10 to 20 years would give him plenty of leverage in his forthcoming negotiations with Walsh.

Jack headed back to the hotel to check out and on the way decided to call Roland Bannister from a phone booth to give him the news. "Time to celebrate Roland because Walsh got 10 to 20 years for manslaughter."

"It's not what we expected, but it's a good result Jack, now we can start working on his wife. I've asked Bantry to find out where he will be sent. It will probably be Florida State, which is a medium security jail, then we can get the ball rolling."

"I don't know if you've noticed Roland, but the ball has been rolling for some time now."

"Don't be touchy Jack. You know what I mean. We've been given the green light and now our destiny is in our own hands."

"Does that mean we shouldn't take risks?"

"Yes of course it does, we don't want to blow this deal now."

"Then why put Frank and Lou onto Al?"

Jack heard Roland take a sharp intake of breath on the other end of the line. "This isn't something we should be discussing on the phone and you know it. If we are going to see this thing through, then there must be trust between us Jack."

"Trust is a two way thing Roland, don't forget it."

Part 2
The Best Laid Plans

1

Simon Walsh sat hunched on the seat of the prison bus taking him to the Florida State Correctional Facility, with his ankles shackled and his wrists cuffed in front of him. He stared blankly out of the window without taking in the flat and featureless Florida scenery, lost in a black despair over his predicament. Tavistock was preparing a High Court appeal to overturn his sentence, but the process would take time even if the appeal eventually turned out to be successful. His lawyer had gone to great lengths to assure him that the basis of the appeal, claiming that the jury had lost their objectivity and independence because of the pre-trial publicity, had been successfully used on other cases. Walsh wasn't holding his breath on the outcome. Although he didn't fully understand the subtlety of the legal argument that was being proposed, he instinctively knew that it would take more than legal gymnastics to get him out of jail and that he couldn't rely on his lawyer's endeavors alone. He didn't know what alternatives were available, but decided that he would explore other possibilities after getting settled in prison.

Walsh had boarded the bus with a handful of other prisoners in the early hours of the morning from the Miami retention center, after only having a cup of coffee and a dry waffle. Everyone was feeling a little fractious because of the early start and their impending transfer to prison. Casually he glanced around the bus at the six other passengers. In front of him was a good old boy from Alabama who had been convicted of killing a black shop assistant after being told to leave the store because his drunken behavior was disturbing the other customers. He had thrown the shop assistant through a plate glass window and one of the shards of glass had cut into the man's jugular vein, resulting in a massive amount of blood being pumped out of his body in a few minutes. A dark pool of blood enveloped the head of the shop assistant as he lay on the pavement, but the customers that he had been so concerned about all panicked after the show of violence and ran away from the shop, leaving him to bleed to death on the pavement. When the police arrived the shop assistant was dead and the Alabama boy was found unconscious in one of the aisles inside the shop. After the shop had cleared he had drunk himself into oblivion.

At the front of the bus was a white business accountant who had defrauded his company of one and a half million dollars by generating fictitious employees in his department and paying them handsome salaries. It had started in a small way but when he found that people could easily get lost in a large company without anyone questioning their function or role, he began to expand on his fraud. He was caught in a random search when the security guard at the gate found fifty pay slips in his brief case. The accountant's build and demeanor were the complete opposite of the big Alabama redneck, being very slight and introvert, with wire-framed spectacles. Although Walsh didn't anticipate an easy passage through his sentence for himself, he felt strangely comforted that there were some people around who he suspected would have a worse time than him.

Walsh straightened his body and turned to look around the back of the bus and saw the face of a black man staring directly back at him. The man was young, in his late twenties or early thirties, with strong handsome features and very dark skin. The intensity in the man's eyes was intimidating and after a few seconds he began to feel uncomfortable and resumed his position to face the front of the bus. Walsh had kept in touch with local news events to try and get an insight into the prison he was on his way to, and the people who could get sent there, but the man was unfamiliar, and he hadn't read anything about him. He had heard from one of the other prisoners that he had killed a mugger outside a Miami club. Walsh could still feel the man's eyes piercing the back of his head and the burning intensity of that feeling unsettled him and caused old anxieties about being locked up to re-surface. Getting more and more irritated with each mile of the journey, he put any further thought of the man out of his head and again cast his eyes towards the horizon of the land stretching out around the bus, gazing at the scenery with a blank mind. His father had often told him that he couldn't just ignore problems and hope that they would go away, but that he had to meet them head on before they developed into something more serious. Simon never confronted problems head on and through his early life had always relied on his father to sort them out.

When the bus arrived at Florida State Correctional Facility it stopped at the outer security gate, which opened automatically. The bus drove through the gate and stopped just inside the perimeter of the prison to be greeted by the guard manning the gate. The guard climbed onto the bus and counted the number of prisoners on board, comparing the number to names he had listed on a clipboard. The situation reminded Walsh of a vacation courier checking the number of passengers before departure, and he smiled to himself at the irony of that comparison. The guard at the rear of the bus, who had accompanied the prisoners on their journey, walked to the front to talk to the driver and gateman. The three men shared a joke about the Governor being caught fondling his secretary and the gateman got off the bus to let it continue to the final part of its journey. After the details of the prisoners were transmitted to the administration center and confirmed as being correct, the bus was ushered through a second security gate and let onto the main grounds of the prison.

The bus pulled up outside the administration building and the guard signaled the prisoners to disembark. They shuffled off the bus, finding it difficult to walk with the leg irons. "Don't worry boys we'll remove your jewelry once you're inside," laughed the guard. When all of the prisoners were in the building and the outer door locked, the leg irons and handcuffs were removed. The relief of the prisoners was audible as they rubbed their wrists and shook their legs to exercise muscles that had been restricted from their full range of movement for such a long time. The prisoners were then ushered into a large room and told to sit on the plastic chairs provided. The guard from the bus remained at the back of the room and they noticed that another guard was waiting for them in front of the seating area. The bearing of the new guard exuded a silent but unquestionable authority, and his body language and facial expression told the prisoners that this was a scene he had played out many times before. He was obviously senior to the guard who had brought the prisoners into the room and he expected the prisoners to recognize their ranking. He motioned the prisoners to take their seats. No words were spoken and a cold silence descended on the room. Both guards settled into an "at ease" stance with feet slightly apart and their hands clasped behind their backs.

The prisoners sat quietly for about 10 minutes before a suited man entered and walked to the front of the room to stand next to the senior guard. The suited man nervously cleared his throat to address the prisoners. "Good morning gentlemen," he began, "my name is Governor Small and I run this little establishment. None of you are considered to be dangerous or a high security risk so you've been assigned here. This is a medium security prison and you will find out that you will be accommodated in dormitories, without bars or locks on the doors. There is a perimeter security fence around the grounds and a secondary security fence outside that. The ground between the two security fences is kept clear and is guarded and monitored 24 hours of the day. If you are foolhardy and try to escape from here you will be sent to a high security prison and there you will find that life is very different to here, and that many of the horror stories you heard about prison life are in fact true. But I won't dwell on that because I expect that you all clearly understand the importance of following prison rules and will be as determined as I am to make your stay quiet and uneventful."

"Ten years ago you would have found that my counterpart would have had a long pedigree in penal institutions with fixed attitudes on how to deal with prisoners. Now I like to think we are more enlightened and we manage this facility a little more humanely by encouraging you to take more responsibility for your own actions. The fundamental principles behind the operation of this prison are based on those of any outside commercial organization and you will either be assigned to the workshops or an external labor detail. In the workshops we make garden furniture and ornaments from any material donated by the County or other kind benefactors. If the raw materials are of sufficiently high quality we also make household furniture, coffee tables and the like, which have proved popular with the locals. Anyone with carpentry skills inform the guard and you will be automatically assigned to one of the workshops."

"Those of you without carpentry skills or any aptitude for that kind of work will be assigned to a labor detail. Our main client is the County and we quote for the work just like any other contractor, and have done everything from digging ditches to constructing small buildings. The work is varied and reasonably interesting and will get you out and about within the community. The locals are very friendly and will accept you working amongst them, provided you all behave yourselves. As I said before, if we find that our trust in you has been misplaced you'll be shipped out to a more conventional prison where you'll find life a lot more difficult. Are there any questions?"

Governor Small paused for a few moments waiting for a response from the prisoners, which had never been forthcoming in virtually all of the induction talks he had given previously. Walsh had no particular craft skills and assumed that he would end up on a labor detail and decided to ask if there was any clerical work he could do.

"Excuse me Governor," Walsh began, "I was a company executive on the outside and I am a qualified accountant, so I wonder if there is any clerical work or book keeping that I could do to help the running of the prison?"

Small turned to Walsh, surprised that any of the prisoners had the temerity to ask a question. "We have adequate administrative staff and besides I believe that you men should toil at physical pursuits to expend your natural energy, and hopefully suppress some of your baser urges."

Walsh was about to press his case further when the prisoner next to him grabbed his arm firmly to restrain him from any further utterances. A familiar silence once more reigned over the room, which was eventually broken by Small saying, "Very well, just remember that if you have any problems you can always speak to me or one of the guards." He then instructed the senior guard next to him, "Jim get these men kitted out with their clothes, take them to the canteen for some breakfast and then sort out their accommodation."

The instruction to the senior guard was for the benefit of the "new fish" who may not have been in a correctional institution before. The guard nodded and the Governor left the room. The guard then turned to the prisoners, "the Governor didn't introduce me – I'm Chief Guard Norton, you will address me as "Chief" or "Sir"…Do you understand? The other guards you will address with the prefix

"Mr." in front of their surnames. If you don't know their name you will also refer to them as "Sir". Do you understand?" Each time Norton had asked the prisoners if they had understood his instructions, he had only briefly paused without really waiting for confirmation. Eventually the prisoners nodded in agreement, a little taken back by the change in style between the Governor and Norton.

"This is a quiet prison, nothing much ever happens and I'm sure that we'll all get along very well. I don't want you going to the Governor with your little problems, despite what he just said. If you people can't live together amicably it reflects badly on me and I don't want that to happen. We're all grown men and I'm sure you can sort out your own problems between yourselves. Provided you don't end up knifing or killing each other we give you the freedom to live together in harmony. If you need an arbitrator I will be only too happy to oblige. I've been in charge here for the last eight years and there have been no serious incidents in that time. I'm sure you will want to keep it that way, won't you?"

Again the prisoners nodded in agreement, beginning to understand that life in Florida State was not going to be as uneventful as the Governor had indicated, but it would be tolerable as long as they accepted and played by the rules. Norton's tone was slightly menacing insinuating some awful consequence for any wrongdoing without actually making a threat. Most of the prisoners were old hands and therefore knew what and what not to do. It was necessary to keep Norton happy and then everyone would have an easy life. Discipline had to be maintained to ensure that tolerable boundaries were not crossed and therefore the prisoners would punish any minor transgressions. The guards would only get involved if the crimes committed were of a more serious nature. It was "new fish" like Walsh that would have most difficulty in trying to adapt to their new environment.

The prisoners were taken to the clothes store where they were kitted out and also given a spare set of underclothes. They were told they could wear their own clothes in their leisure time. Then they were taken to the canteen where they filled in a questionnaire asking for details of their personal history, education and work experience.

Walsh didn't have any craft skills and was assigned to one of the outside work groups as a laborer. After breakfast he was taken to his dormitory, or as the Governor liked to think of it, "his accommodation".

The men in Walsh's dormitory all worked on the outside labor details, and he wasn't too pleased to find that the Alabama redneck had been assigned to the same dormitory and same work gang. Walsh still had difficulty in accepting that his status inside the prison was the same as an uncouth, illiterate white thug, but he would soon come to understand that he didn't have the skills or connections in the prison to raise him above the bottom "grunt" level. The rest of the day was free and the men were given a tour of the prison and shown the workshops, recreational and activity areas. He quickly came to the conclusion that the only leisure activities would be watching TV, playing pool or table tennis, playing touch football, running or weight lifting, and decided that a much more suitable way to relax would be to rekindle his childhood enthusiasm for reading.

Walsh grimaced to himself as he lay in his bunk that evening, thinking that previously he had headed a pre-eminent international financial corporation, and now he was destined to dig ditches and do the fetching and carrying for the craftsmen in the work gang. He closed his eyes and thought briefly of Bridget in an attempt to comfort himself. She had remained loyal to him throughout his awful ordeal and he believed that the only promising thing to come out of this mess was the prospect of repairing their relationship, and making their marriage work. With that thought he closed his eyes and tried to blank out the world around him.

2

Jack and Roland were sat in the bar of the "Blue Cockatoo", discussing the next move of their game plan. After the murder of Al Ferrino both men were wary of each other. Bannister thought that Jack had been too soft with Ferrino, and could therefore have jeopardized the conviction of Walsh. Contrarily Jack thought that Roland had been heavy handed in killing Al and that the situation could have been controlled by letting Ferrino know that he was pushing too hard against the wrong people instead of going straight to the ultimate solution. The little guy certainly knew he had played a bum deal now!

"Look Jack, we've still got a long way to go with this Walsh thing before we can both get what we want from this deal. We can't let this issue come between us, especially now that we've successfully completed the most difficult stage of our plan. Let's forget about our differences over Ferrino and start firming up on the best way of getting news of Elsa to Walsh and starting our negotiations with his wife," said Bannister after taking a sip out of the large glass of brandy in front of him.

"It's not just that you killed Al, Roland, it's more because you did it without telling me. We need to avoid conflicts like this by talking to each other and not making unilateral decisions without discussing it together first." Jack felt a little hypocritical as Elsa had not been consulted on any matter that had arisen between him and Roland since going to Boston.

"I know, I'm sorry for that Jack but we were so close to the end of the trial that I was afraid Ferrino was going to fuck things up for us. I tried to talk to him but he wouldn't be swayed. There was just no reasoning with him."

"He was an awkward customer alright, but I'm sure we could have got him to understand it would've been bad for his health to continue with his blackmail. He was all "huff and puff". There was no real need to kill him Roland, he was harmless."

"I don't know how you survived on the streets for all those years because you've got such a soft center, I can see your halo from here! Look we're aiming high with this one Jack, it's not one of your penny ante shakedowns and we can't afford any kind of slip up, no matter how well intentioned your motives. Besides he could have shot off his mouth at any time, before we got our hands on Walsh's money, which would have been the same as his telling the police his story before the end of the trial."

"I'm as keen on this plan succeeding as much as you are Roland, but if Frank and Lou had botched things, we would have found ourselves in an even bigger mess than in just letting Al blow his mouth off. Both Elsa and me would now be implicated in his murder. Gene Tanner suspects that Al's death was the result of a professional hit because of the stiletto through his heart, but he hasn't made a connection with Walsh…..yet. I was quick to say that I knew Al because he gave evidence against Walsh, to hopefully throw Gene off the scent by being open about my connection with him. But Gene's no dummy Roland, we'll have to be very careful on how we deal with him from now on. I can't see him getting anything on Al's murder, so hopefully his investigation will hit a brick wall."

"OK Jack, the police will have to investigate the murder but I'm 100 percent sure they won't come up with anything, because Frank and Lou have been doing this kind of thing long enough without being caught. But there is a lesson to be learned by both of us. I accept that and hope you do too. Let's put Ferrino behind us and start planning our next move." With that the two men shook hands, which cemented an uneasy peace between them.

"Alright," said Jack. "Walsh is in "Florida State Correctional", which is a medium security prison that's run by a gung ho character called Bill Norton. He's the Chief Guard over there and was expecting to be made up to Governor, when a socially aware, politically correct individual called Graham Small was brought in over his head. These two men come from opposite ends of the prison management spectrum and are also complete opposites in every other respect. As I said, Norton is really the one who runs the prison the way he sees fit providing there are no serious incidents or anything that could reflect badly on Small, who has intentions of pursuing a political career when he retires from the prison service."

Jack took a swig from his bottle of Bud and continued, "Although it's a relatively low security prison the place is run like any conventional prison of twenty years ago, despite the propaganda pedaled by Small. The discipline is harsh and Norton lets the inmates sort out their own problems, as long as they are discrete. That means he draws the line at mutilation or murder, but anything else goes. His safety net is the sharpshooters positioned on the perimeter fence, who practice daily on the surrounding wildlife to let the inmates know that escape from the prison is unlikely. One prisoner was killed shortly after Small took over as Governor but it was explained as the extreme action of the prisoner involved, whose wife was having an affair with his brother. Complete hogwash of course, but all parties were handsomely paid to give the story credibility. It also put Small in Norton's debt."

"I can see that it's a difficult place to relax in Jack, but how does that help us get to Walsh?" asked Bannister.

"We'll put some pressure on Walsh from the inside to make him understand just how intolerable living conditions really are in there. Like every other correctional facility in Florida, or in the USA for that matter, inmates stick to their own, whites with whites, blacks with blacks, and spics with spics. In order for a nice white boy like Walsh to have the protection of his own group, he needs to have a sponsor, somebody high up in the white community. We've made sure that the man he gets close to, and will rely on to protect him inside, is working for us."

Jack continued, "Vincent Tuzio, Leonard's cousin, is doing time in the same place and he's let Wesley Green know that if he allows him to get close to Walsh that there'll be something big in it for him. Green runs the white quarter and has complete control over the white inmates, so nothing happens without his approval. Green in turn has to get the OK from Norton who will also be cut in for his share of the action. I haven't told Vincent the high stakes we're playing so his cut, along with Green and Norton, won't be that big. They'll be thinking of a hundred thousand bucks not a million. I'll also make sure we have the money in our hands before I pass on their share to their families," added Jack.

"Tuzio will tell Walsh that he and Elsa were going together before he was locked up and that she had kept in touch with him regularly, until her reported disappearance. His most difficult job will be to convince Walsh that she wrote to him after her disappearance explaining why it would be difficult for her to visit in the future. Tuzio used to have regular visits from his girlfriend before Walsh's boat incident and her name by coincidence was Lisa. Tuzio stopped her visits to reinforce our story, in case Walsh checks the visitor's register. Revenge will be the reason for Elsa staying in hiding and Tuzio will suggest that he might be able to get her to go to the police if they could agree an appropriate sum for his services and for Elsa's goodwill. Tuzio will suggest that I act as mediator with his wife to confirm the agreed price with Elsa and monitor the transaction. Walsh won't know me from Adam because I wasn't mentioned at the trial or by the media. Paying the girls in the club not to mention me when they were questioned about Elsa was a wise move!"

"So, as far as Walsh is concerned it will be Vincent who's pulling the strings?" asked Bannister.

"That's right, because he will persuade Walsh that he can bring their "past relationship" to bear when trying to persuade her to go to the police and clear his name. I will merely be the go-between hired to negotiate a price between Bridget and Elsa. Provided I can convince Bridget that I'm not party to the blackmail, I might win her trust and get beneath her guard. She's a hard bitten business woman, who won't be easily convinced to part with a lot of money to spring her husband. She'll be looking for guarantees," replied Jack.

"What's going to make her believe that you're not running the scam? After all she may not be able to detect the subtleties of your plan and will think that you're all in it together," queried Bannister.

"Yeah it's going to be the most difficult part of our negotiations. She's no mug, so I'll have to move fast so she doesn't have too much time to think about it. I'll arrange for the money to be paid in an account in Elsa's name. Bridget and Elsa will meet to discuss and finalize terms and Elsa will give Bridget her bank details. As far as Bridget is concerned I won't have any direct contact with the money and won't be an obvious beneficiary, but I know what you mean, it does sound pretty tenuous," said Jack pausing to re-run it quickly through his head. "The basic plan is sound enough, but I may have to call on all of my acting and storytelling skills to swing it with Bridget," he smiled.

"Well if anyone can do it, you can," replied Bannister reassuringly. "And don't worry about any more of my interference, from here on in I'm going to take a back seat and let you do all the running around," he added finishing off his brandy. "I've got things to do before we open tonight Jack, see you later."

Jack watched as Bannister walked away, towards his office. Although he had told him of his plan to get the money out of Walsh, they hadn't really cleared the air over Al Ferrino's killing. This was their second meeting since the end of Walsh's trial and it had certainly gone much better than the first. The first meeting was held on the evening that Jack had returned to New York from Miami. He had stormed into Roland's office to ask for an account of the events leading to Al's murder. Matters were made worse when Frank and Lou came to Bannister's aid after hearing them shouting at one another from the bar. Their intervention only served to raise Jack's level of agitation.

Frank and Lou were all for roughing Jack up and then throwing him out of the club. Bannister stopped them, not just because he didn't want to see Jack hurt, but also because he knew he needed him to plan the next stage of their strategy to screw Walsh. Finally Jack had agreed to come back later after he had cooled off. It had taken a week and Roland was beginning to think he would have to lean on Jack to get him to behave himself.

Jack was happy to let Bannister think that he was back under his control and that they were buddies once more. Bannister's killing of Ferrino had shown Jack just how ruthless the man could be and that he would have to watch, or try to second guess, what he was doing in the background, particularly after they all had received their pay offs. He got up from the table he was sitting at and saw Frank and Lou at the bar mumbling to each other.

"Well it's nice to see you two gentlemen again, what are you discussing? Politics? No the arts....". Jack paused as if in a deep mind search to find a topic worthy of their intellectual might.

"Fuck off, Jack," said Frank sharply, "Before I give you something that's really worth thinking about, like a broken neck!"

"There's no need for that Frank, I was only trying to be friendly. Don't forget you need me in one piece to finish this job." Jack paused on the way to the exit and turned back to Frank and Lou, "and please don't try to follow me it would be embarrassing watching you two try to blend inconspicuously among normal people."

Jack laughed at the pair scowling at him and made for the street. Outside the club he took his cell phone out of his pocket and called up the administration office at Florida State Correctional to confirm his visit to Vincent Tuzio.

Jack hailed a taxi to take him to his parent's house, they had asked him to come over for dinner as he hadn't dropped by for some time. He gave the driver his parents address and sat back to relax during the drive to their house when his cell phone rang. It was Elsa.

Elsa rang him frequently as she was bored up in Boston and her impatience with him to move things along was growing. "Hi baby" said Jack warmly, but his amiable banter was stopped before he could continue in the same vein.

"Cut out the sweet talk Jack, just tell me how long have I got to stay banged up in this house. I hope you can understand that I'm doing time as well as Walsh, and it's slowly driving me crazy."

"I've just confirmed my visit to Vincent Tuzio this coming Saturday, so we can start the ball rolling," replied Jack, trying to give her a reason to lighten the conversation.

"Well how long, then?" demanded Elsa sternly.

"I can't put a time on it yet, not until the heat's put on Walsh and I get a chance to talk to his wife, but at worst it would be two or three months."

"Having me hang around this dump for another two or three months is not an option! Do you understand that?" asked Elsa, whilst progressively getting more and more emotional, but maintaining a steady firmness in her voice.

"Look we can't talk about it now, I'll fly up to Boston after I've seen Tuzio and we can go through the schedule then."

"OK Jack, but you had better come to me or I'll come to you. And that's a promise!"

"I understand Elsa, bye," said Jack weakly, it seemed that he was at loggerheads with both Elsa and Bannister. What should have been a sweet deal was going sour and he couldn't really understand why his partners were not being as objective as he was about it.

He could sympathize with Elsa to a degree as she'd been out of circulation for the best part of a year. Initially he had thought she would have been pleased about not having to perform every night at the "Blue Cockatoo", but he was now beginning to think that she actually enjoyed doing it and that he was unable to provide anything worthwhile as a replacement. Neither had he been to see her since the end of Walsh's trial, which only made the situation worse as Elsa was also feeling unloved and neglected.

3

Jack had been to visit Tuzio before the end of Walsh's trial and had explained events on the day of Elsa's disappearance and her near death. The likely extortion figure was not mentioned but both men acknowledged it would be significant, bandying about a minimum amount of one million dollars.

After the meeting Vincent Tuzio was in no doubt of the kind of measures that would be necessary to make Walsh come to heel. He had good contacts in every ethnic quarter of the inmate community, which meant he could easily get someone to intimidate Walsh for the right price. All it would take was a little cocaine. He had already cleared the action with Green and just needed to pick the right man for the job. Martin Abraham presented a fearsome figure that was respected by all inmates because of his raw animal strength and for his reputation of having a vicious streak, which was generated by the folklore circulated from the other penal institutions where he had served time. Despite Abraham's violent history he was sent to Florida State Correctional for a drunken traffic accident. He was found unconscious at the scene of the accident and was in hospital with a police guard before he realized what was happening. Tuzio decided to approach Abraham during the evening recreational period to talk about Walsh.

That evening Walsh came into the dormitory aching and tired after digging ditches for drainage pipes all day. The skin on the palms of his hands was sore and his back felt as rigid as a board that complained sharply with the slightest movement. The prison had a communal shower and washroom, which included baths, and Walsh decided to have a long soak in a hot bath to try and relax his abused muscles, and relieve the pain in his back. He collected a bar of soap and a towel from the cupboard by his bed and headed for the washroom.

Provision of a dedicated washroom was seen as a modest, but innovative, advance to improve the conditions of the prisoners by Governor Small, but by modern standards it was very basic. The entrance to the building went straight into a change area with benches around the outside walls for getting undressed and back-to-back lockers in the center of the area. Clothes and personal items were put into the lockers and the keys taken by the prisoners while they showered or bathed. Off the changing room were two shower areas and one bathing area with five baths lined side by side. The baths weren't used very often as most people preferred to shower, so Walsh hoped he would get some time to himself.

As Walsh entered the washroom he could see that there were only a few people getting changed. He walked over to a bench and dropped his towel and soap on it and started to get undressed. After taking his clothes off he wrapped the towel around his waist, gathered his clothes and walked to one of the lockers. As he was opening the door of the locker he noticed the young black man he had travelled with on the bus, come into the changing room. The young man turned to Walsh and walked directly towards him. Walsh smiled nervously wondering what to expect and was just about to say hello when the man struck him hard in his solar plexus.

Walsh felt a deadening pain below his rib cage and found himself struggling for breath as the air seemed to be sucked out of his lungs. He dropped to his knees and the towel around his waist became undone leaving him naked and feeling vulnerable. He bent over double wheezing and gasping for air, and was barely conscious of the man talking to him.

"You may be wondering why I've just hit you Walsh as you don't know me and I don't know you. But you do know my sister, her name was Mariana and she was a beautiful girl. Do you remember her?"

Walsh shook his head from side to side animatedly, still sucking in breath and unable to talk.

"No I don't expect an important guy like you would remember her, after all she was only a hooker. But not any common streetwalker though; she was a high-class prostitute who entertained dudes like yourself for a thousand bucks a night. You know you don't find girls like her on street corners; so you can't tell me you still don't remember her? You paid her three grand to spend the weekend with you."

Walsh remained still, beginning to feel a bit nauseous and on the verge of having to vomit.

"You asked my sister to come with you for a weekend of skiing at Aspen, where you'd hired a lodge. But when the pair of you got there she found that there were three other guys at the lodge and of course she was expected to screw them all. She may have been a prostitute, but she didn't spend her time in the gutter with vermin like you. She was used to entertaining the rich and famous, or society people. Her time was spent in the best hotels or at big social functions. That way she was always in control of everything that happened and was never too far from other people. She told me that she sometimes had a little difficulty from one of her punters drinking over the odds, but never found herself in a tight situation. She was innocent because she hadn't experienced any of the things some other whores have to endure from a lower class of clientele. She knew nothing about the kind of animals that men become when they get together. Just like you and your friends."

"She hadn't signed up to take you all on and didn't want to take part, but you all raped her just the same. Each man after you waiting their turn and cheering each other on with every new brutality you heaped on my sister. Not content with that you kept her in the lodge for the whole of the weekend. There wasn't any skiing done; as you and your friends were only interested in abusing and humiliating her. You kept her naked, made her crouch on all fours and then put a collar around her neck. You gotta be starting to remember now Walsh?"

Walsh couldn't control his nausea any longer and vomited the few contents of his stomach onto the floor.

"You then put her on a leash and dragged her around like an animal, making her eat off a plate on the floor and not letting her go to the toilet without your permission. You all still found time to abuse her by fucking her in every orifice, sometimes with two or three of you at a time. She came back broken and ashamed and couldn't face her friends or family, not going out but staying by herself in her room. She started a drug habit to try and forget what had happened to her and the only time she went out was to get a fix. The drugs made her forget and after a short time she needed more money to pay for them, so she sold herself to anyone who could get her the next fix. She became the whore you made her be in Aspen and slept with anybody with enough money to get her the drugs she needed. She got bad stuff, overdosed and died aged twenty two, only a year after you and your friends got your hooks into her."

"I'm sorry," whined Walsh, vainly hoping to pacify his attacker. "I didn't know she died. I thought your sister knew the score. Believe me, I didn't mean to hurt her."

"Shut up Walsh, I'm not interested in what you thought. In my eyes only an animal would treat a woman the way you treated my sister. I want to make you pay for the pain you inflicted on her and every ounce of pleasure you and your friends exacted from using her. You're going to pay every day you're in here because I'm going to treat you like an animal every time I see you. If I see you walking around me I'm going to put you on your knees like now. If I see you eating from a table I will put your food on the floor and make you eat it like a dog. Remember that and keep out of my way."

Walsh looked up pleadingly and the young man kicked him in his stomach. The pain was excruciating and Walsh keeled over crying and clutching his abdomen, while lying in a fetal position. He lay there for a long time and was too frightened to look up and see if his attacker was still hovering over him. Eventually he staggered to his feet, picked up his towel and walked over to a bench to sit down. His whole body ached and he was dreading the thought of having to dig ditches again the next day. Walsh started breathing slowly to calm himself and steady his nerves. Then, wanting to soothe his aching body, he stood up to have the bath he had been promising himself.

At that moment one of the guards walked into the washroom and said, "Hurry up Walsh I'm locking up in 5 minutes, and clean up that mess you've made on the floor."

The next morning Vincent Tuzio sidled up to Walsh as he was eating his breakfast. "I heard about what happened to you last night Simon. How are you feeling?"

Walsh was feeling even worse than when he first went into the washroom the previous night. His fatigued muscles were screaming at every movement and now in addition to his stiff back and muscle fatigue, the left side of his rib cage hurt with every breath that he took. He didn't know how he would get through the day, as he couldn't even straighten up properly. "I'll be alright," he replied cautiously not knowing or caring why Tuzio was interested. The thought of finding out how he could be protected from another attack crossed his mind and he wondered who Tuzio was connected to.

"You can't do any heavy work in the state you're in, I've arranged for you to change with Shaughnessy, so you'll be on the latrine detail today. It's not very pleasant, but it is easy work and you won't have to strain yourself too much. But first of all you had better go to the medical center, in case you have a cracked rib. Don't worry they're used to such injuries."

"Thanks, but why are you bothered about the way I feel?" asked Walsh cautiously.

"I know this is your first time inside and it takes a while to learn the rules and find out how to look after yourself. You've got to stay on the right side of the people who matter, otherwise you'll wish you were dead, or worse, end up dead."

"But what about the speech the Governor gave us about this place using modern techniques for rehabilitation and the protection of the guards?" asked Walsh.

"They'll turn a blind eye to anything as long as it doesn't need to be reported. That gives anyone with a grievance a lot of scope, provided they don't end up seriously injuring or murdering someone. The blacks will intimidate you unless you have the protection of the white community. In this place that means you've got to stay on the right side of Wesley Green."

"How do I do that?"

"In here drugs and cigarettes are the currency, although you can arrange to pay money into someone's personal bank account if you need a big favor. You will have to pay a quarter of your weekly allowance of cigarettes and anything you receive from the outside as a retainer. Don't double cross Green or you'll only live long enough to regret it. Just stay cool and I'll get you in with Green. In the meantime stay away from your friend and I'll see you later," replied Tuzio.

Tuzio wasn't sure why Mathew Caine had roughed up Walsh, he didn't really care as it had produced the result he was looking for in making Walsh frightened of every inmate in the prison. He concluded that he would have to keep a close eye on Caine, in case the man was trying to muscle in on his territory, and also made a mental note to call off Abraham.

4

Bridget Walsh was content and living the life she had always wanted, now that Simon was locked away and would no longer have any involvement in her life or in the business for the foreseeable future. She had played the dutiful wife during his trial but had now decided to end their marriage and try to come to some amicable arrangement in their working relationship when he got out of prison. After all she had been running the company since Simon's arrest and after several years in prison he would probably be in no position to take over the reins for some time. Since Bridget's arrival at the NMP she had gradually taken over the Finance Department and actively looked at the running of other departments to improve co-ordination and the overall management of the company. She also updated the 5 year Development Plan with the approval of the Board of Directors. Simon was more interested in his leisure pursuits and had never really shown any aptitude in the management of the fundamental tools required to run the business, when he took control after the death of his father. His talents lay in steamrolling the other board members to get his way and bullying unsuspecting claimants like her father.

She knew from Simon's dependency on her during his trial that no matter what his future role in the company eventually turned out to be after his release, he would always rely heavily on her good will and support. She had worked hard after Simon's arrest to maintain the confidence of major clients and convince them that the Company was still able to handle their investments efficiently. With her drive and determination to protect the business she managed to get herself accepted by the staff who initially were reluctant to give her credence. She wasn't going to let go of all that she had worked for, or return to a position where Simon was the figurehead. He would have to agree to become the junior partner in the future and accept the changes in their business relationship brought about by his arrest.

The trial had shocked her and no matter how well she thought she knew Simon, she had found it hard to accept that her husband really was a killer. That was another reason why they could no longer live together. Up until Simon's arrest, Bridget had been supremely confident in her dominance over her husband, and his acceptance of her position. That perception had been shattered since she had learned of his attacks on Rita Alonzo and Elsa Bartelli. She couldn't be sure that in some extreme circumstance he would not be violent towards her. Besides her uncertainty over his volatile nature, he was now mixing with the low lives of prison, which could lead to him developing a severe character change that would overcome his natural cowardly streak.

She had spent a few minutes with him on the evening of the day he was sentenced, before he was transferred to prison and had seen him during the following week to sort out personal and business financial details. A special meeting of the Board of Directors had voted in favor of her taking the role of acting Chief Executive responsible for the running of the NMP and Simon had to countersign the mandate giving Bridget the authority to be the major signatory on all financial and legal documents. Simon also gave Bridget the power to act on his behalf for any transactions required for his personal bank accounts.

Bridget had remained independent as far as her own financial status was concerned, living off her own earnings. Simon paid for their living expenses from a home management account, but also had a personal bank account for his private use. She was flabbergasted to find that Simon had less than $100,000 in his private account. He had money in property he had inherited from his father, but Bridget had to smile to herself when she realized that the whore who had tried to rip him off had more ready cash at her disposal than he had. Her husband's "leisure pursuits" had obviously been a big drain on his finances.

After the fallout from the trial had settled, Bridget was emotionally and physically exhausted and hadn't appreciated the strain she had obviously been working under. The night she returned home after Simon had been sentenced she collapsed into an armchair and not woken up until five the following morning. The weeks after the trial also took their toll on her, as she had to work seven days a week to maintain control of the company and ensure things were running smoothly. She decided she could do with a break and after putting things in order at the NMP and booked a two-week vacation in Mexico to wind down. It was a two-center vacation, split between

Acapulco and Cancun.

During the first week in Acapulco she spent most days on the beach or around the hotel pool, soaking up the sun and relaxing. She liked to read on the beach and took with her Joseph Heller's novel "Catch 22", which she had read many times before, but nevertheless always managed to find some new meaning in the story that had previously escaped her. She had first read the novel as a teenager at school and was blown away by the simple truths on freedom and love expounded in the story with such good humor, and couldn't understand why it was not recommended reading in her literature class. As she grew up and became more cynical, she began to understand that the book's anti-establishment philosophy would not be acceptable to any modern school or college that generally relied on obedience and thought control to function. She now saw schools as sausage factories producing a standard product to a rigid specification.

She added a 3 day trip to Mexico City at the end of her second week in Cancun and went shopping, visited museums and art galleries, and toured the city admiring the architecture in the older buildings. She enjoyed bartering in the markets, whether it was for an item of clothing, jewelry or a bag of fruit. Travelling alone in Mexico made her a target of many Latin Lotharios and she enjoyed the attention, and being flirty, without any commitment. Simon Walsh had robbed her of her innocence and any romantic notions she may have had about meeting a soul mate. Now that he was in prison and they would soon be divorced, she felt she could restart her life and travel on the path she had been destined to follow before meeting him. She would erase the memory of her life with him, as if it had never happened.

5

Jack eventually decided to drive to Boston to see Elsa. He thought the drive would give him time to think about how he could convince her of the need for her to remain in hiding a little longer. He couldn't understand why she was being so awkward when they were so near to success. Their relationship had seriously deteriorated since her secret visit to Miami near the end of Walsh's trial, so he was determined to rebuild bridges and try to regain the closeness they'd shared with each other before getting involved with Walsh.

Elsa and Julie were living in a rented house on the outskirts of Boston, in a quiet suburb. This was of course a complete contrast to the lives both women had lived in New York and the environment of the "Blue Cockatoo". When Walsh was convicted Elsa's picture had made the national press, but now she was "yesterday's news" and of no interest to Joe Public. It was difficult to disguise her appearance because of her black hair and dark complexion, and strikingly beautiful face and stunning figure, which automatically attracted attention. Nevertheless she had made some attempt to mask her "glamorous" image by cropping her hair close to her head, not using make up and wearing everyday loose fitting clothes.

Elsa was distraught about her lack of exercise when she found out that she had put on 10 pounds in the first months of inactivity and was beginning to lose her muscle tone. After all she hadn't expected to be inactive for such a long period of time. The fact that Julie had put on at least 20 pounds and seemed to do nothing but eat junk food all day made matters worse. Jack had suggested that they put some exercise equipment in the basement of the house, but Elsa refused saying that she needed to get out of the house to maintain her sanity and get away from Julie's "feeding frenzy". Jack reluctantly agreed and Elsa enrolled at a local health club that was reasonably well equipped and also had yoga and aerobic classes, besides the usual weight training equipment and a swimming pool.

Jack insisted that when Elsa went out she did not wear makeup and dressed down. She normally went out wearing an ill-fitting sweatshirt, jeans and sneakers. Even with short hair, no makeup and casual clothes, she couldn't disguise her obvious good looks, although she did look very different to the nightclub image given in the papers. Most of the people frequenting the health club during the day were young wives who had children at school, or men and women who had retired and wanted to keep in shape.

When Elsa enrolled she was shown around the gym by a young male instructor, in his early twenties, who couldn't get close enough when showing her the mechanics of using each specific piece of equipment. Elsa smiled at the predictability of men and because the young man's disguised attempts to "inadvertently" brush against her brought back distant memories from her days at the Blue Cockatoo. She made a point of maintaining a good distance from him after that, in case he got the idea she was actually interested in him. She introduced herself to other members of the club as "Lisa" and told them that she was recovering from a severe illness and was trying to rebuild her fitness. Some of the more astute members were amazed at the vigor she displayed when going around the gym or working out in the aerobics class. She soon got back into shape, which made her even more impatient to get her old life back.

Jack parked his car in the driveway of the house and walked around the back to enter through the kitchen, where he saw Julie with the fridge door open, trying to decide what to eat. She turned her head quickly as the outside door opened and smiled at Jack as he came into the kitchen. "Hi Jack, what brings you out here to the backwoods."

"Oh, I just thought I'd come see how you ladies of leisure were making out," Jack replied sarcastically.

"Don't say that to Elsa, because I don't think she would find it very amusing."

"Well how are you doing, you're certainly looking…..healthy."

"There's no need to be polite Jack, it doesn't fit you too well. I know I've put a few pounds on, but what the hell I can't stop eating out of boredom. Anyway I've now got even more to grab hold of, do you want a piece," she teased thrusting her right hip towards him.

Jack made an exaggerated lunge towards her, checking himself at the last minute, but still grabbing hold of her to give her a kiss on the cheek. "I know," Julie said, "you just want to be my friend."

"Where's Elsa?" asked Jack.

"She's down at the health club working out. She's there about four or five times a week. I think she goes to break the monotony of being stuck in the house, but it's doing wonders for her and she looks terrific."

"Why don't you go with her?"

"You must be crazy to think I'd be interested in punishing my body the way Elsa does. The only places I want to work up a sweat are on the dance floor or in bed!"

"I'm glad Elsa's doing well, it seems ages since we've had fun together."

"What kind of fun are you looking for?" interrupted Elsa as she came into the house through the back door.

"Hi," said Jack, obviously pleased to see her as he walked over to give her a hug. Elsa dropped her sports bag and returned Jack's embrace and they kissed warmly. Jack could feel her firm body beneath her clothes and pulled her tightly into him. Elsa enjoyed the intimacy and let her body become pliant.

"If going to the gym can do this for you I think I may try it out as well," said Jack, "I feel my body will be a disappointment to you after "feeling" yours next to me."

"Hold on you two," chipped in Julie, "it's bad enough not having any TLC without having to watch you two eat each other."

"Slow down Jack, we'll have to put our emotions on hold until we can get a little privacy," said Elsa pulling away from him. Elsa could almost feel the reluctance with which she was released, and she felt elated by the sexual tension straining every fiber of Jack's body, which was reminiscent of the way their relationship used to be.

That evening Elsa, Julie and Jack went to a local Italian Restaurant. Elsa bumped into one of her friends from the Health Club and introduced Jack as a long lost childhood friend who had called her up out of the blue, and was staying for s short while so they could rekindle some old memories. The evening was relaxed and warm with Elsa and Julie recounting old stories from their time at the "Blue Cockatoo" working for Roland Bannister. Roland was financing their sojourn in Boston and was getting anxious about the length of time it was taking to get the result they were all waiting for. Elsa and Julie knew just how serious minded their old boss was about money.

Julie recalled the time one of the punters got more than a little drunk while she was on stage. He climbed upon his stool and was trying to put a 5 dollar note in her garter when he stumbled and knocked her over. This led to a roar of laughter from the other punters; as it ended up with Julie flat on her back and the drunk on top of her, face down with his head in her crotch. On hearing the commotion Frank came rushing across to the stage, grabbed the back of the drunk's collar and lifted him off Julie. The man couldn't stand up and kept collapsing to Frank's annoyance. There was no firmness or structure to the drunk's body as he kept slipping out of Frank's grasp.

The crowd were now in an uproar and Roland came out of his office to see what the commotion was about. As Bannister came to the front of the crowd the drunk fell towards him sliding down his body and again collapsing in a heap on the floor. Roland wasn't too pleased about being manhandled by the drunk, straightened his jacket and told Frank to throw him out. By this time Frank had decided that the only way to handle the drunk would be to throw him over his shoulder in a fireman's lift and carry him out of the club. Frank dutifully hoisted the drunk onto his shoulder, strode out of the club and threw the man onto the outside pavement contemptuously. Later that evening Roland discovered that the drunk was play acting and had lifted his wallet and the $2000 inside it. He was livid and sent Frank out to find him, but by this time the drunk was long gone.

They all laughed as Julie described how Roland's face had gone puce with anger as he found that everyone else in the club was amused and probably had some admiration for the impudence of the man in pulling off such a daring trick. Roland had to cancel all his credit cards, which were also in his wallet, which added a nuisance value to the humiliation of his loss. Julie was a good storyteller and never failed to entertain her listeners even though Elsa and Jack had already heard most of her stories, and in some cases were the ones to relate them to her in the first instance.

Back at the house Jack opened a bottle of wine and poured a glass for each of the girls and one for himself. Julie picked her glass up and discretely bade Jack and Elsa goodnight and went upstairs to bed. Jack brought Elsa's glass over to her and sat beside her on the sofa facing the fire, which was the focal point of the room. Earlier it had been a bit chilly and Elsa had lit a fire before they went to the restaurant to warm up the room, and now they both stared into the glowing embers.

"Shall I build up the fire," asked Jack.

"No it's not cold," replied Elsa, "and besides we can keep each other warm if the temperature drops."

Jack put down his glass and took Elsa's from her, and then he pulled her towards him to kiss her. Jack could feel his head spinning as they kissed; it had been such a long time since they had been together. Elsa felt the same way, burying her fingers in his hair as he pulled her face towards his. When they eventually parted from their kiss Jack almost gasped audibly, which made Elsa smile.

"Are you laughing at me?" said Jack with mock anger.

"Would I do that to you?"

"I don't know. I don't care either because you've brought me to boiling point, but I don't want to blow too quickly. Tonight we'll have to take it easy to get the most out of our enforced period of abstinence." Jack then reached across and put his hand on Elsa's knee, then slid his hand under her dress, up the outside of her thigh to her panty line. He tugged at her panties and Elsa lifted her hips to assist him in removing them. She was wearing a figure hugging wrap around dress and Jack undid the tie holding the two sides of the garment together. He lifted the overlapping side of the dress off Elsa's body, undid the internal tie and opened the other half of the dress. This time he did gasp as he gazed on her naked body. Her figure was perfect from the curve of her thighs to the full roundness of her breasts. He knew he couldn't live without her and would remember this image for the rest of his life.

The love in Jack's eyes and his excitement gazing at her, excited Elsa and she felt the clock had turned back. The gentle touch of his hands running over her body made her move in anticipation. His tongue on her nipples sent electric shock waves through her body and she could feel herself losing control of her actions. She just wanted her body to become one with his so they could share the sensations they were both feeling. She unbuttoned his shirt and started kissing his chest and biting his nipples.

Jack lay on top of Elsa's reclining body and reached for the back of Elsa's neck to draw her into him for another kiss. As they kissed Jack's other hand stroked her breasts, stomach and thigh. Elsa moaned slightly as Jack lightly pinched one of her nipples. She looked up at Jack inviting him to take her. He began kissing the rest of her body, feeling her nipples get harder as his tongue caressed each of them, feeling her thrust against him as he ran his tongue over her well contoured stomach. He sat back on his haunches and began moving upwards along the insides of her thighs, as she moved in anticipation. Delicately he ran his tongue upwards between the lips of her labia, and on her downward movement he parted her outer lips to explore her sex. Elsa moaned pushing strongly into his face as Jack tasted the moisture from her orgasm. He then teased her clitoris precipitating dramatic responses from her body with every caress because of its increased sensitivity after her orgasm.

Jack undid his trousers and lifted Elsa, bringing her body towards him and he entered her. They kissed as they thrust against each other. Elsa moved up and down on Jack's member, teasing and exciting him in the same way that he had done to her with his tongue. Despite the sexual tension in his body, Jack was trying to restrain himself from ejaculating too soon as he wanted to sustain this moment as long as possible. He felt the same sensual explosion in his body that he had during his first time with Elsa, when he'd felt a surge of sensations and emotions that were completely different to anything he'd experienced before. No other woman was like Elsa and he could feel their bodies fusing together in their sexual frenzy, and as he finally exploded inside her, she also reached another climax.

They lay together in front of the fire. Elsa removed the remainder of Jack's clothes and they caressed each other gently as they kissed. They knew that their deep desire for each other would soon start to build again and that they could look forward to a long night of lovemaking.

"This is wonderful Elsa. I was a little worried after Miami, we seemed to lose something."

"If we did, we've got it back again now. Let's not let other things get between us. You and I are all that really matters, the rest of the world can go to hell," replied Elsa.

"You're right we're the only ones that matter. God I can't remember the last time I felt so good."

"When can I move back to New York then? I can make you feel like this every night."

"You know when baby. We're so near the money now."

"Jack you've been saying that for the last three months. Will I have to wait another three months just to hear the same thing again?"

"No, things are moving at a pace now. We've had an unexpected stroke of luck. There's some guy locked up with Walsh who has a serious grievance against him. He roughed him up in the showers and now our man is petrified of having to endure another attack. With Vincent putting him under pressure as well, Walsh will soon cough up the money."

"Walsh could get hurt, Jack. I wouldn't want that on my conscience."

"Don't you remember what he tried to do to you? How can you feel any sympathy for a low life like that?" Once again Jack was amazed that Elsa felt any compassion for Walsh in his present situation, but at the same time he couldn't help but admire her.

"If he's kept in prison that means he won't be able to assault some other poor, unsuspecting woman, whether she's respectable or a street walker. The best place for him is prison, but there's no need for us to make it any worse for him than it has to be," said Elsa reinforcing her position. "What we're doing is morally wrong. Not just in extorting money from Walsh, but in letting him back out on the streets."

"Don't talk like that Elsa, you're starting to worry me. You've said it yourself; you can't stay in hiding forever. The plot is simple. We put pressure on him to make him fully appreciate the hazards of life in a penal institution and then he finds out you're alive. This gives him the incentive to pay us to bring you to the law so that he can escape his intolerable situation. Then he walks. That's how it's got to be," said Jack, beginning to get agitated.

"I don't really care about the money, Jack. We've got each other and we're the only ones that matter, that's what we just said to each other. We can set up house somewhere else, where no one knows us. We can do whatever we like." Secretly Elsa now yearned to start a family but had been afraid to approach Jack in the past for fear of finding out he wouldn't want to make such a long term commitment.

"No we can't," interrupted Jack, "doing anything costs money. Without Walsh's cash life could be very difficult, and I'm not going into some shitty job to work my guts out and live on a pittance. Don't you see we need the money to make the right kind of start?"

"So when you agreed that we were the only thing that mattered, you really meant and the money too."

"Of course we matter, but we haven't come this far to throw all the work we've done away. We're nearly there baby. You've just got to wait a little longer.

"I hope the money's worth it Jack," snapped Elsa. She stood up and pulled her dress around her and walked into the master bedroom slamming the door behind her.

Jack sat up staring at the fire blankly, totally flummoxed by what had just taken place. The love and warmth that had filled the room only minutes earlier had now completely gone. This bitter after taste at the end of each meeting or conversation between them was becoming too familiar.

6

Simon Walsh was feeling more than a little nervous after his meeting with Caine and was anxious not to run into him again. In the few days since their meeting in the washroom he was beginning to forget what the man looked like. "Shit all the niggers in here look the same", he thought. Walsh hadn't taken much notice of Caine before he assaulted him, and during the assault he was in too much pain to focus on his attacker properly. He had noticed him on the bus but in his panic and fear he was unable to marshal his thoughts and recollections clearly. Walsh was now afraid that he could run into Caine unwittingly by not quickly recognizing him in sufficient time to avoid another beating.

A soccer match had been scheduled between the guards and the inmates. This was an annual event that was mainly good natured, but was also known to occasionally erupt into some violence if any inmate on or off the field decided to even the score with one of the guards, or vice versa. Inmates who had tried to cripple or injure any of the guards during the game had ultimately suffered the retribution from every member of the opposing team and had usually ended up hospitalized. Such naked brutality had acted as a deterrent over recent years, but nevertheless there was always an air of expectancy from the spectators. Walsh had little idea of the history of these matches and was happy to give way to other inmates seeking the best vantage point.

Vincent Tuzio spied Walsh standing alone and self-consciously at one end of the soccer pitch, nervously looking around at the other spectators rather than watching the match, which had just started. Tuzio decided to inform Walsh that Elsa was alive. He didn't know whether to be direct or adopt a soft approach to gently ease Walsh into understanding the truth. The last thing Tuzio wanted was to have Walsh storm away from him in an angry fit. He quietly walked up behind Walsh and patted him on the shoulder. Walsh flinched from the unexpected contact. "Calm down man," Tuzio advised him. "There's no need to be so jumpy, Caine ain't gonna try anything out here in the open."

"Oh yeah Vincent, but how can I be sure of that, I can't take another beating like the one he gave me last time. This kind of existence is new to me and I'm still trying to adjust to it. The ground rules are difficult to understand and then there's the constant brutality and hardship of everyday life. I have to get out of here or it will kill me," he whined.

"I know what you mean, man. I'm used to walking in these sewers, but I've spent a lifetime putting up with the kind of shit that we have to take in here. Now there's no need for you to feel exposed any more 'cos I got you in with Green."

"What's that going to cost me?"

"Well he wanted a little more than his usual fee. You gotta give the man your respect and half of your tobacco allowance."

"You said that he'd want a quarter, not half," replied Walsh.

"I know man, but he said you were a new fish and that you had to earn a little respect before he'd accept a quarter. That's just the way it is man, and I ain't gonna argue with him."

"I don't like the shit they give us in here anyway," laughed Walsh. "He could have it all for all I care."

"There's something else we need to talk about, man. We can't talk here, let's take a walk and get a little more privacy."

"OK but why?" he asked suspiciously.

"Something that may be to your advantage," replied Tuzio herding Walsh away from the crowd of spectators watching the game. "What you in here for man?"

"You know very well Vincent."

"Yeah, but tell me again."

"For the manslaughter of Elsa Bartelli."

"How did you kill her?"

"I accidentally shot her on my boat. We had an argument, which turned into a fight and I grabbed my gun to protect myself. It accidentally went off and she got hit and was knocked overboard and drowned. Nothing's going to change what happened, so what's this all about?"

Tuzio looked around where he and Walsh were standing before replying, to make sure nobody could overhear their conversation before giving an answer. "I knew Elsa before being sent here. She was my woman when I was on the outside."

Walsh stepped back in surprise, again showing a look of fear and anxiety. "What do you want from me?" he stammered, expecting Tuzio to attack him.

"Don't go gaga on me Simon, I haven't got any grudge with you because Elsa's not dead."

"What do you mean she's not dead? I left her in the water. She must be dead!"

"Look man, Elsa is a strong swimmer, you could say she was an all-round athlete in and out of bed," replied Tuzio giving Walsh a knowing grin, trying a little humor to make him relax. "She kept in shape being a dancer and she liked to keep fit by going to the gym and swimming every day. You only nicked her when you shot off your gun, but you didn't hurt her enough to prevent her from swimming back to the shore from where you left her."

"Then why didn't she come forward during my trial? She could have cleared me. I would have made it worth her while."

"Listen man, you pissed her off. She was expecting some money from you for your afternoon jaunt. After all she is a working girl and she'd been after you for the whole of the week. You shouldn't have shot her man."

"I didn't mean to shoot her, I told you that! The gun went off accidentally. She's probably told you the way it happened. All I want to know is what will it take for her to come forward now?"

"Now you're getting the message, man. She wants money and lots of it. You must be a very rich man, who can afford to pay out a little of your wealth to a worthy cause. She hasn't given me a figure but it will be far more than what you would have spent if you had just paid her for sex instead of trying to rape her."

"I don't understand. I offered her money and more, but she didn't take me on. I didn't think she was a hooker. She certainly didn't look or behave like any hooker that I've been with before. Give me a break! I'm no mind reader!"

"You're just naive man. She's expensive and always likes the cash up front, not promises."

"This doesn't sound right to me! So she was a hooker, but I still can't see you two together. Forgive me Vincent, but you just don't look like the kind of guy she would hook up with."

Vincent Tuzio gave a mock hurt expression. "I appreciate what you're trying to say man. Me and Elsa don't naturally complement each other. I'm a bum from the streets and she's so refined and looks like an angel. Well you know what she's like man, but you don't know what she's like in the sack. She's great and so imaginative."

"You don't need to tell me what I missed, I can imagine. Don't side track me, convince me you and her were together and tell me how you know she's still alive?"

"Outside I was a bouncer at the Blue Cockatoo, where Elsa used to dance, and my job was to keep the punters under control. Elsa and the other girls would be up on the stage doing their thing and there'd always be someone trying to get more than an eyeful. After a few drinks some of the punters would try and maul the girls and wouldn't take no for an answer. All the girls got their fair share of attention, especially Elsa. She was the main attraction and got the most hassle, but she could normally handle herself quite well. There's always the exception though, and one night she got a real mean bastard who tried to cut off her panties with a switchblade. He turned nasty when she pushed him back into the crowd and I think he would have cut her face if I hadn't stepped in. He was too big for me to handle on my own, but I did enough to delay him until the other guys in the club got to him. I also ended up getting stuck with his blade. It was a minor wound but Elsa was impressed and our relationship grew from that."

"You don't strike me as being particularly brave."

"I'm not brave man, but I'm smart. That's why I do alright in here and keep the right side of the important people. I'm a survivor and if you stick with me you'll be a survivor too. Just don't give me this crap. If you don't want to play then don't. She's got some other dude on the outside now and I'll not make much out of looking after you."

"If that's the case why has she come to you to make the arrangements?" asked Walsh

"Well it helps I'm in here and Elsa knows she can trust me. She told me what she wanted through one of the other dancers at the Blue Cockatoo who we both know. Julie came to visit and told me what Elsa wanted. It doesn't hurt me and besides I like to keep the right side of everyone cos you never know when you're going to need a favor. I'm giving more here than I'm getting, and when I get out I'll get my payback. Whatever that may be," answered Tuzio.

Walsh scrutinized Tuzio for a moment and then satisfied himself that he was probably telling the truth. Besides, what choice did he have? He had no other friends in prison and Elsa being alive was the only real hope he had of getting out of the place. "I'm sorry Vincent. Of course I'm interested in anything that will get me out of here. You've told me she wants money, what happens now?"

"She wants a guy called Jack Cates to arrange a meet with your wife so he can tell her how much Elsa wants and where to pay the money into.

"What's in it for Cates?"

"He could be the new man in her life or they've got their own arrangement. If he is the new man, he's kept her hidden since that afternoon on your boat. You'll need to agree to pay Elsa whatever she's asking for, but she said your wife wears the trousers so it'll be up to her to decide if it's gonna be paid out or not."

"I don't care how much money it costs as long as I get out of here," replied Walsh ignoring the comment about Bridget being the boss in their relationship.

"Alright man, you call your wife and tell her to get in touch with Cates. He's a private dick in New York so he should be easy to find. Cates will contact Elsa through her e-mail address and find out how much she wants."

"OK I'll call Bridget. I still can't see you with Elsa. You were one lucky motherfucker."

"Don't be fooled by appearances. I was her bit of rough on the side. We didn't have a conventional relationship man. It was really just the sex and she liked that rough too. That's one of the reasons she was pissed off at you for shooting her. She was getting hot from the way you were treating her and may even have given you a freebie." Tuzio wanted Walsh to feel better about himself, and the thought that he hadn't been so far off the mark with Elsa. He felt it might act as an added incentive.

Walsh smiled to himself, finding comfort in the knowledge that he'd got the measure of Elsa, and but for an unfortunate accident, may have spent an enjoyable and gratifying afternoon with her. There would be time to find out what he'd missed after he got out of prison, he thought.

That evening he rang his wife. "Hello Simon, why are you ringing? Is there anything wrong?" answered Bridget, with an inquisitive, rather than concerned, tone.

"Well I'm lonely and you've not exactly been the dutiful wife since I've been locked up, have you? Why can't you visit occasionally?" Walsh heard himself whining and wished he'd asked the question in a different way.

"I've written to you Simon, explaining how difficult it is for me to get down there. I am running the business among other things, which means I'm looking after your interests where it matters. There are some documents that need your signature and I was planning to bring them down to you on the next visiting day."

"Well I'm not there and the work has to be done, so I do appreciate your efforts," replied Walsh insincerely. "The other Board members won't do didley squat, except complain. It's up to you. Anyway, it's not as if we were exactly lovebirds before I went to prison. But never mind that for now, there's something important I need you to do for me. I've been told today that Elsa Bartelli is still alive and will go to the police to clear me of manslaughter, if we give her enough money." Walsh looked around him to make sure there wasn't anybody listening in to his conversation. The queue for the telephone was fairly sparse for a change and no one was paying any attention to him.

For once Bridget was left open mouthed, without a smart answer for her husband and she unconsciously lowered the phone in a trance. This news from her husband had come like a thunderbolt and the shock waves had effectively immobilized her whole body. The prospect of Simon getting out of prison was the last thing she wanted to hear. On the other end of the line Walsh became impatient waiting for his wife to answer him and began shouting down the phone. The distant shouts came through the receiver, sounding like an argument in the next room, which snapped Bridget back into consciousness. "Yes Simon, I'm sorry it was just such a shock to hear the woman was still alive. I needed a bit of time to digest the information," replied Bridget.

"I suppose I felt exactly the same way when I heard it. But the good thing is, she can get me out of this dump."

"Who told you? How do you know it's true?"

"The guy who told me about her was her lover before he got sent down. He knew too much about what happened on the boat not to have had contact with Elsa. You've got to get in touch with a private investigator called Jack Cates. I don't know his involvement in all of this, but he may be Elsa's new man. If he is then he's probably kept her in hiding, so I guess they could have planned this rip off together."

"How much does she want?" asked Bridget.

"I don't know and I don't care. Just pay them whatever they want and get me out of here!"

"There's only so much ready money that I'll be able to scratch together, I just hope that it will be enough. There's no use speculating, I'll get in touch with Cates and find out how much they're asking for. How will I find him?"

"He's a private dick that operates out of New York, so he should be easy to trace. Look I know things haven't always been great between us Bridget, but please do this for me. If I have to serve out my sentence in this place, the only way I'll ever leave here is in a coffin."

"Don't worry Simon, I won't let my personal feelings stand in the way of doing what's right. I'll arrange to see Cates as soon as I can, and also arrange a prison visit after our meeting. Goodbye Simon."

Bridget put down the phone, went over to the cocktail bar in the corner of the lounge and poured herself a large gin. She sat down in one of the armchairs cradling the glass in both hands, lost for the moment in her thoughts. Initial feelings of shock and disbelief were now being replaced by tinges of guilt. Bridget knew that Simon was a habitual abuser of women, and after the trial she had convinced herself that he was also a murderer, so she had mentally exorcised him out of her life. She now wondered if she had been unfair in her judgement of him, and that her attitude formed on the basis of her own experiences with him, rather than on the facts given during the trial. She took a large gulp of gin and the sharp bite of the liquor on the back of her throat abruptly halted her foray into self-doubt.

There was a lot happening for Bridget at the moment with even brighter prospects on the horizon. She was only just coming to terms with the loosening of the shackles of her loveless marriage and wasn't going to throw away all she had achieved since Simon's incarceration, particularly on the strength of wishful thinking based on the promises of an inmate. How confident could she be that Simon's informant was trustworthy and that all of this wasn't just some elaborate hoax to extort money? And even if Bartelli was still alive, all it proved was that she had somehow managed to survive her ordeal and not that Simon was really a regular guy. She picked up the phone book and found a small advert for Jack Cates, "Private Investigator – all matters handled confidentially and with discretion, care and attention". Well this was one matter that would require his best care and discretion, she thought, as she picked up the phone to dial his number.

7

"I'm not sure how much we can trust Mr. Cates, so we will need to keep an eye on him," said Roland Bannister taking a puff from his Havana cigar. "He believes he's running this little operation single handed. We agreed that we would work openly together, but he's not keeping me informed."

"I know boss," replied Lou, "I've never trusted that guy, he's an ex-cop and too smart for his own good."

"I know what you mean Lou. He needs to be careful if he thinks we're just going to sit around doing nothing, while he carves out a nice deal for himself. The man could be too sharp and end up cutting himself. I want you two guys to follow him. You're the only people I trust," said Bannister looking at Frank, "so you'll have to work in shifts. I don't want anyone else involved."

"That's OK," said Lou, "the two of us can handle it. I'll start tonight and stake out his apartment. If I don't make contact Frank will start at his office tomorrow morning. It won't be long before we pick him up and then we'll stay on his tail."

Lou and Frank had worked for Roland Bannister since the lawyer had taken over the Blue Cockatoo. Prior to that, they had worked for Leonard Tuzio who had been the previous "owner" of the club, and working for Tuzio also meant that they owed allegiance to Mario Pallacio. The pecking order was straight forward with Pallacio, at the top as head of the syndicate, with Leonard Tuzio second in command as his right hand man. Lou and Frank were some way down the hierarchy and did what they were told, but knew who to listen to in the rare instances of conflict between Pallacio's lieutenants.

Leonard Tuzio's name was not on the deeds of the club, which was officially owned by one of his oldest friends Barry Summers, but Leonard had bought the place using Barry as the front man. Lou and Frank both provided the necessary muscle in the regulation of Tuzio's entertainment enterprises, but when Tuzio bought the Blue Cockatoo he wanted them to work full time at the club to ensure it remained clean of drugs and any other petty criminal interference.

At the time Tuzio took over the club it was a seedy strip joint, which had a reputation as a place to go for an easy lay. The strippers openly went with the punters for the right price and hookers hung around outside the club late at night to catch those that were leaving empty handed. The first thing Tuzio did was refurbish the internal and external décor of the club to give it a feeling of opulence rather than the garish red and gold livery associated with the décor most strip clubs had at that time. He brought in an interior designer who used subtle pastel colors to impart the illusion of space and refinement, and replaced all of the furniture and removed the traditional stage. The stage was rebuilt in the center of the main function room and was equipped to rotate, oscillate or thrust its central platform upwards. The tables were positioned around the stage to give the audience the best view of the shows. Sex was still the main attraction of the club, but instead of the conventional "bump and grind" routines of the strippers Tuzio created sexual fantasies by having the performers act out sexual themes. The opening night performance was of two girls washing each other in a large bath mounted on the stage. The lighting was soft and intimate and the girls began by undressing and gently fondling each other. Eventually they made their way to the bath and began soaping each other down. The stage began rotating slowly, which added to the voyeuristic excitement of the audience, with their gentle ministrations developing from a mild fondling to simulated lovemaking. The crowd went wild at the end of the show and the club was an instant success and provided a solid platform for Bannister to build on later.

The club soon became one of the most sought after venues in town. The police often visited the place to see if the shows crossed the line from erotic entertainment to illegal lewd acts. Tuzio was careful to only use girls in the shows to prevent the risk of penetration during the simulated sex scenes. The police enjoyed the shows as much as the rest of the audience and Tuzio always ensured that they were well looked after during their visits. The finances of the club were looked after by Summers who was a qualified accountant and concentrated on ledger rather than female figures. During this time Mario Pallacio was unaware of Tuzio's "extra-curricular" venture and it seemed unlikely that the club would come to his attention with Summers as the owner.

Frank and Lou had done a good job in policing the club and the punters. Summers was a quiet retiring man who was scared of Frank, his opposite in almost every respect. Where Summers was quiet and diminutive, Frank was loud and very big. Tuzio felt comfortable in the belief that Summers' fear of Frank would stave off any temptation of manipulating the accounts and helping himself to an unequal share of the profits. The bank account of the club was held in Summers' name but Tuzio had access to it.

The partnership worked very well and the club became very successful, but as its success grew it eventually came under the scrutiny of Mario Pallacio. Pallacio had Summers picked up one morning coming out of his apartment and it wasn't long before he discovered that Leonard Tuzio was his silent partner. There was already friction between the two men and Pallacio saw Tuzio's involvement in the club as a gross lack of respect by his deputy. Pallacio knew that any failure to discipline Tuzio over the matter would be construed as a sign of weakness by his peers and subordinates.

Pallacio scared the life out of Summers who was let go about his normal daily business with the promise that he wouldn't mention the meeting to Tuzio. Summers was more frightened of Pallacio than he was of Frank and he decided to keep quiet, even though he knew Pallacio was planning something nasty for his partner. Pallacio called Lou and instructed him to bring Tuzio to his house that evening, explaining that he wanted to reorganize the drug distribution network and that they needed to discuss details. The drugs issue had created bad feeling between the two men when Pallacio explained that he wanted to break into the High School market by employing school kids already hooked on dope as pushers. Tuzio had made it clear that he didn't want any involvement in pedaling drugs to school children. Lou was aware that this was not an invitation but a command, and immediately telephoned Tuzio and arranged to pick him up at the club.

Tuzio was more than a little concerned after Lou's call, and his gut instinct told him that something was seriously wrong, and that if he went to see Pallacio that evening; he would never leave his house alive. He decided to call on Roland Bannister whom he trusted and thought he could rely on for his discretion. The two had been involved in many shady deals together and, although they were from different ends of the social spectrum, had developed a mutual respect and trust in their working relationship. He explained the situation to Bannister and after a 30 minute discussion and several subsequent phone calls invited the lawyer to join him at the club. Tuzio offered to pick Bannister up from his apartment at three in the afternoon. Frank was in the office with Barry Summers when the two men arrived. As they entered the office Summers began questioning Tuzio.

"Whoa, slow down Barry let me get my breath. I need to sort something out with Frank. Frank I know you and Lou are close. Did he tell you what Pallacio really wants from me tonight?" asked Tuzio.

"It wasn't much boss, but his tone of voice did sound as if he was rattled. Firstly Lou can count the number of times he's been called by Pallacio in 20 years on one hand. Secondly the matter of fact and business-like instructions were strange. On the few occasions that Pallacio has called Lou he usually makes some crack about some gaff he made in his early days with him. All he said was get Leonard over to my house by eight o'clock sharp this evening. He said he didn't want any excuses because of the short notice and that it was essential to sort out any differences over the drug issue because he wanted you to take over that side of the business and leave "entertainment" for Braggio to manage." The tier of lieutenants below Pallacio was flat, but everyone knew Tuzio held seniority, and most importantly it was also recognized by the top man. He was the closest thing to a Consigliere, but unlike his Sicilian counterparts he participated fully in the day to day business of the organization. Braggio envied Tuzio's closeness to the boss and was working his way into Pallacio's favor because he wanted Tuzio's position.

"Mario knows my feelings on pedaling that shit to kids and how much I loathe Braggio, who is the last person I'd want to run the entertainment business. He wouldn't have the first idea on how to handle the job. Mario's been deliberately difficult to hook me and reel me in, expecting me to go to his house with all guns blazing. He's up to something, but the only thing I've done that could have pissed Mario off is my involvement in this club. Barry have you seen or heard of anyone making any enquiries about the club?"

All eyes turned to Summers and he thought for one moment that he was going to be physically sick. "What do you mean?" he stammered.

"Don't act dumb Barry. I just want to know if anyone's been sniffing around here trying to get any information on the takings or the owners or anything else that doesn't involve eating, drinking or staring at tits and ass," retorted Tuzio.

"No, why should I have? I would have told you if anything suspicious had happened."

"Look, I'm not accusing you of anything Barry, I'm just trying to get an angle on my meeting with Mario. We seldom socialize and for him to invite me to his house out of the blue indicates that something is seriously wrong."

"How come you're so nervous?" chipped in Frank brusquely, putting more pressure on Summers.

The sound of Frank's voice made Summers jump and the men around him immediately believed it was because he was hiding something. Barry was normally an edgy person, but this degree of nervousness made everyone suspicious that he knew more than he was telling.

"You were in late this morning Barry. Usually you're first here and you open up, but this morning I had to open up. What delayed you?" added Frank.

Summers couldn't hold out any more and blurted out what had

happened to him. "Leonard I was scared to death," he tried to reason with Tuzio. "I got picked up this morning by a couple of Pallacio's heavies who took me to his town apartment, where he was having breakfast. He asked me to join him and started quizzing me about the club, mainly about turnover and profits. He went on to say that certain establishments suffered from outside interference, citing the case of the "Pink Lady" where the manager was knifed during a disturbance at the bar. Finally he suggested that if he became a partner in the "Blue Cockatoo" he could protect me from that type of incident."

"That's Mario's standard approach to wheedling his way into a business. He usually starts modestly as a minority partner and then gradually intimidates the other partners until he can muscle himself into the prime position," interjected Tuzio. "What did you say to him Barry?"

"Pallacio was very courteous up to that point, but I let slip that I already had a partner. He knew the ownership of the club was in my name and started to dig, making veiled threats about not letting me go until he got the truth out of me….one way or another. At first I told him that a wealthy businessman had bankrolled me, who didn't want his name associated with a strip joint. Pallacio then asked for a name. How could I give him a credible name? I had to give him your name Leonard or he would have killed me."

"Don't be melodramatic Barry he wouldn't have killed you until either he'd got all of the information he wanted, or got the club," replied Tuzio adding, "you know that there's nothing to stop him killing you once he gets his hands on the deeds of the club. Come to think of it, there's no way any of us can stop Pallacio from doing whatever he wants and that makes us all expendable. I'm feeling under pressure because we're at odds over the drug distribution and if he knows I'm involved in the club he'll take it as a mark of disrespect."

"I should finish you off now for ratting on the boss," cut in Frank. Summers was trembling by this time but Tuzio shook his head at Frank to prevent him from carrying out his threat.

Roland Bannister stepped in between Frank and Summers saying, "Barry is the legal owner of the club, so if you kill him Frank what happens to it?" Frank nodded his understanding of Bannister's argument. "We can't leave the ownership of the club in Barry's name otherwise Pallacio will just steam roller him and take control," continued Bannister. "Now if Pallacio knows Leonard is the real owner he'll have to kill him or lose his credibility in the organization. We have to protect the club and get Leonard out of the country."

"Not necessarily in that order," cut in Tuzio. "I have a greater interest in saving my own skin than keeping the club out of Mario's clutches."

"Of course you do," smiled Bannister. Turning to Lou and Frank, he began to explain the schedule they would have to follow for the evening. "Leonard and I have already spoken about saving his skin, because he suspected from the start that Pallacio's invitation had an ulterior motive. He's going to fly out to Rio de Janeiro and then disappear. He has tickets for the 8:15 flight tonight. By the time Pallacio realizes Leonard isn't going to keep their appointment, Leonard will be on his way to Brazil."

"What if the flight gets delayed?" asked Frank.

"We've thought about that," answered Bannister, "I've also booked tickets on the 8:45 flight to Mexico City. It's not my first choice because Mario has some connections in Mexico, but Leonard can use it as a backup plan if he has to."

"The first thing we have to do is transfer ownership of the club from Barry to me," continued Bannister, picking up the threads of the plan he had constructed earlier with Tuzio.

"Why you?" said Frank bluntly.

"Well there aren't many options. Could you manage the club, look after the running of the place, keeping the right side of the authorities, handle the entertainment and deal with Pallacio?" replied

Bannister.

Frank looked a little indignant until Bannister mentioned Pallacio's name. In truth he knew that he didn't have the knowledge or education to manage a business with a turnover of 4 million dollars a year. Besides Pallacio didn't know that he and Frank had been moonlighting at the "Blue Cockatoo" instead of taking care of his business under instruction from Leonard Tuzio, and he was still paying them a wage.

"The only previous connection I have had with Pallacio is the defense of Leonard and some of his other lieutenants against a variety of criminal charges. Through Leonard I've served his organization well and Pallacio will realize that I know a lot about his business. If I'm going to run the club I'll have to give up my practice. I'll also take care of Leonard by making sure he receives regular payments to wherever he decides to stay."

"If Lou doesn't bring the boss to Pallacio, what's going to happen to him?" asked Frank, looking for guidance from Tuzio.

"We won't tell Lou of our plans," answered Tuzio. "It's the best way to protect him. If you tell him to time things so he gets to Mario's for quarter past eight. On that schedule he'll have to pick me up from my apartment at seven thirty, but when he gets there I won't be at home. He'll probably wait for about 10 minutes and will then assume that I'd gone to Mario's house on my own. Mario will be mad but he won't kill him for being dumb. If they make a connection between me not turning up and the possibility of me leaving the country they may check flights, but won't be able to get to the airport in time to stop me."

With that all eyes turned to Summers, Frank said, "Don't worry Boss I'll make sure he is incommunicado for the rest of the day," secretly wanting to make him disappear permanently.

The plan worked well. Pallacio was mad at Lou and slapped him around a little, but the only real injury was to his pride. Bannister went to see Pallacio the next day to talk over the running of the club.

Pallacio graciously accepted him as the registered owner and manager and would leave him to run it unhindered, provided 20 percent of the club's profits were paid into the numbered offshore account he gave him. There was still the thorny matter of Tuzio's lack of respect for his mentor and he wanted some retribution even though it wouldn't be Tuzio.

Lou took Summers to the docks late the next day for another meeting with Pallacio. Summers was told that Pallacio had looked over the books of the Blue Cockatoo and had been impressed by their neatness and accuracy, and that there was a position for him in his organization. Innocently Summers went to the meeting, relieved that he was now on the right side of Pallacio. Pallacio arrived at the docks ahead of his men as he had told them he had wanted to handle Summers himself mano e mano. He couldn't have Tuzio, so he cold -bloodedly murdered Summers in front of Lou and by the time his men came to collect the body to dump it out at sea, it was already bagged and weighted. Pallacio bragged on how he had killed that ungrateful sonofabitch Leonard Tuzio and everyone readily accepted the story, as Pallacio's honor had been satisfied. Pallacio agreed that Frank and Lou should work for Bannister to "protect his interests."

8

Frank drove his car to Jack Cates' apartment block and parked a discrete distance from the entrance. It was 6 o'clock in the evening and Frank had no idea of Jack's whereabouts, but decided that this would be as good a place as any to start as the man would have to come home sometime, even if it was just to change his clothes. Frank was expecting a long night and had taken some garlic sausage and a couple of bread rolls for the stake out. He had also taken his hip flask, which was full of Russian vodka, to keep himself warm.

Lou was due to relieve Frank at 8 o'clock the next morning and would call his partner on his cell phone first to check his whereabouts. Frank didn't really know what to expect from tailing Jack Cates and expected to be dragged all over town. His knowledge of Jack went back to the time that Roland Bannister first took control of the Blue Cockatoo. The ex-cop started working on a few investigative jobs for Bannister, or checking the background of some of the applicants seeking membership of the club. It was all penny ante stuff, but it didn't take long for Cates to inveigle himself into Bannister's confidence and into the beds of the girls working at the club. Frank didn't mind Jack fooling around with most of the girls, but when he got involved with Elsa he considered that he had over-stepped the mark.

The big man felt like a schoolboy with a crush around Elsa and was smart enough to realize that in addition to the huge difference in their ages, he was too big, too ugly and too coarse to be attractive to her. The smart-ass ex-cop had eventually dragged her into his sleazy shakedowns of the rich and famous, damn near getting her killed during the last outing. When he thought of those men mauling Elsa he started to boil deep inside. Taking a hip flask from the glove compartment, he unscrewed the top and gulped down a large slug of vodka and vowed to himself that no matter what Bannister or anybody else wanted that smart-ass ex-cop would pay dearly for what Elsa had suffered.

Frank didn't know Jack was trying to cultivate his relationship with Bridget Walsh. Earlier in the day Bridget hadn't been able to get through to Jack Cates on either his business line or on his cell phone, so she decided that she would ring Cates from work and arrange to see him during the day. A few hours ago her life seemed organized and planned, and focused in the direction she wanted it to go. Now it was a tangled mess, threatened by the prospect of Simon coming back into her life, which was the last thing she wanted.

She hadn't slept well and had woken up with a headache as a result. She didn't normally have a big breakfast and today would be no exception. Hurrying to make an early start for work and beat the morning rush, she grabbed a coffee and took an aspirin to try and ease the pain in her head. By the time she got to her office the headache was beginning to subside. Her personal assistant, Jackie, brought her a cup of coffee and a cheese bagel. As Bridget was launching into the bagel Jackie went to her desk, came back with the morning post and laid it on Bridget's desk. "What kind of weekend did you have?" Jackie enquired casually.

"Don't ask. It seemed to start off well but turned sour yesterday."

"I'm sorry Bridget. What happened? Is Simon alright?"

"Yes, of course he is. Nothing has happened to Simon. I spoke to him yesterday and everything's fine. Well as fine as life can be in prison. Don't worry, it's nothing that I can't handle." Bridget was amazed that most people within the firm still thought of Simon as a regular guy and believed him to be a victim of circumstance, rather than the architect of his own downfall.

"Well if there's anything I can do, or anything you need, just call me," said Jackie leaving Bridget's office.

Bridget took her pocket diary out of her handbag and turned to the page where she had made a note of Jack Cates' telephone number. She picked up the phone, dialed for an outside line and then punched in the number. The call connected but all she got was the answer phone with a pre-recorded message apologizing that no one was available to take the call and to leave a name and telephone number. Bridget put the phone down without leaving her details. She wanted to talk to the man, not to his machine. After trying another couple of times she finally decided to leave her name and number. There was a finance meeting that afternoon and she doubted whether she'd get another chance to call Cates that day.

By the time Bridget returned to her office at five thirty that evening she had forgotten about Jack Cates and was taken aback by the message on her desk to ring him. Jackie finished work at five and had left a hand written message about the call giving a mobile number that Bridget could reach Cates on. The message brought home her present predicament and suddenly she felt the energy drain out of her body, and slumped resignedly into her chair. At that moment the phone rang and startled her. Tentatively she picked up the receiver and answered the call, "Hello, Bridget Walsh."

"This is Jack Cates, Mrs. Walsh. I returned your call earlier this afternoon, but you were out. What can I do for you?"

"Don't be coy Mr. Cates, I'm sure you know what I'm ringing about. I've had an instruction from my husband to call you about getting him out of prison, so I'm sure that you've been expecting my call."

"I don't think it's a good idea to talk about this over the phone Mrs. Walsh. I suggest that we meet. When would be convenient for you?"

"The sooner the better Mr. Cates."

"Well I'm outside your building, so if you've got time to grab a drink we can talk it over now."

Bridget was infuriated because she felt that he was playing with her, but she didn't give him any hint of her anger and calmly agreed to meet him in the coffee shop around the corner in thirty minutes. Bridget had finished her business for the day and could have met with him straight away, but decided to keep him waiting. It was a trivial thing to do, but it gave her a sense of wresting control from Cates. Nevertheless she felt that she'd have few victories in her dealings with this man and decided to take advantage of him whenever she could, no matter how petty.

By the time she entered the coffee shop it was nearly six thirty and she felt smug at the thought of Cates waiting for nearly an hour. The shop was quiet at this time of the evening with most people on their way home, or rushing to get somewhere for a date, or searching out their evening's entertainment. She looked around the shop, which was quite small with a split-level floor and room for about fifteen tables. On the upper level there were two or three couples sitting at separate tables, killing time before going out for the night. On the bottom level was a man sitting by the window reading a paper and drinking a cup of coffee. Bridget decided that he must be Cates as he was the only single person in the coffee shop and she walked over to him to introduce herself.

"Hello," said Bridget, "can I join you?" The man looked up from his paper, nodded and then continued reading. Bridget stared at the other side of the paper waiting for the man to put it down. He just kept on reading and Bridget again found it hard to keep control of her impatience and temper. Finally she said, "Excuse me, but I believe we have something to say to each other."

The man put down the paper and looked long and hard at Bridget and her anger changed to embarrassment under his scrutiny. He smiled and said, "Look honey if you've got something to say to me don't keep it to yourself go right ahead and say it."

"My husband wants to get out of prison…."

"Now I understand," cut in the man, "you're on your own and you need a man. Don't worry you've been lucky and found the right person."

Bridget was stunned by the interruption and by what the man had said. "Look I don't understand what you're saying and I haven't got time to play around, let's get down to business…"

The man stood up indignantly, "Well I'm sorry I misjudged you. You've been trying to proposition me, well I'll be damned. I'll let you know that I've never paid for sex in my life and I never will, so you can go and peddle your merchandise somewhere else."

Finally Bridget realized that they were talking at cross-purposes and the man she was talking to was not Jack Cates. The other customers in the coffee house turned and looked at the pair, either giggling or giving Bridget a look of contempt or disapproval. Bridget flushed a deep red, excused herself and stood up to leave, strode to the exit, looking at the ground and keeping her head down. She walked straight into another man who was walking over toward the table. "I think you're looking for me, Mrs. Walsh," said the man, "I'm Jack Cates."

Bridget looked up and stared into the clearest, bluest eyes she'd ever seen, paused for a second and then pushed past the man to leave the coffee shop. Jack chased her and caught her by the arm before she had taken more than a few steps back towards her company's offices. She turned angrily towards him. "I suppose you were more than a little amused by that charade in there," she hissed.

"I'm sorry about any misunderstanding Mrs. Walsh, but I'd had so much coffee waiting for you that I had to go to the john. I didn't see you come in and when I came out of the john you were sat at the table with that guy. I didn't know if he was a friend of yours so I waited. When he got up and called you a hooker I realized my mistake."

Bridget suddenly burst out laughing as much to relieve the tension as from the humor of the situation. She continued laughing as she walked down the street, trying to stop herself from her emotional outburst. Regaining her composure she finally said, "Alright Mr. Cates where can we talk?"

Jack tried not to smile and courteously nodded and replied, "I know a little bar around the corner where we can get a little privacy." As he turned from Bridget to lead the way a sly smirk crossed his face as he saw the potential of being able to have some fun while doing business. Any idea of having fun was completely opposite to his preconception of Bridget, who he previously considered to be a cold, unemotional, highly professional businesswoman. He had thought that she was more likely to bury her head in a company ledger rather than read a good novel or peruse a gossip sheet. A starched shirt more likely to follow serious pursuits than take any opportunity to be frivolous. But she was feisty and, so far, their dealings together had shown that she was capable of handling the negotiation for her husband's release and would not be intimidated by anyone.

They went to a quiet bar a couple of blocks from the NMP offices and Jack took the opportunity to try and find out a little more about Bridget. She didn't want to talk about herself, or about her husband, or his trial. The bar was in the theatre district and Jack ushered Bridget to the back of the room and asked her what she wanted to drink as she sat down at one of the tables. Bridget asked for a soda and lemon drink and watched Jack as he walked over to the bar, wondering how long their meeting would last as she was starting to get hungry. Returning with their drinks, Jack explained to her that the bar could get busy, but generally Monday was a quiet night and they should get privacy.

He was not what she had expected. Instead of a seedy man in a crumpled suit with stale breath she found a handsome man, who didn't fall into the private eye stereotype and who conducted himself with considerable helpings of charm and humor. Bridget pulled herself up sharply when she found herself being drawn to Cates and had to accept that he was the kind of man that attracted her. Besides his obvious gifts he had the manner of a strong determined man. She reminded herself to be cautious as apart from trying to extort money from her, he may also have played a part in framing Simon for murder.

Lifting her drink to take a sip Bridget said, "Thank you Mr. Cates," regaining her business facade. "Let's not delay matters anymore, how much will it cost me to get my husband out of prison?"

Jack winced as he sat down as if he'd just received a heavy body blow. "You don't beat around the bush do you, Mrs. Walsh?"

"What were you expecting Mr. Cates? I assume you want me to give you a lot of money in return for telling the truth, and producing the slut who tried to compromise my husband in the first place. What do you want? Social banter before we start digging into the sewage?"

"Slow down," said Jack trying to calm Bridget and not attract attention from any of the other customers in the bar. "Look, I'm just doing what I've been paid to do. You're assuming that I'm going to benefit from your money but, other than receiving my fee from Vincent Tuzio, I am not," Jack lied. "I know Tuzio from some of his petty criminal activities, when I was a cop. I think he wants me involved because he trusts me and doesn't trust the Bartelli woman to give him his fair share of the money after you've stumped up."

"Simon told me that you were probably seeing Bartelli and that she had ditched Tuzio. That means you're up to your armpits in this filthy mess, so don't act the innocent."

"Of course Tuzio told your husband I was the new love interest so he could separate himself from the people behind what is essentially a blackmailing scam. As soon as Simon arrived in prison, Tuzio began trying to ingratiate himself with your husband to become his friend. That does two things. Firstly he gains his trust and appears less threatening when making his demands, which makes the shakedown a lot easier. And secondly stops your husband from trying to retaliate or go to the police as he will have come to rely on Tuzio for his protection from any of the other inmates. Simon is completely out of his depth in prison, but I wouldn't blame him if he wanted to get his own back, but believe me he's not equipped to take on Tuzio and would probably end up with a knife in his back. He's already had a bit of a beating for getting the wrong side of one of the other inmates."

Jack's last statement really deflated Bridget, who had initially felt depressed and angry at Simon for putting her in this position. This emotion quickly turned to guilt on hearing he was suffering in prison from an attack by one of the inmates, never mind the mental and physical trauma of actually being beaten up. This was a strange world to people shielded from the harsher realities of life in the gutter. It was odd hearing the news from a stranger and for the first time since this whole messy affair had blown up, she felt compassion for Simon and an even greater sense of urgency to get him released from prison.

"Are you alright Mrs. Walsh?" asked Jack, noticing that she was pursing her lips and that she had mentally withdrawn from the conversation a little.

"Yes I'm fine thank you. I really don't buy your position, because if you're not involved I can't understand why you don't go to the police and tell them that Bartelli is still alive?"

"I would do, if I knew where she was, but I don't. It would be my word against Tuzio's because I've got no proof that she's alive. She must be alive because Tuzio wants me to arrange a meeting between the two of you, so she can tell you where the money is to be paid. She obviously doesn't trust me. Elsa may be dead, but if that's the case Tuzio is going to come up against a brick wall as I have to verify her identity. Why would he waste his time?" Jack was trying to throw more into the mix to confuse Bridget and get her off the track of tying him in with Vincent and Elsa.

"This is getting too complicated for me. Just stop hypothesizing on the various possibilities of the situation and cut to the chase. How much do you want?" demanded Bridget.

"I was only trying to spell out the options Mrs. Walsh. If you decide to pay Tuzio you'll be parting with a lot of money, so I wanted you to understand the risks. If she is alive and you don't pay her, you'll be condemning your husband to serve out a sentence for a crime he didn't commit in an environment where he's already struggling to keep his head above water. I guess it's a risk either way, but only you can decide the right course of action to take."

"You're right. I can't take that chance because I couldn't live with myself if I found out that the Bartelli woman was still alive."

Jack hoped the sudden release of tension and feeling of relief that flowed through him on hearing Bridget's words didn't show on his face. It was his turn to now switch into business mode. "Tuzio told me he wants between five and ten million bucks. He doesn't really know what your husband's worth so he doesn't know how high he should aim. I told him to go for the lower figure, as it would be hard for you to get such a large amount of ready money. How long will it take you to collect 5 million dollars?"

"You must be joking! How much ready money do you think I have at my disposal? That kind of money isn't just lying around waiting to be picked up. For God's sake get real."

"It's not me demanding this amount Mrs. Walsh. I'm just the messenger."

"Simon has less than a $100,000 dollars in his bank account. I have about one and a half million, but that still leaves us a long way from what you're demanding. I'm sorry, I can't raise what Tuzio's asking for quickly. I'm going to have to sell something. Simon has some shares in the company, but it's not a good time to sell. With the shares and the boat I should be able to scrape together sufficient money, but it's going to take time."

"I'm sure Tuzio has got all the time in the world, but your husband hasn't. The quicker you get the money the better the value you'll get from it, as Simon is at risk every second he's in prison."

"Well that's not your concern Mr. Cates," replied Bridget coldly. He may be trying to be helpful, she thought, but he's still too goddam presumptuous.

The sharpness of the rebuff stung Jack and made him understand that he could never relax with this woman. "Call me when you've got the money together and I'll make the necessary arrangements with Tuzio for the meeting with Elsa," he said, adding, "I'll walk you back to your office."

They got up together and Bridget went ahead as Jack settled the bar tab. Bridget's mind was racing, trying to figure the quickest way of getting the money together, so she didn't notice the hooded man on the corner as she ambled toward the NMP office buildings. It was now seven fifteen and the streets were still quiet. Automatically she hit her full stride not realizing that Jack was settling the bill at the bar and hadn't joined her.

Bridget suddenly felt one hand over her mouth and the other pulling her backward towards an alley. The force pulled her off her feet and she found herself being dragged along, being hauled by a muscular arm around her neck. Her mouth became free and she shouted to be let go with no response. She tried to scream and found the sound stifled from a hand placed over her mouth, while she was being pushed against a wall deep into the alley.

"Shut your fucking mouth or you'll be breathing through a gash in your throat," said her attacker as she felt the point of a sharp implement at her neck. She stopped struggling immediately. "That's better now hand over your handbag."

The man snatched the handbag from her as she handed it to him. Bridget couldn't make out the man's face because of the shadows cast by the hood, which made him look even more menacing and her even more fearful of her situation. "Just take the thing and leave me alone," said Bridget, hoping to persuade him to run.

"Maybe I want more than your money," came the voice from the hood. The man dropped the handbag and lifted his knife towards her throat again. "Now just be a good girl and I'll let you go without hurting you."

Bridget was trapped against the wall and she pushed her body back trying to move far enough away from the knife and weighing up the risk of making a dash for freedom. She could smell garlic on the man's breath as he came closer. His body was now against hers and the edge of the knife against her neck.

"You want me really don't you?" said the man. "I know you do. You smell nice. Do you taste nice?" With that the man licked the side of Bridget's face, and she started to feel nauseous. The man was unable to carry on further because he was yanked backward by Jack and fell roughly on the ground. He looked up at Jack and smiled, "What's up man, she's got enough for both of us."

"Get to your feet before I'm tempted to kick your head the length of this alley," spat Jack.

The man rose slowly keeping his knife hand behind his back. He suddenly lunged toward Jack, trying to stick him in his stomach. Jack pivoted his body to one side, deflecting the blow, using the momentum of the man to send him sprawling on the ground again. This time he landed on his hands and knees and cursed at the pain. He seemed distressed as he sucked in air but he had sufficient presence of mind to quickly lift himself up and dart to the opposite end of the alley.

"Stop him!" shouted Bridget.

"What for?" said Jack as the man disappeared, "the guy's a habitual petty thief. He'd be banged up for the night. Then what? He may get sent down, but more than likely he'd never show up in court. It's a waste of time and effort." Jack felt a sharp pain in his side, ran his hand over the painful area. He lifted his blood stained hand and realized the man had cut him and that he was bleeding.

When Bridget saw the blood on Jack's hand she insisted he come back to her office to dress the wound. Her office was on the top floor of the building and had a panoramic view of the city skyline. Jack was standing by the window, taking in the view of the city by night, when Bridget came over to him with a First Aid box. "Take off your shirt," she ordered.

As Jack took off his jacket and then his shirt Bridget went out of her office and came back with a dish of warm water. She took Jack's arm and turned him to the side to examine his wound. "It's just a nick, but the skin is lacerated. You won't need stitches, but it will be painful for a couple of days." Taking a pinch of cotton wool Bridget bathed the wound and Jack's body stiffened slightly, but not as much as when she cleaned it with iodine. "I'm sorry but this is all there was in the medicine box."

"I'm sure you're enjoying this," moaned Jack.

"If you were Vincent Tuzio I'd definitely be enjoying it, but I don't think he would have tried to save me. I'm sorry I've been so abrasive with you, but I'm sure you can understand the reason for it. I just don't know who I can trust." Bridget put clean muslin against the wound and fixed it in position with elastic dressing.

"You can trust me, I'm an ex-cop," joked Jack. "I understand what you're going through. You're whole life is in turmoil, first of all hearing the charges against your husband and then seeing him being sent down for at least 10 years. Most women would be coming apart at the seams by now."

"I've got to be honest with you Mr. Cates, Simon and I didn't have the best of marriages. I won't go into details, but let's say that we are not close. The trial and Simon being sent to prison has been more stressful than I would have believed, but I've taken over the running of his company and I'm able to loose myself in my work."

"That's not unusual these days, there's no need to explain anything to me."

"I'm not explaining ANYTHING to you! I was just correcting your earlier premise about the affect Simon's conviction was having on me," retorted Bridget. Why is this man trying to be so nice and understanding when at the same time he's screwing me and my husband for 5 million dollars, she thought.

"I'm sorry. Look I don't seem to be able to do or say anything right, so I'll go now and expect to hear from you later."

Bridget immediately felt contrite because she had over reacted to his remark, which was probably a sign of the strain she was under. "Wait a minute, I'm sorry," she apologized. "Look let me make it up to you by treating you to dinner tonight."

Jack was stunned by her change in attitude and nodded dumbly. This woman was anything but predictable. What a nice change, he thought.

"Don't relax too much I still might bite your head off every now and then," said Bridget as they made their way to the elevator. She began to feel that there definitely was chemistry at work between her and Jack Cates. She couldn't decide whether to keep herself in check or just go with the flow.

"I'll need to change my shirt first, it's covered in blood," said Jack as they reached the basement car park.

"Don't worry about that," replied Bridget, "I'll drop by my apartment and you can use one of Simon's shirts. You're about the same size as him, just with different packaging," she smiled.

Jack picked up on Bridget's last comment and felt pleased that he was finally starting to communicate with her and that she had relaxed her adversarial stance. The thaw was gradual, but definite, and it was coming from both directions. Jack found that he wasn't just warming to Bridget as a person, he was beginning to see that underneath her brittle façade she was a terrific woman. So she didn't have Elsa's beauty, or body, but women like Elsa are rare, and Bridget had more than just looks. She was funny, smart and quick witted and kept cool under pressure. Most women would have gone to pieces from an attack with the ferocity of the one she had just experienced. Her attacker used raw violence to try and intimidate her, and naturally she had been frightened, but through it all she never lost her composure. The woman would be hard to handle in the boardroom, or in any situation and Jack now understood how Bridget was able to take over the running of the NMP after Walsh had been sent down.

Jack suddenly realized that he was in danger of letting his feelings get in the way of business and he wasn't going to let that happen after so many months of planning and preparation. Nevertheless he couldn't help but compare Bridget with Elsa. He was a natural predator of women and although Elsa had gotten much closer to the real him than any other woman before her, she never really changed this instinct in him, or stopped him from taking advantage of other potential conquests if the opportunity presented itself. After only a short time with Bridget he was beginning to see a new dimension to women that went beyond their obvious attributes.

Jack felt more than a little uneasy putting on one of Simon Walsh's shirts, in the bedroom of Walsh's apartment, and about to go out to dinner with his wife. He hadn't figured on the affect that getting so close to the people he was trying to rip off would have on him. In all of his previous dealings he had maintained a safe clinical distance from his victims. Getting underneath Bridget's skin and relating to her as a person also had its pitfalls, which could make the final task of getting money out of her more difficult if there were complications and he needed to exert more pressure on her. He couldn't let his feelings influence his business sense.

They went to a quiet restaurant and spent most of the night talking about anything and everything except Simon Walsh. Before he left Jack advised Bridget not to quote the exact figure Elsa was demanding from her husband, as Tuzio was still unsure about the amount he could squeeze out of Walsh. If she had trouble getting the whole of the 5 million, he would offer Tuzio a lower figure. Jack said it would be in her husband's best interests if he didn't know how much Elsa was asking for as it would give them more flexibility in completing negotiations with her if they needed to persuade her to take a lower amount. The real reason was because Jack didn't want everyone in the loop to know all the details, particularly Vincent Tuzio who was not expecting such a large sum of money. Bridget was already thinking about options for getting the money and planning how to float Simon's shares in the NMP to get the best price.

9

As Bridget drove to Florida State Correctional Facility from Miami Airport she had mixed feelings about seeing Simon again after two months. She thought that he would try to make an issue about her not coming to him sooner, but she hoped that any complaints from him would be short lived because they had more important things to talk about. It was a gray day, which matched her mood and she could feel herself beginning to tense as the prison came into view. During her separation from Simon she had felt relaxed and at peace with herself, but now her old animosities and resentments began to bubble to the surface once more.

Since her meeting with Jack Cates, Bridget had searched for the best way of coming up with the 5 million dollars that Tuzio wanted. Simon had some property, land and the sports cruiser that she could sell. The sports cruiser would only fetch a few hundred thousand dollars and the process of selling property or land could be long and drawn out. Bridget decided the best way of getting the money quickly would be using the shares Simon had in the NMP, but to do that she would have to talk numbers with her husband.

Bridget was searched before going into the visitors' room. She had brought a couple of books for Simon to read, some bread rolls, cooked ham and a jar of French mustard. She was also carrying her handbag and a large brown envelope and was having to juggle the items in her hands as she showed them to the guard. The guard look quizzically at the mustard and Bridget volunteered that it was a particular favorite of her husband. The guard nodded and ushered her forward.

The visiting room was open with several tables strewn around the room, some which were already being used. Bridget walked to a free table near the right wall of the room and took a seat, feeling that it would be more private than one of the tables in the open area. Simon appeared in the doorway in the wall facing the table where Bridget was sitting. He gave Bridget a broad smile and walked over towards her eagerly. Bridget remained seated as he got to the table and turned her cheek towards him as he bent forward to kiss her. Simon paused for a moment, pecked her on the cheek and took the seat opposite.

"How are you Simon," said Bridget with as much enthusiasm as she could muster.

"I guess I'm as well as can be expected," replied Walsh "It was all very strange when I arrived here but Vincent Tuzio has been showing me the ropes and now that I know the way things are done in here, I feel more confident about looking after myself."

"Jack Cates said you had been beaten up. Why didn't you tell me about it?"

Walsh looked at his wife for a moment and wondered if she would have felt the slightest concern about the incident. "It was a simple misunderstanding, I was mistaken for somebody else. Now that I'm in with the right people it shouldn't happen again."

"What do you mean? People that can protect you in here?"

"Yeah that's exactly the way things work in here. You've got to have a "mentor," he replied smiling to himself at the absurdity of what he had just said.

Bridget handed over the books and food. Walsh looked grateful when he saw the jar of French mustard and nodded thanks to Bridget at her thoughtfulness. "Jack Cates has also told me how much money Elsa Bartelli wants to spring you from prison." Bridget paused waiting for her husband to get his mind back on track, "she wants 5 million dollars." Bridget restrained herself from mentioning that Vincent Tuzio might be controlling things in the background. If Tuzio was keeping Simon safe, she wanted things to remain that way.

The expression on Walsh's face quickly changed. "Where on earth am I going to get that kind of money?" His mood quickly changed from joy to depression because he knew he didn't have quick access to anything like that amount of cash.

"I've been juggling with different strategies for getting the money since being told what Bartelli wants by Mr. Cates, but I think that there's only one way to come up with that big a sum. We can sell some of your shares in the NMP. You have a 5 percent shareholding in the Company worth about 10 million dollars at today's rate. I've spoken to the other Directors and we've all agreed to buy half your shares to give you the 5 million dollars."

"I can't do that," spluttered Walsh, "it's the family stake in the business that I'd be selling out. What about the property and land Dad left me?"

"You could go that route but it would take months instead of weeks to get you out of here. You'd still have a 2.5 percent shareholding and I would buy a three quarter percent of your stake, which would still leave us with over 3 percent in the Company."

"Now I understand your real strategy. You just want to get your claws into my Company," retorted Walsh, looking for a hidden objective behind Bridget's offer to buy some of his shares. His innate insecurity was beginning to show itself and the fact that he was naturally suspicious of anything he didn't have a direct control over only served to heighten his paranoia. Walsh's insecurity and suspicion were feeding off each other and Bridget questioned why she was going to this trouble for such an ungrateful bastard, but could understand his feeling of failure and letting down his father. His hands started to tremble and he began to stutter. "Don't take away my company Bridget," he pleaded.

Bridget held back from giving him a sharp answer, understanding the pressure her husband was under, and the isolation and vulnerability he must be feeling while in prison. She spoke to him firmly, but gently. "Simon, first of all it's not your Company. There are several shareholders with more money invested in the company than you have, and the major battle at the next AGM will be in persuading them not to get rid of me to install a new Chief Executive, who is not named Walsh. I've been working nearly every hour around the clock to show that business has increased since your trial and that the Walsh name has not had an adverse effect on public confidence in the Company. Your release from jail will send out the message that you committed no crime and that the Company is in safe hands."

Walsh paused to reflect on what his wife had just said. The tremor in his hands subsided and he began to take control of the downward spiral his mind had started to follow. He tried to rationalize his situation. He knew he would end up serving less than 20 years, but even if he only served the minimum 10 years of his sentence, it was still a death sentence because he was never going to tough it out for the next 2 or 3 years. Up to now he had steered clear of Caine since their meeting in the washroom, but he couldn't keep avoiding him forever. Despite his natural tendency to avoid confrontation, he decided it was essential that he took control of his own destiny and acted positively to get out of this hell hole. "You're right. I'm sorry honey. I know you've only got my best interests at heart, so can you arrange it? I'll give you power of proxy to sell the shares."

"I've got a proxy mandate here," replied Bridget taking a piece of paper from the brown envelope and a pen from her handbag. "We can get one of the guards to witness it."

There were other things for Walsh to countersign, as he was still officially the key signatory for the NMP. Bridget was the acting Chief Executive but she couldn't sign legal documents or contracts without Simon's counter signature.

Bridget prepared to go after Walsh had finished signing the documents she had brought with her. "Can you manage to come here a little more often? It's been so good seeing you again," said Walsh, trying not to sound too needy.

Bridget's stomach dropped. She thought that she had escaped this scene and was caught off guard. "I've told you how hard I've been working trying to maintain your association with the Company and keeping the Walsh name intact," she replied defensively.

"I've been here over 2 months and this is only the second time that you've come to see me, and this visit has only happened because there were some business documents you wanted me to sign. I know we're not as close as we should be and I've got no right to expect more, but since we got married I've grown to love you. I had hoped you'd grow to love me too." Walsh could see Bridget begin to tense when he proclaimed his love for her. Desperately he added, "I only went with those other women because you were so cold to me."

"This isn't the time or place to go into this right now," interrupted Bridget, "we can talk about our future when this is all over and you're free."

"I need some sort of commitment from you here and now. There's nowhere else we can talk about it," retorted Walsh, peeved at having to justify his sexual indiscretions. If she had behaved the way a wife should have he may have stopped his philandering.

"The only commitment I can give you now is to promise to sort this mess out for you. Now that you've given me the go ahead to sell some of your NMP shares, I'll get you out of here as quickly as I can. After that we can talk about what happens to us." As far as Bridget was concerned they didn't have any kind of future together. When Simon got out of prison she was now determined that she would demand a divorce.

Bridget picked up the envelope with the documents and her handbag and got up to leave. Simon grabbed hold of her free hand and looked up pleadingly, "You will try to come more often won't you?" he asked.

Bridget smiled weakly and nodded and then pulled away from him. "I'll call you when the shares have been sold and arrangements have been confirmed for Bartelli to go to the police. You'll be out of here soon, I promise." She leaned over and pecked him on the cheek and left.

"She still had some visiting time left," said one of the guards to Walsh as he left the Visitors Room.

"Yeah, but she had a flight to catch back to New York, otherwise she would have stayed longer," replied Walsh.

Walsh went back to the recreation area where several prisoners were sitting around talking. One group were pumping weights, and there was a game of touch football being played on the far side of the sports field. Walsh sat down on his haunches with his back against a small brick wall bounding the concreted area of the yard. He started to think about Bridget's plan to sell his shares. He wasn't happy but in his present situation there was little he could do but accept her plan.

"Hey man, how's the missus?" said Vincent Tuzio, squatting down to join him.

"She's much the same as the last time I saw her, when she first visited. I tried to make peace with her, but she's still a cold hearted bitch."

"Don't let any woman get to you man, that's the quickest way to self-destruction. Be cool, the important thing for you right now is to get through the rest of your time here safely, get yourself free and then you can have a say in how she acts or what she does. Did she say how much Elsa wants to get you outta here?"

"She wants more than I can get my hands on. I'm going to have to sell some of my shares in NMP."

"I wudda thought you could muster a couple of hundred thou or so without too much trouble."

"Two hundred thousand wouldn't have been any trouble, but 5 million is a bit rich for most people's blood."

Vincent Tuzio was stopped in his tracks. The amount Walsh had mentioned bore no resemblance to the figure that Jack Cates had given him. He suddenly felt that he was being played for a sucker. He was getting 40 thousand dollars and Green and Norton were getting another 20 thousand each from the deal. He expected that Jack and Elsa would be getting about 120 thousand, because they had set up the deal. This was different. If the payoff was 5 million dollars he should be getting a lot more.

10

Jack was in the shower when he heard his phone ringing. Normally he would have just ignored it, but he was expecting Bridget to contact him about the progress she was making in getting the money for Walsh's release. He quickly ran a towel over himself and then wrapped it around his waist before rushing into the lounge to answer the call.

"Hello, Jack Cates."

"Is that the Jack Cates who lies and cheats his friends out of money?" came the sharp response.

Jack was taken aback by the accusation and it took him a few seconds to register that it was Vincent Tuzio's voice. "What the hell are you talking about Vincent?"

"Don't play the innocent Jack. You know when you was with the NYPD you were straight. Everyone knew that. What happened to you? Now there's more twists and turns to you than there is in a pretzel. I thought you were after a couple of hundred thou from Walsh."

Jack listened intently to find out if Vincent really knew the sum they were demanding to get Walsh out of prison, or taking pot shots in the dark. Bridget had been told not to tell Walsh the amount of money being asked for Elsa's reappearance. He could sense the anger in Vincent and feared that his plan would fail without the good will of Tuzio. Al Ferrino crossed his mind and gave him an overpowering feeling of déjà vu. The immediate risk was that if Vincent felt he was being cheated out of money, he could spill the beans to Walsh out of spite. Jack acted dumb; "How can I answer you if I don't know what you're talking about? Take a deep breath and tell me what's behind this call."

"Don't play the innocent 'cos I know how much dough you're trying to squeeze out of Walsh. I'm talking about 5 million dollars man and you taking me for a chump."

"I've asked Mrs. Walsh for 5 million dollars, so what?"

"That's a lot more than the 200 thousand dollars you spoke to me about when you first roped me into this. I guess you were planning to tell me all along about the jack up in price?"

"For starters we never fixed a price. We said it could be 200 thousand bucks or it could be a million."

"I know but this seems way higher than what we talked about," replied Tuzio.

"What price did you think I would start at? I don't know what Walsh is worth. I've asked for 5 million because that seems about right, given the way he throws money around. But it's just an opening shot. At the trial he didn't have much in the bank but he's got to have other assets. And what do I do if he can't come up with that kind of money? Call it a day and let all my hard work come to nothing? No, I find out what he can afford. You've got to learn to trust your partners, otherwise we might as well end it right here." Here we go again thought Jack, I'm getting tired of this speech.

"I never said anything about quitting, man. I just want a fair share of the pot."

"Alright just stay calm Vincent, otherwise you'll blow the deal and we'll all end up with nothing."

"What about Green and Norton?" asked Tuzio.

"It's pointless getting them wound up, besides they're getting paid well just to let things happen."

"I guess things are OK then, but God help me if Green finds out about this."

"Just keep cool and nobody will be any the wiser. If I get the 5 million I'm asking for, I'll make sure you get your fair share, so don't worry about it."

"Well I haven't really got a choice, so I'm gonna have to trust you, but don't cross me Jack because I can always go to the cops. It don't matter to me 'cos I'm already inside, but you guys could end up joining me."

"I've got the message loud and clear Vincent. Goodbye."

Jack put down the receiver and sat despondently on the sofa to reflect on his conversation with Vincent. Bridget must have had a good reason for telling Walsh the sum that was being asked for. Jack had hoped that she would be vague about the details and just get Walsh's agreement for her to take whatever action was necessary to get the money. This complicated matters and Roland would not be pleased at a fourth party getting a large slice of the cake.

Jack remembered the way in which Roland had dealt with Al and decided he couldn't tell him about this latest development with Vincent. That is until it was unavoidable.

What Jack didn't know was that Frank had bugged his telephone and had been listening to his conversation with Tuzio in his car outside Jack's apartment block. Although Tuzio had threatened to blow the deal, Frank couldn't help but feel pleased that Jack's plan wasn't going as smoothly as he promised. The guy was too cocksure as far as Frank was concerned and needed to be brought down a peg or two. Roland wouldn't be happy hearing this news, but he and Lou firmly agreed they would be more than willing to bring Jack to account.

Frank and Lou had been following Jack for over a week now and they were beginning to think that nothing would come from it, but now Frank thought he had something worth reporting to Bannister. After listening to Tuzio's call to Cates he decided that he wouldn't follow Jack around town for yet another night and went back to the Blue Cockatoo instead.

Roland was interviewing a young woman for a job as a dancer when Frank went into his office. She was running through her stage routine and stopped abruptly as Frank burst into the room.

"I'm sorry Boss but I've got some important news I think you'll want to hear straight away."

"That's alright Frank. I think I'd seen enough of Carley's act anyway. Put on your clothes dear, you can start tomorrow night." Turning to Frank and taking him to one side Bannister whispered quietly, "This girl's got something. She's not as good as Elsa, but she's damn close. Hopefully she can start drawing some of the punters back."

"What's wrong? Is the club struggling?" asked Frank.

"I wouldn't say it was struggling, but it's certainly not as healthy as it was when Elsa was here. Sometimes I wonder if this fucking deal of Jack's is worth the effort."

Carley came over to Roland and thanked him for the job and left the office excitedly.

Glancing at Carley as she left the office, Frank commented, "She's good, but she won't be good enough to replace Elsa."

"I know but I keep on hoping. Anyway what have you got to tell me? It must be important for you to come straight over?"

Frank related the telephone conversation between Jack and Vincent and watched as a wry smile crossed Roland's face.

"I knew it would be a problem keeping the details of the money side of things quiet. The plan is too complicated and relies on everyone behaving in the way he expects. Jack couldn't possibly control what was said between Walsh and his wife, no matter how well he thought he'd be able to manipulate her. So Tuzio has got to find out how much the deal is worth. It will be interesting to see if Jack decides to tell me about this latest development, after all we are partners." Turning to Frank he added, "What do you bet?"

Frank shrugged, "What if Green finds out about it? He's one mean bastard and he wouldn't think twice about killing Walsh or Tuzio."

"Maybe that's a fact that can work in our favor, Frank. You know him from old don't you?"

"Yeah, but not very well, just well enough to steer clear of him. He was on Pallacio's payroll for a while, but none of the guys could get on with him. He was let go before he got too deep into the business. He was a loose cannon that could go off anytime and for any reason"

"Why? Couldn't he mix with the rest of you guys? With all due respect Frank, I wouldn't have thought you were working with a sensitive group of people, or that the group would need any kind of bonding."

"The guy was far too unpredictable and violent. He enjoyed hurting people and would resort to violence, I mean serious violence, for the slightest reason. I've learned it's best to be sparing when you dish out the pain because it's the threat of pain that gets results, not the hurt it causes. After the first few shocks it usually numbs the body and mind. OK so you have to make an example of someone every now and then, but it's just business. With Green it was pleasure."

Bannister was surprised at the clarity and homespun truth in Frank's statement. It gave him another insight into a quiet, secretive man that he knew he would never fully understand. "If young Vincent is in danger of upsetting the apple cart, we may have to call on Mr. Green's services," replied Bannister.

11

The day after seeing her husband in prison, Bridget went to the office early. She had already approached a few of the other Company Directors about buying some of Simon's shares. Initially they had been surprised, but three of them had the available cash and were interested in taking Bridget up on her offer. She instructed her broker to make the transaction and promised to send over the proxy mandate signed by Simon as proof of her authority to sell his shares.

She put down the phone after talking to her broker and it rang immediately. She was puzzled, not expecting anyone to call her outside her normal office hours, "hello" she answered tentatively.

"You don't sound on top of your game this morning Bridget. Should I call back?"

Bridget was about to ask who it was on the other end of the line when she realized it was Jack Cates calling. "Jack! I'm in the process of getting your money you'll just have to be patient."

"Don't be so defensive, I'm not hassling you about the money. I was just ringing to ask how Simon took the news. Has he got a plan for raising the cash?"

"I've provided him with a plan, but I had to go into the numbers in some detail because it involves selling some of his shares in the NMP. As I said, you'll get your money but it will take a little time. I have to talk to some people, but don't worry I'll let you know when I'm in a position to pay. Come to think of it I've never considered that, how do you want the money paid?"

"I keep telling you it's not down to me, I'm just the middle man. Vincent and Elsa want it paid into a numbered bank account in the Bahamas. Elsa will give you the details when you're ready. When she's certain the money is in her account she'll agree arrangements with you for going to the police."

"Alright, it shouldn't take more than a couple of days to tie things up. I'll get in touch with you then."

"Not so fast! I thought I might return your generosity of the other night and treat you to dinner tonight."

"I don't know Jack. It wouldn't really be a good idea in the circumstances."

"What circumstances? What's the problem? I really enjoyed your company the last time we met and I got the impression that the feeling was mutual. Just because we're both wrapped up in this business to get Simon out of prison, it doesn't mean we can't have a little fun along the way."

"Don't get any ideas about us Jack…"

"I'm not. You don't have to jump into bed with me just because I've bought you dinner. I thought you might need a little bit more of an incentive than that!"

Bridget laughed involuntarily and said, "If we get into some kind of relationship with each other it will only complicate things, and things are complicated enough as they are."

"Look in my line of business it's hard to find anyone that's genuine, never mind someone I can connect with so easily, and I just want to forget about everything else that's happening and spend a bit of time with you. Is that so hard to understand?"

Despite the circumstances in which they met, Bridget was pleased that a man like Jack was interested in her. He was obviously an inveterate womanizer, but she didn't care. It had been a long time since she felt like a woman and, more importantly, felt desirable. She decided that she would enjoy the attention and flattery as long as it was there to be had. "I'll ring you later and let you know if I can make it for dinner. I've got a busy day ahead and don't know how long I'll be at the office."

"OK" replied Jack, "but just remember I don't mind eating late."

Jack smiled to himself as he switched off his mobile phone and put it on the coffee table. He didn't think Bridget was just trying to put him off and he felt confident that she would give him a ring. He walked over to the window of his apartment and stared out at the street. He knew from Vincent that Simon Walsh was going to sell half of his stake in his father's company.

It worried him that Vincent would not keep his newfound information to himself and that Green and Norton might discover the amount of money at stake. If that happened all hell would break loose and then there would be no winners. He checked his personal organizer to see what business he had on for the day.

The only job currently on the books was the usual tailing of a suspected adulterer. When didn't he have some man or woman to follow all over the town, only to end up in some seedy hotel? This was the staple currency of his business and infidelity was rife. These days it was not fear of the shame of being caught that motivated people to go to a private investigator, but the need to put the blame on your partner, before it could be put on you. Money drove these people to Jack as the allocation of guilt could have a significant influence on the divorce settlement.

Today Jack was to follow a Tom Bartlett who was in town with his secretary to attend an IT convention. Bartlett sold computer systems to businesses and followed up by providing technical support with troubleshooting and maintenance during operation. He started his own business in the mid-eighties when PC computer systems were starting to get a hold. It grew steadily, if not spectacularly through to the early nineties and he eventually sold out to a larger company that wanted his contacts. He stayed on in sales because he enjoyed the work and was hooked on the adrenaline rush he got after a big sale.

Bartlett's secretary was Helen Broadbent, a sassy good-looking girl who probably saw her boss as a stepping-stone to the bigger players in the company. At 23 she was 35 years younger than Bartlett and Jack wondered how anyone of Bartlett's age could delude themselves that any good looking young woman would be interested in anything other than getting whatever benefits they could from such a relationship, before moving on . The convention was scheduled to run for 2 days and Bartlett was manning his company's stand. It would be easy for Jack to mingle with the crowd and follow his man after he left the convention. There was no need to get to the convention until late afternoon, so Jack decided to visit his Mom and Dad before starting work.

Jack's dad was a retired cop, who had been in the police force for over thirty years. Franklin Cates hadn't distinguished himself in service, as his main occupation during his long career seemed to be the arrest of drunks, vagrants and prostitutes. His superiors considered him to be dependable rather than dynamic or innovative and he watched others leap frog over him in the promotion stakes, while he stayed pounding the streets. Many of the rookies he had broken into the service ended up being his superiors, with some making it to Lieutenant and Captain, but it didn't seem to bother him. His true worth was never fully appreciated as he spent most of his time taking preventative measures to avoid difficult situations developing. In his time with NYPD he built a finely honed knowledge of the streets and a deep understanding of people, but this approach is now a thing of the past.

Jack walked into the kitchen of his parent's house and his childhood years came flooding back as the familiar sights and smells of his home filled his senses. "Anyone here?" he shouted as he picked up a warm cookie from a plate on the kitchen table and walked into the lounge. His dad was catching forty winks on the sofa and his mom was reading the paper while sat in the armchair next to the fire. "Don't you ever lock the door?" he asked his Mom.

"Only when we go to bed. We've lived here for over 25 years and our door is always open to our friends and neighbors. Besides they all know that Frank's a cop."

"Used to be a cop," corrected Jack. He smiled at his mother and bent over to kiss her on the cheek. She graciously offered her cheek without taking her eyes off the article she was reading, but she was always overjoyed when Jack visited. Emily Cates was the mother of 3 children, 2 boys and a girl. Jack was the youngest boy and had always shown a wild spirit that was the envy of his siblings. Frank Jnr, his older brother, had gone to New York University and eventually became a corporate lawyer. His sister Kate became a medical secretary and settled down with one of the doctors at the practice where she worked. She eventually moved out to Idaho with her husband and Jack had only seen her once since the move. She brought her family back to New York for Christmas a couple of years after leaving the Big Apple.

"What have you been doing lately, or shouldn't I ask?" said his mother, pausing to look over the rim of her glasses. It was a penetrating look that always made Jack feel uncomfortable, as if she knew he had something to hide. Emily couldn't possibly have any idea of the distasteful activities her son was involved in, but her undoubted love for him didn't blind her to his frailties and the kind of world he moved in.

"Nothing in particular. I came over to find out if dad would help me with tailing someone on a divorce case. A business man is banging his secretary and his wife wants me to get a bit of dirt on him."

"Why do you do this for a living? I wasn't happy when you were with NYPD but the work was a lot more respectable than the things you're taking on now."

"It was also a lot more dangerous with NYPD and it's this kind of work keeps me in business. Without it I'd have to get some other job, probably working in a stuffy office somewhere and slowly going mad."

"What do I get for helping you?" chipped in Jack's dad.

"It's rude to eavesdrop on conversations," retorted Jack.

"How can I help but eavesdrop if I'm in the same room? Besides you should have known that any policeman, sorry ex policeman, worth his salt is always listening out for everything and anything. What's the job?"

"There's an IT convention across town and a couple of people are using it as an excuse to get their rocks off. Tom Bartlett's a senior salesman who's manning one of the stands with his attractive PA. His wife suspects that something is going on and she's hired me to find out if there's any foundation to her suspicions and to get proof if there is."

"What's his wife like?" asked Jack's dad.

"Don't know. I've only spoken to her on the phone. She called me up and asked for a quote for a couple of days work. I gave her the bottom line and she followed it up with pictures of her husband and his secretary, a brochure for the convention and most importantly a check."

"What do you want me for, it doesn't sound too difficult a job?"

"Bartlett and his secretary are booked into separate rooms at their hotel, it might help to follow each of them if they don't stick together. If nothing else it will prevent me running between the two hotel rooms and missing both of them. Mind you they're bound to come together sometime, but in which bedroom?"

Jack's Mom gave him a stern look and his Dad tried to suppress a smile. "Good enough Son," said his Dad enthusiastically, "I wasn't doing anything so let's go!"

"You know there's no stopping him if he can play policemen again," interjected Emily derisively.

By the time Jack and Franklin got to the IT convention it was three thirty. Bartlett's wife had written on the convention brochure the number of the stand that her husband would be manning. The two men got their bearings and decided to separately move toward the stand from opposite directions. It was unlikely that Bartlett would have any inkling that his wife was onto him, but Jack thought it better that they separate as he didn't want to raise his suspicions by arriving at the stand "mob handed". Jack would portray himself as a company man looking for a new accounting / payroll system, whereas his Dad would act as an enthusiastic amateur trying to keep up with the latest technology. Jack hoped that neither of them would get involved in any deep conversations as their combined knowledge of computer technology would be unlikely to convince the average nine year old that they had any idea of what a PC should be used for.

Jack arrived in the area of the stand first and saw Bartlett talking animatedly to a couple of business types. Bartlett sat down at a desktop PC and started to punch the keyboard furiously, obviously needing to demonstrate some feature of the accounting system he was trying to sell. The men seemed impressed with the information they were being given, occasionally nodding to show their understanding. Jack looked around for Helen Broadbent but couldn't see her on the stand or in the immediate area. He wondered if she had already gone back to the hotel and cursed himself for not coming to the convention earlier.

He walked around the area scanning the crowds hoping Helen would be browsing some of the other stands. He felt a tap on his shoulder and turned to see his Dad making an access way for a young lady carrying a tray of cups filled with coffee. "Thank you sir, just let the young lady through," and turning to the young woman he added, "Careful dear you haven't carried the tray this far to drop it now."

With that he put his arm around her shoulder and steered her to Bartlett's stand.

Of course the young woman was Helen Broadbent and Jack's Dad had ingratiated himself by helping her navigate through the crowd safely, whilst carrying two cups of coffee. She was extremely attractive and her coloring and well defined features reminded Jack of a younger Elsa. Her pairing with Bartlett seemed even more incongruous as the man had no physical attributes that would seemingly appeal to someone like Helen, who must be able to pick and choose from a host of younger men. Jack's Dad followed her to the stand and was about to take his leave when Helen offered him one of the coffee cups. He politely refused but Helen insisted and he eventually accepted her offer. Franklin and Helen chatted while Bartlett was dealing with his customers.

Bartlett seemed to successfully conclude his sales pitch, taking business cards from each of the men. He walked over to where Franklin and Helen were standing and was introduced to Jack's Dad. The two men shook hands and spoke for a while. Eventually Franklin finished his coffee, bade farewell to the couple and walked off. Jack collared his Dad when they were out of the view of Bartlett and Helen. "OK. What was that all about?"

"It was pure chance. She was struggling with the coffee tray and I just helped her through the crowd."

"Well you seemed to be talking for a long time. What did she say?"

"She's a very nice girl Jack. I just can't believe she's the type of girl that you think she is. I'm a good judge of character and she's no flighty piece playing games with Bartlett. She obviously thinks a lot of her boss, but it's out of concern for his welfare, nothing more. I'm telling you she's a nice girl."

"Look Dad you were only talking with her for a few minutes. You can't possibly make any accurate judgements about the type of person she is, or on the relationship between her and Bartlett, after such a short time."

"I know people Son. Thirty odd years dealing with the good and the bad taught me how to differentiate one from the other. She's a good person. There's something not right about this. I can feel it."

"Never mind your feelings. We'll find out if you're right when we follow them back to their hotel. If they split up you'd better take Bartlett, now that you've made such a good impression with Helen."

The next hour dragged and Jack was beginning to wish he hadn't taken the job when Bartlett started to shut down the computers and Helen busied herself by tidying the stand. Throughout the time Jack had observed Bartlett and Helen he hadn't noticed any signs of intimacy that might have betrayed any romantic feelings towards one another. Bartlett was certainly a tactile person and obviously cared for his PA, but his contact with her was simply affectionate in a caring, almost fatherly, way.

Jack and Frank followed their targets to their hotel. Helen had booked herself and Bartlett into separate rooms and Jack wondered if the action was a deception to conceal their relationship from their business colleagues. After checking in at the hotel reception they went to their separate rooms.

"I don't think it's worth carrying on with the surveillance. I think you're right Dad, there's nothing going on here. I'll just make out a report for Mrs. Bartlett and get shut of this case," said Jack, as he and Franklin sat in the hotel lobby.

"What are you so tetchy about? Is it such a surprise that a man and a woman can be good friends without sex rearing its head?"

"It's not that, Dad. In a way I'm pleased that this job hasn't followed the usual sleazy pattern, with me trying to eavesdrop on their pillow talk. I think I've had as much of this type of work as I can stomach."

"That's as maybe but if you're being paid to do a job you're going to do it well. OK?"

Jack was a little startled by his Dad's gentle reprimand and smiled inwardly at his concern over the quality of the service his son was providing. "It's just that I've got better things to do tonight. If I thought that these two were really having an affair and that I could get some incriminating evidence for Mrs. Bartlett, then I'd stay 'til the bitter end. But that's not going to happen and I'm going to end up sitting here all night for nothing, when I can spend it in a much more pleasant way."

"Oh I see. You've got a date lined up, well I'm glad to see you're starting to have some fun after Elsa. Since her death you've been quiet in that department."

Jack was amused at his Dad's quaint turn of phrase and hated lying to him about Elsa, but knew his father was too honest to condone blackmail. Franklin was also unaware of Jack's other activities with Elsa to squeeze money out of gullible punters looking for kicks outside their marriage. The less he knew the better thought Jack. "You're right of course, I've met this woman who has turned me on my head. We've only known each other a short time but I already feel different towards her than to any other woman I've met, including Elsa." Jack spoke the words without thinking about their meaning until he'd finished talking and suddenly found that he was really speaking from the heart. Strangely his Dad, rather than his mother, was always able to tap into his true feelings and Jack was comforted by the fact that he was non – judgmental.

"This woman must be special, Son. I've never heard you speak so affectionately of anyone before. You go and meet her and I'll carry on with the surveillance so that you don't let down Mrs. Bartlett."

"Dad I can't…."

"Don't be stupid. You said yourself that there was nothing to this case. Besides it will make me feel like a policeman again."

Jack warmly shook his father's hand, thanked him and left. It was now seven-thirty, too early to call Bridget, which gave him time to get back to his apartment to freshen up before meeting her later.

12

When Jack got back to his apartment he heard the bleep of his answer phone. He pressed the playback button and heard Elsa's voice telling him to call back. He took off his jacket, threw it on the sofa and reluctantly dialed Elsa's number. Julie answered the phone and shouted to Elsa that Jack was calling.

"Hi Jack. I'm so grateful that you've found time to give me a call. I know how busy you are," said Elsa with her now familiar sarcasm.

"C'mon don't be like that Elsa, I've been out all day on an adultery case. Except that it's not adultery, just two nice people who get on well and care about each other. Y'know the way we used to be."

"What do you mean?" demanded Elsa.

"Nothing Elsa. It's a poor joke and too complicated to go into over the phone. All I can say is that I can't wait to quit being a private dick because I'm starting to develop a social conscience. Don't worry that's not important, what do you want?"

"I've told you what I want often enough Jack, do I have to tell you again? I want to get my fucking life back," Elsa shouted into the mouthpiece.

"OK I hear you loud and clear. We're nearly there baby, just be patient a little bit longer. Bridget is selling some of Walsh's stock in the NMP to raise the money we want. There are a couple of people on the Board of Directors who are very interested so it shouldn't be long now."

"So it's Bridget now. I didn't realize you were getting so close to her. It didn't strike me that she was your kind of woman, after all you're a tits and ass man aren't you?"

"Look there's no need for that kind of talk Elsa. Yes I am friendly with her because there's no sense in making this thing more difficult than it has to be. Everybody's tense because we're so close to the end. We've just got to keep hold of our nerve a little bit longer."

"I hear you Jack and believe me I've no intention of giving up at this late stage of the game. So when will you be visiting me again, it's been nearly 3 months."

"You'll be coming to me down here. It's only going to take Bridget a few days to secure the money and I'll arrange a meeting between you and her so that you can give her your new bank account details."

"Why me! I don't think our meeting will turn out to be a very pleasant experience for me. After all I'm the cause of her husband being locked up."

"We've already spoken about this," said Jack patiently. "Bridget mustn't think that I'm involved in the blackmail, otherwise I'll never get her trust and she may end up going to the police behind my back. She'll then rely on me to make arrangements with you to go down to Miami and report to the police."

"OK Jack, I wouldn't want to be the one to sully her high opinion of you!"

"Once the money's in the bank I'll be up there to celebrate with you and Julie. Perhaps we can get Roland to let his hair down too."

"Gee, I can't wait," replied Elsa with mock enthusiasm, putting the phone down abruptly.

Jack pulled the phone away from his ear and stared at it intensely for a few seconds before slamming it down angrily. God knows he sympathized with Elsa's situation and at times wished he'd never embarked on this venture, but now they were so close to the end it was pointless letting emotions take control. She was like a dripping tap always coming out with the same thing over and over. It wasn't as if it would make things happen any sooner. He didn't really appreciate that time was moving much slower for Elsa than it was for him.

Jack delayed calling Bridget until he was calm, as any anxiety in his voice would be easily detectable over the telephone. He decided to take a shower to give him time to cool down. By the time he'd finished showering it was eight fifteen, which was time enough to wait for a call from Bridget. She had said that she would call, but he didn't want to risk leaving it too late in case she forgot or simply decided not to ring him. He picked up his cell phone and found that Bridget had sent him a text message, asking him to meet her at nine – thirty at the Pacific Pearl in Chinatown. Jack wasn't overly fond of Chinese food, but that wouldn't stop him keeping the date. He walked into the Pacific Pearl restaurant at nine twenty to make sure he got there first.

Bridget arrived at the restaurant 10 minutes late, apologizing that she was delayed because of a telephone call she'd received from her broker confirming the sale of Simon's shares. She explained that one of the buyers was reliant on the sale of other shares to finance his purchase. She herself had bought a three quarter percent interest in the Company and finally felt that she was an integral part of the organization. She felt happier than at any other time since meeting Simon Walsh and also felt that she had gained a hard earned independence from him.

"Well in that case, tonight we should celebrate," said Jack, feeling a hollow ring inside himself after his earlier promise to Elsa. "When will you be able to pay Elsa and Vincent?"

"Either tomorrow or the day after."

"Good, I'll arrange a meeting between you and Elsa," said Jack. "She's sent me instructions by e-mail. So on whichever day you're ready we're to take the interstate North at 10:00 AM, drive for an hour and then call her to get further instructions on where to meet. I'll confirm the day and time with her as soon as you say that I can."

"That's the business done with, now let's get on with the rest of the evening," said Bridget. "I've developed a powerful hunger from all of this high powered wheeling and dealing, and seeing as you're footing the bill, I think I'll indulge myself," she added.

When the waiter brought the menus, Bridget could see the discomfort in Jack's face and asked him if he was familiar with Chinese cuisine. Jack shrugged his shoulders and said he was from good Irish stock and if his food didn't come from a cow or wasn't in a stew he was in trouble. Bridget laughed and offered to order for him and Jack readily accepted. When the waiter brought Jack a bottle of beer he felt more at home and his mind sought refuge with the bottle, not for the drink inside it, but as a familiar landmark in this culinary mystery tour.

Bridget enjoyed watching Jack trying to come to terms with chopsticks and was pleased that he resolutely persevered rather than give up on the complexity of trapping a small morsel of food between two wooden sticks. He tried each of the dishes that were put in front of him cursing under his breath every time he dropped a piece of food. He joked about the idea of using chopsticks for every meal to lose a few extra pounds of weight, as he was bound to drop more food than he would be able to put in his mouth. Both Jack and Bridget were enjoying the meal at the restaurant and each other's company. Their mood was light and relaxed and as it developed Jack and Bridget became more and more intimate in their conversation.

"It's funny," said Bridget, "I'll be giving you 5 million dollars tomorrow or the day after, but I feel as if I haven't got a care in the world. A great weight has been lifted from off my shoulders and it's all I can do to keep my feet on the ground. I can even handle the prospect of Simon being released, which is something I've been secretly dreading ever since he first told me to call you. I guess that sounds pretty awful, doesn't it?"

"No not at all. You're forgetting I got a pretty good impression of what he's like from what I read in the papers about the trial. What will you do when he comes out?"

"Well we won't be living together again as man and wife that's for certain. Not that we ever did have a proper marriage. He can stay with me until he finds somewhere else to live, but I'm going to file for divorce as soon as I can get a lawyer onto the case. I've been living a lie for far too long."

"It's obvious you don't love him, and maybe you've never loved him, why did you marry him in the first place?"

"It's a complicated story Jack and I don't want to change the mood of the evening by relating the sordid details to you now. I'll save that for another time. What about you? Is there a little woman somewhere that you don't want to tell me about? I can't believe a man like you hasn't got a string of beautiful girls waiting for you to call."

"Well it would be pointless of me to try and convince you that I've led a sheltered life, if that's what you mean? But I can truthfully say that I've never felt as spiritually close to anyone as I do with you right now. Yes, I've slept with a lot of women, but that doesn't mean a thing because we never really got beyond the sex. It's different, with you. I don't just want your body, I also want the person inside. This is a new experience for me, because honesty doesn't come easily, but I want you to know exactly how I feel."

Bridget was hanging on his every word. She was reliving the innocent dream she had cherished before Simon Walsh had shattered it. After her years with Simon and the loss of her innocence, the cynical side of her nature was screaming that she should not to let this man wheedle his way into her affections. Deep down she knew that any kind of relationship with a man like Jack Cates could only end in grief, but she didn't care. To hell with being level headed, she thought, she was going to enjoy the moment.

Jack was getting a little nervous because Bridget was sitting quietly soaking up his words without interjecting or reinforcing his belief that she had any similar feelings about him. "I think I love you," he stammered before he realized what he was saying. It was the first time he'd ever opened himself to another person and suddenly felt very vulnerable and afraid of her rejection. He wanted to say more but held back for fear of sounding clichéd or hollow.

Bridget had been looking deep into Jack's eyes during his out pouring and could feel the strength in the sincerity of his words, and that they were coming from deep within his soul. Her mind was racing trying to come to terms with the roller coaster ride of her emotions. A silence descended over them until finally her mouth turned up at the corners in a warm smile and she placed her hand on top of his, "I don't know why, but I feel the same way about you Jack. I've tried to hate you for so long because of your involvement with Tuzio and Bartelli. I don't care about that or anything else and I'm going to trust my feelings and go with my heart. Let's pay the bill and go back to my place."

Jack felt elated and took hold of Bridget's hand and called over the waiter to pay the bill. By the time they reached Bridget's apartment it was twelve-thirty and her maid Francesca had gone to bed. Bridget put her straightened index finger against her lip, indicating the need to be quiet to Jack. He smiled knowingly, while at the same time trying to control the urge to grasp Bridget and crush her in a smoldering embrace. They stood in the hall staring at each other and gently kissed for the first time. An electric charge passed between them slowly releasing all the pent up frustration they had both been feeling over the past few days.

Bridget gently pushed Jack away and went into the kitchen to reappear with a bottle of wine and two glasses in one hand. She grabbed Jack's tie with her free hand and led him to the bedroom door at the far end of the hall off the lobby. Jack opened the door and lifted Bridget up into his arms and carried her over the threshold to the bedroom and walked over to the bed. He began to kiss Bridget on the neck and she nestled Jacks head affectionately feeling the tension drain from her body. Jack placed one knee on the bed and gently lowered Bridget onto the covers and leaned lightly on top of her as his kissing became more passionate.

Bridget eased herself further onto the bed, stretched over to put the wine bottle and glasses onto the bedside table and then quickly started to remove Jack's jacket, tie and shirt. Jack started to reciprocate by undoing the clips on the back of Bridget's dress. She stopped him and rolled him onto his back, hitched up her dress and sat astride his hips. Then she crossed her hands to grab the hem of her dress and slowly lifted the garment over her head and threw it to the floor, leaving herself in her bra and panties. Jack sat up and put his hands either side of her face, and pulling her towards him began kissing her again.

Bridget released herself, moved down in the bed and started to hurriedly unzipped Jacks trousers as he kicked off his shoes. She discovered that he was wearing a pair of tartan socks, which made her laugh out loud unconsciously, but she quickly checked herself in fear of waking Francesca. Jack took the opportunity to remove his pants and socks and then grabbed Bridget and fell back onto the bed. He quickly removed the remainder of her garments and their naked bodies entwined as they explored each other with their hands and mouths. Bridget was floating on a sensual cloud, responding to every touch, kiss and caress from Jack. Her back arched towards him as he slowly ran his hand across her breasts and stomach and let it nestle between her legs, teasing her clitoris. She eagerly tried to thrust herself into his hand wanting to feel him inside her.

Jack could sense that Bridget was sexually inexperienced and wanted to give her as much pleasure as he could before she climaxed. They both writhed and moaned as they explored each other's senses and finally joined in a crescendo of passion as their bodies exploded. They cuddled and caressed each other as the passion subsided and then got under the covers content just to be close to each other.

They both lay silently, locked in each other's embrace trying to believe that the impossible had just happened. Eventually they withdrew from their trance and sat up against the headboard. Jack poured wine into the two glasses and handed one to Bridget. They smiled at each other, clinked glasses and took a sip of wine. Jack put his free arm around Bridget and she nestled into his body. Jack bent his head to kiss Bridget on the lips and whispered, "I love you."

"That won't get you off the hook," replied Bridget, "I've got a lot to make up for, so recharge your batteries because I'm going to attack you after I've emptied this glass!" Jack smiled and poured the last dregs of his glass over her breasts. Bridget tensed as the cold wine touched her skin, but instead of retaliating she pushed the sheet back and slowly poured her wine over her naked body and said, "OK tiger, lick it off." Jack winced when he remembered that Elsa had done the same thing just a few months earlier.

13

In the end everything happened more quickly than Jack had expected. Bridget rang him to let him know that all the financial details of the share transaction had been finalized and that she was now in a position, albeit reluctantly, to pay Elsa. Jack put down the phone and immediately called Elsa to arrange a venue for her meeting with Bridget. They decided to meet at a roadhouse, roughly half way between New York and Boston. The next day Jack picked up Bridget from her apartment and they began their drive along the Interstate.

"What do you think she's really like?" asked Bridget.

The meeting between these two women had worried Jack, initially because of the current temperament of Elsa, but now he had added another layer of complexity by falling in love with Bridget. He had considered the meeting between the two women as an essential piece of the strategy to convince Bridget that he was not one of the blackmailers and that he could be trusted to make sure Elsa reported to the police, as promised. He hadn't expected to win Bridget's confidence so completely and that she would reconcile herself to having to talk to Elsa and pay the money into her offshore bank account so readily. After receipt, the money would be moved through a number of bank accounts to hide its trail, just in case Bridget went to the police after Simon's release.

In hindsight he realized he had been stupid to get so involved with her, because there was no question that in the long run it would cause major problems, not only between him and Elsa, but also with Roland. He had given him more latitude than he had expected, probably because of his infatuation with Elsa. But without Elsa he was vulnerable and if she wanted him dead, Bannister would surely be only too happy to oblige. Bridget's question focused Jack's mind on the upcoming meeting and the possibility of something going wrong. "What do you think she's like," countered Jack, avoiding the request to give his opinion of Elsa.

"She's a common prostitute, that's been established in court, but I'm still unclear on the real reason she searched out Simon. It can't have been simply to turn a trick, because she was a long way from her home patch. I know Simon has a reputation, but there must have been better ways of trying to compromise him than getting him alone on his boat, which worked against her when things turned sour because she had nowhere to run. She must be dumb to boot to put herself in such an awkward situation," Bridget concluded.

"Well she's doesn't seem so dumb now, she's getting 5 million bucks out of Simon." Jack didn't like the derogatory tone in Bridget's voice when she spoke about Elsa and couldn't stop himself from making the jibe. He immediately regretted it and braced himself for a tongue-lashing.

"I guess you're right," replied Bridget calmly, "but the fact that she's still around and able to extort money from me, may have more to do with dumb luck in the way things happened. She may have swum back to the shore, but I think it's more likely that Simon's boat was followed and she was picked up later. Her savior could be Tuzio, the "brains" behind the scheme, or whoever has kept her in hiding all of these months. That's why I was so suspicious of you, but now I don't really care. The machinations of the people behind all this just washes over me and I'll be glad when it's all over," said Bridget relaxing in the car seat. "Now that I'm resigned to paying the money, I don't want to spend too much time thinking about it."

Jack began to relax until Bridget added, "But I've often wondered what Elsa's like as a person. I couldn't do what she does for a living, lap dancing or prostituting myself. What makes a person stoop to do that kind of thing?"

Jack detected a softening in Bridget's attitude towards Elsa, but was still worried that she might start moralizing or talking down to her when they met, which really would set the fur flying between them. If he could nurture a feeling of compassion in Bridget as they travelled to the roadhouse it could make the confrontation with Elsa a lot easier. "There are probably good reasons why she chose the kind of life she leads. Don't let the caricature built by the media influence your opinion of her. I know that there's all sorts of pressures that can make women do things which are much worse than lap dancing," he ventured, hoping that the mellowing of Bridget's attitude would minimize the probability of friction between the two women.

Bridget fell silent, staring out of the car window to study the landscape, and Jack wondered whether she had tired of the conversation about Elsa or if she was trying to think of something else to ask him about her. "Would you still love me if I were a lap dancer?" she asked suddenly.

"What kind of thing is that to say?" replied Jack, deflecting the question and suddenly feeling flustered and under pressure. He was becoming more and more afraid of what was going on inside Bridget's head and her question was too close to home to feel comfortable.

"Don't get uptight just because I've threatened your male ego. Vincent Tuzio was Elsa's partner before he went to prison and now she's probably with this other guy who's been hiding her. They must both know what she used to do for a living, so in their intimate moments how do they handle the knowledge that her body is an open book and that she used to thrust her crotch into other men's faces?"

It was now Jack who was silent. He had seen Elsa on stage and the affect she had on the customers of the Blue Cockatoo, but he had never related what she did on stage to anything sexual between her and the punters. He didn't like to think of Elsa sharing an intimacy with these men, no matter how remote. Suddenly he began to feel jealous of all the men who ogled her or pushed money into her panties or bra. She was his and he had blinded himself to the hunger lust of these voyeurs, who all wanted to bed her. Now he was getting really confused. He loved Bridget, but he now knew that he still loved Elsa.

"Don't sit on the fence," cut in Bridget, "you must have an opinion?"

"Well I don't know what my opinion's worth! You can't be surprised at that because you know how shallow we men can be. What would you think of a man who loved you, but didn't mind you doing that kind of job?"

"That's a sneaky way of getting out of answering me. OK I'll give you my opinion first, but then you've got to tell me what you think. If a man really loves a woman he wouldn't want to share her with anyone, even if it was just stripping on a stage. I couldn't bear to think of anyone else with you and I hope you feel the same way about me."

"Of course I do," replied Jack. "Besides you probably wouldn't earn as much money as a lap dancer as you do now as a company executive."

Bridget laughed and lightly punched Jack on his leg. She was too much in love with him to notice his unease and now couldn't imagine how she had ever allowed herself to associate him with the criminals who were now going to be on the receiving end of 5 million dollars. Apart from the time she spent with Simon before they were married, she had led a fairly trouble free life, with little to mar her idealistic vision of the world. Her appreciation of the kind of people that Jack mingled with daily were stereotypes from films and TV. The harsh brutality of the underworld that she was now learning about second hand was difficult to put into any kind of context.

They pulled in at the side of the road and Jack made a call to Elsa on his cell phone. They had already rehearsed what they would say and went through their lines easily. Elsa was already at the roadhouse where they had agreed to meet and Jack and Bridget were about fifteen minutes away from the rendezvous. "We're to meet her at the roadhouse near the junction with the 537 called Pete's Eating Place. She said that she knows what you look like and that you're to go into the roadhouse by yourself. When she's satisfied that you've come alone she'll approach you."

"Why do I have to meet her by myself?" asked Bridget suddenly panicking at the prospect of the encounter.

"She's worried about her safety and the chance that you might have brought the police with you. She knows who I am but doesn't want me present at the meet. There was also a warning that if she sees a load of cars pull up to the roadhouse she won't show. It's likely that she'll pick a table near the window so that she can see us arrive and will have paid someone to watch me to ensure that I stay in the car. You've come too far to get cold feet now and you have got to do this to get Simon out of prison. Tell me that you're going to be OK?"

Bridget nodded and they drove on to the roadhouse, saying little and pondering on the outcome of the meeting. It won't take long, thought Bridget. She's only going to give me her bank account details, how long will that take? Jack was hoping that Elsa would be calm and not try to make the meeting difficult. Elsa knew that he had been seeing a lot of Bridget over the last few days and he was worried that she might be a little petulant with her. The fifteen-minute drive seemed like an hour.

Jack turned his car into the forecourt of the roadhouse, which was reasonably busy with several cars and a few lorries parked in front of the diner. He pulled into a parking spot and turned off the engine. Bridget sat quietly for a moment, then turned to Jack and kissed him lightly on the lips before getting out of the car. Jack didn't say anything and just smiled weakly at Bridget as she left. All he could do was hope that Elsa had not seen Bridget kiss him.

Bridget walked into Pete's Eating Place feeling very self-conscious and looking around animatedly, expecting to see a sultry temptress in every corner of the diner. She saw an empty table next to the window, close to the entrance and positioned herself on the side of the table from where she could see Jack's car. He had gotten out of the car and was leaning against the side of the bonnet looking towards the diner. Bridget had an impulse to wave to him but restrained herself. She settled into her seat and eventually a waitress came over to her to ask for her order. Bridget asked for a black coffee and the waitress hurried off to place her order. The roadhouse was busy so Bridget didn't expect the waitress to come back in a hurry.

The décor of the place was bright and functional with plastic covered tabletops and a tartan cloth on the bench styled seats. The coffee bar had stools around it with stainless steel legs and the same tartan material over the seats. Bridget glanced idly around feeling more conspicuous with every second that passed. The waitress eventually came back with her black coffee, but she also brought a cappuccino coffee with her. As the waitress placed the two drinks on the table Bridget said, "Excuse me, I only ordered a black coffee."

"The cappuccinos for me," came a voice from behind Bridget, who turned quickly to see who it was talking to her. Elsa brushed past Bridget before she could get a good look at her and took the seat opposite. "Don't look so surprised! Surely you didn't expect me to be waiting at a table with a sign to greet you as you arrived?"

"No, I didn't know what to expect," answered Bridget meekly. She looked over at Elsa and could immediately see that the pictures of her had not done her justice. She was the most beautiful woman that Bridget had ever seen and found herself admiring her face.

"Is there something wrong?" asked Elsa; unsettled by the look Bridget was giving her.

"Oh no!" said Bridget feeling embarrassed, as if she were a child that had been dipping into the sweet box. "You are going to give me your bank account details aren't you?" she added wanting to end the meeting as quickly as possible.

"What's wrong? Are you in a hurry to get away? You might as well wait until you finish you're coffee," replied Elsa. "We can talk."

"What do you want to talk about? We don't have very much in common, so I can't see what there is to talk about."

"Well apart from us both being women, we have your husband in common. Aren't you a little curious about what happened between us on his boat and why I ended up in the water?"

"Not really, what he does or doesn't do when I'm not with him is none of my concern. Besides you put yourself in harm's way by going off with someone you didn't know. Why was that?" Bridget wasn't going to be bullied by this woman.

"It wasn't for the reasons given at Simon's trial. I'm not a prostitute and I wasn't looking for a trick while on vacation! Neither am I a thief. Everything your husband said at the trial, apart from us being on the boat together, was a complete lie. He tried to rape me and when I resisted he shot me. Then he left me for dead."

"You can't tell me anything about Simon that I don't know already," replied Bridget quietly, once more looking at Elsa directly in the eye. She wasn't really shocked by Elsa's brief synopsis and had suspected that Simon had probably tried to force himself on her, and by doing so precipitated the chain of events that ended with Elsa being shot. Bridget broke her gaze to stare into her coffee noting the blackness of the liquor in contrast to the white cup. The coffee mirrored the color of Simon's heart.

Elsa had expected a strong challenge from Bridget and was surprised she had accepted her version of events so readily. "What do you mean?" asked Elsa intrigued by Bridget's compliance.

Bridget looked up at Elsa again and could see that she was bemused by the response she had been given. "I don't know why I should tell you this," Bridget began, "but seeing as we'll never meet again I suppose it doesn't really matter. Simon raped me. I was forced to sleep with him to protect my father, who was in the middle of a large insurance claim with Simon's company. Simon threatened to expose negligence on my father's part, which would have been grounds for not paying the claim and could have ended up with my father going to prison."

"In that case, why did you marry him?" asked Elsa, even more confused.

"Simon had used my father's circumstance to get to me and I suffered his abuse until the claim was settled. I paid my dues so I decided to get what I could out of him. He wanted to marry me, so that I would be the token wife of a successful business tycoon. The night of our wedding I laid down the rules, which were that he gave me an executive position in his company and that he never touches or comes near me again. He agreed and we decided to continue with the marriage, but have maintained separate lives ever since. The business with you on the boat, and other revelations unearthed during the trial, convinced me that I've got to divorce him when he gets out of prison."

Elsa felt compassion and admiration for Bridget because of the way she had turned an intolerable situation to her own advantage and on her realization that the woman wasn't the cold and unfeeling bitch she was portrayed to be. "You won't believe this, but you and I are not so different. We operate in different ways because we have different talents. You've got the education my parents couldn't give me but I use what I've got, and I can tell you that I was the best lap dancer in New York. I drew the line at being touched or groped and never went with any of the customers or did private shows," said Elsa beginning to empathize with Bridget.

"But I can't understand how you can use your body in that way. It's so crude….." Bridget stopped suddenly, worried that her attitude to Elsa's occupation may offend her.

Elsa smiled with an expression that told Bridget she had heard similar remarks many times before. "Do you think women are born sluts or that they become sluts? And for that matter do you know what makes a woman a slut?"

Bridget shook her head negatively not wanting to say anything more that could antagonize Elsa.

"I'm no slut because my body is and has always been private. Nobody touches or uses my body without me wanting them to and I don't let them do it for money, only out of love. I've only slept with one man in my entire life and I've no intention of increasing that number. Showing my body, no matter how crudely is of no consequence. Film stars get paid millions for taking their clothes off and they don't get called sluts. When you're standing in front of an audience of men that are anything but attractive, believe me, I have to act every bit as much as any film star you care to name. I'm only doing it until I can get enough money to train as a dance teacher, which you will provide. Thank you!"

Elsa spoke without emotion but with an authority borne from coming to terms with the hard decisions she was forced to make to survive in the rat race. Bridget was sorry that she had been self-opinionated in her judgement of her. Elsa's assessment of the two of them was right. In essence they were very much alike in their determined approach to life, and even in their love life. Bridget too had only loved one man and could never sleep with another. What Bridget didn't know of course was that they both loved the same man.

"I'm sorry for what I said Elsa. I had no right to judge you or your lifestyle, please forgive me." Elsa would have been unaware of the honor Bridget was paying her, because it was the first time she had apologized for anything since marrying Simon Walsh.

"That's not a problem. I'd like to talk some more, but we've both finished our coffees and you're chauffeur may be getting a little impatient. I think you want this," said Elsa handing Bridget an envelope.

"Y'know I don't even mind about handing over the money. After all it's really Simon's money and I think you've earned it. I guess that's our business over with, good luck."

"Just before you go, Bridget, finish your story. What happened to your father?"

"My father retired from the business a broken man. The insurance claim provided him with enough money to finish the job and pay off all his workers, but he never recovered from the shock and died shortly after I married Simon." Bridget was amazed that Elsa had the compassion to ask about her father. She really had misjudged her.

Elsa smiled sadly remembering her own father, got up from the table, walked over to the coffee bar and climbed onto one of the stools.

They had reached the end of their business and Bridget stood up and walked to the exit. Elsa watched as Bridget left the roadhouse and walked over to the car where Jack was waiting. Her smile froze as she saw Bridget kiss Jack before getting into the car.

"How did it go?" asked Jack.

"It went well," replied Bridget showing him the envelope. "And there's no need to worry that I'm going to press you for an answer to the question I asked before we got here."

"What's that?" asked Jack dumbly.

"I wouldn't expect you to remember anything I said half an hour ago. So let's just say I can understand why a man would love a woman like Elsa, even though she's a lap dancer."

14

Simon Walsh replaced the phone on the receiver after hearing from Bridget that she had managed to sell his shares and get the 5 million dollars to pay his blackmailers. A tremendous sense of relief spread throughout his entire body as he contemplated that he would soon be free. He had been anticipating his release since Bridget's visit and thinking about what he would do on the outside. Seeing Bridget again had made him appreciate just how lucky he was to have her. He was going to change and be a proper husband by convincing her that he was deeply in love with her and would always respect her. He knew that Bridget would find it difficult to accept him as her husband because of their history together, and his patchy history with prostitutes, but he would try to win her over slowly.

Walsh picked up his washing bag and headed for the laundry. He had arranged to meet Vincent there to discuss the payment to Elsa and was relieved that they could start making plans for her reappearance. In truth Jack and Elsa had already decided that she would go to the police in New York and also formulated an explanation for her not showing up at Walsh's trial. If it became necessary for her to go to Miami, Jack would discuss the matter with Tanner.

Jack told Vincent to keep the "money pot" boiling by giving Walsh the impression that he had an input to the planning of Elsa's surrender to the police. The old Simon would already be planning a way to get even with her, but now he didn't care because he just wanted to get this horrible episode in his life over and done with. He was comfortable with his newfound sense of perspective and hoped it would show Bridget that he was a changed man.

As Walsh opened the door to the laundry he could hear muffled voices in the washroom and as he got closer they got louder. His first instinct was not to get involved and to get the hell out of the place, until he heard Vincent Tuzio's voice. Slowly he inched to the door of the washroom to find out what was happening. The door wasn't fully closed as the catch hadn't been engaged properly and Walsh could clearly hear the conversation between Vincent and someone else. The anxiety in Vincent's voice made it clear to Walsh that his friend was in a difficult situation, but he knew he couldn't tell one of the guards, because he would be putting his own neck on the line.

"Nobody was trying to cheat you, man. What I said about the amount of money coming from Walsh was straight up. I'm just the middle man in all this, I don't have all the details or know everything that's going on," said Vincent anxiously.

"That's not the way I heard it. I heard you're squeezing a few million out of Walsh and I want my fair share. You know the rules in here if I don't get the cash I take it out of your hide. Martin here will be only too happy to oblige."

Walsh deducted that there must be two men with Vincent and one of them was Martin Abraham, which was not good. Walsh thought the man talking could be Wesley Green, but he wasn't certain.

"Look man I'm not stupid, haven't I always paid my dues in the past? I wouldn't mess with you. You know that!"

"I would like to trust you Vincent, but this is a lot of money and you might just be tempted to cheat me. Now tell me the truth. How much are you getting from Walsh?"

"I don't know man cos the final sum ain't been agreed. All I was told by Jack was that it would be upward of two hundred thou."

So Jack Cates is up to his armpits in this thought Walsh. The understanding that the whole thing had been a set up from the start suddenly began to dawn on him. He knew his meeting with Elsa was not by chance, but he hadn't realized that she was just one link in a very long chain. Her purpose was to compromise him and place him in an awkward situation that would allow Cates to squeeze him for money. In this day and age infidelity, even with a prostitute, is not considered to be a mortal sin, but if they took any embarrassing photographs or made any recordings of the liaison, it would be hard to explain his actions to shareholders and the Board of the NMP, and even harder to keep his position of CEO in the company. Whatever their original plan, it must have gone wrong because he had taken Elsa on his cruiser, and then things really got out of hand because she had departed from the script and there was no way to catch him "delicto inflagrante". The "witnesses" coming forward and the sudden police interest were all triggered by Cates, it was all beginning to make some sense.

"Somehow I don't believe you Vincent, because a little bird has told me that the sum involved is 5 million. Do you believe him Martin?"

"No Boss."

"Well let's try a little persuasion to encourage Vincent to tell the truth. Just the body for now, not the face, I don't want his speech impaired."

"Don't do this man," begged Vincent in a high-pitched voice which was suddenly cut off.

Walsh heard the sickening thud of several blows into Tuzio's body and the low growling moan of Vincent as he fell to the floor. It reminded Walsh of the beating Caine had given him, but it sounded much worse.

"You've broken my fucking ribs you big bastard! There's blood coming out of my mouth for Chrissakes," screamed Tuzio. "Look man I can't tell you what I don't know," he added turning to his interrogator. "If you kill me the deal will fall through and you won't get a fucking penny."

Walsh heard another dull thud and a whine from Tuzio.

"You fuckers. You mother fucking bastards, you can go and fuck yourselves before I tell you anything," screamed Tuzio looking up at his assailants coughing and spitting out copious amounts of blood.

Walsh heard a sharp crack followed by silence.

"You shouldn't have kicked him in the head Martin, you've broken his fucking neck. What's Wesley going to say now?"

Walsh felt a large, strong hand on the back of his neck as he was propelled through the door. "Wesley's not too fucking pleased," said the man holding onto Walsh. He thrust Walsh into the room sending him scrambling onto the floor as he tripped over Vincent's body. He sat momentarily with his back against a washer looking disbelievingly at Tuzios lifeless body, his head lying in a pool of blood and his eyes staring at the wall.

The other men in the room were Martin Abraham, Wesley Green and Chief Norton, the head guard. Green looked at his partners contemptuously, "I told you to watch Martin, Norton, and that he was likely to get carried away. Now we're fucked because Tuzio's dead and we've got a witness."

"Look don't worry about me I forget what I see very quickly, and instead of paying the money to Cates I'll pay it to you," whimpered Walsh, looking for any angle to get himself out of this mess. Walsh had never been this close to Green before and was amazed at the sheer size of him; he even dwarfed the muscle-bound Abraham. His eyes were intelligent, but cold and Walsh knew he would have to give him a good reason to let him go.

"Unfortunately, Mr. Walsh, it's not just a matter of money now because a man has been killed and the law will be crawling all over this place to get to the bottom of it. With you as a witness all of us are at risk……but then there is the money."

"Don't be sucked in by that Wesley," interjected Norton. "It's been several years since we've had a murder in any Florida prison, never mind a medium security place like this. The Feds are gonna know there's more to Tuzio's murder than a simple falling out between inmates. We've got to kill him to protect ourselves," said Norton looking at Walsh. "He's an outsider and there's no way that he's gonna keep his mouth shut. Look at him, if anyone puts him under pressure, he's gonna blab." Norton was now standing over Walsh and sneering down at him.

Walsh lay on the floor unable to move because every muscle in his body was frozen with fear. He thought that he probably wasn't going to leave the washroom alive. Abject terror made him wet himself involuntarily, leaving a dark patch on his "sweats". With this added humiliation he slowly got to his feet and pressed himself against the washer, the warm urine ran down his leg and out onto the floor.

"The mother-fucker's wet himself," laughed Abraham pointing at the wet spot on the floor.

"You can see my problem can't you?" said Green walking over to Walsh, who was now visibly shaking. "Do I kill you and cover my tracks, or do I kill these two and let you pay me a lot of money?"

Abraham stopped laughing and looked uncomfortably at Norton.

"I don't know what to do," continued Green grabbing the sides of Walsh's head. He smiled apologetically at Walsh saying, "I'm afraid it's you," as he twisted Walsh's head sharply and instantly broke his neck. Turning to his colleagues he said, "Now look what you've made me do."

"Well that's the money gone, "lamented Norton.

"We've all got to take the hit so stop your whining," retorted Green. "OK let's decide how we're going to clean up this mess. Norton, didn't you say Walsh had a disagreement with Mathew Caine over some outside matter?"

"Yeah, I don't know the precise details but I heard it was something to do with Caine's sister. One of my guys found Walsh worse for wear throwing up on the floor of the washroom, after passing Caine as he was leaving. The incident is on record as an entry into the daily log. We keep a record of such minor incidents for reference. They're not reported to the Governor, and are only used to monitor what's going on, so we can make a judgement on the undercurrent and prevent anything major from happening."

"The details don't matter. All that matters is that others are aware of the friction between the two of them. Abraham you get Caine down to the laundry by telling him that Walsh is badmouthing his sister. I know his sister's dead, and I imagine she must have been fucking Walsh. Don't be too graphic; just tell Caine he's being disrespectful. Knowing what a hot head he is he won't stop to listen to the details anyway. Norton you've got to get some men down there a couple of minutes after Caine to catch him red handed."

"What reason should I give?" whined Norton.

"Think of something!"

As he left the washroom Green's disappointment at losing money was tempered by the pleasant thought that Roland Bannister was going to lose a hell of a lot more. Bannister had contacted Green to tell him the sum of money involved in getting Walsh freed, but the shyster only thought of things in black and white, as profit and loss. In prison things were different. If anyone found out that he was being taken for a mug he would lose all credibility with the other inmates. His strength would give him some protection but it wouldn't help if some of the inmates decided to gang up on him and he ended up with a "shiv" stuck in his back.

Bridget was preparing to meet Jack when she got a call from Governor Small. She was told that Simon was murdered by one of the inmates in a long-standing dispute. He apologized profusely that the incident had happened, saying that it was completely unexpected and had never happened in one of his prisons previously. He closed by giving her the name of a welfare officer who would be in touch about releasing Simon's body and would help making the funeral arrangements. He advised her to contact the welfare officer if there was anything else she needed.

Only some of the words percolated through to Bridget's consciousness. She felt guilty about not being distraught at the news and not having paid the blackmail money to Elsa in time, but even guiltier about her affair with Jack Cates.

Part 3
The Reckoning

1

After the memorial service, the drive to the cemetery was long and miserable. Bridget sat in the back of the second car in the funeral train, with the only Aunt and Uncle of Simon Walsh who were still alive. The last time Phil and Betty had visited was when they buried Simon's dad and they were no better company then than they were now. She thought about Jack, but quickly chastised herself for thinking of him at this time of grief. She felt like a hypocrite pretending to mourn over her murdered husband, as the only tinge of remorse that pulled at her heart strings was for the unnecessary death of a human being in such appalling circumstances, not the loss of a loved one.

That morning Francesca had laid out a black suit, purple blouse and black hat and veil. It felt unreal to be putting these clothes on for the funeral of her husband who was only thirty six when he died. She never expected to live the rest of her life with Simon but she would have made almost any compromise to prevent his murder, and had in fact conceded quite a bit of ground in agreeing to the sum of money demanded by Elsa. It was just a matter of timing. If she had got the money a couple of days earlier then Simon would have been released or at the least he would have been sent to Miami for a the review of his case. She blamed herself for not getting the money quickly enough and also for getting involved with Jack Cates. Had she unconsciously slowed down the process just to spend more time with Jack?

The car pulled into the cemetery gates and followed the hearse to the plot where Simon would be buried. The hearse stopped and the funeral train pulled up behind it. Solemnly the four pallbearers pulled Simon's coffin from the car and carried it over to the gravesite, followed by the mourners. It was a grey sky, which matched the mood of the ceremony. The mourners followed the coffin in silence, some quietly acknowledging to themselves that this would be their fate one day. By the time the retinue arrived at the grave, the pallbearers had placed the coffin into the mouth of the neat hole dug to receive it, ready to be lowered to its final resting place.

The priest who had conducted the funeral service at the church said a few kind words at the graveside and unexpectedly turned to Bridget and asked if there was anything she wished to add. Everyone turned to look at her and she felt very conspicuous, not just because the priest had put her in the spotlight but also because she knew that she didn't paint the picture of the grieving widow that everyone had been expecting to see. She shook her head resolutely and the priest signaled to the pallbearers to lower the coffin. The priest gave the coffin a blessing and slowly the mourners left the grave site, each throwing a handful of earth into the grave.

The priest came over to Bridget and asked if there was anything he could do to help her come to terms with her loss. She smiled and thanked him for his concern and told him that she would be all right as she had gotten used to living without Simon while he had been in prison. The priest looked a little alarmed at her answer, but accepted it and bade her farewell. Francesca linked arms with Bridget and walked back to the car with her.

She had telephoned Jack after finding out about Simon's death and he said it would only take fifteen minutes to get to her as he was already dressed and ready to go out, expecting that they would be going out to dinner for the evening. Bridget stopped Jack from coming over to meet her and explained that it would probably be better if they didn't meet for a few days, and would give him a call when she was ready to see him. Jack had accepted that she needed to be alone for a while, for appearances sake if nothing else, and said that he'd wait for her call.

Bridget travelled home after the funeral with Phil and Betty and they had lunch together. She asked if they planned to see a little of New York now that the funeral was over, and if they would like to stay with her. They both looked disapprovingly at Bridget for being so frivolous at this time of grief and she was deeply relieved when they refused her offer. That evening she sat in front of the fire with a gin in her hand contemplating the future. Normally her first consideration would have been for the welfare of the NMP, but now she could only wonder if she had any kind of future with Jack. She felt guilty for not mourning the loss of her husband and only thinking of her lover, which was compounded by the fact that they failed to get Simon's release before he was murdered.

Across town Jack was in a bar sucking on the end of a bottle of Bud. He had called Elsa after Bridget's phone call and told her the news of Walsh's death. Elsa started laughing; all she could do was mock Jack and ask him why his meticulous planning hadn't allowed for the possibility of Walsh being murdered in prison. She then asked Jack if his murder was a direct result of the scam they were trying to pull.

"No it was s fluky thing. Walsh ran into the brother of a girl he'd mistreated in the past and the guy took his revenge on him. He's denied it, but it's an open and shut case. The guards caught him virtually red handed."

"What am I going to do now? Walsh is dead and I'm supposed to be dead. How can I return to New York now and pick up my life as if nothing ever happened?"

"Well you can just turn up the way we'd always planned you would. In fact we can use Walsh's death to our advantage, we can say you were in hiding for fear of reprisals and that now Walsh is dead you were free to come out in the open. How does that sound?"

"It sounds like the last year of my life has been a complete waste of time," replied Elsa caustically.

"Well it's been the same for me. I've spent a long time trying to run this scam smoothly and it's all been for nothing, zilch! No Simon, no money"

"Well it's not been a complete waste of time for you. After all you did get to know Bridget along the way."

"What's that got to do with anything? I told you that I had to win her trust to persuade her to get Walsh to stump up the money."

"Tell me how you won her trust. Was it by fucking her?"

"Why are you going down this road? Whatever I did I did for us," replied Jack unconvincingly.

"Yes you hated every minute of it, didn't you? Don't be a hypocrite Jack. I can take anything except you telling me that you fucked someone else for the both of us!" When Elsa realized what she had said, she burst out laughing but quickly ended up crying. "I can't talk to you now," she shouted down the phone and slammed down the receiver, not for the first time when talking to Jack about Bridget.

Jack had tried to call her afterwards, but he found that Elsa had taken the phone off the hook. He knew that she would make sure he couldn't get in touch with her until she was good and ready to talk, and that could take a couple of days. That night he had gotten very drunk and ended up sleeping in a doss house, because he felt incapable of making his way back to his apartment. He wasn't so drunk that he didn't know that he was also vulnerable to anyone trying to even up old scores and he knew no one would think of looking for him among a bunch of drunks and vagrants.

He planned to get drunk the next night, because when he got drunk nothing mattered, not Elsa, or Bridget, or the money. He thought again and decided he wasn't going to get too drunk as he was going to Vincent Tuzio's funeral the following day. He felt sorry for Tuzio, who had somehow got involved in the fight between Walsh and Caine and ended up getting himself killed, probably trying to protect Walsh. It was a big price to pay thought Jack and a wave of guilt flowed through him as he remembered that he was planning to short change Tuzio on the payout of the blackmail money. People like Tuzio always ended up losers, but with Walsh dead they were all losers, especially Roland who had now forked out at least a 100 thousand dollars to keep the scam running over the last twelve months.

Roland may have shelled out a lot of cash, but he would have got a good return on his investment if things had gone to plan. They were so close to getting the money that Jack could almost smell it. He knew he would never get another chance to get his hands on that kind of money again. As he sat at the bar draining his bottle of beer, he could feel himself sinking down in a whirlpool of depression once more, and decided that he wasn't going to let the situation get on top of him and that he had to do something to lift his spirits. He couldn't go to see Bridget and Elsa was still in Boston, so the only other options were to either go to the Blue Cockatoo or just browse the bars.

Going to the Blue Cockatoo could be more than a little problematic, thought Jack, as he hadn't spoken to Roland Bannister about Walsh's sudden demise and had been putting off the inevitable until he had nowhere else to turn. Jack remembered the little speech Roland had given him months earlier about being a winner and not being seen to be a loser. His own sense of image and the respect that other people had for him were the key indicators he used to measure his status in the underworld community. Of course Roland would be more than a little peeved by the fact that he had put out a lot of money without getting anything back on his investment. But that setback would be nothing compared to the prospect of becoming a laughing stock in the underworld fraternity.

Thinking about his impending confrontation with Bannister sobered Jack up very quickly, not that he had consumed a great deal of alcohol by this stage of the evening. He knew any meeting with Bannister would be difficult, even unpleasant and could also carry an element of risk to himself. He also knew that he had to make Roland see that Walsh's death couldn't have been foreseen or avoided, as the chain of events that led to the murder were down to a freakish twist of fate. The chance of Walsh meeting Caine in prison must have been enormous, a million to one, and surely Roland would have to agree that Jack had no chance of predicting what happened, never mind of saving Walsh.

Finally Jack decided that it would be better to see Roland on his own volition, before being summoned to the Blue Cockatoo. If he went to Bannister with his tail between his legs, after being dragged to the Blue Cockatoo, he would find it very difficult to reason with Roland and get him to see things from a realistic or balanced perspective, which of course is the way Jack saw them. Jack made a mental note to call Roland after Vincent Tuzio's funeral and arrange to see him the following evening, just as he felt a large hand grasp his shoulder.

Jack turned to see Frank grinning at him. His large ugly face was sporting an uncharacteristic smile, which Jack found more unnerving than the enormity of his physical presence. Frank was clearly enjoying watching Jack squirm and anticipating the inevitable order from Bannister to beat a little sense into him, or worse, see he couldn't do it again.

"Hello Jack, I thought I'd find you in here drowning your sorrows. Did things not go the way you expected them to? Mr. Bannister was expecting a call from you, and he's been wondering why you haven't been in contact with him yet."

"Frank, what a nice surprise, seeing you that is!" replied Jack summoning all his mental reserves to avoid looking worried or frightened. "Strangely I was just thinking that I must ring Roland when you grabbed me. I just haven't had the chance yet."

"Walsh died ten days ago Cates. What's kept you so busy for the last ten days that you couldn't find time to make a little phone call? At one time we couldn't keep you out of the club, but now you're never there. Maybe now that Elsa's coming back we'll see a little more of you. Don't matter how busy you are, Mr. Bannister wants to see you."

"Give me a break Frank, I'm just chilling out before going to see Roland. I'll be over in a couple of days," replied Jack annoyed that he had let this situation develop and had lost the initiative before actually going to see Bannister. "What did you say about Elsa coming back?"

"Elsa called Mr. Bannister yesterday and asked him to clear her coming back to New York with the DA. He made a phone call to Bantry today and told him Elsa was frightened of coming forward during Walsh's trial, and even more frightened afterwards of being charged with perverting the course of justice. I don't know the ins and outs except that Bantry said Elsa wouldn't have to face criminal charges but she would have to go to the DA's office to make a statement and that the New York office would be OK."

"When's Elsa coming back?" asked Jack, disappointed that she hadn't spoken to him before speaking to Bannister.

"I don't know, probably in the next couple of days. You'd better come over to the club before the end of the week because Mr. Bannister is getting impatient. Don't make me come for you Cates. I don't mind the aggravation, but believe me, you wouldn't like it," said Frank sternly, before leaving Jack at the bar.

2

Elsa swept into Roland Bannister's office at the Blue Cockatoo as if she had never been away and was just checking in to talk to the Boss at the start of another working day. Inside she felt more than a little nervous and was unsure of the reception she'd get from Roland as they hadn't seen each other since she went to Boston. She had taken great care to make the right impression on her entrance by wearing stylish, rather than sexy clothes. There would be plenty of time to don the body clinging garments she used to regularly peel off while dancing at the club. The outfit she chose was eye catching but practical, as Roland had arranged to take her over to see the DA after lunch. She wore a tight fitting blue-black skirt, pale blue silk blouse, with a maroon wrap around soft black leather jacket. She completed the ensemble with a pair of patent maroon high-heeled shoes that displayed the curve of her calves to perfection.

Elsa's hair was much shorter than it had been when she was last at the Blue Cockatoo and it was now a waif's cut that was brought forward at the front to frame her face and tailed at the back into the nape of her neck. She had never felt better physically, which showed in the firmness of her body and the flow and grace of her movements. Roland rose speechless from his chair and walked over to greet her with a kiss on the cheek.

"My God, Elsa you look tremendous. It's so good to see you again." Roland was unusually at a loss for words because Elsa's sudden appearance had completely disorientated him. She was early for lunch and he was completely bowled over by the way she looked.

"It's good to see you too Roland. I wanted to call you during my exile to let you know what was happening, but you know Jack, he didn't want me to make any unnecessary phone calls because of the risk of someone finding out where I was."

"Forget that Elsa. Let's move on now because you've been away too long and I'm keen to get you involved in the club again."

"Well, I've been working on some routines so it won't take long for me to pick up the loose ends and get back on stage. Besides I doubt the punters are looking for too much artistic merit in my dance routines!"

"I don't want you up on the stage again. I want you to manage the girls, the entertainment and the bar. I want you to help me manage the club!"

"But I've got no real experience..........."

"You can do anything you want to do, you're a smart kid," said Roland encouragingly. "What experience do you need? You've been dancing here for five years now and you know what the punters want. You can keep the girls delivering to the clients and audition new blood. If you don't know what the dancers should be doing, then no one does. Frank will help you with the bar and make sure the guys working it don't try to take advantage of you while you're learning the ropes. He and Lou will take their orders from you for the day to day tasks. Besides you're too good for those meatheads out there, they don't appreciate class! They just want flesh."

Elsa was dumfounded and stood frozen in amazement. She knew that things would not be the same when she returned, but what Roland was suggesting was completely unexpected. She wouldn't be sorry about keeping her clothes on. She had changed over the last year and knew that she really needed a new challenge and this was an opportunity she couldn't ignore. Having wrestled with depression, loneliness and despair she had taken command of her situation and made decisions on what she should do without consulting Jack. Now she had to make another decision on her own, because only she really knew what was best for her. With Jack sniffing around Simon Walsh's widow, she felt even stronger about determining her own future, with or without him.

"If you're willing to take a chance on me, then I should respect your trust and grab the offer with both hands. Just be patient and I'll repay your trust by making the "Blue Cockatoo" the best nightclub in town."

"Good! Now let's have a drink to seal the arrangement," replied

Bannister. He walked to the bar and asked Frank to pour a glass of wine for Elsa and a brandy for himself. Frank beamed at the request. Roland had discussed asking Elsa to manage the club with Frank, after her initial phone call asking to come back, and he now assumed that she had accepted it. Bannister walked back into his office, took Elsa's hand and led her to the sofa resting against the wall between his office and the bar, where they sat down beside each other.

"I'm glad that's settled, but we need to talk about Jack and the deal with Simon Walsh that's just gone belly up."

"Do we have to Roland? I'm sick to my back teeth about the whole thing. I want to put it behind me as just another bad experience and accept that I should have known better." At that moment Frank came into the office with the drinks, handing Elsa her wine first. "Thank you Frank. I hope I don't get tipsy before I go to the DA's office later."

"You've come a little early Elsa, so unless you're thinking of having a lot more to drink, I think you should have sobered up by the time we go there. Do you think she was eager to come back Frank?"

Unusually Frank smiled, his face taking on a completely different, almost boyish appearance, despite his leathery skin and deeply lined features. "Well I'm glad to see you back Elsa," stammered Frank as he left the office.

"I don't think you'll have any trouble managing him, he's a fan like the rest of us." Bannister paused to taste his drink and then turned towards Elsa. "When you said you were putting everything behind you, does that include Jack?"

"I don't know what I feel about Jack right now. When I went to meet Bridget to give her the bank details, it was clear from the way they were canoodling in the car park that their relationship had passed the platonic stage. I really think that Mrs. Walsh is in love with our Jack, more fool her."

"But where does that leave you? I mean you can't just leave things in the air indefinitely."

"If Jack thinks I'm just going to roll over and let him do what he wants then he'll be disappointed. I've given in to him far too much in the past, doing whatever he wanted me to do because it helped him. Well, from now on that's all over. Before I climb back on his wagon he'll have to convince me that it's worth my while and that he's not still "dicking" around with Bridget."

"That's the thing isn't it? You've spent virtually 12 months in solitary confinement and I've lost a hundred grand in the process, supporting you and Julie and paying off all of Jack's flunkeys. What has this debacle cost Jack? It's cost him very little, apart from his wounded pride, perhaps. We shouldn't let him walk away from this Scot-free. It's only fair that he suffers some of the grief that we've had, isn't it?"

Elsa nodded sipping her wine, really disinterested in Roland's platitudes about fair play. She just wanted to forget about everything that had happened since meeting Simon Walsh and get on with the rest of her life. Her mind was dwelling on her future role as the assistant manager of the Blue Cockatoo and how she could broaden the appeal of the club beyond lap dancing. The club would always rely on sex for its fundamental appeal, but it could put on reviews that had a little more to do with entertainment than merely parading naked women. She was thinking of some of the European nightclubs she had heard about.

"Elsa, are you listening to me?" asked Roland, noticing her disinterest in the conversation. He was trying to delicately find a way to get Elsa to side with him against Jack. The money Bridget brokered for her husband against his shares in the NMP is still there to be had and he also assumed that with Simon Walsh dead, all of his worldly wealth would go to his wife. "I've got a plan, but I don't think you'll like it very much."

"Well, tell me what it is and then I'll tell you whether I like it or not."

"It involves Jack and Bridget. You said yourself that they were more than acquaintances, more than friends even. We have to persuade

Jack to nurture Bridget's feelings and then he can exploit their relationship and get some of that money. I'm not greedy; so it wouldn't be practical to expect him to get the whole 5 million dollars. I just want something back from my investment. A million would be enough for me."

Elsa was thinking about Jack again and couldn't imagine any way he could get money out of Bridget. "How are we going to do that without putting Jack in an awkward position? she asked. "He doesn't have any leverage now."

"Why should he feel awkward, unless he has real feelings for her? It's just a progression of the original plan. Instead of getting the money from Walsh, we get it from his wife. And what's more you and I don't have to do anything but sit back and watch Jack jump through all the hoops necessary to get Bridget to part with a million dollars."

"But it will mean Jack sleeping with Bridget," said Elsa timidly.

"Why do you care? I thought you were going to put yourself first from now on? If he's screwing her anyway, we might as well use it to our advantage," replied Roland.

Momentarily Elsa felt her stomach drop at the thought of Roland's last suggestion. Ironically using Jack as the bait in this kind of scam was a complete turnaround of their earlier arrangement in which Elsa played the sex object. The thought of Jack being used as a gigolo amused her. After all things hadn't been the same between the two of them for some time. "OK why not?" she said more positively.

Roland was relieved because he thought he had gone too far, too quickly in pushing Jack and Bridget together. In his head he had planned to go through the details with a much more measured approach so as not to put off Elsa. The problem was that he loved Elsa and couldn't impress her using his slick lawyer delivery. He found it easy in every other area of his life, but not with her. "That's settled then. Jack's coming to see me tonight; we'll confront him with the plan then. You must understand that we've both got to be united in this and that you can't let Jack deflect or cajole you into doing something else."

Elsa nodded and Roland put his arm around her and kissed her on her cheek warmly.

3

Jack woke up with a slight headache. Not as big as the one he would have had, if he had not met Frank, because their meeting prevented him from drinking a lot more in case the big man was following him. He knew that he was now between a rock and a hard place and it was his own fault for not going to see Bannister earlier. Shit, how could something that seemed so good a couple of weeks ago turn out to be so bad? He needed a strategy for dealing with Roland, but he didn't have anything else to offer that could placate him. No tit-bits of information from the NYPD that could benefit him, or anything else that he could trade for his favor. Just as he was thinking that things couldn't get any worse the phone rang.

"Hi Jack its Bridget," came the voice down the line.

"Bridget, how are you feeling? God, I've missed seeing you" answered Jack with genuine warmth. "I was getting a little worried that you were taking Simon's death badly and blaming yourself. You know that you did everything possible to help him, don't you?"

"Yes I know that now. There's nothing to worry about Jack. I haven't been in touch before because things have been a bit hectic since the funeral. First of all I had to attend an emergency Board Meeting to stem the growing lack of confidence in anyone with the name Walsh. Luckily my record is good and the general consensus was that business could only improve after Simon's death as most of the damage to the company name was done by the publicity surrounding him during his trial and when he was sent to prison. Next I had to see Simon's lawyer about his will, or should I say lack of a will. His estate has gone into probate, but that's the least of my worries. Since then I've been busy mending bridges with NMP investors, plus investing in the company myself, and now finally the tide seems to have turned and everything appears to be settling down to the normal routine."

"Oh is that all, I thought you were having real problems," Jack jested.

"I know facing a gang of stony faced Board of Directors isn't as daunting as chasing thieves and murderers, but it can be more than a little scary. With those guys you can't see their guns and knives until it's too late to do anything to save yourself. Now that I'm back on an even keel I could do with some of your special loving to recharge my batteries."

"Er… that might be a bit of a problem tonight because I've got to see a Client," lied Jack, referring to his summons from Roland Bannister. He wished he had elaborated on the need for visiting his Client at night and put a little more flesh on his feeble excuse to make it sound more plausible.

"Funny, here I was thinking you would be looking forward to seeing me again," replied Bridget tersely. "What hours does your Client keep that you're going to be tied up all night?"

Bridget's question gave Jack the opportunity to rectify the situation. "He's a night club owner and he wants me to look at his security systems and do a check on the guys responsible for crowd control. He took them on with the club and he wants me to check that they've got the right qualifications, temperament and experience to do the job." Jack was amazed at the speed at which he could fabricate a story that even he may have believed.

"Oh! I see. So I guess that means you won't be able to come round later. It would be nice if we could spend the night together, I just want to feel you close to me. It doesn't matter what time you arrive." Bridget felt she was exposing her emotional vulnerability to Jack, being so deeply in love with him, but she didn't care. She had spent years suppressing her emotions and now she was going to say what she felt and express her needs.

"We're having dinner first so it might be a bit late," replied Jack wondering if Elsa would have any expectations about him sleeping over with her. "I'll try to get to you before midnight, but if it looks like I can't get away I'll give you a call."

"OK, but it's your loss," said Bridget clearly disappointed at Jack's negative response and apparent lack of enthusiasm. "Bye."

Jack felt bad at the way he had let Bridget down, but he knew he was in for a long night with Roland and that he'd also have Elsa to contend with. He hadn't spoken to Elsa since her return to New York and assumed that Roland would be trying to take advantage of their estrangement. Life was certainly far more complicated now than it was a year ago and Jack was beginning to wish the whole episode had never happened. He loved Bridget, but he also loved Elsa and couldn't understand how he could have such deep feelings for both women.

He had always known that Elsa had never been happy playing the whore and that the money they got from his scams was not really enough for him to accept her degrading herself in that way. "Why did I let her do it? She's far too good to be used like that", thought Jack. He could now see that he had probably not only lost her, but that he'd also lost any protection he had against retribution from Roland. Jack could picture the delight Frank would get out of beating him to a pulp. Unfortunately there was no way he could avoid putting himself in danger by going to the club because his failure to turn up would only result in Frank and Lou finding him and physically dragging him to his appointment.

Walking into the "Blue Cockatoo" that evening was one of the hardest things Jack had ever done. His stomach was knotted at the prospect of being cast aside by Elsa and he was hyperactive expecting strong-arm tactics from Roland. Frank was in the lobby as Jack entered the club and gave him a broad smile in a mock show of friendliness. His teeth gleamed as his mouth opened, but his eyes were warmly anticipating the damage he would be doing to Jack's body in the near future. Jack nodded to him and walked through into the lounge, veering off to the right side of the room to Bannister's office. He walked up the stairs, tapped lightly on the door and entered without waiting for a reply.

Bannister was sitting at his desk as Jack entered and he looked up from the ledger he was checking, surprised at someone entering his office without an invitation. He pushed his chair away from his desk, stood up and walked over to Jack with his hand outstretched. "Jack, it seems like ages. Tell me how are you doing after the Walsh debacle?" Bannister warmly shook Jack's hand, which immediately raised the hairs on the back of Jack's neck because Roland was not a man who liked physical contact with other men, which meant that he was obviously making this show of affection for a reason.

"I'm fine Roland, much the same as usual, eking out a living on the infidelity of a nation. I'm sorry that I didn't get in touch sooner, but after the Walsh thing collapsed I just got so depressed that I couldn't face seeing or talking to anyone for a while."

"Well, I was beginning to wonder when you were going to show your face, but I can understand your depression because you put a lot of time into the "Walsh thing". Before we go any further, let me get Elsa. After all she's a partner and needs to hear what you have to say as much as I do." Bannister picked up the phone on his desk, called the bar and told the barman to find Elsa and ask her to come to the office.

"How has Elsa settled back into dancing at the club? I guess the punters were more than a little pleased to see she was back?" asked Jack

"She's not dancing Jack. She's now helping me manage the club, so the punters will have to remain disappointed, because she won't be stripping for them anymore."

Jack was taken aback at the thought of Elsa managing the club. Not that she wasn't capable, but because it was the last thing he would have expected. He was also envious that Roland could give her something she would value that he clearly could not. "Are you sure she'll be able to handle the job? She hasn't got any real experience of management." The words echoed in Jacks head and he realized how petty they must have sounded to Roland.

"I think so, she's bright and will pick up things quickly. She may have a little difficulty to start off with but there are plenty of people around who care about her and will be able to break her in gently. More importantly she wants to do the job and couldn't wait to get started today after we returned from the DA's office this afternoon."

Jack picked up the comment about Elsa being with people who cared about her and could see that Bannister was replacing him as Elsa's mentor and he wondered if he was also going to be replaced as her lover. "Were you able to speak to Bantry? What did he say about her sudden re-appearance?" asked Jack trying to ignore what was happening between them.

"We spoke on the speaker phone. He knew she was returning to New York because I had spoken to him a couple of days earlier and told him that she had been in hiding, petrified of going to the police because of the fear of becoming a target for Walsh and anyone he cared to hire to take his revenge on her. She explained everything that happened on Walsh's boat, but told him she swam to the shore after falling in the water, losing a lot of blood in the process. Elsa showed the New York assistant DA the scar on her shoulder where the bullet had grazed her. She added that after reaching the shore she caught a taxi to her hotel, changed and flew back to New York that night on a cancelled reservation. She left her luggage at the hotel because she felt too weak to carry it. Bantry asked why there was no record of her flying back to New York and Elsa said that she paid cash for the ticket and used a false name, which she can't now remember."

"What was Bantry's reaction? Did he believe her?"

"Fortunately he had the same dislike for Walsh as us, and as a result may be prepared to stretch credulity a little to put an end to the uncertainty surrounding this case. Elsa told Bantry that she didn't feel safe until she heard about Walsh's murder and thought she should now "come clean" with the police. Bantry won't want to spend too much money extending the case further as he knows nothing of our plan to extort money from Walsh, and he won't be able to see any benefit to himself at the end of it. Julie paid all of the bills in Boston so Elsa's story that she went to Boston to live with a friend will also be difficult to dispute."

"I couldn't pay any of the bills because, if you remember, I was supposed to be dead," said Elsa entering the office. On hearing her voice Jack turned quickly to see her. As always she looked stunning, wearing a black silk shirt and tight, figure hugging, black cord trousers. The ends off the shirt were tied in a knot revealing a tantalizing length of her mid riff. Their eyes met and Elsa greeted Jack, "Hello Mr. Cates, long time no see."

"Elsa." Jack walked over to hug Elsa but she checked his advance by holding him at arm's length, and gave him an impassionate peck on the cheek before walking over the sofa to sit down. "Don't think you can automatically pick up things from where you left them. People change and move on, especially when they are taken for granted or mistreated, or made a fool of for such a long time."

Jack was stunned by Elsa's cold response, she was acting as if he was just another acquaintance. "How can you be so distant, and why are you taking the high ground? You knew I had to make sure Bridget did what we wanted and whatever I did I did it for….." Jack's voice trailed off when he remembered he was re-running a cliché he had already used when trying to absolve himself of his guilt for sleeping with Bridget.

"What's wrong Jack? Have you got that feeling of déjà vu? I would have thought you would have polished up your excuses by now to make them sound a little more convincing, if not just as hollow. At least you now have the sense of not trying to justify your actions as sacrifices for a greater cause," replied Elsa sarcastically.

"Hold it you two," interjected Bannister "You can discuss your differences in private, which is probably the best place to air them." He paused then in mock religious overtones continued with, "Brethren we are gathered together today to discuss where we go from here after the Walsh debacle, and decide what we can retrieve from the situation."

"What do you mean Roland, "What we can retrieve"? Walsh is dead, there's nothing we can retrieve," replied Jack.

"Simon Walsh is dead, but his forlorn widow still has the money she arranged for the payoff to Elsa, unless her husband cut her off in his will. He had few living relatives and there's a good chance he won't have made a will, so after his estate passes through probate the money will go to his wife."

"OK Roland so Bridget has the money. What good is that to us?" he asked impatiently.

"Don't be so obtuse Jack, surely you can see there must be some opportunities we can use to come out ahead of the game. I understand that you and Bridget got on very well together. Elsa tells me that from her vantage point after her meeting with Bridget at the roadhouse, she could see that the relationship between the two of you was much more than business, and that you acted more like "love birds" than enemies. Surely we can capitalize on this situation and use it to get a little money out of her? We're all losers here and we should do what we can to turn the situation around and get our money back. Or should I say my money back, as I'm the only one who seems to have lost any real quantity of cash in this deal."

"Well how the hell am I supposed to do that? Ask her for it politely and hope that she's so overwhelmed with my charm that she coughs up?" asked Jack petulantly.

"No, it's a bit more complicated than that Jack. You're going to have to marry her! And don't think you have a choice in the matter." answered Bannister sternly, assuming the dominant position. We've tried it your way, now we're going to do it my way."

"Are you joking Roland?" said Jack lifting his hands in a gesture of reason. Roland simply nodded, adding to Jack's frustration. "You must be fucking mad! And what do you think of his plan Elsa?" continued Jack trying to elicit some support from her, and hoping that she still felt enough for him to disagree with Roland's proposition.

Bannister was pleased that he had prepared Elsa for an outburst from Jack, otherwise she may have sided with her ex-lover weakening his position. Naturally she was reluctant at first but Bannister had worn away her resistance by reminding her of Jack's poor treatment of her over the years, but really scored when he reminded her of the callous way he had perpetrated his latest infidelity, with a complete disregard for her feelings. Elsa found herself susceptible to his arguments because of the rift in her relationship with Jack, initially caused by her isolation in Boston and now widened because of his affair with Bridget. Of course his ultimate plan was to get Jack out of Elsa's life, which would give him the opportunity to provide a shoulder to cry on and a chance to make his move on her when the time was right. After all she was the only reason he got involved in this dumb deal in the first place.

"Well as you've assured me that you only fucked Bridget for the success of the scam, it shouldn't be too much of a hardship for you to carry on. And believe me I think she's probably so besotted with you that you shouldn't have too much trouble getting her to the altar." Elsa felt strange talking to Jack this way, especially in front of Roland and after all they had meant to each other in the past. She wasn't happy with the prospect of Jack marrying Bridget, but it had all sounded so logical the way Roland had explained it to her, but in confronting Jack she was starting to have second thoughts until her resolve to get back at him kicked in. Her intent was to hurt him in the same way that he had hurt her. He was now the object wriggling on Roland's hook and she had anticipated great satisfaction in watching him squirm, but in actual fact she hurt for Jack in seeing the predicament he now found himself in.

In desperation Jack looked deep into Elsa's eyes trying to find a vestige of the love she once had for him, but she turned away quickly asking Bannister for a drink, who then turned to Jack and asked him if he would like his usual bottle of beer. Jack was still reeling from Elsa's onslaught, knowing that she was prepared to go along with Roland and force him to marry Bridget. He was amazed that her love for him had changed to resentment so quickly and he wondered how long it would be before Roland replaced him in her bed. With his spirit continuing to follow the now familiar downward spiral of despair created by Walsh's murder, he dumbly shook his head, declining Roland's offer.

"What's wrong Jack? Not thirsty? You seem lost for words for once. Does that mean you'll go along with the plan?"

Jack was floored and he couldn't hide it and replied dejectedly, "Well as it's what you both want, I guess I don't have much choice. Something like this will take time so don't expect it to happen overnight."

"Of course not," replied Bannister, "after all we must allow Bridget a respectable period to grieve for her husband, but let's not leave it too long after that. What would you say? Twelve months seems a reasonable period of grief. Give the matter some thought Jack and we can work out a schedule."

"Whatever you say Roland," said Jack despondently. "Well if that's business concluded, I'll go." He looked at Elsa saying, "I guess you and me have nothing else to talk about." Elsa didn't return his look so with that he left Bannister's office.

Hearing Jack bring an end to their relationship made Elsa suddenly feel hot and claustrophobic, and in trying to suppress her natural emotion to cry, she also felt that she was gasping for breath. "Excuse me Roland, I need some air," said Elsa. Bannister nodded and Elsa followed Jack, intending to catch up with him to try to put their separation on a much friendlier footing, but she was intercepted by Frank who asked her to urgently sign for a late delivery of spirits. Frank blocked her path explaining that the driver was waiting and in a hurry to get away. As he spoke Elsa tried to look around his large frame to catch a glimpse of Jack, but he had left the club at a rapid pace and there was no sign of him.

Jack hit the street both hurt and angry. He needed a drink, and quickly. How could Elsa have sided with Roland in preference to him? Effectively she had severed their relationship as surely as if she had stabbed him through the heart, and she didn't blink an eyelid when she did it. He thought back of the intimacy they had shared and found the whole situation too incredible to comprehend.

Apart from his break up with Elsa he couldn't understand how his "partners" could expect him to exploit Bridget by marrying her and then fleecing her of a good proportion of the money she had got for her husband's release? Shit, this felt wrong. He wasn't a man, who fastidiously adhered to accepted moral ethics, but he loved Bridget and because of that the thought of taking her money went against everything he believed in. He didn't mind using Bridget before he got to know her, but now things were different. She was a person; a special person that he didn't want to hurt or put in danger. Jack was too much of a coward to choose between Bridget and Elsa, but knew he couldn't have let things go on the way they were indefinitely. Now Elsa had made the choice for him, well so be it!

4

At three o'clock in the morning Jack was standing, no barely standing, outside the front door of Bridget's apartment. Although he was well known to the night desk clerk, he had to cajole his way into the building because he was obviously the worse for wear for drink. The desk clerk was a retired cop and knew Jack from his days with the NYPD, otherwise he would never have been able to get into the building. The management prided themselves on security arrangements and the exclusivity of the apartments. Despite the difficulty he had in maintaining his balance and focusing his vision long enough to get a bearing on the direction he wanted to move, Jack managed to find and operate the elevator up to the floor of Bridget's apartment and was now leaning against her door, tired and wanting to take the weight off his legs.

Instead of ringing the bell, Jack quietly called out Bridget's name through the door trying to be quiet and avoid disturbing Francesca. In his befuddled mind he may have thought he was calling quietly for Bridget but was, in fact, making far more noise than if he had simply rung the bell. Francesca, whose bedroom was closest to the front door heard Jack calling and on recognizing his voice rushed to open it before he woke Bridget. As she opened the door Jack fell through it and grabbed onto Francesca to try and break his fall. Francesca fell backwards under the weight of Jack who landed on top of her, with his head nestling on her bosom.

At that moment Bridget came into the hall to see Jack telling Francesca that she was the only woman in the world for him, while Francesca was trying to free herself from him by pushing him off her and wriggling away from beneath his body. Her efforts were thwarted because every inch she gained was lost as Jack simply kept pulling her back underneath him. "Jack if you're going to cheat on me, shouldn't you be more discrete?" asked Bridget, gently mocking him in his current predicament.

Jack looked up quizzically at Bridget trying to comprehend how she could be talking to him from another part of the hall and also be lying underneath him. Slowly the reality of the situation began to dawn on him as he looked from Bridget to Francesca and back to

Bridget again. Raising his body he eased his weight off Francesca, as she took the opportunity to escape from him, and quickly rose to her feet, adjusting her dressing gown. "Go to bed Francesca," said Bridget with an understanding tone of voice, "I'll take care of Jack." Francesca didn't need to be encouraged further and quickly disappeared into her bedroom.

By this time Jack was attempting to get to his feet and began to stagger about like a young colt trying its first faltering steps after birth. He stumbled and bounced off the wall, but managed to recover before Bridget caught hold of him. The momentum of his weight nearly knocked Bridget off her feet but, unlike Francesca, she was prepared for the onslaught and managed to arrest Jack's eccentric lurching and guide him to her bedroom. She edged up to the bed and dropped Jack gently onto it so that he was lying half on and half off it, with one foot resting on the floor and the other dangling in mid-air. After taking off his shoes Bridget lifted his legs onto the bed, making sure he wouldn't be able to roll off, and saw he was fast asleep. She gave a wry smile, kissed him lightly on his lips and turned out the light as she left the bedroom.

The next thing Jack became aware of was the bright sunlight streaming into the room, even dazzling him through his eyelids. He squinted to protect his eyes from the blinding light and turned his back to the window, pulling his knees upwards and curling his body into a fetal position. His head was pounding but he was determined to get into a comfortable position and hopefully continue to sleep off his hangover. The next thing he heard was Bridget's voice saying, "Don't get too relaxed Jack, and sit up, I've brought you some breakfast." Reluctantly Jack straightened his body and pulled himself up into a seated position, with his back against the headboard. Bridget was holding a tray and sat down on the edge of the bed before placing it on Jack's lap. "Thanks," said Jack sheepishly, "look I'm sorry if I behaved badly last night, but to be honest I can't remember much about it. I didn't do anything too bad, did I?"

"It depends what you call bad," replied Bridget sternly, teasing him.

"Well you know, did I say or do anything disgusting, or did I simply say or do anything you didn't like?" asked Jack beginning to worry that he might have ranted about the previous evening's meeting with Elsa and Roland. "You know a drunk man is an open book."

"You weren't conscious long enough to say much. You were so drunk you had difficulty doing much of anything. You went out like a light as soon as your head hit the pillow, but not before you plighted your undying love to Francesca. She was overcome with surprise and this morning asked for the day off. You must be losing your touch with women."

"But I know I fell through the doorway and I thought she was you, I can explain........"

"Don't worry stud, I think she'll be able to overcome her disappointment!"

Jack slowly began to see that Bridget was having fun at his expense and started to relax. He obviously hadn't said anything he would have cause to regret, as Bridget was happy to have him with her and clearly enjoying being a tease. "If Francesca's alright, why are you being so hard on me?" he pleaded.

"Well for one thing you were supposed to get here by midnight, but instead you turn-up in the early hours of the morning drunk and incapable. You obviously found drinking with your buddies preferable to spending the night with me. If you're trying to get away from me now, what will it be like in a few months?"

"It's not like that Bridget and you know it! I got wrapped up in the security details for the Blue Cockatoo, the manager was satisfied so afterwards he offered me something to eat and a drink. We started ramblin' on about old times and one drink led to another. You've got to be social otherwise clients don't come back, it must be the same in your line?"

"I may socialize to a certain extent, but I don't get pickled. You must have had one hell of a drinking session. What turned a social drink into a binge?"

"Well after drinking with the manager I went into the bar to check out some friends, but it turns out that they aren't the friends I thought they were. Sometimes when reality hits, you need to soften the blow with alcohol. So that's what I did." Jack was caught off guard and honestly explained the cause of his depression and the reason for him going on a bender. He didn't clarify that the "friends" were actually a friend, who was Elsa. He immediately regretted being so open because it gave Bridget the opportunity to ask further questions.

Bridget was alarmed at the sudden change in Jack's mood and the somberness of his reply startled her. "Did this have anything to do with Elsa?" she asked more out of concern for him than by the fact they had met up again.

"No," said Jack recovering his composure and forgetting that Bridget would make the connection between the club and Elsa. "My Client is the manager, Roland Bannister, who is paranoid about a break in. I've given him a plan for door and window locks, alarms and security cameras. The complete works. I used to drink with some of the staff but now they've sided with Elsa and won't talk to me."

"You look upset. Do you want to talk about it?" Bridget asked gently, not wanting to pry deeper than was comfortable for him.

Jack looked up and smiled, recognizing her concern for him. "I don't want to talk about the past. What's done is done and there's no sense in trying to resuscitate a corpse. I'm more interested in the future and what's going to happen to us. Where are we going? Have we got a future?"

"Do you have to ask? I love you and want to spend the rest of my life with you," replied Bridget leaning over and gently kissing him on the lips. "Why the sudden concern? I'm not terminating this relationship because you turn up late and drunk on my doorstep."

"My experience last night taught me how fragile relationships can be. At one time, one of the people I was talking about was my closest friend, but now there's nothing." Jack wanted to be open with Bridget about his feelings for Elsa, but knew he couldn't tell her everything; for fear that she would end up despising him for tricking her and inadvertently contributing to Simon's death.

"Do you mean friend or lover?" interjected Bridget suddenly feeling uncertain and insecure herself.

Jack had said more than he really wanted to, but had gone past the point of return. He decided to convey his feelings for Elsa through a surrogate. It was pointless now trying to deny there wasn't another woman in his life. "From what I've said, you're smart enough to know that I've not been altogether honest with you. Yes there was someone else. I was seeing her when I met you, and yes we were lovers."

Bridget's stomach dropped and she got up off the bed; arms folded and nervously started pacing the room. "If you have someone else why let me make a fool of myself, and why are you still bothering with me now?" she cried.

Jack put the tray aside, got out of the bed and rushed over to Bridget. He held her by the arms, but she resolutely kept them folded to avoid the closeness of an embrace, as she looked into his face. "If I wanted anyone else I wouldn't be here, with you. I want to be honest and tell you the truth now; otherwise we won't have any kind of future together. When I met you the last thing on my mind was the thought that we would become lovers. You were business that's all, but from the moment I met you I felt the chemistry between us and eventually couldn't resist it. Everything that happened between us went against my best judgement, but I couldn't help myself."

Bridget recognized the way she felt after meeting Jack, with her own emotions going through the same turmoil before she gave in to her natural instincts. "Go on," she demanded wanting Jack to give her a reason to justify staying with him.

"The woman was a stripper at the Blue Cockatoo who I met when doing a security check for an insurance company after an attempted break in. There had been quite a bit of damage caused and the insurers wanted me to check whether the attempted crime had been down to negligence. The club was alarmed but the alarm system hadn't gone off and it was felt that the attempted robbery was an inside job. I worked a couple of weeks behind the bar to try and get to know the staff and get any leads on likely suspects. It was a pointless exercise because the thieves were eventually caught trying to break into another club a few blocks away. But I did get to meet this woman while I was working there."

"What do you mean "this woman"? Can't you give her a name?"

"Her name was Julie," Jack lied. "We got on well, spent some time together either before going to the club, or after closing, and after a few days we were sleeping together."

"Were you still sleeping with her while you were making love to me?" cut in Bridget sharply, getting more and more annoyed by Jack's apparent inability to be aware of her feeling of insecurity.

"If I'm honest with you, I probably would have, but she's not been living in New York for the last few months because her mother was terminally ill. She only returned to New York last week after her mother's funeral." Jack felt bad about having to lie on such a grand scale and now found he was spinning an even broader web of deceit to give an air of credibility to his answers to Bridget's questions.

"Have you seen her recently? Did you go to the funeral?"

"No. I never met Julie's parents. They didn't know she was a stripper. Julie didn't want anyone from New York attending the funeral in case they gave anything away. It was a difficult time for her, but I had to see her as soon as she returned. I had to be sure about the way I felt about you, and to see if my feelings for her had been replaced by my love for you. When we met I knew instantly that I no longer felt the same way about her, although I still care enough not to want to hurt her. Can you understand that?"

Bridget nodded feeling a tear beginning to form in the corner of her eye.

"I tried to explain what had happened between you and me while she was away, but she wouldn't listen to any kind of explanation. I didn't want to hurt her but it was inevitable that I would. Julie told me that she never wanted to see me again and that I had ruined her life. I didn't feel too good after I left the club and couldn't come straight over to you and pretend nothing had happened. So I got drunk." Jack remembered the nausea he had felt in Roland's office when he failed to elicit any response from Elsa about whether she still had any feelings for him. He left Bridget's side and sat down on the end of the bed.

Bridget looked down at the sad figure hugging itself at the end of the bed. "Tell me honestly. Do you love me and no one else?" she asked vehemently.

Jack looked up trying to formulate an answer she could accept and suddenly realized that there was still a chance for him to convince Bridget of his love for her. He stood up and grabbed her firmly. "You know I love you and that there's no-one else."

"Well in that case let's get married," said Bridget calmly, adding, "the sooner the better."

Jack released his grip on her, once again amazed at her audacity. "But Simon's funeral was only last week. What will people think?"

"I don't care what anybody thinks and neither should you. We are the only people who matter and if you don't agree with that, then we don't have a future."

"I'm not concerned about what people think of me. I'm already marked down as being worthless, but you're the head of a big company and have a career.... our getting married could destroy all that. Aren't you worried about the consequences?"

"If you feel the same for me as I feel for you, then the only thing I'm worried about is losing you."

Jack took Bridget in his arms and kissed her passionately. He was overjoyed at her unequivocal pledge of love for him, which lifted the black despair he had felt after Elsa's rejection. He could live without Elsa; Bridget was the only person he needed. Jack pulled away to look at her and suddenly felt that his hangover had gone, but marriage to Bridget would bring other headaches before he could get rid of the burden Roland had placed on him.

5

Elsa, like Jack, was trying to get used to life without the person she had felt closest to for the last few years and it wasn't easy. After the meeting with Jack and Roland she had tried to occupy herself with business at the club to take her mind off the large empty vacuum she felt being alone, without a soul mate. Roland and everyone else at the Blue Cockatoo was being extremely nice so as not to talk about partners or offend her by mentioning Jack, knowing that she was feeling frail and vulnerable. But she couldn't have them walking on eggshells indefinitely so she gathered the bar staff and the dancers in the main bar an hour before opening.

As the staff filed into the bar they were chatting amongst themselves quietly trying to second-guess the purpose of the summons from Elsa. Roland was conspicuous by his absence, but Elsa had already spoken to him about the situation and got him to promise to come in a little later and give her a chance to talk to the staff. Julie was attending to the bar and Elsa had instructed her to take orders and get everyone a drink. One by one the staff grabbed bar stools and chairs, and turned to face Elsa, who was sitting at one of the tables. Frank walked over to her and asked if she wanted a drink, Elsa shook her head, stood up and motioned him to go back and sit with the rest of the staff.

"First of all thanks for coming in a little early, but I had to talk to all of you about my personal situation because you're all going to such great lengths to be extra kind to me. I appreciate your concern, but we can't carry on like this indefinitely, otherwise I won't be able to do my job well and you'll be preoccupied with me instead of the customers."

Julie looked over at Elsa as she was talking and understood how painful talking openly about her private life was to her.

"I won't be dancing anymore because Roland has been kind enough to give me a managerial position," continued Elsa, "and the last thing I want to do is let him down. I'm still green around the edges and I need you guys to put me straight when I go wrong. So help me make a success of this gig and when I put a foot wrong ......tell me! I won't lie about my bust up with Jack...."

"You're better off without the bastard," cut in Julie.

"Thanks, Julie but I can manage on my own. You all know Jack and he's still probably going to be showing his face every now and then so don't worry about what you say to him, any more than you should worry about how you talk to me. Jack and me are all grown up and I'm sure we'll both survive this thing and move on. Has anyone got any questions?"

Elsa paused as she looked around the room. "If you ain't seeing Jack no more, can we hit on him," piped up Colette, one of the dancers.

"If you think there's anything worth having, now that I've done with him, you're welcome," replied Elsa. The repartee between the two women broke the tension and everyone in the room laughed, as much in relief as for the humor in their remarks. "OK if that's all take 15 minutes to finish your drinks and then let's get the show on the road," said Elsa. The room broke into a relaxed buzz and Elsa made her way to the office.

Frank caught up with Elsa in the doorway to the office. "Elsa, I know what you're going through, because you thought a lot of Cates, even though he is a jerk. If there's anything I can do, or if you want me to teach him a lesson, just let me know."

"What do you mean Frank? Beat him up?"

"Whatever you want Elsa, I'd be only too happy to do it. He's too cocky by far and doesn't treat you with the respect you deserve."

Elsa put her hand on the big man's shoulder, "I know you only want to help me Frank, but it doesn't matter what I think or feel about Jack now, I wouldn't want to see him hurt. You understand that don't you?"

"Yeah," Frank nodded, a little disappointed, and went back into the bar.

Elsa walked over to the desk and sat down behind it. She involuntarily let tears form in the corners of her eyes, always a window to her true feelings. She impatiently brushed the moisture away and turned to the stock books to focus on more mundane matters. She was content that they had just received an order of spirits and beer and that she wouldn't have to worry about running short of drinks tonight. Nevertheless she made a note of the number of wine bottles unopened and gave herself a mental reminder to ring the suppliers for another half dozen boxes of mixed white wines.

Elsa closed the stock book and perused the office. It was Spartan with few items of objet d'art to soften the décor. Roland had a couple of token pictures on the wall that were prints of famous masters, which weren't really picked with any purpose and didn't fit into the overall ambience of the office. One picture was Van Gough's "Stars" and the other was a Monet's "Ladies in waiting". Elsa decided that she should resist changing the office décor until she was more firmly established in her new position at the club. She had changed her workplace to suit an efficient way of operating, and had re-arranged things on her desk and in the cabinets and drawers so that she would be able to find any item of equipment or file, in the shortest possible time. The accounts were locked in the safe that was discreetly positioned in the wall, behind an ornate cocktail bar, and was accessed through one of side cabinets in the bar. The safe also held petty cash and the deeds for the club.

She went to the safe to take out the float for the tills before opening time. She and Frank had taken the cash from the previous day's takings to the bank and changed 100 dollars into small denomination coins, to put 10 dollars' worth into each of the 10 tills in the club. Roland would probably come in about nine thirty before the rush at ten and Elsa wanted to show him that she had everything under control. In addition to the coins she took out 50 dollars for each till in twenties, tens, fives and singles. As she went from till to till with the change she was pleased that the atmosphere was relaxed and the bar staff, were talking amongst themselves, hardly noticing her arrival. Except that is, Julie who came up behind her as she was putting the money into her till and gave her a warm hug.

From the bar Elsa went into the dancer's dressing room to see the girls huddled in a group chatting quietly before getting changed into their tiny costumes. "Are you all set to wow'em tonight?" she asked from the doorway.

"You bet" replied Colette, "those boys don't know how privileged they are to gaze on our fine bodies."

"Fine body? You look to me as if you've been putting on weight girl. Have you been spoiling yourself lately, and I don't mean men! I mean wining and dining."

Colette stood up and instinctively half turned to try and catch a glimpse of her rear in the mirror. "Do you think I'm fat? My clothes are hanging off me! And look at that ass, you won't see one better in New York tonight."

"It must be my imagination, Colette, but be sure to weigh yourself and check it out," replied Elsa. "OK girls show the punters why this is the best and classiest club in town." With that she smiled and left the room, enjoying the brief consternation she will have caused Colette before her picking up on the joke. The girl hardly had a spare ounce of fat on her body.

It was now eight-thirty and the doors would open at nine o'clock, with the girls coming out at ten-thirty. It was usually quiet until ten and then the punters would rush in, coming from bars and restaurants in the town. Some came in early to eat, but not many. It was seldom that any drunks got in, not with Lou and Frank manning the doors, but it was common for a drunk to be thrown out before the closing time of two-thirty, usually because they were trying to get too friendly with one of the girls. Elsa suddenly became aware that she was pleased not to be flaunting her body in front of strangers and having to avoid their groping hands or other unwanted advances. She no longer missed the power she'd wielded as a dancer. Or did she only need to exercise that power to balance her relationship with Jack?

6

The weeks and months passed quickly as Elsa settled into her new life managing the "Blue Cockatoo" along with Roland, who took more of a back seat after she became more familiar with running procedures and eventually took over the reins. Jack hardly ever visited the club or called either of them. He was not consciously creating a distance between his former colleagues, but his past life was terminated when Roland gave him the ultimatum to marry Bridget. His separation from Elsa was far harder and he found himself casually recalling their time together without any real reason other than he still missed her. Roland was beginning to get more than a little irritated by Jack's attitude and his failure to maintain a reasonable contact with him.

Apart from his annoyance with Jack, he was feeling smug and content. He had Elsa working for him and she had shaken off, or at least suppressed her feelings, for Jack. Although she might have been smarting a little until she got used to the idea, but she had made the most important choice, which was to be independent. It was funny but Roland had always considered Elsa to be her own woman, probably because of the persona she projected when she was dancing, but after watching her turn herself inside out after Jack's departure he realized how much she had relied on his being around. Magnificent women don't always fall in love with magnificent men, he mused.

He sat back in his hotel room, caressing the glass of brandy he held in his hand. He would miss going to the club tonight as he had other business to attend to first. Jack had shown a lack of respect once too often and, now that the dust had settled, he was going to make him pay. How else was Roland to maintain his reputation amongst his peers? Word had already circulated about the fiasco with Simon Walsh; it was impossible to keep such things secret. Roland knew that there were too many people aware of the scam that Jack was trying to perpetrate using his bankroll for word not to get out. In some circles he would already be an object of amusement. God knows discretion is not a by word in criminal circles.

Roland had been planning his denouement to this regrettable episode since he first got word of Walsh's death, not from Jack, but from Wesley Green. First Jack must be forced to marry Walsh's widow, and then Roland thought he could extract the recompense owed him before implicating his partner in some dark and unforgivable deed. It could be a lover's tiff, ending in Bridget's death, or an unsolicited attack on Elsa or one of the other girls at the club, leading of course to Jack's death. The details didn't really matter Roland knew he would be able to adapt to any given situation to suit his needs.

It would be easy to get Frank to take care of Jack, and he would be grateful of the chance to even some old scores, but that would be viewed as an easy victory facilitated by one of Pallacio's men and would do nothing to reinstate his standing among his peers. Besides, if Elsa discovered that he had any involvement in the harming or killing of Jack then he could kiss goodbye to any chance he might have had to becoming more than just a friend. That's why Roland had arranged to meet an old police friend of Jack's, Gene Tanner.

He had flown from New York to Miami on a late night flight and stayed in the Hyatt Place Hotel at the airport, which he knew from previous visits gave easy access to the center of the city. As Roland sat in the back of a taxi going to Miami Police Headquarters a plan started to formulate in his mind. The shape of events may differ in the implementation of his idea, depending on the path taken, but they would all lead to the same end, Jack's punishment.

"Hello Mr. Bannister," said Tanner as he ushered Roland into a meeting room.

"Thanks for seeing me at such short notice Detective Tanner", replied Roland as he took a chair on one side of the large desk in the center of the room. He made himself comfortable on the chair and crossed his legs, leaning into the backrest.

"I must admit I was a little surprised when you asked for this meeting Mr. Bannister, until you mentioned Simon Walsh", ventured Tanner sitting down on a chair on the opposite side of the table.

"Yes, Simon Walsh. Not a very likeable person, but surely not deserving of the ghastly end he met in prison. I'm on business in Miami so I thought it might be worthwhile talking to you about Walsh while I'm down here." Tanner sat in silence waiting for Bannister to state the real purpose of his visit. "He was a rich man, recently acquiring his father's wealth and the head of a big international company. It's difficult to understand how he fell to the depths he reached before his death", continued Roland.

"Don't feel too much sympathy for him, Mr. Bannister, he made a career out of using and abusing women. The man who killed Walsh was the brother of one of his victims. She was a nice girl who may have worked as a hooker, but took care not to mix with the wrong type of john, until she met Walsh that is. Walsh planted the seeds for her mental and physical destruction after hiring her for a weekend of "fun" with him and his buddies."

"Yeah I read the details of the case in the paper. It all seemed a little too pat for my liking. Mathew Caine, although violent, was not considered to be a potential murderer before the incident with Walsh", replied Bannister. "But that doesn't matter. You're right it's not Walsh but his widow that I'm really concerned about. She's now a very wealthy woman and could be the target of any unscrupulous philanderer."

"What an old fashioned description! I've met Mrs. Walsh and she doesn't seem like the type of person who would be easily taken in by a smooth talking "philanderer". What makes you think she's in any danger?" asked Tanner.

"The girl Walsh took out to sea with him, Elsa Bartelli, manages my club in New York. She was petrified of Walsh but was even more scared of her then partner, Jack Cates. Cates had put her up to soliciting Walsh so that he could blackmail him. The plan took a detour when Walsh took Elsa out on a sea trip, but Cates choreographed Walsh's incrimination for her suspected murder and his subsequent murder in prison."

"How the hell could he have done that!" challenged Tanner rising to the defense of his friend.

"I don't know the details, but I do know that he has ingratiated himself with Mrs. Walsh and that they are planning to marry in the near future. He quickly dumped Elsa after climbing into Mrs. Walsh's bed, the poor kid was heartbroken when she told me that Jack had stashed her away until Walsh was sentenced. She also told me how he planned to get his hands on Walsh's money through his wife. I fear for Bridget Walsh's safety after they marry and she's no longer useful to him."

Tanner sat silent for a while, mentally sifting through Bannister's story and trying to knit the pieces about Jack and Elsa into the chronology of Walsh's trial and term of imprisonment. "Jack's not a murderer", Tanner replied suddenly. "He may bend the rules slightly, but he was a good cop. I know him well and I don't believe he could kill anybody in cold blood. He wouldn't have put the finger on Walsh and I know he wouldn't harm a woman. Anyway, Mrs. Walsh and Jack both live in New York, not Miami, so why tell me about your concerns?"

"For two reasons. One, you know about the Simon Walsh case, and two, as you've said, you once worked with Jack and know him personally. You can talk to NYPD if you think there is any substance to what I'm saying, and if necessary convince them to keep an eye on Bridget. You know I walk on the opposite side of the street to you and I don't want to be seen going into any of the NYPD precinct stations. Besides, I doubt my story would carry any credibility just on my say so."

Tanner had done his homework on Bannister before the meeting, so he knew he had connections with criminals and could understand his reluctance to approach the law with his fears. He did wonder why he was so concerned about Bridget and how reliable his opinions were. But what possible reason could he have for putting Jack in the frame for a possible murder? Maybe he had some ulterior motive for casting suspicion on Jack, maybe not, thought Tanner. Jack may skate on thin ice at times but he would never commit murder, he couldn't have changed that much.

"I can see that your skeptical, Detective Tanner, but just remember two things. It's been some time since you worked with Cates and we could be talking about a lot of money. Look, I'm just concerned about the effect of any unpleasantness on Elsa. Since she finished with Jack, she and I have got close and I don't want any upsets that could hurt her. I know that sounds selfish, but she's one hell of a woman and this could be my last chance of her becoming more than my assistant manager." Bannister shrugged expecting Tanner to be sympathetic to his situation.

Tanner looked at the sharply dressed middle-aged, self-assured man in front of him, who was obviously used to getting his way in business and in life. It didn't sound plausible that a man like this could be so besotted with any woman, but Tanner had to admit that Elsa was no ordinary woman. He was certain, however, that there could be some "funny business" afoot and it would be worthwhile advising his pals in the NYPD of the players and their prospective roles. They should probably keep an eye on Bridget Walsh because she was central to everything, but it would be low key.

Bannister left Tanner satisfied that he had placed a cloud over Jack's head even if he hadn't convinced him that Bridget Walsh was in grave danger. She would marry Jack and one or other, or both, would have something unpleasant befall them and Gene Tanner would remember this conversation and be able to put two and two together to make five.

7

Jack felt apprehensive as he dressed. Not because he had to wear a tie, which he never normally did, but because it was the wrong time to be getting hitched to Bridget, even though she had no reservations. Not that he didn't love Bridget, because he did. But Roland's ultimatum cast a shadow on what should have been a joyous occasion. The wedding was happening much earlier than the timescale Roland had given him and Jack didn't want Bannister to think he was toeing the line because he was scared, greedy or trying to get back at Elsa.

Bridget wanted a quiet wedding ceremony with just a few close friends present. Jack had asked Gene if he could come up for the wedding, just to give him some moral support. Gene had apologized saying he was under pressure because of a high profile case that was going pear shaped and that he was at a critical point in his investigation, so he couldn't afford to take a break, no matter how brief. Jack was disappointed because Gene was one of the few people he could relax with, now that Elsa was no longer in his life. Gene didn't tell Jack about his conversation with Bannister and on reflection thought the whole idea of Jack harming Bridget was absurd.

In the end it did turn out to be a quiet affair. Bridget hired a banqueting suite in the Bryant Park Hotel and true to her word only invited a few friends to witness the legal ceremony, and a buffet and drinks were laid on in an adjoining room to celebrate the wedding.

Even though there were no more than a dozen people invited to the wedding, Jack didn't know any of them, apart from his parents and Bridget's maid, Francesca. She was the only person of Bridget's circle pleased to see Jack and warmly wished the couple well after the ceremony. She couldn't ignore her "mothering" instinct when it came to Bridget's welfare and started handing out drinks and food almost immediately, to the annoyance of the catering staff that had been hired for the occasion.

Bridget stood next to Jack intermittently squeezing his hand as she spoke. The crowd were mainly business colleagues and a couple of school friends. These people came from a different stratum of society than Jack's normal stomping ground and the distance between their worlds was palpable. She suddenly pulled him away from the circle of guests she was talking to and dragged him over to see a small old lady who had entered the room.

"Come with me Jack, there's somebody important that I want you to meet."

The old woman beamed when she saw Bridget and held out her arms encouraging a warm hug. "I'm so sorry I'm late, but my plane was delayed for 10 hours. So instead of arriving here last night and spending a comfortable night in bed, I've been sitting in an airport lounge and then an airplane, and we've come straight here from the airport!" she cried.

The old lady was followed by an elderly man struggling to carry two cases and keep up with events. He obviously wasn't the old lady's husband as the body language between them didn't indicate any intimate closeness. Jack thought he was either in the employ of the old lady or a distant relative.

"Aunty Ingrid, thank God you're alright. I got your fax message. You know it's easier to send texts these days."

Ingrid pulled away and scowled at Bridget replying that she had lived for over 80 years without cell phones and didn't see the need to start using them now. The women hugged again and Bridget turned to Jack and held out her hand to draw him closer. Then turning back to Ingrid she said, "I'm so pleased you made it, even if you did miss the wedding ceremony."

"I'm sorry too dear, but as it wasn't a church ceremony, perhaps it's not quite so important," Ingrid replied.

Pulling Jack towards her she continued, "This is Jack. He's the man I'm crazy about and want to spend the rest of my life with."

Ingrid looked up at Jack and seemed to penetrate his soul with her piercing eyes and limply held out her hand to greet him. Jack took her hand and bent to kiss her lightly on the cheek. "I'm pleased to meet you Aunty Ingrid" he ventured and stuck for anything further to add, raised himself to his full height and smiled uncomfortably.

"At least he's not like the other one. Stinking of alcohol within an hour of the wedding ceremony," said Ingrid referring to Bridget's first husband. "Don't be the shit he was," she said turning to Jack bluntly, "or you'll have me to answer to! Bridget is too nice a girl to be led a merry dance again, so don't start something you can't finish."

"Don't worry Aunty Ingrid, I'll make sure she has a happy life from now on," replied Jack sincerely.

His warmth cut no ice with the old woman. "Be sure you do," she retorted and turning back to Bridget she continued, "Please get me to a chair before I collapse".

Bridget took her hand and said to Jack, "The man with her is her butler, James. Can you sort the cases out with him and get them to their rooms?"

Jack turned to James and said, "C'mon let's get booked into your rooms."

"I did suggest we do that, Sir", replied James "but madam was insistent we come here first".

"Don't bother with formalities James. I can see your life is tough enough as it is" he smiled back as Bridget and Ingrid moved out of earshot.

"I'm more than her bloody butler. I'm also the gardener, driver, and chief bottle washer" volunteered James as he bent to lift up the cases. Jack took one of the cases from him and ushered him to the door.

"You're British," said Jack as they walked onto the landing outside the function room.

"All the best house servants always have been British. The tradition has been passed down through generations. But now we no longer work for upper class families or even aristocracy. We work for Arabs, Russians ....and Americans," replied James with a look of distaste on his face.

"You must enjoy the work otherwise you wouldn't do it," replied Jack.

"I suppose I do", said James, "but things have changed so much since I first started in service. M'lady used to have another 3 servants for cooking, gardening, house cleaning and maintenance, but now it's just me. We're both getting old and crusty together, but I'm determined to outlast her for the annoyance value."

Jack smiled and thought Ingrid must have been quite wealthy in her heyday. He quite liked James and could even put up with "Aunty Ingrid" for Bridget's sake. It would be the first of many concessions he would have to make, now that he was a married man. As a couple they seemed to be assuming a normality of life together that he never expected to achieve, although he still had the shadow of Roland Bannister hanging over him, together with his high expectations.

Jack's sudden quietness made James a little uneasy. "Are you alright Sir?" he asked.

"I've told you James there's no need for formalities with me" replied Jack as they stepped into the hotel lift. "I'm glad to get out of there. I don't really fit in with the crowd Bridget mixes with," Jack smiled as they walked down to reception. "Let's you and me have a couple of drinks in the bar when you get settled."

"Don't let the old biddy smell your breath afterwards or she'll change her opinion of you" answered James. "You're probably still on probation!" he laughed.

8

While Jack and Bridget were getting married, Roland Bannister and Elsa were having a drink together in the manager's office of the Blue Cockatoo.

"Now that Jack is getting married to Bridget Walsh we need to make plans about squeezing him for the money he owes me," said Roland, "he's had it too easy of late and hasn't exactly kept me in the picture. I didn't even get a wedding invite!"

Elsa still found it hard to be casual about Jack getting married, even if the ache of not being part of his life had subsided. "Not very amusing Roland" Elsa replied. "I'm sure Jack will get in touch with you sooner or later to arrange something."

"Why don't you call him Elsa? I'm sure he'd be pleased to hear from you", smiled Roland.

"That's not in very good taste, even if you find it funny," snapped Elsa. She was surprised at Roland's lack of sensitivity as he had been the sole of discretion since she had separated from Jack and had done everything to try and get on the right side of her. Perhaps he was beginning to accept that they would never be intimate. Since her return to the "Blue Cockatoo", Roland had made a few half-hearted attempts to get her into bed, but she had made it clear, as tactfully as she could, that the attraction was one–sided. He didn't push it, initially expecting to make headway as they got to know each other better from working together. Eventually he succumbed to the inevitable conclusion that it wasn't going to happen and he was beating his head against a brick wall.

"OK I shouldn't have been so blunt and unfeeling, but he's far more likely to respond to your request than mine. The problem is that he's not taking me seriously and thinks I'll forget about trying to get money from Bridget. Of course I could refresh his memory by sending him an invitation with Frank and Lou, and you know how much Frank likes Jack."

"Why can't we just forget the whole thing?" pleaded Elsa, not liking the anxiety she was feeling at the prospect of Jack getting hurt by Roland's two pet thugs. Roland had used them as a constant threat virtually from the start of the blackmail scam.

"I don't want to lean too heavily on Jack, but it's a matter of principle. Everybody in our "fraternity" knows what's been going on with Jack and the failed attempt to extort money from Simon Walsh, and that I've bank rolled Jack to the tune of over one hundred grand", replied Roland.

"You don't need the money……" said Elsa before being interrupted by Roland.

"No but being on the wrong end of a joke would be bad for my reputation and business. If I let Jack get away with this everyone else will think they can take me for a ride with impunity. Jack's got to honor his end of the bargain. I know the way things turned out couldn't have been foreseen but that's his problem. He promised a big return on my investment and now he's got to deliver!"

"Jack and I were in this scam together and I feel equally responsible for the current mess were in," reflected Elsa, as much to herself as to Bannister. "You can't put it all on Jack."

"Don't put yourself in the gun sights Elsa. This hair brain scheme was Jack's doing and he was the one making the promises and taking control of things. You just went along with him as you always did when the two of you were together. Really, I could never understood how you allowed yourself to be degraded in that way."

"Rather than pole dancing?" interrupted Elsa. "I'm in the sex industry, which tends to numb your sensitivities."

"OK you were a stripper, but you had class and I wouldn't let any of the punters lay a hand on you, you know that! Jack took away that class and you were branded a whore at Walsh's trial! I used to hate thinking of you in the situations Jack seemed happy to put you in, and I couldn't understand why you always went along with him!"

Roland's voice was becoming agitated and he appeared to be trying to justify the situation in his own mind rather than make Elsa understand his point of view. Elsa was a bit surprised at Roland's strength of feeling. She knew he was attracted to her, but she had always thought it was driven by the fact she was unattainable while she was with Jack; an object of desire that would lose its appeal once in his grasp.

"I never thought any of Jack's scams could end up with me nearly getting killed!" replied Elsa weakly. She felt like a child in front of a demanding father, wanting to say the right words that would please him.

"The past is the past and we can't change it. But I can make sure that the lessons learned from it benefit us in the future, and that is making sure we get Jack to meet his end of the deal. Bridget Walsh is worth millions so I'm sure she can afford to get Jack off the hook for a mere million dollars."

"A million dollars!" gasped Elsa, "there's no way Jack can get his hands on that kind of money. If he asks Bridget for the money, he'll have to tell her about his part in the blackmail attempt. That would knock the bottom out of their relationship and he'd still end up being unable to pay you," reasoned Elsa.

"That was the sum we agreed Elsa. I don't care how he gets the money ...just as long as he gets it."

"But it's pointless putting him in an impossible situation where he's bound to fail."

"You obviously still have feelings for Jack; otherwise like me you wouldn't care what kind of situation he finds himself in. He owes me and he's going to pay either in money or in pain," said Roland firmly. "He's an inventive guy. If he can't get the money by sweet talking Bridget, then he'll have to find some other way. That's why I think it would be a good idea for you to talk to him. Firstly to make him understand the strength of my determination to make him pay and secondly to let him know he only has two weeks to make good his debt."

Elsa felt the bottom drop out of her stomach. A dark dread started to rise within her and all she could see was the broken, lifeless body of Jack lying in a gutter somewhere. She suddenly understood that Roland disliked Jack immensely and suspected that although it had begun because he had a juvenile crush on her, it now went far deeper. She now knew that his feelings for her would no longer stop him carrying out his threat.

"I wouldn't know where to start the conversation," pleaded Elsa.

"It's simple you want to let bygones be bygones but having listened to me rant on about his debt. You want him to appreciate the anger I feel towards him and you can then broker a meeting between us," replied Roland. "I don't want to remind you that you're with me now as a friend as well as an employee. And before you say anything.......yes you do a good job, but that doesn't eliminate my need for satisfaction in this matter."

"Look. We both work in an unforgiving world where compassion is viewed as weakness. Even if I wanted to forget about everything that has happened over the last few months, I couldn't. Why? Because sooner or later somebody would hear about it, conclude I'd lost my nerve and come down here expecting to muscle in on my business," continued Roland. "Now are you going to make that call?"

Elsa nodded meekly, got up and left the office. She went out to the main bar and saw the club staff busying themselves by filling stock levels and putting washed glasses on the shelves underneath the bar for the evening ahead. She enjoyed being the Manager of the Blue Cockatoo, much more than being a dancer, but if she compromised herself by allowing Jack to become Roland's whipping boy, she couldn't carry on working there. Yes the best thing would be to talk to Jack to make sure he fully understood his situation and the need to come up with either a plan to pay Roland, or get out of New York.

Suddenly she felt alone. Normally in difficult circumstances she would talk to Jack who always picked her up and put things in perspective for her, leaving her in a better frame of mind than before. That wasn't possible now and she had lost the intimacy she had with Jack, feeling desolate by the prospect that she would never get as close to anyone else as she had been with him.....and now his life was being threatened, she knew that she still loved him.

9

Jack picked up his cell phone and realized immediately that Elsa was calling him as her name flashed on the screen. He paused before saying, "Hi Elsa, it's nice to hear from you," in his brightest voice.

"Hello Jack," Elsa replied flatly. "I think we should meet for a talk about Roland, and his determination to make you to come up with the money he's demanded you get from Bridget."

"What's he been saying?" asked Jack. "I haven't really had the time to come over to the club with one thing or another," he added delicately not wishing to mention his marriage to Bridget. "I can come over to the club today or tomorrow. I haven't got much on at the moment. The private eye business isn't what it used to be," he continued trying a little levity.

"I need to talk to you before you see Roland," explained Elsa. "I don't think you fully understand just how fired up he is about bank rolling us without a return."

"He knows he'll get the money back. He'll just have to wait until I can scrape something together," Jack interjected.

"Look Jack, it's gone beyond that now. He wants more than his bankroll he wants the million dollars he's asked for, and now he's put a timescale on it," said Elsa, mentally urging Jack to understand the gravity of the situation.

"When he mentioned wanting me to get a million dollars from Bridget I didn't really take him seriously. That's a lot of money, when does he want it?" said Jack anxiously.

"I don't want to talk on the phone. There isn't much privacy at the club. Let's meet tomorrow to discuss it properly."

"OK," replied Jack. "Where do you want to meet?"

"Not at one of our usual places. We need somewhere quiet where we're unlikely to run into anyone we know. There's a good coffee shop between 5th and Madison Avenues called Birch Coffee. It's easy to get to on the subway, so let's meet there." instructed Elsa.

"What time?" asked Jack.

"Half twelve," replied Elsa and cut off the call. She realised that her hand was trembling as she put the phone into her handbag. Stupid bitch she thought. Why get uptight talking to that bastard. From his tone of voice it's obvious he's not missing me. Why should he? He has Bridget now.

Frank had heard Elsa's telephone call and went into the Manager's office to tell Roland.

"It's OK Frank. I asked Elsa to call him and fill him in on why he should start trying to get the money off his wife ASAP. I painted a clear picture for Elsa of what would happen to him if he doesn't pay up."

"I think Elsa got upset calling him," replied Frank.

"Yeah, unfortunately she's still carrying a torch for him. God knows why. Do you know when and where they're meeting?"

"Yes Boss," confirmed Frank.

"Well why don't you keep an eye on Elsa to make sure Jack doesn't upset her again," said Roland.

Frank looked a little bemused when he left the office, but Roland knew that he'd follow Elsa and if necessary prevent her and Jack getting too comfortable with each other.

10

"What are you going to be doing today?" asked Bridget leaning on her elbow in bed.

Jack turned to her blankly and said, "I don't know really. I'll check in at the office and see if anything has come in and take it from there." He hadn't slept too well, thinking too much about his upcoming meeting with Elsa, and now was feeling guilty about not telling Bridget. He still had strong feelings for Elsa and knew he couldn't turn them on and off like a tap, no matter how much he would like to.

"Why don't we meet for lunch about one? That way I can have something to look forward to while I'm grinding through the paperwork this morning," replied Bridget.

"I don't know hon. I promised an old friend of mine in NYPD that we would meet for lunch. He's looking to retire and set up as a private dick and asked me to fill him in about the procedure for getting a licence."

"Well he'll obviously be able to tell instantly how well you're doing and want to start as soon as he can," replied Bridget cynically.

Jack playfully pushed Bridget's head into the pillow, rolled her over onto her back and pinned her to the bed. "Don't be smart, I'm a dedicated professional whose only ambition is to serve the community," said Jack and kissed her firmly on the mouth. Feeling aroused Jack started fondling Bridget and kissing her with more fervour.

"Hold your horses Mr Professional. I've got a meeting first thing and can't be late as I'm the chair person," said Bridget trying to push Jack off her. Jack ignored her and carried on attempting to get Bridget aroused, but his ardour was halted by Bridget's insistence to get out of bed.

"I see this is the beginning of the end," mocked Jack. "Married less than a month and already the magic has worn off!"

Bridget scrambled out of bed and said, "I'm working for both of us, not just me. I want to earn enough so we will be able to put our feet up and relax in the not too distant future."

"You don't need the money," answered Jack.

"Simon was a multi-millionaire, but all of his money is tied up in assets. "I bought into the NMP to build my holding to 6½% of the stock, so all I have in the bank is 'two hundred thou', which I know is a lot. But it's not enough to live the rest of our lives in carefree retirement. I've still got to work for that."

"But what about the payoff to get Simon released from prison?" asked Jack.

"That was swallowed up by my investment in the NMP after Simon's death. It was the only way to convince the Board of my commitment to the company," replied Bridget and with that she disappeared into the bathroom, so Jack put on his dressing gown and went into the kitchen.

Francesca was busy doing Bridget's breakfast and greeted Jack asking if he wanted anything to eat. Jack confirmed he didn't and walked over to the bubbling filter coffee pot, grabbed a cup and poured himself a black coffee. He wasn't a big breakfast person as most of his working time spread from the other end of the day to the early hours of the morning.

"Don't you think Bridget works too hard Francesca?" asked Jack, leaning against a cupboard.

"We can both be grateful that she does," replied Francesca. Jack didn't like the inference of her remark and was about to expound on how he was an independent man able to support himself, when the maid added, "I don't care what you do or how you do it 'cos I've never seen her so happy. Don't mess up!" She turned and smiled at him as she placed an omelette on the breakfast table for Bridget.

Within 30 seconds Bridget came into the kitchen wearing her dressing gown and with a towel wrapped around her head, and sat to the table to eat the omelette. Their morning routine was timed to the second. "Thanks Francesca" she said after tasting her first mouthful. Francesca smiled and walked over to the table with the filter coffee pot to pour her a cup. Her breakfasts were more measured since her marriage to Jack, which Francesca thought was a definite improvement.

"If you can't meet for lunch how about dinner together, Jack?" asked Bridget looking up at him.

"I've got to go over to the Blue Cockatoo to see Roland Bannister. It shouldn't take long and then I'll give you a call," answered Jack.

"Well don't meet me drunk," said Bridget remembering Jack's visit in the small hours of the morning after he last went to the club.

It had been nearly 6 months since Walsh's death and Jack's life with Bridget had settled into a regular pattern. He still worked nocturnal hours but he and Bridget managed their time to ensure they had at least one day a week together. It would be nice to break the pattern for an unexpected evening together.

11

Elsa saw Jack come into the coffee shop and drew in her breath for a moment, but quickly regained her composure not wishing to give him any indication of the huge effect he still had on her emotional state. She attracted his attention and he smiled at her as he walked over to the table.

"Been here long?" he asked in an apologetic voice.

"No, I was only a couple of minutes ahead of you," she replied.

"Let's order then," said Jack. "I'm starving, didn't have much breakfast," he lied.

"I'm not hungry," replied Elsa. "I'll just have a cup of coffee."

"OK I'll have the same," said Jack and called over the waitress to place their order. She was puzzled, expecting them to have lunch, but nodded politely and went to get their coffees.

"You're looking great Elsa, obviously life is good. How are you coping as manager of the Blue Cockatoo?"

"Jack can we just talk about Roland" replied Elsa firmly.

"You mean we can't be friends?"

"No. You have your life and I have mine. Let's leave it at that." retorted Elsa.

"If you don't care about me, why all the concern about what Roland might do?" asked Jack.

"I'm not concerned about you. I'm concerned about the trouble Roland might get himself into," Elsa lied.

Jack felt that familiar kick in the pit of his stomach from one of Elsa's unwelcome declarations of her affection for Roland, and took a couple of seconds to compose himself. He didn't like to think of her being closer to Roland than to him, but realised that he would have to accept it. He just held on to the hope that she wouldn't become his lover.

"OK with that settled, what has Roland been saying about me?"

"I don't think you understand just how mad he is at you and I'm worried that he'll go to any lengths to show that he's not going to let you make a fool of him," replied Elsa.

"I'm not trying to make a fool of him. I had a plan, which seemed fool proof, but against all odds it fell through. We both took a risk, which didn't pay off."

"He doesn't see it that way. He believes you owe him money and on top of that have disrespected him. He's wants you to more than cover the one hundred thousand dollars he "invested" and remember he's expecting you to come with a million dollars to compensate him for the damage to his reputation."

Jack looked at Elsa with a resigned expression on his face. "How on earth does he expect me to come up with that kind of money? I'm not going to try and hustle it from Bridget, so he might as well set his dogs on me now because there's no chance of me coming up with that."

"He's convinced that Bridget can bail you out," said Elsa. "Because Walsh got killed in prison he's convinced she's still got the five million dollars from the blackmail money she didn't have to pay out. And because she's the boss of her company he feels that whatever her financial circumstances she has access to a large pot of money."

"She's re-invested the 5 million dollars in her company and may get paid well but hasn't got a personal fortune. She had to sink the blackmail money into the business after Simon died to show her commitment to the company. It was necessary to satisfy the Board and Investors to get their support for her taking the permanent position of Chief Executive. And she certainly isn't going to fraudulently "borrow" money just to satisfy Roland," replied Jack. "Besides I haven't told her about my part in sending Walsh to prison.

I've wanted to, but somehow never seemed to find the right moment."

"Well what are you going to do about it?

"I don't know," said Jack looking genuinely concerned.

"Roland is in all afternoon. Why don't you go over to the club and try to reason with him. Maybe there's some other way the two of you can come to an agreement that won't end with you hospitalised or dead! Isn't there some other scheme you can come up with that could make him money, without him having to invest more," said Elsa.

"I don't have any answers Elsa, but it might be worth talking to him just to calm him down. I don't think I can make him see reason but it's pointless making him even angrier by trying to avoid him."

Jack got up from the table and wanted to hug Elsa because he realised from her last outburst that it was him she cared about, not Roland, but in his heart he knew that time had passed. He smiled, squeezed her hand gently and left the coffee shop.

As he walked into the street he was tempted to look behind to see if Elsa was watching him leave. He didn't turn to look back and carried on walking, mulling over what she had told him. He smiled thinking that he had told Bridget he was going to the Blue Cockatoo, and now that was just what he was going to do. He didn't know what condition he'd been in after going there but would enjoy his evening with Bridget, even if he was on crutches!"

12

While Jack was anticipating a cosy evening with Bridget, Roland Bannister was gradually getting more and more irritated about Jack's lack of concern in paying his debt and his ongoing failure to take appropriate measures to get the money from Bridget. The malevolent ire he held for him was growing daily and remained constant in the background of all of his waking thoughts.

"It's pointless relying on Jack to take control of the situation so we're going to have to do something.... now!" he finally said as much to himself as anyone in earshot, emphasising the word NOW.

Frank and Lou were in the room with Roland and they looked blankly at each other wondering if Roland was expecting them to respond. Roland was talking to himself and began to formulate a plan to coerce Jack into doing exactly what he wanted, when he wanted it to be done. The only thing that would grab Jack's attention would be a threat to Bridget. Although Roland was sure Jack still loved Elsa he couldn't use her for leverage against him. He was now convinced he would never get her to want him and had given up trying to persuade her, so he would save her for later, but only if it became necessary.

"You've been following Jack for some time now, haven't you? While doing that did you find anything out about Bridget's movements?" Roland spat out at Lou and Frank. They both nodded dumbly. "Have you been able to find out if she has a routine?"

"We've lost Jack a few times and sometimes had to pick up his trail at Bridget's offices. She's pretty consistent," replied Lou. "When Jack doesn't meet her after work she generally seems to works late, 'til about eight. But every now and then she'll meet Jack earlier and they will go on to eat somewhere."

"Do they go to the same restaurant every time?" asked Roland.

"No it varies," replied Lou, "but they're all more or less within a 5 to 15 minute walk of her office"

"What does she do on the evening's that she doesn't meet Jack?"

“Generally she catches a cab outside her offices to her apartment.”

“OK here’s what you’re going to do,” said Roland unconsciously lowering his voice in a confidential tone. Lou and Frank knew this was a sign that he wanted some dirty work doing. “Keep watching her until the evening she meets up with Jack. The next day I want you, Lou, sitting in a cab outside her offices. As you drive off towards her apartment you’ll undoubtedly get stopped at the traffic lights two blocks down from where she works. Frank you’ll be waiting at those lights and will jump into the back seat.”

“Boss, how am I going to work it so that my cab is at the first in the taxi rank?”

“Get there early and pass customers onto the cab behind you. That can’t be too difficult. If anybody’s awkward give them money or use a little muscle! Whatever the situation demands!” shouted Roland. He didn’t like being distracted in the middle of his thought process and resumed with his plan.

“The warehouse building on Wharf 10 at Jersey Docks is going to be demolished shortly because it’s to be replaced with a modern handling and stacking facility on the quay. The existing building’s in a quiet area and has offices where you can hold her while I talk to Jack.”

The light suddenly went on in the heads of Lou and Frank and they both nodded simultaneously.

“We’re going to have to show our faces, which means we may have to kill her after we’ve taken care of Jack,” continued Bannister. “After you’ve grabbed her I’ll call Jack requesting an exchange of Bridget for one million bucks. If he’s not co-operative about an exchange of Bridget for the money then I’ll let you use your imagination on the best way to persuade him, but I don’t want any rough stuff until then. I’m seeing Jack later today and I’ll give him his final warning, but I’m not expecting much from him as he still won’t take me seriously until after we’ve grabbed Bridget. I don’t like doing this. Deep down I want to like Jack but he’s forcing me to act like this, which makes me even more annoyed!”

13

It was mid-afternoon and Jack caught a cab to the Blue Cockatoo. The traffic in and around the Hell's Kitchen zone was always busy. He hoped he wouldn't run into Elsa again. Hearing her voice on the telephone had cheered him and seeing her sitting at the table in the coffee shop had raised his spirits even further. He didn't know how he could continue living without her in his life and was pleased that he now knew her prime concern was not for Roland, but for him. When he squeezed her hand leaving the coffee shop, he was convinced that she had responded warmly.

Roland's expectations were unrealistic, but Jack had to risk agitating him even more by explaining the economic facts of his situation. Elsa was worried things could turn bad and now he was going to get it first hand from Roland himself. If things turned violent he would end up collecting more than a few bruises. Frank was a big man and would probably take delight in hurting him, but he would defend himself to the best of his ability. He felt he'd be able to knock a few lumps into the big man before going down.

It was pointless taking a gun because that would only escalate the situation, as they were unlikely to kill him without getting the money. He concluded that if he had a beating coming the best thing was to take it and try and stall Roland for as long as possible. The depressing thing was that he didn't have a plan for getting him the $100,000 he had lost, never mind the million dollars he was expecting.

As the cab pulled up to the club Jack was tempted to tell the driver to carry on, but against his better judgement he paid the fare and got out onto the pavement. Jack walked around to the back of the club and saw deliveries being made. The double doors were open as the delivery man carried through crates of spirits on a pallet truck and Jack eased passed him to enter the club. He continued through the corridor linking to the main dance and bar area and crossed the room to the stairs leading to Roland's office. The difference in the dance room during day and night times always amazed him. At night the floor and bar were lit up, dance music was loud and pervasive and with the girls gyrating the place was electric. During daylight hours it looked dead and uninviting.

As Jack approached Roland's office he heard talking and knocked on the door. The talking stopped and Roland shouted "Enter". As Jack walked into the room he was surprised to see Roland and Elsa standing side by side, but not half as surprised as Roland was to see Jack.

"Where is my money?" he sneered menacingly causing Elsa to recoil from him. Jack's entrance had flipped a switch inside Roland's brain making him act irrationally and he was becoming obsessed with the situation, losing his sense of perspective. Jack was beginning to wish he had brought his gun, because he was convinced that it would all end badly.

"Slow down Roland, you haven't even offered me a drink yet", smiled Jack trying to calm a potentially escalating situation. "Can't you put things into perspective? We had a deal going and it blew up in our faces. It's no one's fault, it just happened. There's nothing I could have done to prevent it happening."

"Yes, but it didn't cost you money Jack and it cost me 100 grand!" asserted Roland.

"No I didn't lose that much money, but it did cost me time, a lot of time," replied Jack, adding ".... and I lost Elsa."

Elsa didn't expect such a sentiment from Jack, who rarely spoke of his emotions or feelings towards her throughout their time together, and definitely never to Roland or anybody else.

Jack was rattled and scared of what might happen if Roland could not be pacified. After Roland's demand for money Jack had taken a sub servient role to try and appease him, but now he had to try and relieve the tension between them, which was close to breaking point. At one time he would have had more leverage to humour Roland because of their friendship, but that counted for nothing now. His consolation was that the body language between Elsa and Roland, and her reaction to his demand for the money confirmed they were not spiritually or emotionally close.

"You've married Walsh's widow and she must be loaded. Use your charm to wheedle the money out of her. If she loves you enough she'll hand it over," retorted Roland.

"Elsa tells me you want a million, there's no way I can get my hands on that amount of cash, and....."

"Don't give me any sob stories Jack. You either get me the money you owe me or your future is going to be very short", interrupted Roland.

"But why has the sum grown?" questioned Jack meekly, noting the first direct threat from Roland.

"Interest Jack. It's been over a year since I started to lay the cash out and I need to be repaid the interest you owe me! I could get Frank in here to encourage you more than my mere words, but I want you fit and able to do what you have to do to get my money! I'll give you two weeks and if it's not forthcoming I'll send Frank around to get what he can out of you, which may be painful or even terminal!" If the money is to be had a week would be plenty of time thought Roland. He planned to wrong foot Jack by demanding the money within a week following the kidnap of Bridget.

"Roland please don't let things get to this......we were all friends not so long ago. Give Jack a bit of time, or let him work for you to pay off his debt," pleaded Elsa.

Roland was more than a little disappointed to hear the passion behind Elsa's plea, which added to his conviction that she was still in love with Jack. "He's had time Elsa and has done nothing to convince me that he has any intention of honoring the debt. He hasn't got time to work off one million bucks and my patience is exhausted, so he'll just have to use his famous ingenuity to come up with the money."

Roland's voice was calm in his explanation to Elsa, but the look in his eyes convinced her not to challenge him further.

Jack was relieved to hear that he wasn't going to get a beating from Frank but clearly understood that he'd be "dead meat" if he didn't deliver the money to Roland before the deadline. In fact, he wasn't even sure if he'd survive the week if he couldn't convince him that he was able to get that much cash by then. It was pointless trying to reason with Roland and he wasn't in a position to argue about the stupidity of his ultimatum. Jack realised that it wasn't the money Roland wanted, it was to make an example of him, and that his ex-partner probably wouldn't be happy until he was dead.

Jack's brain was racing to come up with a plan for a quick exit when Roland said, "I take it you're clear Jack, on what I need from you and there is no misunderstanding?"

"Yes", said Jack looking at Roland's smirking face. His eyes were alive at the prospect of killing Jack. Perhaps he needed to kill him to reinforce his position in the criminal fraternity and also because deep down he had resented Jack's way with women and his popularity in the underworld, despite being an ex-cop.

"Elsa, please show Mr Cates to the door and make sure he leaves the premises. He's not welcome here without an invitation," said Roland in his most diplomatic tone, which resonated with echoes from his days as an attorney.

Elsa nodded and she and Jack filed out of the office. Once out of earshot Elsa asked Jack what he was going to do.

"I don't know. There's obviously no point in trying to dissuade Roland and I don't want you to try changing his mind any more. He's obsessed and unpredictable, so even you won't be safe if you get on the wrong side of him. From the way you both acted in there I take it you two are not....er "a couple"?" asked Jack hesitantly.

Elsa looked up at him with fire in her eyes, "You have no right to ask me that and don't get to thinking I still care because I tried to intervene. I'd have done the same for any dumb animal!"

Jack was taken aback by the intensity of her words, "Elsa, I'm sorry I........"

“Forget it Jack”, said Elsa more calmly, seeing the hurt in his eyes. “Jack I do still care about you so whatever you do keep safe and don’t let Roland catch up to you.” As they reached the exit Elsa squeezed Jack’s hand and ushered him out of the building. The reality of Jack being killed in the next 14 days suddenly hit her and she felt a physical pain in her chest from the escalated thumping of her heart. She didn’t go back to the office but went to the bar for a strong drink.

14

Jack hit the street unconscious of the noise, people passing him by and the traffic on the thoroughfare. He hadn't got his ribs or nose broken, but he was on death row waiting for his execution. Frank would make short work of him and was known to be an expert with a stiletto. Roland would probably want him to suffer a little before the end so Jack didn't know what to expect before he felt the blade between his ribs.

He would have to leave the country, ideally just as effectively as Leonard Tuzio who had disappeared into thin air. He would get a false passport and other documents, including a birth certificate, to take on his journey to help him get re-established elsewhere. Suddenly he realised that he didn't know how he would tell Bridget. He knew he had to protect her and the best way would be to get out of her life.

Bridget wouldn't want to go gallivanting around the world with him. She had poured herself into the NMP and wouldn't want to throw it all away for a life of hardship and uncertainty on the run. And of course she was unaware that Jack was the man mainly responsible for Simon Walsh being sent to prison and the brains behind the attempt to extort 5 million dollars from him. Just when he thought he had reached rock bottom after losing out on that scam, he found there was always room to slip a little further.

Jack decided he wouldn't tell Bridget anything. It would be better if he just disappeared and let her get on with the rest of her life. It would hurt her at first but she would acclimatise in time and he would write to her when he got settled explaining the reason behind his departure and why she will be better off without him. He had wanted to tell her the truth about Simon's imprisonment for some time because she deserved to know what really happened, and to rid her of the guilt she still felt at not being able to get Elsa to clear her husband before his death.

Jack caught a taxi to the NMP Building and called Bridget from his cell phone. "Where are you?" he asked when she answered his call, "I'm waiting outside and I'm hungry". Jack didn't feel light hearted but he couldn't let Bridget know what was happening. They had less than two weeks together and he was going to make them the best weeks of her life.

Bridget tidied up her desk and went straight down to the street. They asked in reception if she needed a taxi, she shook her head and said she was being taken out to dinner, and with a broad smile opened the door into the street.

Bridget ran into Jack's arms and they kissed and hugged warmly. She felt at home in his arms and didn't want to let go. After reluctantly leaving the warm embrace she turned to walk in the direction they normally took to their usual eating houses, but was halted by Jack. "It's too far to walk," he said.

"Well where are you taking me tonight", said Bridget as they turned towards the taxi rank.

"It's a surprise. I've spent the whole day canvassing restaurants to find the one you'd like best." They got into the taxi at the front of the line and Jack gave the address he wanted to go to. He didn't notice that the cab behind the one they got into was being driven by Lou. He had persuaded Gus Shepherd to let him use his cab for the next week. Gus was a little reticent at lending out his cab but Frank had persuaded him with a small amount of violence and Lou had reinforced the "request" with money. They were a perfect match.

The cabbies identification card was falsified and Lou had picked up the cab from Gus at five to get into the routine Roland had demanded earlier in the day. He would get further instructions from the Boss tomorrow about kidnapping Bridget.

15

Roland called Frank and Lou into his office. He was finally going to get things moving after over a year of being made to look a fool by Jack. He didn't expect Jack to come up with the money voluntarily and therefore he was going to bring Bridget into the game, whom he could use for leverage. Kidnapping her and probably having to kill her later didn't sit well with him, but against his better judgement he was going to see this thing through no matter what the cost.

Lou entered the office first with Frank trailing behind. Frank suspected that Roland wanted them to put a little pressure on Jack but knew that the normal strong-arm stuff would not be effective. Frank had no love for Jack, particularly because of the way he had treated Elsa, but he knew he would take a beating without complaint and would not be intimidated by it. It was illogical as there was no advantage to be gained from the use of force. Roland's plan to kidnap Bridget opened other opportunities.

"Close the door Frank", said Roland, "I don't want Elsa to hear what I'm going to say to you."

Frank did as he'd been instructed and took a chair in front of Roland's desk, next to Lou.

"Did you arrange for a yellow cab to be on hand this evening, Lou?"

"Yes Boss, I had a dry run last night and saw Bridget Walsh meet Jack outside the NMP building. They use the taxi rank rather than calling a cab from Bridget's office"

"Good. She's Bridget Cates now Lou and that's why I want you and Frank to pick her up tonight and take her to Jersey where they have any number of moorings and harbours for their commercial trade. As I said, they're also in the process of refurbishing the old container storage area. With modern containers there's no need for warehouses and so they're demolishing the old container store on Wharf 10. You pick her up and take her over to Jersey...and be gentle. I don't want her to be injured in any way because I want to use her in mint condition as the perfect hostage to make Jack more pliable."

Frank looked a little bewildered but understood what was required of him. He didn't like treating women roughly, but had done it when necessary in the past.

Lou asked if they could get easy access to Wharf 10. Roland confirmed he had already paid off the security guard to let them in and out of that area of the docks. The buildings on Wharf 10 are derelict and presented a health hazard if squatters found a way in. He added that demolition contractors were currently tendering for the work so the area should be deserted, but for the occasional site visit from contract competitors.

"As soon as you've got her safely into the old container store I'll give Jack a ring. He's going to be more accommodating when I tell him we have Bridget. She must be loaded as the CEO of the NMP and if nothing else she can sell a few shares to get Jack out of trouble. A million bucks is nothing to her."

Both Lou and Frank sat staring at Roland dumbly nodding intermittently to let him know they had gotten the gist of what he wanted and understood his instructions.

"No doubt Jack will want to talk to her to be sure she's safe and more importantly to find out how he can get the money, unless he has another trick up his sleeve. There are offices in the container store and a backroom, with a cot where she can sleep. The two of you can take turns to babysit her until I'm ready to let Jack talk to her. The cocky bastard can squirm for a day or two."

"We'll have to prepare the room in advance and get some foodstuffs in", interjected Frank.

"It's not a fucking hotel Frank!..........OK just take a couple of blankets a flask and some sandwiches. I suppose it will be a bit mucky after being empty for the last eighteen months", replied Roland conceding to Frank's point. He didn't want Bridget to suffer on Jack' behalf, but he thought it may be necessary to rough her up if his ex-partner didn't see things the right way. He still had the idea in the back of his mind that if they ended up killing Bridget he could always frame Jack, who being dead wouldn't be in a position to defend himself.

"I've spoken to the other cab drivers and I'll sit at the head of the queue at the rank to make sure Bridget comes to me when she leaves her offices. They don't mind giving way for one fare and besides Frank was standing beside me when I asked them!"

"You both know what you've got to do so don't let me down," said Roland finally.

As Frank and Lou stood up Elsa knocked on the office door and walked in to talk to Roland about ordering new stock. A hush fell over the room until Roland told her the boys were going out to run an errand and pointed to one of the chairs they had been sitting on. Frank was always pleased to see Elsa and smiled at her broadly. She returned his greeting as he walked out the door.

"What's the reason for the big pow-wow", she asked and then added hesitantly, "you promised Jack two weeks."

"Don't worry Elsa, they won't be going anywhere near Jack", replied Roland.

16

Jack was busy in the process of getting false documentation, starting with a passport. He went to a photo booth and got 4 passport sized photographs, put them in an envelope for safe keeping and then caught a cab over to Queens to see Freddy Bartholomew.

Freddy was an ex-con who did time for forgery. He had made some plates of 5, 10 and 20 dollar bills, which were perfect and undetectable by all except treasury employees, who even then had to confirm any doubts with a chemical analysis of the dyes used in the production of the bills. He was arrested after the warehouse in which they were making and storing the bills was raided by the police. He had told his partners not to flood the streets, or use the money at their regular haunts. His advice was ignored and one of the dumb asses on the production line was identified as passing the bills at his local bar and led the police to the warehouse.

Contrary to popular belief there is no honour among thieves and his partners gave up his name without resistance. He found the police waiting on his doorstep when he returned home after buying groceries. Luckily there was no evidence of his current projects in his apartment as his workshop was elsewhere, rented under a pseudonym. His wife kept up the rental payments while he was in prison.

His biggest disappointment was that he had made the perfect plates together with a fool proof production process, which were now worthless. It was his first offence and he was released after 5 years when he continued his business of document forgery, which being a much smaller operation avoided the need for partners.

Jack knew of Freddy from his father who had been part of the task force used to raid the warehouse. His father had felt sorry for Freddy, who he considered to be a consummate professional and gentleman, but who had chosen his partners unwisely. Jacks father had helped Freddy's wife while he was in prison and the two men had remained friends after his release, even though they worked on opposite sides of the track. Jack had sought Freddy's advice when still with the NYPD on the authenticity of a batch of Asian passports he had confiscated during the raid of a drug factory. Freddy was able to confirm which were authentic, and which were forgeries.

The documents Jack needed were standard fare for forgers and he knew if anyone could produce them in the tight timescale required, it was Freddy.

Freddy opened the door to Jack and beamed when he recognised his face. "What a nice surprise I'll put the kettle on."

Walking into the kitchen Freddy started to make a pot of china tea. Freddy had introduced Jack to tea and he had found the taste different but agreeable and every time he visited him he had a cup of the strange brew. "I'm afraid it's not a social call, Freddy, I'm in trouble."

Taking a seat at the kitchen table Jack watched as Freddy poured out two cups of tea and brought them over to his friend. "Jack, you know if there's any way I can help I will gladly do it. Tell me what kind of jam are you're in."

As he listened to Jack's story beginning with Elsa meeting Simon Walsh he felt the situation was unusual, as in their previous times together his friend always seemed confident and self-assured, but now it was obvious he felt vulnerable and was worried about the safety of his wife.

"Is Bridget aware of your full involvement?" asked Freddy.

"No", replied Jack, "and now I'm sorry that I didn't tell her earlier. There's a lot I'm sorry for, but I thought it was a fool proof plan, and when Walsh was sent to prison I was certain everything would come together."

"You didn't allow for the human factor. When I'm working on documents I'm perfectly at ease as the success of the outcome is solely dependent on my skill. It's only when the human factors are introduced to the mix that the unexpected occurs. I know that from bitter experience."

The forger found it hard to believe that Jack was no longer with Elsa, but knew that things change in life and you have to adapt. "I wondered why you and Elsa broke up. You both seemed so right for each other", continued Freddy.

"Yeah that's a big regret, but there's no going back now. Bridget is brilliant and I do love her, but she's not Elsa."

"That's a hard lesson for you, but you could be due for an even harder one if I don't get you a new passport. I would suggest you fly to Mexico City on your true passport and use the one I give you for going on from there. There's so much corruption in Mexico no-one will be too concerned about whether you have the right passport or not. Other countries may not be so lax. It just depends on where you go. You don't want to go anywhere where you will need a visa, not initially. When you get established you will eventually have to get a work visa, but in some countries it's a lot easier than others."

Jack handed Freddy the photographs he had taken at the photo booth. Without saying a word Freddy took them off him and put them into the pedal bin sitting next to the sink. He went into the living room and came back a few seconds later with a camera in his hand. "This isn't amateur night. Let's do things right."

Freddy left the room and brought in a shirt, tie and a tweed jacket. "The objective is to make you look as natural as possible and give you a different physical appearance. That includes dress, hairstyle and any other facial characteristics. I don't normally advise wigs or a false moustache, which can never be made to look completely natural, but we can give you a pair of spectacles. Now strip to the waist."

Jack did as he was told and Freddy handed him the shirt and tie. Again he left the kitchen and came back with a pair of spectacles, which he gave Jack to hold after he had put on the tie. "You will notice its clear glass without any magnification factor, so don't let anyone else get hold of them."

Without waiting for a reply Freddy continued to remodel Jack. He found Jack's hair to be thick and brushed straight back. The natural waves gave it body and shape but Freddy was interested in changing it in a way that would bring out the sharper features in Jack's face. He pulled a comb from his pocket and parted the hair on the left side of Jack's head, but his hair naturally wanted to spring back to its original position. Again Freddy left the kitchen and came back with some gelatine. He rubbed it into Jack's hair and the parting remained in place. He combed Jack's hair to lie flatter and tighter against his head.

"Right put on the jacket and glasses and I'll take a couple of photographs," instructed Freddy.

After checking the quality of the photographs he asked Jack the nationality he wanted on the passport. "The problem is you have too much Irish in you to pass for Latin or Asian so your options are European or Canadian. The only European countries you could safely represent are Eire or the United Kingdom."

"I think Canadian would be safer as most foreigners won't be able to differentiate the North American dialects," said Jack. Freddy agreed and gave Jack a picture of his transformed self as he left.

"Give me 3 days. I'll get you a Canadian passport and your photograph chipped, which is the most difficult part of the job."

Both men shook hands warmly as Jack left. His next job was to look for flights to Mexico City. Jack didn't make purchases on the internet, preferring to deal with people rather than a computer. He caught a cab into town and made a bee line for a travel shop and booked a flight leaving for Mexico City in 10 days' time. He would call Roland from Mexico and erase his trail from there onwards.

With only a few days left Jack wanted to see as much of Bridget as he could. He rang her to arrange to meet for lunch. She was rushed off her feet because auditors were due and she had a pile of accounts to get through, adding that she would have a working lunch and probably wouldn't get home until ten. Jack was disappointed but warmly encouraged Bridget to get her nose back to the grindstone and signed off saying that he would bring some goodies back to the apartment for when she got home.

17

It had been a long day for Bridget, checking accounts ledgers, invoices and bank statements to make sure everything was in order for the auditors who would be arriving in two days. It was 9:30PM and she stretched in her chair to relieve some of the stiffness generated by her sitting in the same position for hours. She recovered her sitting position and rubbed the back of her neck. She needed a hot bath to soothe the aches in her body. Her job was demanding and sometimes she regretted taking the helm of the company, especially when it meant missing a dinner date with Jack.

The computer beeped as she turned off her console and switched off the power to the printer. George the night watchman had already been to her office once to check on her and ask if she needed anything. She thought that he would have finished his checks of the rest of the building and should be back in reception, so now would be a good time to go. The remaining loose ends could be finished in the morning, still in plenty of time for the arrival of the auditors.

Normally there were two auditors who fell into good and bad cop roles. Bridget wasn't sure if this was their intended modus operandi but felt it was unnecessary as for years the process had been quick and clinical because of the high standards set by the company's new Finance Director, who was already on his way home because his wife insisted on never eating later than nine in the evening.

Bridget pushed her chair away from her desk, wearily got to her feet and walked over to the coat stand by the door into the office. She put on her coat and went back to her desk to pick up her handbag. Night lights came on in the corridor as she made her way to the elevator and saw that it was raining outside. A miserable end to a miserable day! Why she always put so much effort into checking everything was a mystery to everyone in the finance department, but she had overall responsibility for the welfare of the company and was committed to ensuring its records were healthy.

She left the elevator at the ground floor level and walked over to the reception desk to say goodnight to George. He was drinking a cup of coffee and smiled at her as she walked towards him.

"It's ten o'clock Mrs Cates and time you went home. I wanted to shoo you out of your office an hour ago."

"I had to finish off George. It's just as well as now tomorrow and more importantly the next day, will be plain sailing."!

"It's been raining for the last half hour; shall I call you a cab?"

"No, don't worry George there's always a queue of taxis outside the door. I'm not the only one who works late. No sneaking off at 2:00 in the morning for a quick cigarette – it's bad for you! Goodnight."

George bade Bridget goodnight as she turned and walked to the front doors of the building. She used her pass to open the side door and stepped out onto the street. It was raining persistently, but lightly and Bridget looked over at the taxi rank and signalled for the lead taxi to come over. She stepped into the taxi and gave her address to the driver. She exhaled deeply as she lay back into the seat and closed her eyes for a few seconds to relax and let the comfort of the pliant cushions of the taxi seat flow over her. She opened her eyes and realised the taxi had veered left instead of right and was travelling in a different direction to her normal journey.

"Excuse me I think you've taken a wrong turn", she said to the diver. He didn't respond and after a few seconds she repeated herself. When the driver still failed to respond she started to get agitated, but then the cab pulled up at some traffic lights. She moved to open the cab door but before she could reach the door handle it opened and a large man pushed himself into the back of the cab. Simultaneously he put his left hand over Bridget's mouth and forced her into the far corner of the passenger seat.

"Bridget, be a good girl and don't make any trouble for yourself," the man said as the taxi pulled away from the traffic lights. He was strong and half lay on her so that she was powerless to move. She felt a stab of pain in her side and looked down to see a gun in the man's other hand now pressed into her ribs. "Now when I take my hand away you're not going to scream are you?" the man asked. Bridget shook her head in compliance to his request and the man lifted his hand from her mouth.

She started to speak and the man put his finger against her lips to stop her talking. "I don't want you asking any questions right now and the only thing I'll say is that we are going to take you somewhere and hold you there for a period of time. The length of time you're there will depend on your husband."

"Jack! What's he got to do with this?" thought Bridget. She went to speak again and the man stopped her once more. He took her handbag and motioned her to sit back in the seat comfortably. As the man moved off her she attempted to open the cab door, which was locked. The man grabbed her arms and turned her towards him. As she faced him his right hand released her arm and he slapped her hard across the face. The blow was powerful and the slap stung her cheek, turning it red.

"That's your first and last warning," said the man, "don't try to escape again." He motioned Bridget to sit back in the seat, which she did holding onto the side of her face.

Frank looked at Bridget with fire in his eyes giving her a visual warning not to try to escape again. He could see the tears welling in her eyes, but there was no way that she was going to cry. She was a gutsy girl, but Frank knew he could put the fear of God into her. "Do you understand?" he said firmly and Bridget nodded affirmatively. Lou looked into his rear view mirror and could see Frank looking at Bridget, and Bridget looking out of the cab window. "The big lug. He always feels uncomfortable hitting ladies," thought Lou and he hoped Roland would not ask them to kill her.

The rest of the cab ride was carried out in silence and Bridget realised she was being taken to the dock area of Jersey. Lou drove up to the gates of a fence, got out of the cab, unlocked the gates and opened one leg. They drove through, still in silence, and Lou stopped, closed and re-locked the gates.

Bridget was not afraid for her own safety. This certainly wasn't a sexual assault as the big man had not made a move on her in the back seat. Besides he seemed to be courteous of her space and didn't try to brush against her or touch her in any way. For that she was grateful, but being unaware of Jack's involvement she was worried about his safety, being sure that they wouldn't be as "gentle" with him.

The cab pulled up outside a storage building and Frank took Bridget by the arm and pulled her out of the car. Bridget remained silent and accepted being manhandled. The men went to a side door, unlocked it and took her inside the building. It was a large cavernous structure that obviously hadn't been used for some time as it was covered in dust and cob webs. There had once been a crane in the building for stacking containers but it had been removed. The building had been used to provide additional security for containers carrying valuable items but had become redundant with the development of container design making them secure in any environment.

In the far corner of the storage area was an office sitting on a mezzanine floor, with a steel staircase and access platform leading to its door. Frank ushered Bridget to the office leading her as they walked across the empty floor area. She preceded him up the steps and he pulled her back at the door into the office as he searched for keys to open it. Bridget was surprised anyone bothered to lock the door given the state of the place and the fact that there didn't appear to be any valuables in the office. An internal door at one end of the office led to a backroom, which Bridget discovered was a small bedroom with a small cot, obviously for use by a night watchman when the building was active.

Frank and Lou had been silent for the most part of the journey to the warehouse, but now Frank sat Bridget on the bed and squatted down in front of her. Even in his squatted position his head was higher than hers. "I know this has been traumatic for you," he began, "and I don't want to make the situation any worse than it is already. You have been kidnapped so that we can get money rightfully owing to us from Jack Cates."

"But what has Jack..." Bridget began to interrupt before Frank again put his fingers gently to her lips. Bridget stopped talking not wanting to incur his wrath, remembering the slap he had given her.

"Good, now just listen. Someone else will visit us soon and he will tell you everything you need to know about Jack and the reason for your kidnapping. Until then just stay quiet and get some rest here."

Bridget looked around her and didn't look forward to the prospect of lying on the bed mattress. The room wasn't particularly dirty, but the mattress was stained and showed signs of its age and the many people it had serviced over the years. There was no sign of a toilet.

Frank sensed Bridget's discomfort and said. "There's a toilet you can use across the yard. We'll take you there and back, but no funny business otherwise you'll have to cross your legs!"

Her distaste must have been transparent when Lou piped in, "Take a look at the lady – she doesn't seem to like the accommodation we've provided. Please stand up milady and let me take your coat." Lou gestured for Bridget to stand and when she did he slipped her raincoat off her shoulders and hung it on the hook at the back of the door. The end of the hook had been broken off and the coat slipped off the hanger on Lou's first attempt, however there was still about two and a half inches of metal on which to hang the coat.

She was dressed in a white satin blouse and straight skirt, her standard office attire. "Are you going to be warm enough in just a blouse and skirt?" Frank asked.

"I can put on my raincoat if I get cold", answered Bridget. She did have a jacket with the skirt but left it on the back of her chair in her office because she thought it might rain, and it was too warm to wear underneath her raincoat.

Frank stood up and looked condescendingly down at Lou. "Have you finished!" he demanded. Lou nodded meekly looking down at the floor. "We've prepared for our stay here and have coffee, milk, sugar, bread and fruit. Is there anything you want?"

"Can I have a cup of coffee?"

"Yes, how do you want it?"

"Black, no sugar, thank you."

The scene was surreal. Bridget the kidnap victim was having coffee made for her by her kidnappers. There was little tension between them although Bridget was wary of angering the large man.

Frank turned to Lou, instructing him to put the kettle on. He followed Lou out of the bedroom and closed the connecting door, adding "be quiet" as he left.

Bridget took her raincoat off the door hanger and laid it on the bed. She wanted something between her and the material of the mattress. Frank and Lou were muttering outside. Bridget got up and put her ear to the door to listen to their conversation. Initially it was difficult to distinguish the words from the sound coming from the office, but she quickly tuned into the voices of the two men and was able to piece words together.

Concentrating hard on what was being said, Bridget suddenly realised the big man was coming with her coffee. She turned from the door, which gently struck her shoulder as it opened. There wasn't much room between the edge of the bed and the wall, and large movements were difficult in the cramped space.

Frank looked at Bridget quizzically. "I don't know what you were doing but remember the less you know about us the better for you. I don't want to have to kill you," he continued flatly, "so don't give me a reason to change my mind." He paused and then asked for her cell phone. Lou had carried her handbag from the taxi and it lay on the bed. Strangely neither of her captors had rifled through her bag and she unzipped it to search for her phone. Frank took it off her as she pulled it from her bag, turned it off and put it in his pocket. He didn't think of searching her handbag as normally his targets carried guns, not handbags!

She felt stupid for not pulling her phone out of her handbag when alone, but she was disorientated at the speed and nature of events, and now the gravity of her situation suddenly came clearly into focus. She couldn't stop her hand trembling and was embarrassed that her nervousness became obvious as she held the mug of coffee. Frank threw a packet of Oreos on the bed, turned and left the bedroom.

18

Roland was relieved that Bridget's abduction had gone so smoothly and he decided to call Jack in the morning. A night of worrying about Bridget's whereabouts would make him far more compliant and ready to accept his terms for an exchange. Roland liked to manipulate people and it was the one aspect of his time as a lawyer that he enjoyed. Pressure is a good tool to use in getting people to do what you want, but controlling their thoughts and implanting your will as their own is far more effective. Jack would have to follow instructions if he wanted to see Bridget alive again, although he didn't know that it was unlikely either would survive the night of the exchange.

Despite the current turn of events Jack would have to die. He had not shown an ounce of respect towards Roland in his handling of events since Simon Walsh's death and would be happy to let his debt continue indefinitely. At one time Roland wanted Jack dead at any cost to satisfy his hurt pride, but he now looked on his demise coldly as a business transaction that needed to be carried out to reinforce his authority in the criminal community. He was already regarded as being lightweight by many of his peers and Jack's attitude would only serve to confirm this widespread opinion.

He would not get Frank or Lou to kill Jack as they were too close to home and any mistake on their part might be traced back to him. He would have to get a professional hit man who would be trustworthy as well as efficient. He needed one of Mario Pallacio's contract killers and picked up the phone to call Michael Braggio, Pallacio's senior lieutenant. Roland didn't like Braggio who was a man absent of scruples and certainly without honor.

When he finally got through to Braggio he opened the conversation with, "Hello Michael, apologies for the time but I thought it would be better calling late at night." Roland decided to be friendly to help get on Braggio's right side, although it went against his nature. "It's been a long time since we last met, how are you?"

"Yeah. I'm fine Roland, what do you want?"

Roland wasn't really surprised at Baggio's abruptness but carried on in a warm vein. "Straight to business that's why you're so successful. I need someone taking care of and will pay whatever is necessary to get the job done properly."

"That's no problem, who's the lucky person?"

"Jack Cates" answered Roland.

"I thought you and he were good buddies, but if you now want him dead that's OK by me. Business is business."

Roland was relieved that he wasn't questioned further on his motives as he didn't want to have to explain to Braggio of all people that Jack had made a fool of him in trying to extort money from Simon Walsh. "I've kidnapped his wife and I'm asking for an exchange at the docks for money he owes me with a little interest. When he hands over the money I want your man to kill him. There are a number of good vantage points, particularly the cab of the old dock crane, which overlooks the area in which the exchange will be made."

"That's OK. It will be 100 grand, cash in advance" replied Braggio.

Roland whistled, "That's steep......."

"You want the best and the best costs" interrupted Braggio before Roland could complete his sentence.

"OK. The money is immaterial I just want the job done. I'm going to arrange the timing of the exchange tomorrow so it will probably take place the day after tomorrow. I'll forward the information as soon as I confirm details with Jack."

"A day's notice is cutting it a little tight I don't know where my man will be coming from. I'll make some phone calls after we've finished. Give me a solid date and time by tomorrow morning," replied Braggio.

Roland agreed and put the phone down. Ten percent of his money would be going to Braggio, but he didn't care as long as he got rid of Jack. The deep bitterness Roland now felt for Jack had completely replaced the friendship they had built up since they first started working together. Their collaboration was mutually beneficial and had started shortly after Jack had left the NYPD and although Roland hadn't made a fortune out of the transactions he had involved Jack in, he was comforted by the information that had been given him, allowing him to avoid potential disasters.....until now. He had rewarded Jack by giving him the run of the Blue Cockatoo and most of the girls there, including Elsa. Elsa had been Roland's greatest disappointment, firstly that she had fallen for Jack like many of the other girls, and secondly that he couldn't fight his way into her affection after she and Jack separated.

Elsa was still in love with Jack and so she would be the last person to find out about the arrangement he had just made.

Roland decided he would make sure Bridget knew of Jack's part in the prosecution of Simon Walsh, which would remove any need for her to celebrate his life after his death, and may avoid the necessity to kill her.

19

Jack had rung Bridget earlier on her cell phone without response and also called the apartment to check if she had got home safely only to be told by Francesca that she hadn't arrived yet, nor had she heard from her. Jack tried the apartment again an hour later and on being given the same message decided to go to the NMP offices in case she was still working, now that the switchboard was closed. She often got distracted when wrapped up at work and lost all sense of time.

He walked into the reception area to be met by a security guard. He was told that the building was empty, that all of the staff on the executive floor had gone home, and that Bridget had left around 10:00PM. Jack was now beginning to get more than a little worried as it was not like Bridget to go anywhere without letting him know that she would be late, or where to meet her.

He called the local precinct station and spoke to the duty officer on the front desk. Again he got a negative response when he asked if there had been any accidents in the area. It had been a quiet night so far without incident. Finally Jack rang the hospital feeling irrational but nevertheless compelled to do it. The answer he got was expected, that no–one with Bridget's name had been admitted. He felt uneasy and couldn't imagine what was happening until he got a call from Roland.

"Hi Jack" said Roland in a breezy manner, completely different to the tone of voice he had been using the previous day when talking to him, which automatically put Jack on edge. "I was going to call you in the morning, but couldn't wait to tell you my good news."

"What do you want Roland? I'm in the middle of something can I get back to you later?"

"I may be able to help you," replied Roland. "If you're looking for your wife I'm on my way to see her. Is there any message you want me to give her?"

Jack heard the words but couldn't make sense of them. They spun in his head without forming any comprehensible meaning. After a short pause he demanded, "What's going on? Where's Bridget?"

"Calm down Jack. Bridget's safe....for the moment, but if you want to keep her that way you had better get the million dollars you owe me by the day after tomorrow."

"If you hurt her Roland, I'll fucking kill you. I swear I will." Even in this dire situation the words sounded like a cliché to Jack but he spat them out without thinking of how they would be received by Roland.

"C'mon Jack you can do better than that!" mocked Roland, extracting as much joy out of Jack's dilemma as he could. "I know you're a tough guy, but I don't think you understand that I am not prepared to wait any longer for the money you owe me. I don't care what you have to do to get it.....just get it! If you need help from Bridget you can talk to her later."

It was pointless for Jack to tell Roland he couldn't get access to Bridget's bank account without her, or that he couldn't beg, steal or borrow the amount of money he was looking for. The best thing to do was to play along with him and do whatever was necessary to free Bridget when he handed the "Money" over. He would have to deal with Frank and Lou, so would have to go armed and be prepared to kill them if necessary.

"OK Roland, you have the whip hand. You were right all along, I can get the money, so where shall we meet?"

"I'll call you an hour before the exchange to let you know where it is to take place. It'll be either tomorrow or the day after. Don't be foolhardy Jack. You know how determined I can be, so don't think I won't let a little bloodshed get in my way if I think that it's necessary. Don't make me kill Bridget!"

Before Jack could respond to Roland's threat, Roland cut off the call. Jack felt his heartbeat getting stronger and stronger until he thought the thumping organ would burst out of his chest. He leaned against a wall and put his head in his hands trying to form the basis of a plan that would get Bridget out of this mess. She wouldn't be held in the Blue Cockatoo, he thought, which would be too obvious even with the protection of Lou and Frank. But Elsa might know where Bridget is being held.

Jack hurriedly called the number of the Blue Cockatoo. It was answered by one of the bar staff and Jack asked to speak to Elsa. "What is it Jack, I'm busy," she answered on getting to the phone "You know how hectic it gets this time of night."

"Roland has kidnapped Bridget and he's threatening to kill her if I don't stump up the million bucks he's decided I owe him."

There was a pause on the other end of the line. Elsa was stunned by the news and astounded that Roland should resort to such heavy handed tactics, automatically accepting Jack's word. She had seen Roland get more and more agitated over Jack's "debt" and had been worried about him getting Frank to persuade Jack to pay up, but now the stakes had gotten even higher with the kidnap of Bridget, and the greater threat of her murder.

"Roland can't be serious about killing Bridget. He may be a lot of things but surely he's not a murderer."

"Do you know where she is or where he might be keeping her?" asked Jack, ignoring Elsa's reply.

"Of course I don't! Do you think I would be part of such a thing?" Elsa paused to control her rising anger. "Roland's not here right now" she continued, "but I'll tackle him the moment he gets back."

"I'm sorry Elsa, but the question had to be asked. Besides, I'm so worried about Bridget I'm not thinking straight. She doesn't deserve this. I was the one that started the half brained scheme to get money from Simon Walsh and now after the fiasco of that botched job, her life is on the line," spluttered Jack.

"Don't be so dramatic. I feel as guilty as you about Bridget's predicament, but I can't see Roland going through with this when he finds out you haven't got the money. He's just trying to teach you a lesson," said Elsa not fully believing her own argument. She knew Frank would be involved and he had a long history of carrying out dirty work for both Pallacio and Bannister, including murder. She didn't know if she would be able to persuade him not to hurt Bridget, which would put him at odds with Roland.

Frank didn't shrink from hurting women but drew the line at gratuitous violence. Many years ago Frank had gone against Pallacio in settling a score that involved scarring a pretty, young whistle blower who worked as a dancer at the Blue Cockatoo. Pallacio wanted not only to hurt her, but to also take away her beauty as punishment. He reasoned that this would be a better deterrent to others than killing her. Frank was instructed to beat her up and scar her face, and when he refused Pallacio struck him so hard it broke off two of Frank's front teeth. Frank held his ground and Pallicio treated him with a grudging respect after the incident. Franks chivalry was to no avail as Pallacio, got someone else to do what he wanted.

20

While Jack was talking to Elsa, Roland was on his way to the docks to see Bridget. He wanted to talk to her, partly out of his curiosity to see the woman who fell in love with the man who had framed her husband (albeit ignorant of that fact), and partly to get some comfort that Jack would be able to get his hands on her money.

Bridget heard Roland climbing the stairs to the mezzanine floor and put her ear to the door to listen to the conversation between the newcomer and her kidnappers. She could hear the large man assuring him that their captive was well and sleeping in the bedroom. Suddenly the sound started getting louder and she then moved away from the door, but again not quickly enough. As Lou opened the door it caught against her leg, spinning her onto the bed.

She sat on the bed looking at each of the faces of the 3 men staring down at her. She was not going to be intimidated by any of them and didn't shrink from their gaze.

"She's been listening at the door again," said Lou "I told you not to do that" he spat at Bridget in his most menacing tone of voice. As he moved forward, Frank caught his arm and shook his head, which was enough to deter Lou from making any further movement towards her.

"Let the Boss talk to her," said Frank.

"I apologise for your current circumstances," interjected Roland, "but unfortunately it's the result of a long standing quarrel I've been having with your husband. He and I go back a long way and when he came to me with a business proposition I agreed to fund it provided it would result in a healthy return. He assured me it would and so I bank rolled the project."

"If it's just money, I....."

"No Bridget it's more than money. It's about respect. In the circles Jack and I move in, respect is a very important factor in dealing with our peers. Without respect we lose our credibility and that renders us useless in our chosen field of work. Jack may not have intended the turn of events that have taken place, but he had commitments and his failure brings consequences."

Bridget was surprised at the newcomer's articulate delivery, although he hadn't really given enough information for her to understand the root cause of his disagreement with Jack. She shaped her mouth to ask a question but Frank, standing behind Roland, signalled for her to remain silent by putting his index finger vertically across his mouth.

"You're probably wondering about the project Jack and I worked on together and what went wrong to create this rift between us. It started with Jack running a penny ante scam to compromise rich married men into paying large sums of money to him for either remaining silent or to stop him from causing them injury, after being caught with his woman.

Jack ran the scam with Elsa Bartelli, who was and is far too good for him, but nevertheless she agreed to support him in the scam, which generally worked well with little risk. Unfortunately with your first husband, Simon, things went wrong. Elsa ended up on Simon's sports cruiser without Jack in the wings to provide security. Your first husband was a brute and he tried to force himself on her, which ended up with her being shot and falling into the water. Jack recovered Elsa and hit on a plan to make Simon pay for what he had done to her."

"But Jack acted as a go between Elsa and me to get Simon released from prison," interjected Bridget.

"Yes but first he set the wheels in motion to build a circumstantial, but substantial murder case against him, which ultimately put him in prison!" replied Roland.

Apart from the initial shock of the kidnap, Bridget had managed to control her emotions throughout her ordeal, but now she suddenly began to feel hot and uncomfortable. She could not believe that the man she had fallen in love with was responsible for Simon's imprisonment, and therefore also his death, and despite that, he had managed to inveigle himself into her life. Although her marriage to

Simon was loveless, her overwhelming sense of guilt and helplessness deepened, together with an emerging hatred of Jack.

Frank studied Bridget as Roland told her of Jack Cates part in the framing of Simon Walsh. He could see the impact Roland's message was having on her and admired the way she was maintaining her composure, despite the barely discernible trembling of her hands and the small pools of water welling in her eyes. How did Cates manage to get a hold over women such as Elsa and Bridget who were far and away too good for him?

Roland carried on with the rest of the story explaining the extent of Jacks' involvement and the rear guard action taken after Simon's death for him to marry Bridget. By this time the colour had drained from Bridget's face and she sat on the bed impassively staring at the ground. She no longer cared what happened to her as the love of her life had been proven to be a sham and their life together was based on a one sided love affair.

"What I need to know Bridget is that Jack will be able to take a million dollars from your bank account and hand it over when we make the exchange tomorrow night," boomed Roland.

Bridget nodded affirmatively without lifting up her head. She didn't know what Jack would do to get the money and didn't care. Her life had no further meaning to her. Success in the NMP was scant compensation for losing what she thought would be her partner for life.

"Good!" said Roland, "let's hope we can get this thing over and done with as quickly and painlessly as possible. With that he turned on his heels and went out of the room. Lou followed him to discuss arrangements for the night of the exchange.

Frank looked down at Bridget with a friendly, compassionate smile. "It's an expensive lesson but when this thing is over, move on and forget about Cates."

"Frank" called Roland, "where are you?" Frank walked into the office and Roland added, "No matter what you think of Bridget, remember she is only the means for us to get the money owed by Jack. Don't you two worry, you'll do very nicely out of the deal also. I'll call you tomorrow to confirm arrangements. Remember she has seen our faces and knows where to find us. You know what that means."

Frank and Lou nodded obediently to Roland as he left the office. Neither man was happy with the situation and the prospect of having to kill Bridget, but they would do what was necessary when the time came.

Early in the morning, hours before the opening of the club, Elsa was sitting at the bar of the Blue Cockatoo with a long cool drink in her hand. She was trying to decide how to confront Roland over the kidnapping of Bridget. The unease she felt over his obsession with getting money from Jack had now become a fear of him sliding over the edge of a dark precipice leading to the murder of both Jack and Bridget. The murder of Jack was already on the table and Roland must know that if he hurt or killed Bridget his ex-partner would come after him. She could try and get information out of Frank, but she really had to ask Roland directly to try to pull him back from the precipice, and to help save Jack.

21

On the morning of the exchange Roland breezed into the Blue Cockatoo with a swagger that had been missing for some time. He felt in control once more and had arranged the evening's events to re-establish his position as a major player in the criminal fraternity and end up with a handsome payday as a bonus. Modest by the standards set against the revenue of his club but nevertheless substantial by the kudos he would gain through the manner of its collection. By the end of the day Jack would be history.

Elsa had arrived early so that she could talk to Roland before things got out of hand and someone, most likely Jack, ended up dead. The alternative of finding what she could from Frank never materialised as he hadn't been at the club for a few days and she didn't want to talk about it on a cell phone. She had no idea that Jack's death was already central to Roland's game plan. When she saw him enter the club she waited for a few minutes and then followed his path up the stairs to the office. She paused at the door and realised Roland was on the phone, so she waited outside the door.

"Michael make sure your man gets to the docks at nine o'clock, one hour before Jack arrives. I haven't told Jack the location or time of the exchange, which I will leave to the last minute to keep him guessing. Your man will have plenty of time to prepare and I will make sure he has access to the docks and the crane cab."

"OK, that's all I need to know" replied Braggio and put down the phone.

"Peasant" thought Roland and looked towards the door as Elsa knocked and walked into the office. "Hello Elsa, this is going to be a wonderful day," beamed Roland.

"Why is that Roland? Because you've put the screws on Jack by kidnapping his wife?" she blurted out, immediately regretting being impulsive. She had sat on the information since being told by Jack and just couldn't contain herself.

"I suppose you got the news from the horse's mouth!" snarled Roland, "I've given him plenty of time Elsa, which has now run out."

"How the hell do you expect him to get that amount of money?" replied Elsa, pleading with Roland to use his common sense.

"Y'know I don't really care!" replied Roland. "I'm not too worried because his wife is well heeled. As always Jack can rely on his women to look after him."

"And what about Bridget? What's going to happen to her? If Jack can't come up with the money are you going to kill her?" continued Elsa.

"Don't be so bloody stupid. I'm not a murderer and you know neither Frank nor Lou would do it," reasoned Roland. Elsa didn't know that he had already discussed the possibility of having to kill Bridget with them and in truth wasn't sure how it would all end, apart from Jack's death.

"Well that's a relief," said Elsa feeling the tension in her gut easing a little. "What time are you going to make the exchange?" she asked.

"I've not made my mind up yet," lied Roland. He didn't want to tell Elsa his plans in case she went running straight back to Jack with the information. He was beginning to think that he could no longer afford a manager with allegiances outside his interests, which meant they were outside the interests of the Blue Cockatoo. He thought it unlikely that she would want to continue to work at the club after Jack's death. He could plead ignorance and claim Jack had tried to double cross him, pulled a gun and ended up being shot by one of Braggio's men who he had been brought in to oversee the exchange. The trouble would start if she insisted on going to the police. Roland remembered his conversation with Detective Tanner in which he told him that Elsa was petrified of Jack, which was the only reason she agreed to taking part in his scams. Initially he had been sowing seeds with Tanner to frame Jack for any harm done to Bridget, but it may also prove useful if Elsa should become an inconvenience.

The heated exchange between Elsa and Roland brought Julie into the office. "Is everything alright with you guys? She asked.

"Everything's fine," answered Elsa, "let's start getting ready for tonight." Elsa nodded to Roland as she left the office giving the impression they had a mutual understanding, which was far from the truth.

Roland sat back in his chair thinking deeply about Elsa's future, wondering if Braggio's man could do two jobs for him. He put the thought behind him and called up Frank. "Hi Frank, the exchange will take place tonight at 10 o'clock. I've arranged for Braggio's man to be positioned in the cab of the crane at the south end of the dock. We'll enter through the security gate at the north end, meet up at the warehouse and then Lou and me will bring Bridget to the rendezvous point for the exchange. You and Cates will come from the opposite end of the pier and he will hand over the money, then we will hand over Bridget. As Jack is making his way back to his car he will be shot dead!

"What about Bridget", exclaimed Frank involuntarily.

"Don't worry big guy. She'll be shocked but unhurt provided we can make her see sense," replied Bannister. "When I spoke to her she was unable to think straight because of what she learned about Jack's involvement in sending Walsh to prison, but she may have had time to dwell on that and not be feeling anything for him by now. But remember she can finger us to the law, so my gut instinct is to finish her off after Jack, but we'll see how she reacts."

After the call Frank relayed Bannisters instructions to Lou, who was playing a game on his iPhone to kill time. While they were talking Lou looked past Frank casually and noticed the door to the bedroom was slightly ajar. It was open enough to let Bridget hear their conversation more clearly. "I've told that snooty bitch not to eavesdrop several times. Now I'll give her a scare," thought Lou. He darted around Frank shouting at the top of his voice, "You're in trouble now, girl," and making a charge for the bedroom, threw the door open. This action was followed by a piercing scream and a thud against the wall.

As Lou entered the room the door was restrained from opening to its full extent and he could see Bridget's legs sticking out from the bottom of the door, trapped between the door and one of the bed legs. Cautiously he stepped over her legs to peer around the door and let out a gasp. Bridget was sitting on the floor with her back against the wall and her head slumped forward. A trail of blood was dripping down from her face onto her white blouse. The red was a striking contrast against the white of her blouse, even though it was grubby after its three days of wear.

Lou lifted Bridget's head and saw her right eye was a congealing mass of blood and her left eye was staring straight at him. He looked up at the stub end of the coat hanger, which had bits of her eye and blood hanging off it. By this time Frank was standing behind Lou to see what the commotion was about and stared down at the lifeless form of Bridget in disbelief. He threw Lou aside and cupped her face in his large hands to inspect the damage and then felt for a pulse in her neck, "she's dead," he uttered in disbelief.

"It was an accident! She was listening through the gap at the door frame. As I threw open the door she must have turned away in panic and the stub of the coat hanger swung into her eye." Lou was reconstructing the event although he still couldn't believe what had happened. He leaned forward and put his hand on Frank's shoulder saying "How are we going to tell Roland?"

Frank looked at Bridget's staring eye and suddenly stood up saying, "All of the running around over the past two weeks has been for nothing! Just because you wanted to scare a woman! And now we'll have nothing to show for it!" With that he turned and put his big hands around Lou's throat. As he squeezed Lou didn't have time to protest but spluttered to suck in air. The look in Frank's eyes was demonic, burning holes into his skull. Frank's face became blurred and Lou blacked out.

When Lou regained consciousness he found himself lying on the floor face down. His neck was sore and he took deep breathes not believing that he was still alive. He went on all fours and then stood up shakily, and turned to see that Frank had put Bridget on the bed and covered her face with his jacket. Frank was sitting in the office with his head in his hands.

Warily Lou moved into the office, but kept his distance from Frank. He didn't want to set him off again because if he did there was no telling if Frank would be able to stop. After a while Frank became aware of Lou's presence in the room. He straightened up in the chair and turned to look at Lou. "You stupid bastard. We were supposed to look after her, not fucking kill her! She was the only innocent person in this whole sorry mess and she's ended up dead. What does that tell you?"

"We were probably gonna have to do it anyway," he replied timidly.

"Maybe so, but she didn't deserve to go out like that. I'd have done it easy so she didn't know what was happening. A stiletto into the heart like I did for that guy trying to blackmail the Boss."

Lou didn't think Frank wanted his opinion and kept quiet.

"You, me, Bannister and Cates, we're used to squirming around in the gutter but she wasn't and somehow got sucked into this mess through no fault of her own. It just shows we must be in the right business – 'cos only the strong survive."

"I'm sorry Frank, I didn't mean to fuck things up. If I'd known something like this could happen I never would have…."

"I know," interjected Frank, "but you know me and my hair trigger temper. For a moment there you were on thin ice, but more importantly, I don't know how we're gonna to tell Roland."

"We can't give him this news over the phone. We'll have to go in and tell him. God knows how he'll react. I created this mess so I'll go to Roland's apartment and take the flack. You stay with Bridget." Lou replied.

Frank didn't speak and just nodded his agreement.

22

Jack found that waiting for Roland's call was intolerable. He knew that he needed a plan to deal with Roland and his goons. Once they discovered he had gone to the meeting $995,000 dollars shy of the million bucks they would definitely turn nasty. Jack's main concern was for the safety of Bridget, therefore he decided to enlist the assistance of the law and made a call to Gene Tanner.

"Hi Gene," greeted Jack with as much enthusiasm as he could muster.

"There's a coincidence. I was talking to your buddy Roland Bannister a few days ago about Simon Walsh and you marrying his widow. He wasn't very complimentary towards you and warned me about you defrauding your wife out of her money, even going as far as to say you wouldn't stop at her murder!"

Jack was astounded by what he heard from Tanner and couldn't believe how much ground Roland had covered in planning his retribution. "He's kidnapped Bridget! I think he's unhinged and I don't give much for her life or mine," he stammered.

"I thought it strange at the time but if he was planning to kidnap Bridget, he must have been preparing the ground to frame you for her murder. It would be difficult for you to deny doing it, if you're already dead!"

Jack was taken aback that Bannister had even spoken to Gene, never mind his insinuations and obvious intentions for the future. "I'm no angel, but I draw the line at murder. I hope you know me better than that Gene," ventured Jack.

"You've stretched legal boundaries, but I think I know you well enough not to believe that you have the capacity to murder. But where do you draw the line?" asked Tanner.

Jack decided to tell Gene about the whole sorry affair of trying to blackmail Simon Walsh that ultimately resulted in his marriage to Bridget. He ended up by telling Gene that Bannister had been responsible for Al Ferrino's death because the little man had tried to get more money out of him during Walsh's trial. "You were right it was a professional killing. On our instructions Al had started the ball rolling on Walsh's prosecution by drawing out the witnesses to her disappearance, but realised there was a lot more at stake than the 10 grand we gave him and wanted more. Bannister had his thugs murder him before he let the cat out of the bag. Walsh of course was murdered in prison and now Roland is aggrieved that he's out of pocket by 100 grand. He's kidnapped Bridget and is demanding I bring him a million dollars for her release."

"Before we go any further, you realise that when this is all over I will have to take you back to Miami as an accessory to murder," interjected Gene.

"Gene, I didn't know what Roland was planning. I just wanted to stall Al until the end of the trial and then scare him out of his demands."

"OK, but there is going to be some comeback on you. We'll settle on the details later, after Bridget's safe," insisted Gene.

"I don't care what happens to me Gene. I just want to get Bridget free of Roland's clutches and back with me, safe and sound," replied Jack.

"OK, where is the exchange to take place?" asked Gene.

"I don't know. I don't know the time either. All I know is that it will be sometime today," replied Jack. "Roland is making me squirm and he doesn't want me ready for exchange, he wants to keep me on my toes. He said he'd call me an hour before the exchange is to take place."

"In that case I'll alert NYPD and get a tail on you so that if anything unexpected happens we'll still be able to keep close. I'll get a flight up to New York straight away and give you a call when I arrive."

"Thanks Gene," responded Jack feebly.

"It's not for you it's for Bridget," said Gene and closed the call.

Jack had taken precautions to protect himself during the exchange. He couldn't handle Roland, Frank and Lou together, in fact he doubted he would be able to handle Frank on his own. For insurance he would take a double action, 38 calibre Smith and Wesson revolver with 7 rounds. It was light and a single bullet in the right place would even stop Frank. He also had a bullet proof vest, which he would wear under a sweatshirt. It would be a little bulky but now that it looked as if the exchange would take place at night, it wouldn't really be that noticeable. The final piece of armoury would be a double edged boot knife, with his jeans pulled over his boots. The knife would be hiding behind a rip in the material for easy access.

After taking $5000 out of his bank account, Jack had virtually fully drained his financial resources. He had taken out one thousand $5 bills to make up 50 hundred dollar bundles. He would have to convince Roland that he was carrying five hundred $2000 dollar bundles. The additional four hundred and fifty bundles would be made up with plain paper. After preparing the bundles of money and paper, Jack placed the money and the dummies in an archive storage box and wrapped it with plain brown paper, using an inordinate amount of scotch tape to make it more difficult to open.

He didn't want to resort to violence but expected an all-round assault when the package was opened. His greatest concern was to ensure that Bridget wouldn't get caught in the crossfire.

23

After talking to Jack and taking in all the nuances of their discussion, Gene called Captain Joe MacDonald at NYPD headquarters. Joe was the highest ranking police officer that Gene thought he knew well enough to discuss Jack's case without prejudice and would allow him to come to New York to work alongside his team. He was lucky enough to get him on his direct line. "Hi Joe, its Gene Tanner," he said after Joe's initial response.

"Gene. This is a surprise we haven't spoken in an age. It must be 5 years at least."

"I was up in New York about 18months ago and asked for permission to speak to Simon Walsh about a potential murder investigation."

"Yeah," replied MacDonald. "Wasn't he the guy that got murdered in one of your jails?"

"Yes. I'm afraid he did and it's connected with the reason I wanted to talk to you. Simon Walsh was framed for the murder of Elsa Bartelli by Jack Cates. In fact there was no murder because Jack hid her away in Boston after he fished her out of the sea. His idea was to demand money off Walsh for the reappearance of Elsa, but his plan was upset by Walsh's murder."

"Cates was in league with Roland Bannister, who runs the "Blue Cockatoo" in New York," continued Tanner, "and he was not best pleased at the cock up. He twisted Jack's arm to marry Walsh's widow, who he had negotiated with to secure her husband's release, on the understanding that Jack would get money from her to balance the books, but with a little interest. The money was not forthcoming so Bannister has kidnapped Bridget and expects Jack to stump up a million dollars for her release."

There was silence on the other end of the line for several seconds and MacDonald finally said, "If a kidnap's involved we should go to the FEDs, but we haven't got time to get them up and running at such short notice. You know the red tape they need to go through before kicking off, so I'll turn a blind eye until tomorrow morning.

It's interesting, but let's hope recovering Bridget safely by tomorrow morning is the final twist in the story."

"Believe me it's even more complicated than I've explained. I've given you the abbreviated version," replied Tanner.

"I'm surprised Jack Cates is involved. Although I don't know him well, he always had a reputation for being straight. It's a pity he went off the rails," added MacDonald. "I know Roland Bannister better. He operated as a smart ass lawyer for every petty criminal in New York before taking over the "Blue Cockatoo". The transfer of that place from Barry Summers to him is still a mystery, as is Summers' disappearance."

"Joe, I've promised to help Jack so can I come up North to work on your team?"

"That's no problem but you'll have to be sharp, time's running out," answered MacDonald.

"I've checked the flights to New York. I can still catch the 14:30 plane from Miami International to New York, which means I should get there before 17:30 and to you by about six. We will need a SWAT team on standby to pour water on what could be a highly volatile situation when the exchange takes place. Can we go through it in more detail then?"

"Sure" replied MacDonald. "It would be good to tie up a few loose ends for a change."

"Jack doesn't know the time or venue for the exchange but by the time we meet that will hopefully be settled. It may be wise to put a tail on him in case something unexpected happens. He knows about the arrangement and won't try to make things difficult. See you later."

24

"OK, tell me what the problem is," said Roland as he opened the door of his apartment to let Lou in.

"It's not straightforward Boss," stammered Lou, standing awkwardly in the lobby. "Something unexpected has happened, which changes our plans for Cates."

"Well come into the kitchen", replied Bannister good naturedly "and we can discuss it over a cup of coffee."

In the kitchen Bannister motioned Lou to sit at one of the stools at the breakfast bar and began preparing the filter coffee percolator by putting in filter papers and a Brazilian coffee blend. "Fire away Lou".

"Well the circumstances are difficult to explain, but Bridget is dead", replied Lou.

"WHAT!" exclaimed Bannister, and immediately stopped what he was doing. He rushed over to Lou grabbing him by the lapels of his jacket, "how the fuck can she be dead? .You were just baby-sitting her until the exchange!"

"It was a freaky accident. I thought she was eavesdropping on me and Frank talking about arrangements for tonight and wanted to give her a scare, cos she had been doing it all the time. I ran to the bedroom and threw the door open and the coat hook went into her eye with such force, it must have stuck into her brain and killed her instantly", explained Lou.

Bannister was aghast, for once not knowing what to say.

"I guess the exchange is off, then?" continued Lou timidly wanting to get a reaction from Bannister.

Bannister walked back to the percolator in a trance, turned and threw the cup he was holding at Lou screaming, "You stupid bastard you've managed to make me look even more stupid than I did before! How on earth can you botch up a simple baby-sitting job, especially with so much at stake? I should kill you for this!"

"Sorry Boss. As I said it was…."

"Shut up!" snapped Bannister "I'm thinking. Elsa is about the same height and build as Bridget and she could possibly pass for her in the dark, with the right camouflage and clothing. Dark glasses, with a scarf over her head should hide her face, and if she's dressed in clothes like Bridget's, underneath her raincoat she may just pull it off. It's not as if Cates is going to have a great deal of time to take stock of what's happening. We'll keep Elsa in the background until the money is checked and by then Braggio's assassin will have Cates in his sights and should be able to pull the trigger before things get awkward", continued Bannister with his usual penchant for understatement.

"Do you think Elsa will agree to do it?" asked Lou.

"It would be a good way to pay me back after all I've done for her since she came back. She's bound to be shocked by Bridget's death, but I think I can persuade her to help. It's her reaction to witnessing Jack's death I'm more concerned about. Let's go over to the club", said Bannister reaching for his coat.

On the way to the club Bannister rang Frank. "Are you still with Bridget at the docks?" he asked.

"Yes," replied Frank.

"I know this is a terrible thing that has happened, but there's nothing else we can do for Bridget now, so I would like you to go over to Cates' apartments about 9:30 and pick him up for the exchange. He'll be expecting a phone call from me for the place and time of the meet, but I don't want to give him any time to prepare for it, particularly if he's planning to bring along any friends. I want Elsa to pretend to be Bridget so the exchange can still take place."

"I don't want anything to happen to Elsa", replied Frank in a mildly threatening way.

Bannister was prepared for his reaction to Elsa's involvement and assured him that she would not be placed in any danger, and that Cates would be dead before he realised what was going on

.

25

Archie Lemon sat comfortably in his car driving from New York City to Jersey. He would take the Holland tunnel to make the crossing and park his car as close as possible to Wharf 10, before making his way there by foot. He was pleased that the exchange point was a little isolated, but he still wanted to inspect the area thoroughly and establish his main and back up escape routes before setting up in his vantage point for the shoot. He thought there should be plenty of confusion after he'd taken his shot, which would allow him to make his getaway easily. In the event of either something going wrong or an unexpected happening, he always carried a pistol with him in case he needed to shoot his way out.

There were plenty of port parking opportunities so Archie had no difficulty finding a car park close to the exchange location and a convenient spot to leave his hire car. "If necessary I needn't go back for the hire car", he thought, as he'd paid for it in cash and using a false driving licence as means of identification.

He was dressed like a port worker in blue gingham casual checked work shirt, jeans and lumber jacket, dark brown safety boots and a ribbed beanie cap that he pulled down to his ears. His weapon was a semi-automatic, large calibre marksman rifle, which he would have to assemble at his chosen vantage point. Archie had studied a map of this area of the commercial docks and had a reasonably good idea of his game plan. There would be plenty of time to iron out the rough edges. It was a pity to leave the gun behind as it was a beautifully crafted and very high precision weapon with a high magnification sight. The gun and case were inside a large duffel bag, similar to a sailor's kit bag.

The security guard let Archie in to the cordoned off area of the docks and he meandered over to Wharf 10 and saw the relationship of the derelict warehouse and an old dockside crane mounted on rails to roll up and down the edge of the wharf for the loading and unloading of cargo. It was an old crane capable of lifting 35 tons, but hadn't been used in several years. The cab, some 20 feet off the deck was supported on braced legs and the jib used for lifting and luffing was also a braced frame construction. Archie climbed onto the crane and could see that from the cab he had a clear view to the derelict warehouse and as the exchange was to take place on the wharf, would also have a clear view of his target. He opened his kit bag and pulled out the gun case and realised immediately he would have to stand the gun on something to raise the level of the barrel sufficiently to clear the bottom of the front window frame of the cab.

Archie walked over to the derelict warehouse to try and find something secure on which to place the rifle stand. The door to the warehouse creaked as he opened it and shone a torch into the blackness. Even in daylight the light inside the warehouse was poor as the windows were all at high level and dirty.

Inside the office Frank heard the door open and sunk down on his haunches to avoid the chance of being seen from the ground. He scuttled over to the door and opened it slightly, careful not to make a noise. He could see Archie waving his torch around, but was not sure if he was the security guard or someone else….but who? Frank thought it could be the assassin that Roland had hired from Braggio but needed confirmation in case the exchange had been rumbled by the law. He decided that he would not confront him inside the warehouse unless he came up to the office, as this could end up with one or other of them getting shot.

Archie found a sturdy 55 gallon steel drum with a lid that he could use to support his rifle. Its height was sufficient to clear the window frame with room to spare, but he would have to take out the operator's seat in the crane cab to fit it in position. He carried the drum by holding its top and bottom and was pleased that it wasn't too heavy. Archie walked over to the warehouse door, which opened outwards and he leaned on it to push it open and stepped outside.

Frank decided his best opportunity to get the better of this man was while he was carrying the drum. He ran down the stairs of the mezzanine platform and over to the warehouse door, opening it as quietly as possible. By this time he already had his gun in his hand and ran up to Archie just as he turned on hearing movement behind him. "Hold it!" yelled Frank. Archie stopped and turned fully to face him.

"Can I put this barrel down? It is heavy you know", replied Archie.

"No you can hold it for a little longer so I can see where your hands are", instructed Frank. "I think I know who you are but you need to confirm it by telling me who you're working for."

"I'm from out of town to do job of cleaning out some dirt. It's a specialist task with specialist equipment. I can't tell you who I'm working for as that would be poor etiquette on my part, but let's say that what I do is permanent and I haven't had any complaints from other customers", answered Archie. Frank cocked his gun and Archie spluttered "OK, it's Michael Braggio".

"Put the barrel down", said Frank. "We're on the same side. What are you doing now?"

"I'm setting myself up for the exchange but I need a something stable to stand my rifle on. I'm gonna use the cab of the crane cos it's the best place to give a clear sight along the full length of the berth. I'll also need to take the seat out of the cab and the glass out of the front window."

"Don't worry about that", said Frank, "I'll get them out for you".

Archie looked at Frank. He was a giant of a man who he imagined would have great strength. He didn't have to wait long for proof as Frank strode over to the crane and ripped the seat from its moorings in a single jerking action. There were restraints in the floor but Frank grabbed the barrel pulled out the lid and turned it over with its open end on the floor. This gave a stable platform on which Archie could mount the gun. He then got outside the cab, climbed onto the jib bracing and pushed out the glass panel of the front window. Frank then got back into the cab to remove the window pane.

After making sure the access was clear, Frank vacated the cab and Archie climbed in with his gun case. He opened it and carefully started to assemble his rifle. Frank was amazed at the precision with which the components of the rifle fitted together. "I've already calibrated the sights so we're ready to go", said Archie at the end of his task.

"Roland wants me to collect Cates at 9:30 PM, so we'll get here about 10:30. By that time he'll already be in place outside the side door of the warehouse that we've come through. He'll walk over towards the edge of the wharf to a point approximately 100 yard from this cab. Is that OK, or is it too far?" said Frank.

"No that's a snip for this rifle" replied Archie.

Frank went back to the warehouse and Archie pondered on the error of anybody crossing this man as he could truly kill a person with his bare hands.

Braggio had briefed Archie thoroughly sending a photograph of his target and giving him a step by step picture of events leading up to the exchange. He now had a clear idea of the scene that would unfold and was confident of a successful kill. The end of the gun barrel was visible in the cab in the daylight, but by ten o'clock tonight it would be hard to see.

It was important that he do a good job as Mr. Pallacio was taking an interest in this job as well as Braggio, so his reputation was dependent on him doing a good job.

26

Bannister marched into the "Blue Cockatoo" with Lou trailing behind him. "Go and find Elsa", he snapped "and ask her to come to the office. Then stay away until I call you about tonight's arrangements".

Lou scurried off to find Elsa and Bannister started thinking about what would be necessary to convince her to stand in for Bridget. She would obviously be shocked by Bridget's death, but would surely understand the need to get something out of this whole sorry affair. I've done a great deal for her since her return from Boston, he thought, not that he would want to overstress her dependence on him. He knew her to be a proud woman and that being heavy handed would probably result in a breakdown of the negotiation. Roland deeply regretted after her breaking up with Jack that they had not become closer, but she had made it clear they could only be friends. Another disappointment due to Jack.

There was a rap on the office door and Elsa walked in and said, "Hi Roland. Can you make this quick as I'm trying to finish the weekly orders for booze and food?"

"This won't be a five minute chat Elsa. Something very serious has happened and I'm going to need your help. Go and tell Julie to finish the orders, while I pour us some drinks", Roland replied firmly. Elsa could see that he was in no mood to be disagreed with and went out of the office to instruct Julie. In the meantime Roland poured himself a large brandy and followed with a gin and tonic for Elsa. "Let's sit on the couch" he said to Elsa when she returned and picked up the drinks as he walked around the office desk.

Elsa didn't say anything and was slightly worried that Roland was going to come onto her again. "There's no easy way to say this Elsa, but Bridget is dead!" The shock of Roland's statement left Elsa aghast and open mouthed. Roland continued to explain the circumstances of her death as Lou had told him.

"The poor woman", Elsa finally said taking a big gulp of her drink. "Her kidnap is now murder. Let's stop this thing before matters get even worse."

"Don't exaggerate Elsa. It's not murder. It would be manslaughter, however the fact that it happened during her abduction means that it would carry a pretty hefty sentence. I'm not worried about that because we're not going to get caught," replied Roland.

"Jack will be more than furious when he hears about it. You know he's going to go after Lou and that could lead to him taking on Frank as well. He's in an intolerable position," countered Elsa.

"Why should you care about the position he's in? If he hadn't made such a botch up of looking after Simon Walsh he wouldn't be in this situation now," said Bannister getting a little agitated. "Our welfare comes before his and don't you forget it," he added, "and we'll make sure we're protected against him seeking some kind of retribution."

"Well the exchange is off," replied Elsa, "because Bridget is dead!"

"Well I think we can get round that if you disguise yourself and take Bridget's place," answered Roland.

This proposal shocked Elsa even more than the news of Bridget's death, "but I don't look anything like her," Elsa stammered. "Besides Jack will recognise me!"

"Don't worry it will be dark and if you wear her raincoat and a scarf over your head Jack won't be any the wiser until it's too late," responded Bannister.

"What do you mean, until it's too late?"

"I mean until after he's handed the money over. We'll keep you in the background until the handover is complete and then tell him about Bridget." Of course Elsa didn't know that the success of Roland's plan would mean that Jack was dead, and she couldn't imagine what his reaction would be when given the news of Bridget's death."

Elsa was getting a little frightened as Roland was becoming more and more assertive in his insistence she pretend to be Bridget at the exchange. She kept quiet as Roland added, "As I said, you'll be kept at a distance until Jack has handed over the money and if he gets violent on the news of Bridget's death Lou and Frank will be there to take care of him."

"Of course he'll get agitated when you tell him about Bridget, and probably violent too. Are you intending to kill him also?" shouted Elsa.

Roland grabbed Elsa's arm and squeezed it hard until she winced. "Your allegiance is with me now, not him. If you don't do as I ask I will just get Lou and Frank to kill Jack now. At least this way he has a chance of life depending on how he reacts," lied Bannister. He knew for certain now that Elsa still loved Jack and nothing was going to change that and also knew that she would hate the man responsible for his death.

Elsa relaxed against his grip realising that she was trapped and would have to do as Roland wanted. She needed to tell Jack that his life was on the line and he shouldn't turn up for the exchange, but how could she tell him about Bridget?

While she was lost in her thoughts Roland added, "Just one more thing Elsa, let me have your cell phone, just in case you're tempted to call Jack. I know you can still call him from any phone inside the club, but I hope the extra trouble it causes you will help make you understand whose side you're on. Besides you'll be under close scrutiny for the rest of the day, just to make sure you don't succumb to temptation."

"My handbag's outside let me get it for you", she replied meekly, seeing her best chance of getting in touch with Jack disappear.

At the bar Elsa ran into Julie. "I think Roland is getting paranoid over Jack and is going to do something drastic! I'm caught in the middle", she said while searching through her handbag. "He wants my phone so I don't go telling any tales to Jack".

After giving her cell phone to Roland, Elsa went back into the bar at a loss to know the best thing to do. If she had known of Bannister's intention to kill Jack she wouldn't have any doubt on her best course of action. The other thing bothering her was how on earth Jack could get his hands on a million dollars. He certainly didn't have a nest egg hidden away and was making a fairly basic living as a PI. He must have got the money from Bridget, but how? It then dawned on her that he might be bluffing and if he was, how did he see the exchange playing out? Jack wasn't stupid so he must have some game plan in mind, but again that might fall apart when he finds out about Bridget.

Elsa's head was spinning but she decided that she would call Jack later so he would come prepared tonight. She didn't know the exact time of the exchange, but thought she would ring him early in the evening, as soon as she felt it was safe enough to do so.

27

When Gene Tanner cleared the airport he headed straight to NYPD Headquarters. Joe MacDonald greeted him warmly as he entered his office. "Good timing Gene. I have one man positioned in the car park of Cates' apartment and another in the café across the road. He's in his apartment at the moment and they both have a good view of comings and goings, so they should pick him up as soon as he leaves. He must have gone out earlier in the day as our first sighting of him happened when he returned to the car park".

"That's quick work Joe, but I'm thankful for it because I've got a feeling that things could get nasty. Jack's out in the cold and there really isn't any honor among thieves, so his past friendship with Bannister won't count for anything when the fireworks start."

"Yeah. Bannister has the sophisticated veneer of an educated, successful man, but I think he's as ruthless as any of his underworld peers and won't let Jack off the hook gently. I think there could be some heavy action and I don't want it resulting in a blood bath. I'm mostly concerned about Bridget's welfare as Jack may not be able to protect her against such heavy odds," added MacDonald.

"Its eight o'clock now so something should be happening fairly soon. I can't believe they're holding Bridget very far away so it shouldn't take Jack much more than half an hour to an hour to get to the exchange location, traffic permitting. We can follow Jack at a discreet distance with the SWAT team in tow. That should more than even up the odds", replied Gene.

"It could be a long night Gene. Want a coffee?"

While Joe was advising Gene of his stakeout arrangements, Jack was trying to work out his best plan of action. He had been in some tight corners before but this would be one of the tightest. His main concern was getting to Bridget before Roland realised that the money package only held five thousand dollars. He was prepared to accept whatever happened to him, but he didn't want Bridget hurt. The brown paper package on the table looked big enough to be $1,000,000, but he knew it wouldn't stand close inspection if

Bannister decides to rummage through the package as he will quickly see through the bluff.

Jack knew that he would have to take control of the situation immediately after handing over the package to Roland, by demanding Bridget's immediate release and forcing the exchange. Lou and Frank would probably be armed so he would have to be prepared to take them out quickly if necessary. He didn't want to get close to either of them, especially Frank and thought he would be quicker to get his gun out than they would. The only uncertainty was how to wrest Bridget away from their clutches and the possibility of them using her as a shield.

He decided to ring Gene as much for comfort as anything else. "Hi Gene. Are you in New York?" he asked.

"Yeah" replied Tanner "I'm in NYPD Headquarters with Joe MacDonald".

Jack new MacDonald, but not well. He did know that he was a straight cop and played by the book. His secondary concern was therefore how to evade arrest when the exchange was over.

"Has Bannister made contact yet?" asked Gene.

"No not yet, but it's early. I think the exchange will be between 10 and midnight, then he can easily fabricate an alibi by saying he was at his club. No doubt everyone there will back him up." Maybe not Elsa he thought.

"OK we've staked out the car park and the front of the apartment so we'll know when you leave for the exchange, just in case you find you're not able to call us. Keep tight buddy," said Tanner and put down the phone.

Jack felt a lot more relaxed knowing that NYPD would be ready to step in when necessary.

While Jack was on the phone to Gene, Elsa had tried to ring him from a public phone but got the engaged tone. She had asked Julie to keep an eye out for Roland and let her know if he was coming in her direction. Julie had offered her cell phone but Elsa decided not to use it in case she got caught and ended up getting her friend into trouble with Roland.

"He's coming through," Julie said and Elsa put down the phone and left the booth.

When Roland clasped eyes on Elsa and Julie he said, "I was just coming to get you Elsa. I think it's time we made our way to our dinner date. Get your coat."

"Roland. Wait while I get a blanket", replied Elsa. "I want to wrap Bridget in something to show her a little respect", replied Elsa.

Julie looked quizzical and Roland rolled his eyes, but felt he could wait a few minutes longer to keep Elsa sweet. "Don't forget a scarf", he shouted after her. She returned with a large rolled up blanket under her arm and put a scarf into her coat pocket. She struggled to hold the blanket and Roland took it off her. Lou was waiting at the car and got into the driving seat. Roland put the blanket in the boot and got into the passenger seat, while Elsa made herself comfortable in the back.

They drove to the Port of New Jersey terminals and made for the commercial dock area and Wharf 10. The drive to New Jersey was uneventful and without conversation other than Lou confirming directions with Roland. Eventually they passed through the security gate and headed towards the derelict container warehouse.

Frank stood up when Elsa came into the office ahead of Roland and Lou. In a soft voice she asked, "Where is she?" Frank nodded towards the bedroom, which Elsa entered with the blanket in her arms. Frank followed her into the room apologising for what had happened. "Don't worry, at least she's at peace now," answered Elsa. It was an empty sentiment as Bridget was too young to have died.

Elsa turned to see the blood on the floor and then back to the bed towards Bridget's lifeless body. Frank's coat covered her head and when Elsa removed it she gagged seeing the red hole and staring eye on Bridget's now ghostly pale face. "Help me get her covered properly", she said to Frank. They removed her raincoat from underneath her and wrapped the body from head to toe in the blanket, almost like a mummy. It wasn't easy as rigour mortis had started to set in and her limbs were stiff. Luckily Frank had laid her flat on her back, with her arms by her side and legs together. Elsa had brought some packaging tape with her and wrapped it round the blanketed bundle to keep it together.

She started to cry a little for the passing of Bridget, not knowing why. Bridget had died alone without anyone close to hold her in her final moments. Frank was surprised to see Elsa's reaction. He knew better than question her and just glared at Lou for creating this painful scenario.

Roland looked at his watch, which now read 8:45 PM. "Frank I want you to head over to Jack's apartment. He's expecting me to call but I want you to collect him unannounced so that he can't prepare any nasty surprises in advance. Don't give him any leeway," he said. Frank nodded, left the building and got into the car the others had arrived in.

Archie Lemon was watching the comings and goings from his vantage point on the crane and was pleased he could see the faces of the people clearly with the security lighting. It wasn't cold, but it was a little chilly. Archie had brought a hip flask full of bourbon and drained the last few dregs before putting it back into his pocket. He had been wearing gloves throughout the day, so there would be no trace of him after the event. He had been caught trying to rob a store as a youth so his fingerprints were on file, but there were no DNA records of him. Having downed the last of his bourbon Archie settled down for the main event, which was now close at hand.

28

Jack was finishing off a cup of coffee when he heard a rap on the door. He tucked the revolver in the back of his belt, pulled over his sweatshirt and put the boot knife at the back of his right foot and straightened his jeans. He went to the door and opened it to see Frank's smiling face greet him, "Roland asked me to pick you up. Just to make sure you turn up at the right time."

"I've been sitting here waiting for his call. I want to get this over with as quickly as he does. Let me get my coat," replied Jack.

"OK but be quick about it," rasped Frank.

Jack put on his jacket and went over to the table to pick up the brown paper package. "So that's what a million bucks looks like," whistled Frank.

"Yeah there's a lot of bills, and it's heavy."

Jack knew he wouldn't be returning to his apartment and had already put personal items and documents into a safety deposit box at the bank. He had also seen Freddy Bartholomew to pick up his false passport, together with a change of clothes and the pair of glasses he had worn for his passport photo, which were in a holdall in a room he had booked at the Best Western Bowery Hanbee hotel. The hotel was close to Penn Station, which has good links to JFK International Airport.

"Come on, let's not keep Roland waiting", added Frank opening the door for Jack.

Jack turned to go to the elevator to the car park. "Not that way Jack. I'm parked in the service bay. My cousin works maintenance here and I have the code for the gate. It's quicker to use it in quiet periods."

"I was going to use my car," answered Jack.

"Don't worry I'll bring you back here," replied Frank desperately trying not to snigger.

"We'll probably want to go to Bridget's apartment. That's where I live most of the time."

"Look Jack wherever you want to go, I'll drive you there. Now c'mon it's getting late", said Frank beginning to get a little irritated, particularly with Bridget being brought into the conversation. He didn't like Jack but he thought it better he gets his bullet before learning about Bridget. Normally hits were just business and he was getting irritated about being drawn into the emotive factors surrounding the exchange, particularly with Elsa standing in for Bridget. Some exchange he thought, it's going to be one way traffic.

Jack followed meekly realising there was nothing he could do. There was another tail at the front of the apartment who might see them leaving, so word may still get back to Tanner that things had started to move.

Frank had a key for the door to the service bay and after unlocking it again opened it for Jack to go ahead of him. He's only being careful thought Jack, but his actions although never friendly, were now far more formal than usual and Jack wondered if he was being set up.

Frank keyed in the code at the exit gate, but instead of turning to the main street in front of the apartment block, he took a side road connecting with the main road a few blocks down. "Where are we going", asked Jack.

"We're going over to Jersey City", said Frank. "Traffic should be quiet this time of night so I reckon it'll take about 40 minutes." Jack realized he should have put on a wire so that Gene could hear what was happening, and thought "it's too late now."

Little was said during the remainder of the journey, which worried Jack even more. He expected to hear a lot more from Frank about his being made to come to heel by Roland. Normally he would have taken every opportunity to rub his nose into the mess created by Jack's perceived lack of respect for Roland. They went through the Holland Tunnel so Jack realised they would be driving through the dock area, which may have been a good place to hold Bridget because of the demolition and refurbishment work being carried out there giving the opportunity to hide in empty buildings.

They drove through the dock area until they reached the cordoned off zone of the demolition site. The guard opened the gate and was told to leave it open for the "clean up" team. Frank had been told by Roland to drive towards the dockside crane, turn the car at the rear of the crane and leave the lights on so that they shone in the direction of the derelict container warehouse. Roland didn't want Jack too close to the warehouse in case he recognised Elsa. As they passed the warehouse Jack could see "Bridget", Roland and Lou waiting outside.

Frank positioned the car as instructed and he and Jack left the car and started to walk towards the warehouse. On seeing their movement Roland started to walk in the opposite direction towards them until the three men met midway between the car and the warehouse. Lou kept a firm hold of Elsa by the door of the warehouse. Archie Lemon was watching the scene unfold below him and was adjusting his gun sight to focus on his target, which he could see clearly fixing the cross hairs on his head. Now he would wait until the group of men started talking and were relatively still.

"Jack. I'm so glad you could make it," said Roland sarcastically.

"I didn't really have a lot of choice particularly as you are holding something so precious to me. I want to see that Bridget is OK before I hand over the money", replied Jack.

"No can do", said Bannister. "You're not getting near her until I have checked the money in the package you're holding. If you don't hand it over quietly, Frank will have to take it off you."

Jack was rapidly going over the options to get "Bridget" free in his head and decided to hand the money to Roland who would have his hands full momentarily. With Roland preoccupied with the money package he could then take out Frank before going for "Bridget". It was risky because she was still with Lou, who wouldn't hesitate to kill her if he decided to use her as protection against Jack. He held the package out for Roland with his left hand and put his other hand, furthest away from Frank, on the handle of his revolver.

"Thanks", began Roland, "with your co-operation we can get this over and……." A whistling noise sounded and a hole suddenly appeared in Bannister's forehead. He died instantly and dropped the package as he fell to the ground. Everyone was momentarily stunned.

Jack immediately ran over towards Bridget and Lou. Lou grabbed Elsa and used her as a shield seeing Jack approach with his gun pointing in their direction. "Drop your gun Jack or your girlfriend gets it in the head", said Lou holding his gun to the side of Elsa's head. This brought back memories of Charley Inglewood and his failure to save him. He couldn't fail again.

Frank came lumbering behind Jack, but instead of grabbing him he shouted, "Don't hurt Elsa Lou!" This was sufficient to distract Lou momentarily and gave time for Jack to fire his revolver and hit Lou in the head. Lou fell backwards letting go of Elsa.

"Elsa? Are you alright?" asked Jack. Before she could answer Frank got hold of Jack putting his left arm around his neck and tightening his grip. Jack instinctively grabbed his arm with both hands, dropping his gun, but was unable to loosen his grip.

"I'm going to choke you to death Cates. I don't want you to die quickly", spat Frank

"Frank!" shouted Elsa, "please don't hurt him. I'll do anything if you just let him go. Please just let him go."

"Why do you care?" asked Frank at a loss to understand Elsa's reaction.

"I love him Frank and have done from the first time I set eyes on him. I tried to fight it when we first met and now, but I can't help myself", replied Elsa. "Please let him go."

Frank's grip started to ease and Jack pulled away from him and picked up his gun. "Elsa let's get Bridget and split."

"We can't get Bridget, she's dead", replied Elsa.

"What do you mean dead? Where is she?" shouted Jack wildly

"It was a horrible accident and trust me you don't want to see her," continued Elsa.

Jack was a hair's breadth away from shooting Frank, "You bastard, you bastard, you…." he kept shouting.

"It had nothing to do with Frank! Put your gun down", urged Elsa afraid he was going to shoot Frank. Jack lowered his gun and turned to go into the warehouse, but Elsa grabbed his arm, "trust me Jack, and remember her the way she was".

The pressure in his head that started to build up when he heard that Bridget was dead exploded and Jack fell to his knees and started sobbing inconsolably. Elsa knelt down beside Jack and took his face in her hands. "We've got to go Jack. I'll make sure that Bridget gets taken care of properly".

She turned her head sharply as someone walked into the yard and said "You guys had better get moving before the police arrive".

"Leonard!" exclaimed Frank "what the hell are you doing here?"

"Who do you think it was arranged for Bannister's hit?" he answered, C'mon we can't hang around much longer. I've got a car outside, now hurry!"

Frank ran to the gate and Elsa led Jack away. He was still stunned from the news of Bridget's death and unable to follow without Elsa's guidance. It was something else to feel guilty about because she had loved him unconditionally and now she lay in a derelict warehouse, dead. Despite being the only innocent in the whole affair, she had been dragged into a world of snakes and finally paid the ultimate price.

29

Frank got into the front passenger seat of Leonard Tuzio's car, and Elsa and Jack sat in the back. "Let's get far from here to a place where we can talk." The car headed back to New York without a word being said by anyone. Tuzio drove to a car park close to the New York Hilton Hotel. "I've got a room here," he finally said, "it's in a good position, pretty central. We can chill out and I'll explain a few things. He turned to Frank saying, "use my car and drive over to Pallacio and tell him the job's been done. From now on you'll be working for him again."

Tuzio handed Frank the car keys and took Elsa and Jack to his suite. "What would you two like to drink", he asked once they were inside. Elsa had a gin and tonic and Jack had his usual Bud, although he didn't have the appetite to drink. Tuzio settled down with a large bourbon and said "I guess you two need some answers. And of course you both know that what I'm about to tell you stays in this room or you'll both end up like Bannister." They nodded in unison.

"Bannister was as tricky as they come. Completely untrustworthy and only out to further his own ends. That's OK to a certain extent but the New York families are a close knit group and you have to pay your dues and show respect. Bannister was always talking about respect but showed little to the people he should have been beholding to. I had a fall out with Mario Pallacio over the "Blue Cockatoo" and my undeclared ownership and income, so I know what happens when you ignore the rules. Mario calls the shots as far as New York is concerned and I had digressed. I made Bannister a partner and he helped get me out of the country before Mario could get his hands on me."

"Yeah but what's that got to do with us?" interjected Jack.

"Be patient Jack", replied Tuzio. "Mario accepted an arrangement where he got a cut from the club and didn't ask any further questions on the running of the business or its finances. Bannister was also supposed to send me money on a regular basis to keep me safe in hiding. He started to complain to both me and Mario that the takings had been falling rapidly, particularly when Elsa went to Boston. Mario of course sent a couple of guys to the club to check out the action and they found it was still pretty healthy. After 12 months in hiding I called Mario repenting for what I had done and as he now had a bigger transgressor to worry about we made up. I promised to give up any claim to the "Blue Cockatoo" and so our working relationship and friendship were patched up. I've been in New York for the past few months and secretly resumed my old position in the organisation, and now Michael Braggio reports to me."

"I didn't know much about Simon Walsh until my cousin Vincent told me he was working with you Jack to get money out of him. Vincent was a good kid and excited about making a bundle he could fall back on after his release. He was the lynch pin of the deal but Bannister had other ideas. While you were negotiating with Bridget Walsh, Bannister was going behind your back to Wesley Green," Tuzio continued.

"But he would lose out as much as me?" said Jack.

"Well he would have a lot more people to pay off than you. Now that he was part of the family he would have had to give Mario a goodly proportion of his share. But not only that, he wanted to get rid of you Jack. He had the hots for Elsa and there are probably a number of other reasons he used to justify his actions. He spoke to Wesley Green, an unpredictable bastard who used to work for Mario but was let go because he caused too much trouble. Bannister told Green how much you were asking for and he went off the deep end, which ended up with the murder of Vincent by his cronies. He also killed Walsh, although Matthew Caine got blamed for it. The next I hear from Braggio is that Bannister had arranged this exchange for the kidnapping of Bridget and wanted one of my guys to take you out. Mario and I had a meeting and decided he was going to have to be the one taken out. The rest you know."

"Elsa, Bannister did me a favour when he got you involved in the running of the club. I want you to carry on doing that and if possible take even more responsibility. I'll take Bannister's place, but you won't have to worry about me trying to get into your pants," continued Tuzio.

"I don't know," replied Elsa. "I know nothing about you."

"Well I have greater honesty than Bannister, but that's no hardship. Things will be much the same. I've been the silent owner of the "Blue Cockatoo for a long time, but you just didn't know it," answered Tuzio. "What about you Jack?"

"Gene Tanner may come after me as an accessory to Al Ferrino's murder, so I guess I'll have to make myself scarce. I have my passport and am planning to fly out from JFK to Mexico City before the shit hits the fan on all this, but I'll have to exchange my ticket for an earlier flight. Then I'll have to take things as they come," said Jack.

Tuzio went to a drawer and pulled out his wallet. "My clean up team will clear the docks except for Bridget's body. The police will get a call about where to find her with a tip off that she was murdered by Bannister. They'll spend a long time looking for him but by that time his body will have been incinerated. So will Lou's body. I know this is hard on you Jack but here's $10,000 dollars to help you acclimatise to your new situation."

Jack took the money and got up to leave. "I could use a guy like you. Stay out of the country for 12 months and then come back. We can talk again then," said Tuzio.

"OK" said Jack as he headed for the door.

"Wait for me," said Elsa, nodding to Tuzio and following Jack out of the hotel room. They hailed a cab outside the hotel building and went to Elsa's apartment.

"When did you know about Bridget?" Jack asked.

"I only found out this afternoon. Roland took my phone, but I tried to call you from one of the public phone booths but couldn't get through," answered Elsa. "I had no idea what Roland was planning and only played along because he said if I didn't he would get Frank to kill you."

"I'm so sorry about what happened to Bridget, but I'm also sorry for what I put you through. And all for nothing," said Jack. "Did you mean it when you said you still love me?"

"You know I did, and now I'm ready to go with you to Mexico City."

"I want you with me, but I'm not going to drag you around the world forever looking for the main chance and hiding from God knows who," answered Jack. He took her hands in his, held them up to his face and kissed them. "I'll be flying on my own tonight. You take Tuzio up on his offer. I know you've enjoyed being manager at the club. Carry on doing it and you may find I'll be back after a year just as Tuzio suggested."

Elsa started to cry, despite the fact that she knew what Jack was saying made sense. She would spend the rest of their time together comforting him over the loss of Bridget, and see him off at the airport.

30

The sky was overcast on the day of Bridget's funeral. Everyone was distraught at her fate, especially Aunty Ingrid who had to take to her bed for three days after being told of Bridget's death. The train of funeral cars slowly drove to her grave site. James drove Aunty Ingrid and Francesca, the other cars carried other family members and close friends.

"Thank you for letting me come with you ma'am," said Francesca.

"Don't be silly girl. I know Bridget considered you as part of the family, which is more than I can say for that scoundrel of a man that she married. I knew no good would come of the marriage but she seemed so much in love."

"She did seem happy with him, but he was very hard to figure out. I think he loved her also, but had too many dark places from his past pulling at him to relax with her and enjoy what they had together," answered Francesca.

"Well he's missing now and although he's not being sought for her murder, I'm sure he must have been involved," said Ingrid as the car pulled up on the circulation road of the cemetery. "We'll have to walk from here."

Francesca walked around the car to Ingrid and said, "give me your arm ma'am let's walk down together and think of the light that Bridget brought to our lives."

"Don't make me cry girl," said Ingrid taking her arm and leaning onto her. "I'll need your support at the grave side. Please don't let go of me. James, wait here by the car," she instructed, dispensing with the support he usually gave her. James nodded his understanding of Ingrid's instruction and leaned against the bonnet of the car. He waited until he thought Ingrid and Francesca were far enough away not to notice him having a crafty smoke.

"Don't you know smoking kills!" came a voice from behind. James turned to see a man with short, slicked back hair and heavy full rimmed glasses, dressed fairly casually for a funeral.

James looked closer and said, "Is that you Jack?"

"Sssh keep quiet. I don't want anyone to know that I'm here. I want to see Bridget off so I'll just blend in with the crowd. How is Aunt Ingrid coping?" he asked.

"She's got over the worst, but for God's sake don't let her see you because funeral or not she will kick up hell," answered James.

Jack winked at him and made his way to the back of the crowd that was forming around the grave side. He held his breath when he saw Elsa a mere 10 feet away. Luckily she was looking in the direction of the grave with her head slightly bowed. Jack manoeuvred himself so that if she turned her head, she would not easily see him.

The grave side service carried on and Jack found himself thinking of Bridget's smiling face looking up at him, and her deep blue eyes twinkling with her mischievous grin. A few tears trickled down his face and under his breath he apologised to her for being the unwilling catalyst in the circumstances leading to her death. As the crowd turned away at the end of the service Jack made sure Elsa did not catch sight of him, and let her pass as people surged forward to get back into their cars. He turned towards her and moved close enough to whisper, "And I've always loved you from the moment I laid eyes on you."

It took a few seconds for Elsa to assimilate what Jack had said to her and when she spun around to confirm it was him talking to her there was no sign of anyone behind her. Pulling herself together she quickly walked across the flow of the people believing that he would try and make a quick getaway, but when she got to the edge of the crowd there was still no sign of him.

Her car was up ahead on the main circulation road so she turned back towards Bridget's grave for a final farewell before leaving the cemetery. Fighting back the tears she picked up some soil to throw on the coffin saying, "You were the best of us." Finally she turned to walk to her car and began thinking of Jack. "Yes we will meet again," she thought, took a deep breath and put the moment behind her.

ABOUT THE AUTHOR

Like most people Henry thought he had at least one good book in him and started writing this one about 10 years ago. He spent most of his time working as an engineer on the design and construction of heavy civil works and buildings. This work included motorways, water supply and sewerage, and nuclear facilities. The rigor of this work was a counterbalance to the creative process of writing. He is now writing his second book, which is based on a true story, set in WW2.

21492976R00250

Printed in Great Britain
by Amazon